a spirited life

BOOK ONE IN THE SPIRITS SERIES

B.B. MILLER & LESLIE CARSON

Cover design by: Jada D'Lee Designs
Editing by: (Rebecca— Fairest Reviews Editing Services)
Interior Design & Formatting by: Champagne Book Design

ISBN: 978-0-9982462-8-4

For the ones who won't let their spirit be broken.
The ones who embrace another chance at love, even if it terrifies them.

a
spirited
life

BOOK ONE IN THE SPIRITS SERIES

chapter
one

Sabrina

WEDDINGS OFFICIALLY SUCK.

No...wait...of course this wedding doesn't suck. It's the most beautiful wedding in the history of weddings.

My best friend, Becca Holton, is married to her very own Irish Prince Charming, Liam Swanson, in what can only be described as a picture-perfect wedding.

Harry and Meghan? Please. A distant second.

I mean, come on. We're in Ireland at a 16th century, honest-to-goodness, castle. McGuire Castle is luxury steeped in historic character. It's a fitting setting, given Becca and Liam have officially moved back to Liam's homeland. It also doesn't hurt that I have a project in town that I'm finishing up that my firm has been working on for a year. This is my third international assignment for Freeman Architects, and I love every second of it.

Becca's search for the perfect wedding venue ended the minute she found the stunning pictures and raving reviews for McGuire Castle on-line. It's lavish, romantic, and I dare say, even magical. It's part of Gaelic Irish royalty. Think towering, curved stone walls and turrets, original oil paintings, cozy fireplaces, and intricate carved-wooden trusses, mixed with every modern convenience you could want. The moment you pass the limestone and iron estate gates and travel down the winding lane, curving along a vast lake that leads to this architectural dream, you'll know that there's five-star, and then there's McGuire Castle.

They've somehow made it feel both luxurious and welcoming. We were greeted yesterday in the Grand Hall in front of a roaring fireplace with a whiskey tasting that blew my mind. The whiskey is produced here in small batches in some sort of time-honored secret handed down through generations with barley sourced from a farm just down the road.

And the view? The sprawling four-hundred acres are something out of a fairy tale. Massive rock wall gardens that stretch for days, complete with manicured trimmed-hedge mazes and mature trees holding onto the secrets and ghosts of hundreds of years past. A glimpse of the harbor in the distance can be seen over the rolling moss green hills and jagged cliffs, where a treasure trove of yachts bob in the sea with little white lights twinkling off the languid waves.

My suite (one of forty bespoke suites in the castle, named after some Lord of something or other) is a dream. I had turn-down service last night, complete with little chocolates in a gold box. I'm not going to lie. I could eat that entire box right now. The four-poster bed is a virtual cloud. I could fit my cookie-cutter apartment back in California into the bathroom. I'm in the height of luxury with rich velvet chairs and crystal chandeliers. I'm not used to this level of elegance and grandeur.

The nine-course meal at the wedding reception was a little over the top, but it's what Becca and Liam wanted. The first course, quenelle (whatever the hell that is) of Irish salmon and prawn leeks, gave way to free range/organic everything, goat cheese mousse, and a salted caramel pear tarte. It just went on and on, and sadly, I could barely stomach any of it after what I saw in the darkened hallway.

Which brings me to the lake that sits in front of the castle. It's stocked with some kind of exotic fish, earning oohs and aahs from a few of the guests earlier. Those fish are hungry. How do I know this? I'm currently ruining my peach organza bridesmaid's dress as I wade through the middle of the lake, those fish nipping at my ankles.

I curse, stubbing my toe on a rock. Probably a rock from 1745 that was placed here by some courtly knight as a sign of his steadfast love for a princess.

Love sucks.

I hike the bottom of my full skirt up and take another swig from the green whiskey bottle I snagged from the bar, swaying slightly. It simultaneously soothes and burns my throat going down. If only it could obliterate my memories with it.

Glaring at one of the imposing stone towers in the distance, I wonder if they still have all the equipment needed for a beheading.

It would serve Laird right—the lying, cheating, surfing bastard. I should have known better. There's no way anyone with that wavy blond hair, those ocean blue eyes and that chiseled lean body could keep all that hotness to only one person.

I mean 'Laird'? Seriously? His name alone should have given me a clue how this was going to end. Oh, but he loved to tell me, and everyone within a five-mile radius, how he was named after world-renowned, legendary surfer Laird Hamilton.

"Come on, Brie!" he used to say to me almost every single day. "Surfing is everything. Let's share it together." He'd give me a lopsided grin as he shoved his hand through his insanely wild hair, his chest bronzed from endless hours of surfing in the California sun. Many of those days, I didn't make it to the beach. We would spend the morning in bed until he'd disappear to the call of the ocean, his surfboard tucked under his arm. I wouldn't see him again for days.

To be fair, I did try surfing a few times. But no way, no how was surfing going to be something I was good at, even with the surfing god himself helping me. There are only so many mouthfuls of ocean water you can swallow before you give up.

Also, clearly surfing isn't *everything*. No. *Everything* may now include Alison Swanson—sister of the groom and now officially on my blacklist—being fucked by Laird against the cold stone wall outside the master ballroom after the wedding ceremony, but it sure doesn't include me. Not anymore.

The vision of him pounding into her against that medieval wall is burned into my brain. The fabric of her identical peach dress swirling around them caught me off guard when I went in search for Laird before dinner.

Maybe it was a case of mistaken identity. I mean, we did have the same dress on, and Laird wasn't at the front of the line when they were handing out brain cells.

But Alison's funky raven dark hair and endless curves are the polar opposite to my long blonde hair and below-average height. Even Laird's not stupid enough to mistake Alison for me.

Maybe he'd be hit by a stray bullet during clay shooting tomorrow morning. I give my head a shake, making the darkened lake blur a bit. How much of this damn whiskey have I had? I lift the bottle, squinting to study the etched sailboat on the front.

McGuire's Irish Whiskey— Chapman Reserve— Batch 41. Holy, holy hell, it's strong. Potent and going down faster than it should. But I deserve it, damn it. I've supported stupid Laird and his stupid dream of winning the stupid US Open of Surfing in Huntington Beach for *four years.*

Four years of him not having an actual job and crashing at my apartment. Four years of me paying for everything and cheering him on, of carting his hotness around to every surfing competition on the coast of California in my beloved Jeep that somehow slowly became his.

Four years of me finding myself stranded alone on the highway because he didn't fill said Jeep up with gas. Four years of me trying to explain to him that Vulcan wasn't a real planet.

All of those quirky conversations that I loved at the time, now only serve to rev up my anger.

I wonder how long this has been going on with Alison. We've been planning Becca's wedding for a year, and Alison and Laird have been part of the process every step of the way. It makes my head hurt to think about the number of times the two of them went off together on some wedding emergency errand.

I thought it was sweet—Laird helping out and getting involved in the wedding. It was so rare he thought of anything outside of catching a wave. But he jumped at the chance to go search for Irish-themed decorations with Alison. What an idiot I am.

More nasty ankle biting as I stumble a bit on the rocky lake bottom. I shouldn't be out here. Even in my slightly intoxicated haze, I realize this. I should be having a ball at the ball. The band is fabulous, my best friend is married, and a fireworks display is about to top the night off.

But, I just couldn't take any more. No more of Laird's sideways glances to Alison when he thought I wasn't looking. No more lovey-dovey kisses between every other couple in attendance. Feeling overheated and betrayed, I bolted before the first dance. Ed Sheeran is amazing, don't get me wrong, but even I have my limits.

Stupid Laird and his seaweed dick. I can only hope that somewhere along the way, all that salt water has caused permanent shrinkage. I kick my leg out at the evil fish lurking below. God, how pathetic am I? There's nothing wrong with Laird's cock. It's fine as these things go. Normal. Yes, I did come face-to-dick with some seaweed wrapped around it once, but isn't that to be expected when he spends 80% of his time in the ocean? You know, when he's not drilling a bridesmaid that's not me?

There's not enough whiskey in the world for this feeling.

The castle spins as the first pops of color fill the sky, and I tilt my head back to watch the display. It's breathtaking. So breathtaking I almost don't notice the man stalking across the darkened grounds, making a beeline for the lake. His form is highlighted by the fireworks. I can tell he's tall, his long legs swallowing up the distance between us. He's a man on a mission.

Even though it's June and I'm told unseasonably warm for Ireland, he's wearing a thick cable knit sweater—one of those chunky ones you see on built models in those ads that feature scruffy fishermen. His baggy jeans look like they've been well-loved, and those hiking boots have seen better days, but what do I know? I'm draped in half-soaked organza, my hair a virtual bird's nest, as I try to hold onto the last glimpses of my sanity. I only wish I looked half as good as he does.

His dark hair and cut jaw cause me to stumble a bit, but I manage not to splash face-first into the water. Holy crap. How did I not know David Gandy was invited to this wedding? I hand wrote every single place card, and I think I would remember seeing his name.

Dream Gandy stops at the shore of the lake, hands on his hips, and just glares at me.

I try not so subtly to kick the fish away from my ankles and stand my ground. Where the hell are my shoes? Even if I'm never wearing this peach number again, those shoes I can't deny are fabulous. Wedge heels that bring me up to a solid five-four. I could use that height against good ole David here. He's got to be six-two at least.

"Yer in my lake." Ah, the Irish burr is thick on this one. That accent is hard to understand in my fuzzy head. It kind of reminds me of Shrek's, "Get out of my swamp!" Or maybe that's my friend Batch 41 talking.

A little beagle stands obediently at Dream Gandy's side, his cute tiny tail whipping back and forth. He's smiling—the beagle, sadly not David. Beagles always look like they are smiling and happy to be out and about. Unlike his owner who clearly wishes he was anywhere but here.

"Allo?" Shrek-sounding David calls out. "Are ye deaf?"

I take another healthy swig of the whiskey before holding the bottle up high in the air. "Nope." Another explosion of light hits the inky sky, another fish takes a chomp out of my ankle. These Irish fish are as nasty as the prickly hotness Gandy wannabe in front of me. I start laughing. *Wannabe in front of me.* I'm rhyming now, and I never rhyme. I'm also cackling uncontrollably.

A stream of whiskey escapes the lovely bottle, sadly falling into the lake. Maybe that will take the fish down. I watch as it drops into the blackened water, and I bend over to give a wave to the ankle biters below.

"For feck's sake. Would you stop yer moving? Yer gonna fall right in."

"Maybe I want to fall in." The beagle looks up at his lord and master then back at me.

"You don't. Trust me."

"Listen, Shrek." I point the bottle in his general direction, wobbling slightly. Very lady-like, you see. "The last thing I need is some fisherman telling me what to do." At least that's what I think I say. I may be slurring at this point.

"Fisherman?" He cocks his head and the beagle does the same.

"Yeah." Waving the bottle at him, I start to move forward. "Like you've just come from a Nautica photo shoot on some yacht." In the light of the fireworks, I can see his forehead crease.

He holds his hand up. "Just stand still, woman." There's something about that growly Shrek-like voice. It's deep, annoyed, and just a little tempting.

The beagle inches forward to the water's edge as I feel something slither against my leg. The shriek that follows wakes more than a few ghosts in the lush rolling hills that surround the castle, and I'm jumping, the skirt flailing as I try not to wipe out. My feet slip on the rocks, and then Dream Gandy curses and is moving into the water, the beagle bounding along beside him excitedly.

I'm swooped up and into his arms. Strong arms I can feel even through the thick layer of wool. He's grumbling as I kick my legs, the cool water flying. "Would ya keep yer voice down?" The beagle darts between his legs, and Dream Gandy pushes through the water and back to dry land, carrying me as if I'm the weight of a feather.

"Put me down!" I slur, even as my arms wrap tighter around his neck. It needs to be noted that I do indeed save the evil bottle of whiskey, though it does dangle precariously in my hand.

"Not on yer life." Jesus, he smells good. Something spicy, earthy, warm, and manly. Aged oak and honey. I highly doubt actual Shrek smelled like this. It would be bad to burrow into his warmth. Resting my head on his chest? Also not a wise move, but everything is spinning, and I find my cheek pressed against the soft wool of his sweater.

He tightens his grip against the underside of my legs and marches toward the castle. "Not back to the party. I just can't." At my whispered words, his steps slow. He glances down at me, and I see for the first time the intense color of his steel blue eyes. The hard lines of his ruggedly handsome face are almost too much to take. I have to look away.

The beagle races to a massive door at the corner of the castle, jumping in place. The dog lets out a little squeak that I can barely hear past the blood pounding in my ears. I'm a bit of a fainter—chronically low blood pressure will do that to you– and I recognize the signs now. Skin heating, everything spinning, breathing coming faster. Yep, it's official. The Batch 41/ Dream Gandy combo is going to make me pass out. At least my humiliation will be complete.

"Where are you taking me?" Talking—talking is good. Maybe I won't faint after all.

"Away from the party."

"But my lake…" I take a peek over his broad shoulder to the lake shimmering in the light from the fireworks.

"*My* lake is gonna be full soon." My eyes widen at him. "The bonfire for the happy couple that's about to take place out there? You don't want to be out there like this when that happens."

"Wait, *your* lake?" All of this moving isn't helping my spinning head. Breathe… just breathe. Never mind that a stranger is carrying you who the hell knows where.

"*My* lake. Colin McGuire at your service." He mumbles this, stopping at the door.

Under the lights cast down from the castle, he almost seems to glow. "McGuire…like the castle."

I see the first hint of a smile when the corner of his mouth twists. "The very one."

Another squeak from the adorable beagle.

"Was that a bark?"

He gives me a tight nod. "'Twas."

"Didn't sound like much of a bark."

"He sorta lost his bark." The beagle spins in circles, and then lifts his little front paws up to the door. "Hold yer horses, Tack."

"How did he lose his bark?"

"You ask a lot of questions. And from kennel cough." I frown back at Colin who rolls his eyes at me.

"Not my fault. I rescued him from a shelter. He picked it up there." My heart jumps in my chest. Prickly Gandy rescues dogs? "Seems I'm doing a lot of rescuing these days."

"I did not need rescuing!" I lean back as he pushes the door open with his shoulder.

"Sure you didn't."

He drops my legs and my feet hit the floor. It's like I've entered a time machine. There's an actual coat of arms on the wall. I'm back in time to King Arthur's court, but everything is distorted and spinning. My stomach lurches and I sway backward. Maybe when I'm not so drunk, I can spend some time enjoying the castle. I'm going to be in Ireland for a few weeks, finishing an office redesign, that is if I live past tonight. "Easy." I feel a strong arm wrap around my waist, taking my weight, catching me before I fall. "You donna have yer sea legs yet."

"See what?" Sadly, Colin is fading into a blurry haze. I try to steady my breaths, squeezing my eyes shut, but it's pointless. I know that blissful oblivion is a breath away. Maybe when I wake up, I'll find out this has all been one bad dream. I only hope that my Dream Gandy is in it.

Colin

"For feck's sake."

She was able to stand for only about thirty seconds in the breakfast room before her eyes rolled back in her head and she pitched forward against my chest. I shift her in my arms to get a better grip, while trying not to let her head droop and strain her neck. Who knew that carrying an unconscious woman would be so tricky?

They make it look so easy in films.

"Now what do I do, hmm, Tack?" I ask, in response to an imperious yip near my ankles. I must look a bloody fool. Tack grins up at me, wiggling all over, ignoring my frown. "What am I asking you for? You're just excited to have someone new to play with."

A soft, rumbling sigh comes from the beauty in my arms and she snuggles her head against my shoulder, still clutching the bottle, lost to whatever alcoholic dreams have her. Despite the ridiculousness of the situation, she feels…oddly right in my arms, a warm, sweet-smelling bundle that I can't help but hold tighter against my chest.

The booms and crackle of the fireworks overhead dim as I shove the door shut with my shoulder. I head down the corridor, up the back stairs to the second floor, and past the portraits of my great, greater, and greatest uncles. Reaching one of the guest rooms—the *family* guest rooms, not one of those used for paying visitors—I nudge open the door with my hip and try not to stagger to the bed. She doesn't weigh much, maybe eight stones, but after hauling lines on *Saoirse* all day, I'm about knackered.

She sighs when I lay her down on the mattress, but doesn't wake. I'm not sure if I'm relieved or not. I manage to pull the bottle from her grip, without rousing her or spilling the contents. And thank God for that—it'd be a damn shame to waste any of *Chapman's Reserve*. Taking a sniff from the bottle, I smile to myself in satisfaction before setting it on the side table. Damn fine whiskey, that. One of my better business deals.

After listening to her steady breathing for a moment, I haul the desk chair over closer to the bed, and sink down into it. She has to be one of the loveliest women I've seen in a long, long time. Short little thing. A straight nose that suits her narrow face. Long eyelashes rest against sun-kissed cheeks. Golden curls fall around her face and shoulders, trailing down to nice, full breasts…

I jerk my gaze to my feet. Jaysus, sitting here like a fuckin' creeper…*get hold of yourself, man*. It's not like she's the first woman you've ever seen.

A loud boom outside rattles the windows and draws a startled yip from Tack. I jump up and make it to the window in time to see a burst of yellow and red sparks dissipate and shimmer into nothingness. From here, I can see a crowd of finely-dressed guests gathered to watch the last of the show. I hope the townsfolk are enjoying them as well. They can probably see them across the harbor, too.

One person I know who isn't enjoying them is sitting upstairs, probably with a book and a dram, trying to ignore the pomp and circumstance outside. But before I head up to check on him, I pause at the foot of the bed for one more look at my slumbering beauty. Her dress is a total loss, the bottom of the fluffy skirt drenched and streaked green from the pond. What on earth compelled her to get so smashed? Why didn't she want to rejoin her party? The panic in her light brown eyes, eyes the color of the whiskey she was drowning in, was real and concerning. That was why I made a snap decision to bring her here, the family wing, where no paying guests are allowed. Ever.

What the hell was I thinking?

Shaking my head at my own foolishness, I stride over to the desk and scrawl a quick note with directions on how to get back to her group when she rejoins the living, and then I prop it against the whiskey bottle next to the bed. "Come on, Tack," I mutter, and leave, half-closing the door behind me.

Tack's nails click on the floor as he follows me down the hall to the back stairs. Taking the steps two at a time to the third floor, I make my way to the suite at the end of the hall. At my soft knock, a voice as deep as my own bids me enter.

"Has that strammach ended yet?"

I grin when I see I was right; my grandfather is sitting in his favorite leather armchair, a glass of whiskey on the table beside him, a book open on his knee. His dislike for fireworks stems from his time in the army, but they're popular with guests, and so we live with them occasionally. "Almost. The fireworks are over. They've moved on to the bonfire by the lake."

He scoffs and takes a sip from his glass. "I assume Dermot is keeping an eye on things?" he asks, and waves a hand at the bottle and spare glasses on the cabinet that serves as a small bar. My grandfather doesn't like to go far for a dram.

"Of course." Dermot is one of our chief groundsmen who's usually assigned to the events crew, especially when there's fire involved. He's been with us for years. I pour myself two fingers and take a seat opposite my grandda. Still hale at seventy-six, he's a wonder. An imposing figure with a barrel chest and a full head of snow-white hair, with laser-sharp blue eyes—eyes that I've inherited. I wish I'd inherited his silver tongue, too. The man can talk the birds out of the trees when he wants to. Comes in handy during negotiations.

Tack scampers over and huffs in pleasure as my grandfather scratches his ear. "What happened to you?" He frowns and points to my soggy boots. "You're tramping muck all over the halls? Aileen won't be pleased."

Aileen is Dermot's wife, and she manages the housekeeping staff for the entire castle. We'd be lost without her. And he's right—she'd cuff my ear if I stomped muck on her floors. "I'm not. They're just wet." At his raised eyebrow, I sigh. "I had to fetch a guest out of the lake."

"The lake? What the hell was that about?"

Leaning forward, I brace my elbows on my knees and stare down at the glass in my hands. I should have thought about how to explain this before coming to his suite. "I don't know. She was drunk and refused to rejoin the party, but wouldn't tell me why."

"She?" He shifts in his chair, looking at me with raised brows. "What's her name?"

"I don't know. She passed out before she could tell me. I think she's a bridesmaid, though, based on her dress. I saw a couple others just like it in the group watching the fireworks."

Tack settles down on the rug in front of the fire, as my grandfather tilts his head, looking at me with concern. "Where is she now? And how did she get there, if she's unconscious?"

"In one of the guest rooms. I had to carry her—didn't know what else to do. I couldn't leave her lying on the lawn in front of all those guests." I take a sip, hoping he doesn't make a big deal out of this. I felt like a right idiot with my arms full of a beautiful, but smashed girl, and the last thing I need is for my grandfather taking the piss out of me. "She's safe now. I'll text Aileen and ask her to keep an eye on her," I add, trying to sound nonchalant. Aileen will know what to do.

"*Carried* her? To one of *our* guest rooms?" He squints at me, and then a sly smile steals across his face, which he tries to hide by taking a drink. "Well. Well, well, well."

The amusement in his voice irks me for some reason. "Well, what?"

He leans back in his chair, getting more comfortable, and sets his book on the table next to him before crossing one long leg over the other. His enjoyment of the moment is almost palpable, and my irritation inexplicably rises. "Oh, nothing," he murmurs. I glance up at him, but he refuses to meet my gaze, preferring instead to smirk into his glass. I groan internally.

"Fine." Knowing nothing good is going to follow that smirk, I down the remaining whiskey. "Come on, Tack."

Tack dutifully rises with me and follows as I set my glass down and head for the door. "It's just…" His deep voice stops me with my hand on the knob, and I bang my forehead lightly on the door. I knew it. "How *gallant* of you to carry her to her rest," he continues. "How… positively *chivalrous*. Almost like something out of one of those dime novels the pub maids are always carrying on about."

"Yeah, yeah," I mutter, rolling my eyes at his teasing. "What would you have done? Left her to drown?"

He waves a gnarled hand at me. "Course not. But, Colin," he pauses, making me look back at him. His fond smile warms me. "You could have just as easily gotten someone from her party to look after her, or called Aileen to come down and deal with it. That you wanted to ensure her safety yourself…" I frown at him, and he continues, his voice soft, "Perhaps you should find out who she is."

"Doesn't matter. She'll be gone in the morning," I snap, and then take a deep breath before continuing. "Sorry. I'll see you tomorrow. 'Night, Grandda."

I swiftly close his door behind me and stalk down the hall to my own set of rooms. After checking to ensure Tack has plenty of water for the night, I fling myself into my own leather armchair and stare out the window at the flickering flames of the bonfire below. I can hear muted singing from the crowd gathered around the flames and wonder if the blonde beauty downstairs can hear them too .

A whimper draws my gaze to Tack, who's resting his head on my knee. "Don't worry, boy," I murmur, smoothing his warm fur with my fingers. "She'll be gone tomorrow, another flock of tourists will show up, and life will go on as normal. No more midnight strolls through the pond."

So why doesn't that thought cheer me?

chapter
two

Sabrina

WAKING UP WITH A JACK HAMMER BEATING AT YOUR BRAIN IS
not fun.

Holy, hell. How much did I have to drink last night?

Opening my eyes is a chore. There's way too much light streaming into the room for the amount I had to drink last night. I stretch
out, casting a bleary gaze to the nightstand…correction to where the
nightstand *should* be. In its place, I find some ornately-carved credenza
that looks like it took about ten years to handcraft.

I blink, hugging the million thread count, sateen sheets to my
chest. Hang on…there was not a credenza in my room previously.
Where the hell am I?

Painful as it is, I roll my head to the side, looking for my phone.
My precious phone is nowhere to be seen. I try to tap down the rising panic.

My throat feels like sandpaper, my mouth dry and gross with the lingering remnants of the whiskey nightmare that is Batch 41. The damn green bottle mocks me from across the room—the room that definitely is not mine.

I press a palm over my forehead as pieces of the craptastic night flash back to me in painful strobe-like clarity. No way around it—last night was a train-wreck ending with me being carried by a David Gandy look-a-like. I groan, burying my face in the pillow. It smells heavenly, some soft oaky fragrance that seems to permeate every corner of this castle. I'm tempted to curl up and never leave.

I'll just close my eyes for a few minutes. The crackling fire is too cozy to leave just yet. Plus, I don't want to even think about facing Laird or trying to explain to Becca why I disappeared. Not yet, anyway. I won't be responsible for tarnishing her fairy tale weekend wedding.

We're supposed to have some elaborate medieval brunch today to bid them farewell before they take off on their extended honeymoon tour of Ireland. Liam is beyond proud of his family history that allegedly goes back to a Viking raid in early medieval times that they plan on exploring. It all sounds a little macabre for my taste, but what do I know? My boyfriend, correction my *former* boyfriend, has the maturity of a hormone driven sixteen-year-old.

I blow out a long breath, staring at the dying flames of the fire. How apropos; flames flickering out, turning to ash, leaving a smoldering ruin in their wake. I feel like an idiot—a walking cliché. I'm the loving girlfriend who is obliviously unaware of how her lover spends his free time when he's not with her.

That's probably what hurts the most—the deception. The fact that I wasn't worthy to be told he wasn't interested in me anymore. I'm a big girl—I can take it. In relationships, if you're not feeling it, just be a man and say so. It's so much easier than finding out like I did. A conversation I can handle. This just makes me feel jaded and bitter, and I kind of hate Laird a little bit more for that.

I stare up at the intricate designs carved into the vaulted ceiling, thinking there must be a dungeon somewhere in this place where I could punt Laird. With a sigh, I flip to my side, catching sight of a deep green Celtic cross etched into a stained-glass window. This castle really is a dream. As an architect, I can appreciate the painstaking work that must have gone its building and restoration.

The room is massive, with tapestries adorning the walls. The furnishings include a luxurious plaid sofa, and a carved tea table facing one of the windows.

I run my palm over the bedding, its soothing touch highlighted with accents of green and rose. I roll over and burrow myself in its luxury. Facing the music, the painful truth of the end of my relationship with Laird is just going to have to wait a bit.l

Who knows how long later, a warm, wet nose on my arm and a tentative nudge at my hand remind me I'm not where I should be, though where that even is right now is the million-dollar question. It's definitely not with Laird. Embarrassment washes over me again. As much as I never want to see the bastard again, I'm going to have to. I want to hug my best friend before she moves onto the next phase of her life. I want to remind her of all the crazy and impulsive situations we got ourselves into over the years. I want to tell her that when Liam pisses her off, and he will, I'll be here to listen to her. Laird may have destroyed my trust, but I won't let him take another thing from me. So, I'll face him and everyone else at this medieval brunch, even though I'm still contemplating a beheading, or two.

I crack an eye open, earning me a full tongue lick to the cheek from the most adorable beagle on the planet. He lets out a little squeak as I push up in the bed. "Tack." He tips his head, shifting his paws on the side of the bed as if overjoyed that I know his name. How could I forget? Dream Gandy's accent is on repeat in my head, though some of the words are jumbled, I do remember him talking to his dog.

I pat the bed, and he jumps up beside me as I massage the soft fur on his head. "No licking. I know where that tongue has been." He flops down and rolls over, showing me his belly. "Typical man," I mumble, stroking his stomach. His tail swishes on the bed, a sign he's clearly enjoying the attention.

Maybe a dog is the answer to my troubles with men. Dogs are definitely loyal. Tack here looks like he'd take a bullet for me and we've only just met. My fingers run along his collar to the bone-shaped dog tag dangling under his chin. I read the inscription: *'Tack' Return to Colin*

McGuire—McGuire Castle. I flip the tag over, seeing a little barcode that makes my heart skip a beat. Prickly Gandy not only rescued the dog, he had him microchipped as well. He may come off as an ogre—a tall, hot as hell ogre, complaining about strangers in his lake—but this dog tag tells me there's a lot more to Colin McGuire than he lets people see.

Tack jumps to his feet on the bed, letting out a cute little squawk. "Guess we better return you, Tack." Reluctantly, I throw the covers off, glancing down at my ruined dress with a groan. My shoes are MIA, which is sad on multiple levels. I wanted to wear those again, and now, I'm going to have to tiptoe around the castle barefoot.

I brush my tangled hair back and smooth down the bodice of my dress. Judging from the sound of silence outside the door, I'm guessing it's still pretty early. Maybe I can find my way back to my room unseen.

Tack leaps to the floor, his nails clicking on the limestone as he heads to the door and disappears into the hallway. Even the door is incredible—hand-carved and probably weighing a ton. I try to ignore the fact that it's open a bit. It means I was passed out and vulnerable in an unlocked room. Wild scenarios flash through my brain. I really need to stop watching those true crime marathons.

Shrek—er... *Colin* carried me out of that lake and away from prying eyes last night, which says something about him, I think. If he wanted to take advantage of me, he could have—easily. But instead, I've woken up safe, warm, and in the height of luxury. I hope I can find him today. I want to thank him for saving me from mortifying embarrassment. If the guests of the wedding had gotten a glimpse of me wading around tipsy in the lake, I may have actually died of humiliation.

The stone floor is cool under my bare feet, and I take a few deep breaths as my head complains some more. No more Irish whiskey for me. Even if the rest of my life is a clusterfuck at the moment, of that I'm certain.

A sheet of paper leaning against the evil green bottle that got me into this mess in the first place catches my eye and I pad across the room to inspect it. Underneath embossed McGuire Castle letterhead and crest, is a neatly written, rather elegant cursive.

To get back to the party...

I smile, reading the curt directions I have a strange feeling were written by the ogre himself. No fuss, no muss—just straight and to the point. Not even a name or signature below the instructions from Mr. Personality.

Spying an expensive pen and pencil set to the side, I lift another sheet of letterhead and sketch out a quick version of Shrek standing next to a castle turret, (thank you six years of design school), with a simple note. *Thank you, for everything.*

I wonder if he'll understand the Shrek reference, or if he'll even see the note at all. I hope he does. I hope it makes him smile.

"That shithead!" Becca whisper-hisses as we sit at an obscenely long table at the medieval brunch. I pass her a wooden bowl full of fruit. I finally found my way back to my room, only getting lost once, thanks to the precise instructions from Dream Gandy that got me back to the main ballroom. From there, it was a maze of stone hallways and passages that all looked the same until I came upon the wing with the suites. It felt kind of clandestine, me sneaking around barefoot in the early morning hours with a thick layer of mist hugging the castle.

My perfect suite with an unlocked door and all of my belongings, including my precious phone, were exactly where I left them. You'd be called an idiot in California if you left your door unlocked, but things are different here at Castle McGuire.

There were no signs of Laird. He was probably busy finding more walls and darkened hallways to spend his time in.

A long soak in the claw-foot tub that is officially my new favorite thing about this place, and I was almost a new woman. And then I saw Becca, and it all came out: the awful, stone-wall pounding truth about Laird and Alison.

"That total asshole!" Her eyes are murderous on Laird.

"Shhhh! Keep your voice down," I mumble under my breath as a few heads turn our way. "I don't want to cause a scene." I glance down the mile-long table to where Laird is currently charming the pants off Liam's grandmother. Even the seventy-five-year-olds aren't immune. "Not here. Not when it's the day after your wedding and everything is supposed to be perfect."

"I want to throttle him," she bites out, waving a large drumstick in her hand. "Maybe beat him with this."

"Tempting, but no." I glare at Laird, the vision of him hammering into Alison still fresh in my mind. "I'll deal with him. Don't you worry." I feel another wave of annoyance wash over me. "I'm going to have to get a STD test while I'm here," I bite out through gritted teeth, shooting death lasers in Laird's direction. "That absolute prick. I just had my physical before coming over, and now I'm going to have to…" I don't want to finish that thought. Humiliation at its finest as I have to seek out a clinic in a strange city and ask for a full panel because my ex-boyfriend can't keep his dick in his pants.

She gives me a watery smile, her hand resting on my arm. "I'm so sorry, Brie. Alison is a slut."

"Yeah? Well, she wasn't alone in the hallway. It takes two and all that." Someone fills my goblet, and I take a healthy sip, frowning. It's thick and honey rich, practically searing my throat on the way down. "What the hell is this?" I hide a cough behind my hand.

Becca grins at me over the rim of her goblet. "McGuire's Meade Honey Wine. Apparently, it has powers of fertility." I blink at her.

"You just got married less than twenty-four hours ago, and you're already wanting to get knocked up?"

She shrugs, fiddling with the ends of her hair. "Liam's not getting any younger." She glances down the table where her new husband is laughing with Laird. Liam's forty—five years older than Becca and me.

"It's not like he's pushing ninety or something, there, Becs."

"I know, but he wants to start a family—soon." She lowers her voice slightly as if this is a secret.

"*He* wants? What about what you want?" I set the heavy goblet down, turning in my chair to look at my best friend. My best friend who, less than two months ago, told me she wanted to spend at least four or five years exploring the world with her then soon-to-be husband. Babies were nowhere in those conversations. Even though she's glowing with that new-bride shine, I can see a little nervousness as her eyes dart to her husband before they land back on mine.

A baby? Is that what Becca really wants?

The three-piece medieval band breaks into some Irish folk song and a few dancers in period dress take to the raised stage in front of us. Suddenly, Liam is at her chair, pulling her up and out onto the make-shift dance floor, and I wonder if he's starting to pull her out of my life completely.

"Pull!" I yell and squint behind my safety glasses, following the clay pigeon as it soars into the air. I pull the trigger on the gun. I've never held a gun in my life, but I can't deny it's a little therapeutic, taking my anger out like this. I sway back a bit at the sheer force of the shot. I'm going to have a bruise on my shoulder, but it's worth it.

"It's got a bit of a kick there," Jonathan, the fifty-something instructor, reminds me. Jonathan has been extremely patient with me this morning, taking my mini freak-out of holding a gun for the first time in stride. "You got a real eye for it now."

I smile at him, feeling a little smug. I actually hit the edge of the clay on that last one. I adjust my red headphones, my ears already ringing from the sound.

"You want to give it another go?" he asks, reloading the gun.

I give him a nod, frowning as I see Laird, making his way across the grass to the shooting range in his flip-flops. Even in Ireland, you can't take the surfer out of him. Of course, he has to ruin this for me too. Jonathan turns in Laird's direction, motioning him over. "The more the merrier, I say." Jonathan's voice rises.

"I don't. I don't say." I step around Jonathan, hands on my hips as I stare up at Laird. God, he's pretty—that tousled blond hair, that surfer tan that highlights the lines of his face. *Don't be distracted by the pretty. Remember what you saw last night.* "What are you doing here?"

"I came to find you. You disappeared on me last night, and then at brunch, I didn't want to interrupt your girl time with Becca." This is his explanation. *I* disappeared on him. Never mind that he was otherwise engaged with his seaweed dick inside someone else.

"My disappearing didn't seem to bother you last night." He blinks at my tone. "Did you even try to find me at all?" He opens his mouth, but I plow on. "I mean, I could have been dragged into the forest by wolves or something and you'd never know."

His mouth quirks. "Wolves? Have you been watching those teen movies again?" He reaches to tuck a strand of my hair behind my shoulder. It's a signature move of his. Just before he leans in to kiss me, he's always tucking my hair back, like I'm some delicate flower that he's almost too afraid to touch. I bet he didn't tuck Alison's hair back. No. I bet there was a lot of hair pulling—wicked, raw, needy hair pulling. It's never been like that with Laird and me, but what I saw in the hallway has got me thinking about a lot of things. Like sex.

Of course, Laird and I had sex. But it was always normal, easy, and nothing like the wild abandon I saw last night. He's never fucked me like he can't get enough, and that's what it looked like. He was trying to devour Alison. He's never tried to devour me.

"Um…" He looks confused when I flinch away from his hand. Laird often looks confused, like when I try to tell him about why I love my job, or about why shopping for antiques on a Sunday morning is better than surfing.

"How long?" I ask as he rocks back on his flip-flops. The man lives in flip-flops. The fact that he had actual shoes on for the wedding is a first.

He tips his head to the side when I take a step away from him. "How long what?"

"How long have you been sleeping with Alison?" That easy smile of his drops, his hand rubbing through his hair. He says nothing. Not a single thing. Poor Jonathan clears his throat, backing up a bit, recognizing an impending meltdown, no doubt. "How long?" My voice is eerily calm.

"Ah, what?" His voice is high, his eyebrows even higher.

"I saw the two of you last night." His face goes ghost-white, that pretty tan a distant memory. Ah, to be caught when you thought you got away with it. "Couldn't even wait to get to a bedroom, Laird? Really? Anyone could have spotted you two. *I* spotted you two."

"It didn't mean anything, Brie." He reaches for my arm, and I twist away from him.

"It meant something to me. Remember me? Your girlfriend for the last four years? Did I conveniently slip your mind?" I throw my arms up in the air.

"It won't happen again."

"You're right. It won't. I want you out of my apartment when you get back to the States."

He blinks again. "But where will I stay?" His voice sounds panicked. "I have the Vans Open in a few weeks."

I shake my head, anger simmering dangerously close to the surface. Of course, he's only thinking about himself. "I forgot. Everything is always about you. Well, you should have thought about where you would stay before you fucked someone else." He rears back, his mouth dropping open. "Maybe check with Alison. I'm sure she's got a wall or two to christen." He grimaces, his lips pressing into a hard line. It's then I realize the nasty, ugly truth. "Oh my God. It's been going on for a while, hasn't it? You've already christened all her walls." I bite the inside of my cheek. I will not cry in front of this asshole. He doesn't deserve my tears. "Why didn't you just tell me?" Thinking about it now, when was the last time we had sex? Three, four weeks ago? We've both been so swamped with wedding plans, we've barely seen each other, though now I know what he's really been doing all of this time.

His eyes soften, and he reaches for me. "I thought it was just a phase. That we'd fuck and get it out of our systems." I let out a choke-laugh, trying to ignore the way his words beat at my brain. "She's… I mean…the sex is…" He seems to struggle to find the words.

"Give me the gun, Jonathan," I grind out, blindly holding out my hand as I glare at Laird.

"Ah, 'fraid not, my dear. Haven't had a murder at McGuire Castle in over three hundred years. We're not about to start now."

I take a step forward, my finger punching at Laird's chest. "I want you out of my apartment before I get home. Do you understand me?"

"But, Brie, baby—" He closes his hand around my finger. I yank it from his grasp.

"You do not get to 'baby' me. You and I are thirty-five not fifteen. If you were unhappy, you could have just talked to me, like a normal adult. Instead, you made me feel like this, like I'm not enough." I feel tears brewing behind my eyes. I thought confronting Laird would be the right thing to do, would make me feel better. It's only making me feel worse, so much worse. What a blow to the ego to hear that sex with someone else is so fantastic you can't even find words to describe it.

"It was just sex," he says, like this makes it all okay.

"Well, now you're free to have 'just sex' with whomever you want. And so am I." I step back over to Jonathan, holding my hand out. "Can we continue?"

"Ah… If you'll just step back, sir," Jonathan says to Laird, motioning to the safe zone behind the shooting range.

"Brie, please. I don't want to lose you." I ignore Laird and his ridiculous plea. It's hollow and too late.

"Yer all right to continue?" Jonathan asks, his voice soft.

I give him a nod, and he hands me the gun. "Pull!" My voice is stronger than I expect, despite the lump in my throat, and when I blow that clay pigeon out of the sky, damn does it feel good.

Colin

With a sigh, I sink down on the bench outside the back door and lean against the stone wall of the castle. I usually run five miles, but I pushed myself to eight this morning because I felt guilty about taking too many helpings of Mrs. Sullivan's ham and egg pie for breakfast. It didn't help that she piled a mound of fried potatoes and a slice of my favorite fresh-baked bread on my plate, either. She's been our cook since I was a boy and knows all my favorite foods. Usually I can resist, but not this morning.

Not this morning, when I'm nagged with annoying thoughts of a certain blonde beauty. I thought a good run would clear my head, but no such luck. I yank my shirt off and use it to wipe the sweat from my face before leaning back and closing my eyes. The rough, cold stone on my bare back is a sharp contrast to the sunshine warming my face and chest. I let my thoughts wander and frown when soft giggles and loose blonde tendrils come instantly to mind.

She fit so perfectly in my arms as I carried her upstairs last night. At least, once I got her situated, so her head wouldn't hang over my arm. Huffing a laugh, I contemplate what happened to make her get so snockered. Since she was in that dress, she must have some connection to the bride, but I have a feeling that happiness for her friend wasn't part of the equation.

Pulling my note from out of my pocket, I smirk at the drawing she added on the other side. Does she think I look like an ogre? Or is it just the castle reference? I couldn't resist peeking down the second-floor hallway this morning, and when I saw her door standing open, I deemed it safe. And I'm glad I did, otherwise I wouldn't have such a cheeky piece of artwork to keep me company on my run.

A drop of sweat drips down my temple, and I swipe it away. I wonder what her name is? Sarah? Heather, maybe? She kind of looks like a Heather. She's also talented; the drawing is great, although the ogre thing is weird. Elinor? Nah, not Elinor. Too formal. Maybe one of those earthy names, like Summer or Clover. Or maybe—

With a low groan, I rub my hands over my face, as if to purge her from my memory. *Get over it, McGuire.* Her group probably departed this morning; she's long gone now. No point thinking about things that will never—*could* never—be.

"'Tis a fine thing, Colin McGuire, you sitting here lounging in the sun whilst the rest of us are working our fingers to the bone."

A slow grin spreads across my face and I crack an eye open. Aileen is smirking down at me, one hand on her hip and one of my t-shirts thrust out in her other hand. "Thanks. Are you psychic now?" I ask, taking the fresh shirt and slipping it over my head.

"You're just now noticing?" She cocks an eyebrow, and then laughs. "I saw you come back from upstairs. Figured you'd need it."

"You figured right." I stand and bend to kiss her on the cheek. "Thanks, Ai. One of these days, you know, I'm finally going to convince you to throw over Dermot for me."

She laughs again at our running joke and slaps my chest lightly. "Oh, go on. I can't leave Dermot now—he'd be lost without me after all these years."

"We all would, Ai." I wink at her, and she rolls her eyes. "Where's Grandda?"

"Heading to the malt shed the last I saw him. He mentioned he needs to see you sometime this morning." She tilts her head and peers up at me. "Is everything all right with you? You look a little lost this morning. You're not coming down with anything, are ye?"

I try to smile, but it feels more like a grimace. "Nah, just winded from the run." I rub the back of my neck and try to sound casual. "Um, has the wedding party from yesterday cleared out?"

"Aye, some have. There're a few still about, I think." She squints at me, but I keep a bland expression, hiding the surge of hope that hits me. Maybe Summer-Clover-Heather is still here...not that I care, of course. "There's a fiftieth wedding anniversary party coming in tomorrow. We'll be ready, don't worry."

"Oh, Aileen, I never worry," I say, giving her a reassuring smile. As much as I hate having to rent out the castle for events, I trust Aileen completely with the arrangements. She handles everything so Grandda and I never have to be involved and can ignore it as much as possible.

I shake my head to clear it. It doesn't matter what her name is; thinking about it is a waste of time. "I'll head over to the malting shed, then."

She makes a show of sniffing me and grimacing. "You'd better have a shower first," she says, giving me a knowing look before turning to head back inside. Rolling my eyes, I follow her.

Running a hand through my damp hair, I decide to walk with Tack across the grounds to the malting shed, instead of using one of the golf carts we keep on hand to reach the back lot. Shed is a misnomer; it's a huge, modern building where we malt the barley and other grain before transferring it to the malting floor to germinate. The old buildings where my ancestors made the McGuire whiskey lauded by kings still stand on the property, but they now only serve as historical attractions for the many tourists who pass through the castle.

With a property this size, we'd never be able to keep it afloat on just the whiskey earnings. We've considered several offers to expand and go international, but Grandda and I feel it would lose its uniqueness and become just another pretty label on the shelf besides Jameson, Bushmills, and the rest. We taste every batch ourselves and we wouldn't be able to continue that practice if we had multiple distillery locations—it just wouldn't be practical. We believe that since our name is going on the bottle, we want to be sure it's something we can be proud of.

Most of our profits go right back into the business. So, until we decide to give up some control, we need other ways to pay our bills. Renting out part of the castle helps with the insane costs involved with maintenance, personnel, and taxes. We're wealthy, sure, and we have investments, but no one can sustain this type of property for long on just a bank account. When these types of homes were built, the owners didn't have to deal with fair labor or disability access laws. I'm certainly not complaining; the fact is that life is different now and we need to be creative if we want to keep our home.

I push open the large green door and step inside, smiling at the sound of my grandfather's deep voice. He's just as involved with production now as he was when he was younger. He and one of the shed hands are leaning over the bins, examining the damp grain.

"Is it ready?" He looks up at my question and smiles.

"Aye, it's perfect," he says, brushing some kernels from his hands back into the bin. He says a few more words to the shed hand and gives him a nod, before turning to me. "Walk with me. Tack! Get out of that." Tack abandons the pile of rags he was sniffing and scampers over to us. Clapping a hand on my shoulder, he guides all three of us outside and into the sunshine. "Have a good run?"

"Not bad." I look at him out of the corner of my eye. He's pursing his lips and squinting at the sun, as if trying to phrase his words. "What's up? Is there a personnel issue?"

He takes a deep breath. "Your da emailed me."

My stride falters, but he ignores it. "Where is he now?" There's no question about *what* he wants, just where.

"Spain. A resort in Costa del Sol." I snort derisively, and he continues, "But he's heading back to the Bahamas next week."

My jaw tightens. No wonder he needs an infusion of cash. His friends in the Bahamas are expensive, and he always stays for a month, at least. "Well, at least he's still alive."

"Yes." We continue to walk across the lush lawn toward the pond, the birds playing high above us. "He asked how you were."

My harsh laugh can't be helped. "Oh, he did now? Well, isn't that big of him."

"Colin," he says softly. "He loves you. You know that."

"Do I? After what he did?" A gust of wind chills my scalp, and I scrub my hand through my hair, so it dries faster. I catch his pained expression, and I huff out a breath in exasperation. The hardness in my heart concerning my father isn't going to thaw anytime soon, but it's not fair to take it out on my grandfather. He's hurting as much as I am. He's the man who stepped in to care for me when my father left—both times. I owe him everything.

"I know you don't believe it, Colin, but he will come home one day. He'll exorcise the demons driving him and come home." I'm not convinced, but I stay silent. We reach the pond, and I prop my foot on one of the stones ringing the edge. The fish dart to and fro, just like my father does—he just swims in a bigger pond.

As I watch Tack follow his nose around the edge of the pond, the image of my drunken beauty comes to mind, and I smile despite the fury boiling inside me. She looked like a nymph standing in the middle of the pond last night, the light of the torches that ring the water casting an almost magical glow around her. Unfortunately, the thought of her brings another to mind. I take a deep breath, not wanting to ask, but unable to stop myself. "Is...is *she* still with him?"

A sigh escapes him, and he runs a hand through his thick, white hair. "Apparently so."

"Of course she is." I shake my head, looking skyward. "I can't decide which one is the bigger idiot," I say with a harsh laugh. "Two liars lying to each other."

"Colin—"

I push away from the pond and stare off toward the malting shed. "Do you need me for a while? Thought I might take a walk."

He huffs, resigned. "No. I'll see you at dinner tonight, yeah?"

"Yeah. C'mon, Tack." Without another word, I stalk off, Tack on my heels. I walk and walk, not really paying any attention to where I'm going. I know my grandfather believes Da will come to his senses one day; he has to for his own sanity. I'm not sure I really care or not at this point. I don't know if I'll ever be able to forgive him. Even if she was as much to blame, what kind of man would do that to his son? I mean, that's fucked up beyond belief.

A gunshot snaps me out of my daze, and I realize I've walked clear to the shooting range. Excellent—my body knew what I needed, even if my brain didn't. Jonathan waves at me in greeting and starts walking toward me, so I steer my steps his way. His assistant is standing in front of someone, pointing at something... aw, fuck. A tourist. I usually prefer shooting alone, but whatever—as long as whoever it is doesn't try to engage me in pointless blather, as tourists are wont to do, it'll be fine.

"How are you today, sir?"

I shake his outstretched hand. "Fine, Jonathan. Thought I'd shoot a bit if that's all right."

"Er, not sure if that's a good idea right now, sir." He looks over his shoulder at the tourist—a woman—with the gun. "There was a bit of a lover's quarrel and, ah, the lass is working out a bit of angst, if you know what I mean."

I huff a laugh. Guess I'm not the only one nursing a broken heart. "Quarrel? How do you know?"

He shuffles his feet and scratches his chin. "They, ah, had it out right in front of me, sir. Apparently, her lad strayed and she caught him red-handed." The thought chills me, striking a little too close to home. "There was mention of, ah, *walls* being involved," he murmurs, his ears pinking. "You may want to have Aileen give instructions to scrub down the alcoves."

"Oh, god." I run a hand over my face. What is it about castles that turn people into raving sex maniacs? I'll never forget the time Aileen surprised a threesome going at it on the grand staircase. Poor woman almost had a heart attack. "Well, I'll stay at the other end of the row away from her. Will that work?"

He looks back at the range and nods. "Aye, that'll do. I'll get you a gun, sir."

I walk over to the far end of the range, while Jonathan heads to the gun shack. Tack follows him—he's been trained to wait inside until I'm done. While I'm waiting, I cast a glance over to the tourist, who's fist-pumping the air after blasting another clay pigeon out of the sky. Good shot, she is. Focused. I don't think she has any idea I'm even here. She bends over, giving me a fabulous view of her perfect arse. What kind of idiot would cheat on that? A long, blonde braid swings down her back when she straightens and takes aim again. "Pull!"

Another shot, another smashed pigeon. She's definitely working out her troubles. Jonathan approaches and hands me a gun, so I can work out some of my own. I ready myself and nod to him. "Pull!" I quickly raise the shotgun, aim, and fire. I grin, feeling some of my own tension slip away as the clay disc explodes.

"Well done, sir," Jonathan says, patting my shoulder.

"Shrek!" We turn, and I freeze when I see my drunken nymph gaping at me, shotgun in hand. She struggles to remove her ear protectors with one hand until the assistant takes the gun from her. "Er, I mean, *Colin*."

Fuck me. Even in jeans and a simple jumper, she's more beautiful than she was last night. "You're still here." My eyes fly open, remembering Jonathan's words. *That's* why she got so drunk. Well, I guess I can't blame her. Not at all.

She nods. "I'm leaving the castle tomorrow, but I'm actually staying in Crossmoor for work for a while." She looks at the gun in my hand. "You're a good shot."

Warmth spreads through me. "So are you."

"Sabrina's doing well, especially for her first time," Jonathan comments from behind me, and I flinch, having forgotten him. I look back at her.

"Sabrina?" A magical name. Yes, that's perfect.

She bites her lip and removes her eye protection. "Sabrina Worthington, but my nickname is Brie."

"Like the cheese?" Jonathan snorts behind me, and her eyes narrow.

"Yes," she grits out, and I swallow a smile. My, she's a feisty one. But then she looks down and frowns before facing me again. "Actually, it's good I ran into you. Gives me a chance to thank you in person."

"Oh, um, you're welcome. I'm glad you're all right." Acutely aware of Jonathan's presence, I shut down that line of conversation. "Do you like shooting?"

"It's...it's a great way to work out aggression." She looks out over the range. "Why don't you have to use the headphones and goggles?"

"I'm used to shooting. We're more careful with guests." I look over toward the castle, where one of the castle guides is walking a group of tourists down toward the old distillery. "If you'd rather be alone..."

"No!" she blurts, and then hands the protective gear to Jonathan. "I think I should call it a day. My shoulder is getting sore. Oh—Tack!" She kneels as Tack runs past me with a joyful yip. He's wiggling all over as she rubs his ears and speaks softly to him.

"It seems you've made a friend," I observe, smirking down at them. He shamelessly flops on his back so she can rub his belly. What a pushover.

She tosses her head. "He woke me up this morning," she says matter-of-factly, and I roll my eyes when I hear Jonathan's muted chuckle. Damn it. God knows what's running through his mind now.

"Oh." I swallow, feeling suddenly awkward. Although I shouldn't,

I want to talk to her more, but not in front of an audience. Before I fully realize what I'm saying, I blurt, "Um, have you had lunch yet? Are you hungry? There's a great place down the hill."

Her eyes widen and a smile plays about her lips. "That would be great."

I turn back to Jonathan, who's smiling down at his shoes, but straightens his expression when I hand him my gun. "Thanks," I murmur.

"No problem, sir. Have a nice lunch." He's holding back a laugh as I lead Sabrina away, and I know I'm going to pay for this later when he tells my grandfather.

But when she stands and gives me a radiant smile that I feel down to my toes, I have a feeling it'll be worth it.

chapter
three

Sabrina

I'M LOUNGING ON SOFT FLANNEL CHECKERED BLANKET, IN THE DEEP, lush grass, on a hill overlooking an ancient stone tower that dates back to the Middle Ages. Tack leaps through the long grass, chasing down some beat-up stuffed squirrel that Colin keeps throwing for him.

The sun is blazing, casting a warm glow through the fields, the castle rising like the royal, stone masterpiece it is behind us. It's like a dream. I've almost forgotten about the mess with seaweed dick.

Shrek has laid out a virtual feast of crusty bread, fresh fruit and the most perfect tiny panini sandwiches I've ever seen from a wicker basket he carried to this little spot of heaven. He keeps a safe distance away from me, on the edge of the blanket. He's given me a few side-eyes, particularly when I kicked off my shoes to sink my bare feet into the grass. Other than that, he's been quiet, giving me one-word answers most of the time when I ask questions about the castle.

I guess I can understand his reluctance to talk about the history of this place all the time. Still, even though it's akin to pulling teeth, I'm going to try to get more out of him.

"What was it like growing up here?" I ask, wiggling my toes against the warm grass.

"Cold."

I tip my head to the side. "And here I thought you Irish lot didn't complain about the weather."

He watches the tip of Tack's tail move through the field in the distance. "I wasn't talking about the weather."

"Ah." I'd like to push for more, but something tells me the ogre in him wouldn't appreciate it.

"What's a castle without a little family drama?" he supplies, his tone clipped.

"I ask myself that same question every day."

I can see just a hint of a smile pulling at his lips. He glances off at the sea in the distance, the wind teasing through his thick mass of dark hair. Christ, he's almost too much to look at.

Tack returns with the squirrel, dropping it at Colin's feet, his tail wagging with excitement until he stiffens, turning his head and letting out a yip to the rolling field of green. Colin leans back on his elbows, casting a fleeting look in the same direction before he focuses back on the churning sea.

In the distance, I spot a few fluffy sheep dotted against the emerald hills and try to rein in an excited squeal. "You have sheep?"

Colin shakes his head, tossing the squirrel once more for Tack. "They're not ours. We let a few of the farmers use the pastures." Another layer of the man peels away. I have a feeling the gruff and annoyed Colin I met last night is the result of a rough wall he's built masking who he truly is. I wonder what's happened in his past to make him so guarded. I do know that you don't help a stranger or rescue dogs or let sheep roam your land if you're not at your core a good person.

"The blue spray paint? Does that identify them?"

My stomach tightens as he throws an amused smile at me. "Someone did their research before coming over."

I give him a shrug, trying to ignore the slow heat burning between my thighs. The reaction I seem to have for this man is dangerous for me. "Becca, my friend who got married yesterday lives here now, so I'm trying to learn as much as I can about Ireland. But it makes sense. Wouldn't want to confuse your sheep with someone else's."

"No. You definitely would not." The sheep graze away, and I spot one with an additional red swatch across its back.

"Does that one belong to a different farmer then?" I gesture toward the small flock, and he tilts his head back, my eyes darting to that damn Adam's apple in his throat. Why is that so tempting? Why does it make me want to press my lips against it, to see what he tastes like?

"No. That one's been mated." I stare at him, confused. "The rams have a bag of dye around their necks. Leaves a mark when they mount an ewe."

"So it's kind of like claiming your territory then?" My voice sounds higher and a little breathless.

He gives me a slow nod. "In a way, yes." I try not to think about him claiming me, about me claiming him. How it would feel to have his strong body cover mine, right here, right now.

He leans up and tugs a flask from an inside pocket on his jacket and takes a long sip before passing it over to me.

I sniff at the flask, a strong toffee-like scent tickling my nose. "Mrs. McGuire must love this place." I'm so subtle.

"There's no Mrs. McGuire." His voice sounds hollow, and he turns those steely-blue eyes on me. "You honestly think I'd be sitting here with you if there was?"

"Well, men have been known to be assholes, so…" I shrug and take a quick sip from the flask, covering my mouth as I try to hide a cough. Colin either chooses to ignore me or doesn't care that I'm almost dying from whatever hell is in this flask. Damn, they make strong liquor here.

"There was supposed to be a Mrs., but my fiancée decided she preferred a different generation of the last name."

He holds out his hand, his gaze not wavering from the cliffs. I silently pass the flask back to him. Clearly, he needs it more than I do.

"I'm sorry, what?" Because honestly—what the hell?

He takes a long sip, and I watch the thick bob of his throat as he swallows. "My fiancée preferred older men—my father specifically."

I just blink at him. "Are you shitting me?"

"I shite you not." He shakes his head, dutifully picking up the wrecked squirrel toy and tossing it, yet again, for Tack before muttering, "I can't believe I just told you all that."

"Who's your father? The God of Thunder? I mean come on. Ogreish tendencies aside, just look at you!" I blurt out like an idiot, gesturing in the general direction of his hotness.

He spits a mouthful of whiskey across the grass before letting out a loud, deep laugh. It's a glorious sound.

"Sorry. That was supposed to be my inside voice." I pluck a grape from the bunch on the plate and pop it into my mouth to shut myself up.

He unleashes a half smile at me that dissolves a few of my brain cells in the process. "Don't apologize. I haven't laughed like that in a long time."

Grinning, I wave another grape at him. "Just stick around, Shrek. I'm good for laughs, if nothing else."

Lifting the flask to his lips again, he pauses. "I'm sure there's plenty you're good for."

Damn it. Did it just get hotter out here?

"Thanks for the picnic," I say, my stomach twisting with nervous anxiety. This feels like the end of a date, when you're standing on the porch after dinner, awkward and flushed, wanting a kiss... no, *needing* a kiss and afraid you're not going to get it.

Only this wasn't a date. At least I don't think it was. I might *wish* it was, even though I shouldn't. I'm in no state to be dating anyone at the moment. Even if *anyone* is the hottest man I've ever seen in real life.

"Not a problem. Had to eat lunch, didn't we?" Tack drops the beat-up squirrel at Colin's feet, glancing between us. We've walked in silence through the sprawling maze of gardens, arriving back at the castle that seems more ominous than it did a few hours ago. The sun has disappeared behind the clouds and the smell of impending rain hangs heavy in the air.

"That we did." I glance at up at the massive main doors of the castle, the McGuire name etched above in stone.

"You're leaving tomorrow, then?" he asks, looking down at Tack rather than at me.

"Tomorrow afternoon. I'm staying in Crossmoor for a while. My company has a client there I'll be working with."

He tips his head to the side. "What is it you do, Sabrina?"

Good God why does my name have to sound so sinful coming from his lips? His perfect, full, kissable lips?

"Sabrina?"

"Hmm?" I snap my eyes away from his mouth. "I'm an architect." See? Some brain cells are still firing.

"Ah." He nods, gripping the basket a little tighter in his hand.

Back to the one-word answers. A grunt or two thrown in for good measure feels like a lottery win with him. "Our firm scored a pretty big client with O'Shea Pharmaceuticals last year. They're about to re-open their headquarters. We've been working remotely while construction went on, but it's time to finish the job now." And I love my job. Getting to oversee the closing of this project has me somewhat giddy, if I'm being honest. Our senior architect, a massive control freak, who liked to take credit for everything, left our firm a month ago, leaving management scrambling. They found out quickly that good old Geoffrey Lancaster was actually an idiot who stole everyone else's ideas as his own—namely *my* ideas.

In the month that he's been gone, the team has really rallied around finishing this redesign, without all of the drama that used to orbit around Geoffrey. He was notoriously frazzled, constantly late for meetings, and always forgetting key deliverables, largely due to the fact that he had literally nothing to do with planning them in the first place. It's been like a breath of fresh air for the team to work without his constant cloud of uncertainty.

Colin's eyes seem to flash and darken with something dangerous. I bet angry sex with him would be an other-worldly experience. *Get your mind out of the gutter!* "They bought up a couple hundred acres of land to expand their manufacturing plant," he grumble-replies, grimacing.

I hit a nerve. So, Prickly-Gandy has a soft spot outside of his beloved beagle. "I'm just working on the redesign of their office space." That I feel the need to explain myself is a problem. I'm never going to see this man again—a fact which is beyond sad. And even though I shouldn't care what he thinks, but I do.

"While they destroy a centuries-old forest in the process." There's grumbly Shrek, back in all his fine, imposing six-foot-two glory.

"If it was centuries-old, wouldn't someone be protecting it?" I counter, hands on my hips.

"*Someone* tried to," he lobs back to me. "It was deemed the four hundred acres we own here were more than enough to counter the devastating environmental impact that monstrosity is going to have." Colin starts pacing, Tack tilting his head to the side to watch him.

"If it helps, O'Shea is committed to following environmental policies. They've written a forty-page statement about it. The redesign is focusing on energy efficient—"

That stops him short, and he turns to unleash on me. "Energy efficient, my arse! Patrick O'Shea is a dirty, capitalistic bastard who's only interested in lining his pockets." I raise a brow at his tone, at the fact that his accent gets thicker, sexier the more upset he seems to become. Slowly, I turn my gaze to the row of tour buses lining the stone drive of the castle.

"Ah, hello?" I motion to a large group of tourists congregating around one of the gift shops. "What do you call this?"

He shoots a fiery glance at the throng of people taking selfies by one of the turrets. "That's different!" he grinds out.

"Different how? Is this not capitalistic?" We watch a couple emerge from the gift shop, happily swinging a brown bag with a crest emblazoned on it. It looks vaguely like the coat of arms I saw in the castle last night.

"No! These people are here for the history, to step back in time when things were different. They want the experience, you know? Like your friend who got married yesterday. You know how hard we work to keep this place preserved? How we have to follow every single rule about restoration and environmental treatment, while that prick O'Shea gets away with whatever the feck he wants?" Tack gives a little squeak of approval, backing up his raving mad owner. "We've been welcoming people here since the sixteenth century. It's a far cry from pumping out drugs designed to keep yer erection up."

I just blink at him, my mind reeling from the fact that the word erection fell from his lips like a prayer. "It's not like they're focused on curing diseases that actually matter," he adds, his stone-like face getting redder by the second.

"Pretty sure erections matter to a lot of people," I helpfully point out. I'm just winding him up now. "And you'd be okay then if they were researching something like heart disease? Is that what I'm hearing?"

"Feck no!" He shakes his head. "Yer missing the point." He rakes a hand through his hair, tugging in frustration.

"Hey!" I jab my finger at his chest, meeting solid muscle underneath his jacket. "I'm not the enemy here. I'm just helping to design an environmentally friendly, energy-efficient office space. That's it."

I can feel his chest moving under my hand with his amped-up breaths. Somehow, my palm has ended up flattened against the rugged leather of his jacket. My fingers itch to tug on the leather and pull him closer.

"Christ." He mutters something else that sounds like it's in a foreign language, his eyes darting to my lips. For a second, I think he's going to kiss me. It's fleeting, and let's face it, stupid on every level for me to fantasize about this man laying a kiss on me, even though I know it would take me to my knees.

His throat bobs with a swallow before he dawns that mask of indifference of his again and he takes a long step back. "I'm sorry. I shouldn't have gone off on you like that. You hit on something that means a lot to me."

"You don't say." He has the good sense to at least look somewhat apologetic. I even get a quarter smile. I consider it a win and internally high-five myself. Small victories and everything. "I never would have guessed."

"Just be careful with O'Shea," Colin says. It's like he's struggling to keep his voice even.

"I take it you two know each other?" I ask as we move into the castle and out of the way of the tourists. His jaw twitches, his shoulders tense.

"You could say that. Our families go way back." He clams up, revealing nothing else.

"Way back? As in King Arthur and the Knights of the Round Table way back?" My mind floods with various scenarios of medieval times and jousting for the hand of a fair maiden. This castle really does wield some magic.

I glance up at Colin as he stops in the hallway. He looks mildly amused, the perpetual scowl he seems to sport fading away. "King Arthur? Well, we do have several swords." His mouth twitches. "But there are much more dramatic legends than King Arthur, many originating right inside these very walls."

My eyes widen at the mention of legends. "Really? Like what?"

He studies me with an intensity I'm not sure I can handle. "Best get your legends straight if you're going to be spending any time here. Some of the Irish aren't as forgiving as I am."

I scoff, my laughter echoing down the cavernous hallway behind him. "You're forgiving? You really are something else, Shrek. I'll bear your warning in mind, but my American ass and I are fully capable of slaying our own dragons, thank you very much." I lift my chin in his direction, holding those darkened blue eyes of his. Pompous ass. Though I'm not sure if that's really the case. He may just enjoy pushing my buttons. I can't deny that I enjoy it too. A little too much, given I'm leaving his castle in less than twenty-four hours.

"Of that I have no doubt." He watches Tack scamper off down the hallway. "I'm taking a party out on the *Saoirse* later. You should join us. Slip number twelve at the marina. Pick up a little history of the sea." He starts walking backward down the hall as I frown.

"What's the *Saoirse?*"

He shakes his head. "If you want to know, you and your American ass will figure it out." With that, he turns, stalking down the long corridor after Tack, leaving me slack-jawed and speechless.

It doesn't take long for me to figure out what the *Saoirse* is. The answer? Intimidating as hell. I glance at various framed pictures of the majestic yacht that adorn the wall of one of the activity rooms near the front of the castle.

The thing is massive with billowing forest green and white sails. There are several photos of a skinny-looking Colin celebrating with other wind-blown guys, their arms slung around each other, holding different sizes of trophies.

Seems good old Colin comes from a long line of regatta winning sailors. Terrific. Yet another man in love with the sea. I shake my head at the timeline of yachts dating back to the 1700s. I should just cut my losses now, say goodbye to Becca and Liam as they head out for their honeymoon, and then go to bed early.

Sadly, the things I *should* do are rarely the things I end up doing. It's gotten me in trouble more times than I can count. Laird is a classic case in point. I should have never approached him at the bonfire on Huntington Beach that first time I saw him. There he was, looking every bit the quintessential surfer, practically having to bat away giggling girls in bikinis. That should have been a clue to just go home, but I didn't, and look where that got me.

I'd like to think I'm older and wiser now. Plus, I've never been on a yacht like this in my life. Judging from the smiling faces of all these people in the pictures, it looks like it would be fun. And I could use a big dose of fun right about now.

I'm still raw and emotional from the episode with Laird. I was with him for a long time, and despite the fact that, deep down, I knew we wouldn't go the distance, it still burns to be cast aside for a better lay.

Having made up my mind, I go in search of Becca and Liam. They'll be leaving soon for the next chapter in their lives and then it's time to start my own.

Colin

What the feck was I thinking? Raking my hand through my hair, I stride across the yard, heading for the back door. First, I'm carrying her to the family guest wing, then I'm mooning over her all morning like a love-sick puppy, *then* I invite her to lunch, *and now* I'm asking her aboard *Saoirse?* She's a tourist—here today, gone tomorrow.

I've lost my fecking mind.

Tack trots ahead of me, jumping up the stairs as I take them two-at-a-time. Granddad's rooms are empty, so I continue down to my own suite of rooms. After making sure Tack has food and water, I pour myself a short whiskey and stretch my legs out on the leather sofa in my den. From this angle, I can see the roof of the malting shed out the window.

Leaning my head back against the arm, I stare at the thick wooden beams overhead. I hate to admit it, but I know exactly what I was thinking. Patrick-Fucking-O'Shea, that's what I was thinking.

That bastard's family has been a thorn in our side for centuries. Although blood hasn't been shed between us since the 1800's, they're the one family in town—the whole bloody country, actually—with which we will never get along. Even without all that, Patrick is one of the biggest wankers I've ever had the displeasure to meet. I hate that Sabrina is going to be working for him, even for what sounds like a short time. Hopefully, she won't be dealing with him directly. If so… the bastard better watch himself.

I run a hand through my hair roughly and sit up, making the liquid splash in my glass. I need to get a grip on myself. Why should I care what he does with her?

Sabrina. The cheeky American girl with an ass to die for. Christ, I'd like to run my hands over her plump bottom, squeezing and…

"Oh, for feck's sake," I mutter to myself, standing and downing the rest of my drink. "So she's pretty. So what?" But I know I'm being ridiculous. She's not merely pretty—she's absolutely gorgeous. Whoever her ex is, he's a fecking idiot. I'm rarely caught speechless, but every time the sun found her blonde hair today, turning it into spun gold, I was struck dumb. She's smart and funny. Her eyes danced with mischief, making me want to know what she was thinking, even though I shouldn't. And now I've willingly agreed to be trapped in an enclosed space with her for two hours? I could have kept my mouth shut, and she'd be gone tomorrow, off to go frolic with O'Shea, the fucking twat. The thought of both makes my stomach churn.

"Maybe she won't show?" Tack merely blinks at me. "Big help you are." Shaking my head, I set my empty glass down and shrug out of my shirt on the way to my closet to change. I need to get down to the docks and prepare for the cruise. My friend Allen's parents are visiting from Canada, and he wanted to give them a treat. His father used to be in the Navy, and now I guess they live in a landlocked city and he misses the sea. I was happy to help them out; I can be an entertaining sod when I want to be. Except now I'll also be entertaining a cheeky American beauty.

Which I'm looking forward to more than I should.

It's almost four, and I wave when I see Allen and an older couple make their way down to my slip. Some clouds scud across the sky, but there's no rain in the forecast. If there were, I wouldn't be taking anyone out. I try to ignore the hope in my heart as I scan the docks behind them, to no avail. No blonde beauty accompanies them.

"Hey, man. What's the craic?" I shake Allen's hand as he climbs down, and smile and nod as he introduces me to his parents standing on the dock. We both extend our hands to help his mother aboard, but his father waves my help away as he hops down, more nimble than he looks for his years. His excitement is palpable, and I can't help my grin. It's a joy to sail with someone who loves the sea as I do.

I give them a brief tour, ensuring Allen's mother is strapped into a lifejacket. She's not as comfortable aboard as her husband. After looking one more time down the dock, I sigh; Sabrina must not be coming. I shake my head, pretending the disappointment I feel is indigestion. She probably had a better offer. Turning, I'm about to ask Allen to help me cast off, when I hear the pounding of feet.

Whirling around, I see Sabrina running down the dock to us, hair flying behind her. She's in jeans, jumper, and coat, her trainers slapping against the wood as she runs. Coming to an abrupt halt, she leans over, hands on her knees as she tries to catch her breath. "Sorry I'm late!" She gasps. "I got the dock numbers mixed up."

I can't help my smirk. "Do they use a different numbering system in the States?" Her eyes narrow to slits.

"No, they—" Her presumably smart-ass comment is cut off by Allen stepping forward. He's eyeing her like she's a tasty slice of cake, and suddenly—inexplicably—I want to tell him to back the feck off. Which is ridiculous. Because I don't care. At all.

Right. Keep telling yourself that, my boyo.

"You didn't say we'd have company, Colin," he says, but he doesn't move his eyes from her. He moves to offer her a hand, but I suddenly jolt to life and reach her first. A tiny smile flashes across her lips as she gracefully takes my hand and hops down. At the same time, a small swell rocks the boat, and she loses her balance, falling into my chest with a quiet, "Oof."

My arms automatically go around her, holding her while she regains her footing. She smells like fresh baked cookies; the ginger sugar ones my gram used to bake just for me when I was small. They were my favorites.

"I'm so sorry!" She gives me an apologetic smile, but her eyes sparkle with humor. "I guess I don't have my sea legs yet." I let her go when she pulls away, her cheeks pinking when Allen laughs.

"No worries. I'm glad to see that Colin is making new friends. And an American, to boot." He shoots me a look that tells me I'll be hearing about this again later over a pint. He holds out his hand for her to shake. "Allen Fisher. Pleasure to meet you."

"Sabrina Worthington." She graces him with a polite smile, but her eyes keep flickering over to me. Allen grins down at his feet, and then claps his hands together.

"So, are we all here now?" he asks me. At my nod, he claps once more. "Brilliant. I'm going to check on my mum." With one more admiring glance at Brie, he struts up to the bow, where his parents are standing, looking over the harbor. When I look back at her, her eyes are wide, her brows drawn in alarm.

"Brie? Are you all right?"

"Good God—you look like a walking Old Spice ad," she sputters, flailing a hand at me. "Or a 'Tour Ireland' poster model. Women would definitely mob travel agencies, waving their passports and shamrocks. This is so not fair."

I bark out a laugh and run a hand through my hair, embarrassed. God, she's funny—I like it. I'm hardly dressed to impress. My thick, blue jumper has seen better days, and my jeans are worn, too. Glancing down, I notice my boat shoes are ready to be replaced as well. Not my best turn out. "Oh, ah, well." I rock back on my heels. "Um, would you like a quick tour before we leave? Might be good to know where the head is, and all."

"The head?" Her face lights up with sudden understanding. "Oh, yes, probably a good idea." A happy yip interrupts us, and she beams down at Tack, who's wriggling in joy at her feet. "Oh, there's a good boy! And you have your own little life vest. Very responsible." She nods in approval and bends down to rubs his ears before passing a hand over his vest, checking to make sure all the straps are secure.

"He's not a great swimmer, hence the vest, but he loves it out here. I don't have the heart to leave him behind most days." I hold out my hand, and she rises and takes it; her hand is warm and soft, but there's strength there, too. I lead her past the helm and down the ladder belowdecks. Tack follows, hopping down the steps. There's a small, but nicely-equipped galley and dining area. I point out the head next to the galley.

"How big is this?" she asks, eyeing the galley and the lounge area. Tack runs past us and jumps on one of the lounges, bracing his paws on the back and trying to peer out a porthole. I see Allen's feet walk past outside.

"She's a fifty-one-foot Oceanis yacht with a stepped hull. I have her rigged to handle alone; any larger and it would require another hand aboard. I like the option of being alone sometimes." I smooth my hand over the mahogany trim on a corner, buffing out a small spot with my thumb. "She's my pride and joy."

"I can see why." She's quiet, but her whiskey-colored eyes are taking in everything. I gesture toward the bow, and we walk farther.

"She sleeps six. There are two guest rooms—" I gesture back to the stern, past the galley and the head. "And the master is here." She leans forward, peering into my room. Tack runs inside and jumps up on the bed, lying down and watching us.

"Oh, there's a bathroom here, too. It's got a shower." She peeks up at me, and quickly averts her eyes, blushing again. What's so embarrassing about a head? "This is gorgeous," she continues, stepping over to grasp the edge of my desk. "If I had one of these, I'm not sure I'd ever go home."

I chuckle. "Sometimes I don't. Some days when I return after a late sail, the sky is so perfect, that I just stretch out on the bow and watch the stars come out until Tack tells me it's time to go below."

Her eyes grow large, and she reaches out to touch my sleeve. "That sounds lovely." She's the one that's lovely. Unable to stop myself, I brush a golden tendril away from her face, tucking it behind her ear. She sucks in a breath, the tip of her tongue touching her top lip, and my heart gives a lurch.

"Oi! Colin, are you down there?" Allen's sudden shout makes me jerk away from her. Tack jumps off the bed and scampers between us; in a flash, he's through the galley and up the ladder to rejoin our guests.

"Time to get going," I say, with an awkward smile. "Come on."

It's been calm sailing and a perfect afternoon, aside from Allen's flirting with Brie every chance he got. I think he was doing it to wind me up. Mostly. I thought about tossing him overboard at one point, but I didn't want to upset his parents, who are good people. His mother chatted with Sabrina almost the whole trip. I think she really only came to make her husband happy and was relieved that she wasn't the only woman onboard. Brie was good about keeping her company.

The sails are furled again, and we're motoring through the harbor back to the dock. The day has given me many gifts. The sight of Brie gripping the side rail as spray shot up over the bow. Brie laughing at Tack while playing tug-of-war with him over that ratty toy squirrel of his. Brie standing beside me at the helm, hair streaming behind her in the wind as we came about. Right now, she's curled up on a chaise behind me with Tack snuggled in her lap. Her cheeks are red from the wind and her hair is tousled, but she looks even more amazing.

"Colin." I nod to the former Navy man as he joins me at the helm. "I wanted to thank you for today. It was just what I needed."

"I'm glad I could do it, sir. You're welcome aboard anytime."

He glances back at Brie, who is listening to whatever his wife is babbling about now. "Your girl is lovely. Lovely and patient," he murmurs with a chuckle. "My wife can talk the ear off a sparrow. She's been a blessing today."

"She is that. But, she's not my girl." I chance a peek back at her; her eyes are closed, her face tilted up to feel the sun. She looks like an angel.

An odd warmth creeps through me at the thought. When I turn forward again, the older man is watching me with a small, knowing smile. "If you say so. My mistake." He claps me on the shoulder, and we stand silently as we approach the dock. Allen stands ready to jump to it with a line to moor us. His father walks along the starboard, tossing the fenders over to hang off the side. A couple dockhands meet us and, in a few minutes, we bump gently into place in my slip. By the time we're tied up and everything's secure, the sun is starting to sink behind the hills and that last warm light seems to make everything glow.

"Thanks again for a perfect afternoon, Colin," Allen says, his parents echoing his comments. "Sabrina, a pleasure meeting you. I hope we meet again." He winks at her, and then leans in to murmur to me,

"I didn't think I'd ever see you with a girl again. Welcome back to the world, McGuire." I grip the rail to keep from popping the cheeky devil.

"Thanks," I mutter, with a strained smile. "Let's get together for a pint later this week, yeah?" We shake hands all around, and I help him get his mum to the dock before waving them off. As they trundle down the dock, I turn to help Brie, but she surprises me by hopping to the dock unaided. I frown down at my feet; I'd been hoping for an excuse to hold her hand again, although I probably shouldn't.

Damn it.

"I had a wonderful time. Thanks for the invitation, Colin." She smiles down at me, and I try to ignore how good my name sounds falling from her lips.

Propping a foot on the bulkhead, I try for casual. "Glad you and your American ass could make it." She laughs. God, she has a lovely smile.

"Me too." She toes at the dock. "So, um, is there somewhere we could get a beer and something to eat? As a thank you?"

My eyes pop open. "What, you mean, you want to buy me a beer?" I can't remember the last time a woman offered to pay. *She* certainly never did when we were together. That should have been a tip off, but I was young and dumb and in love. Idiot.

"Well, yeah. And something to eat." She props a hand on her hip. "I'm starving. All that salt air, you know. Can you stand eating two meals with me in one day?"

Her smirk makes me laugh. "I suppose I could." I shouldn't, but at the moment, with the fading sun behind her making her hair glow, I can't resist her. I reach down to remove Tack's vest and lift him on to the dock, where he promptly tries to sit on her foot. She chuckles and easily lifts him to snuggle him to her chest. Lucky mutt.

"Oh, but what about Tack?" She bites her lip, looking at him.

"There's a dog-friendly pub across the street." I tuck Tack's vest away in a locker, and make sure everything's locked. "He's well-known there."

She beams. "Great."

I jump up beside her, remembering that I'd told Grandda I'd see him at dinner. I'll have to text him from the pub. He'll understand. I take Tack from her arms and set him down; he immediately scampers up the dock, yipping at us to hurry.

"It's like he knows where we're going," she says, matching my stride. We reach the slip gate and I unlock it, letting her pass through first.

"He does. I mentioned he's a regular." I let the gate swing shut behind us, giving it a tug to ensure it locked itself. There are a lot of expensive boats here, and we all take dock security seriously.

Back up at street level, Tack runs over to relieve himself against a tree. When he comes back, I pull his leash out of my pocket and attach it to his collar. His tail is whipping around like crazy, and Brie laughs at his impatience. "Come on, before he works himself into a frenzy," I say. We cross the street and reach Steven's pub, The Crown and Sparrow. I open the door, and we're greeted with a rush of warm, malty air that immediately makes my stomach growl.

"Sounds like somebody's hungry," Brie says, her lips drawn up in an impish grin, as she steps in ahead of me. Watching her plump ass sway as she walks, I stifle a groan.

If she only knew.

chapter
four

Sabrina

THE CROWN AND SPARROW PUB IS MOVIE-WORTHY. I CAN'T HELP but laugh at the chalkboard sign welcoming patrons with the message, *'May the winds of fortune sail you, may you sail a gentle sea, may it always be the other guy who says this drink's on me.'*

The pub is warm and cozy with aged oak hardwood trim, stone and brick walls, and a wood-burning fireplace parked at the far end.

I think I'm in love with the cobble stone floor and the tin pressed vaulted ceiling. It's a labyrinth of nooks and crannies, with lots of yachting pictures in miss-matched frames on the walls, but the high-light is clearly the curved bar with a handful of people gathered around it. And booze… so much booze behind the counter. The entire wall is full of bottles.

The live music that was playing abruptly stops when Tack lets out a little yip, signaling our arrival. Tack sprints ahead, making a beeline for the bar, where a tall man is currently filling a glass from one of the many taps that line the solid-wood area.

He slides the tumbler forward to one of the patrons sitting at the bar and turns in the direction of the door. In the muted light, cast from the wooden lights overhead, he turns and breaks out a full-on grin that I'm sure has taken many women to their knees. Lucky girls.

"As I live and breathe." His accent is thick as he regards Colin, head tilted to the side. "If it isn't wee Colin McGuire. Ya missed the last two poker nights, mate. We all thought you must'ave finally fallen into that moat of yours."

"I don't own a moat," Colin replies, surly and annoyed as ever as we move toward the bar. "And I'm not a wee lad anymore." A round of rough laughter fills the bar, and the band starts back up again.

"Coulda fooled me." The bartender leans down to give Tack a welcome scratch to the head before he pulls out a jar of treats and holds one out in his palm. "Tack, it's been a while, boy. Take yer treat." Tack lets out his version of a bark and gently holds the little bone in his mouth before heading to a dog bed beside the bar. He flops down, content to munch away. Colin wasn't kidding when he said everyone knows Tack.

The bartender wipes off the bar top and motions to the stools. "Since this one here has the manners of an ox, I'm Steve Gallagher, lover of foreigners as the name implies, and who might you be?" He tosses the bar towel over his shoulder and leans an elbow against the thick wood. He's the polar opposite of Colin: tall and lanky with un-ruly blond hair, and a sly smirk that seems equal parts dangerous and friendly. He looks vaguely familiar.

"Sabrina Worthington." He takes my hand and lifts it to press a kiss to the back. I'm pretty sure I hear a low growl from Colin, but that could just be my stomach. "Everyone calls me Brie." Except Colin, of course. Though I do have to admit hearing my name with his accent stirs everything inside me up.

"Sabrina Worthington. That sounds positively posh. How on earth did you manage to get yourself tangled up with this ray of sunshine?" He waves in Colin's direction, completely ignoring him as he props his chin up with his palm.

"My best friend got married at the castle." I sigh wistfully. Even if Becca's wedding didn't end in fairy tales for me, it certainly did for her. She was incandescent when I saw them both off before I made my way to the marina this afternoon. Still, in all her happiness, there's a twinge of uncertainty in me. I know I'm not losing my best friend, but things are changing, new phases in both of our lives with a wide-open future ahead.

"Ah, yes." He leans forward, motioning for me to come closer, so I do, thoroughly enjoying his easy humor. "I'll let ya in on a little secret. He doesn't really like weddings all that much."

I feign shock. "You don't say! I never would have guessed that." Steve laughs with a shake of his head.

"Right? He's so good at hiding his emotions."

"Ah, 'ello? I'm right here," Colin grumbles, sliding onto a bar-stool next to me.

Steve continues to ignore him, turning to pull two glasses from one of the shelves, along with that now familiar green bottle I never want to see again as long as I live. "First one's on the house."

I hold a hand up. "Ah, thank you, but no. I'm way too familiar with Batch 41."

He nods, filling one of the glasses and sliding it toward Colin. "Got a bite to it, yeah? It's not for the faint of heart."

"Believe me, I know." I suppress a shudder, my stomach twisting with the foggy memories of that damn whiskey. Never again. "Just a local beer would be great. Something dark?" Maybe one that matches the mood of good 'ole Shrek here. I turn to flash Colin a smile, finding him shooting daggers at Steve.

Steve fills a beer mug from one of the many taps as I study him. "Hey, I've seen you before." His eyebrows shoot up as he passes me the beer. "You're on Colin's wall."

"Now that's a place I've not been before. How am I on your wall?" He finally turns to Colin, acknowledging him.

"In the boat room," I explain, taking a sip of the dark ale. It's malty, bold and rich. In other words, perfection.

Steve's lips twist in amusement. "The boat room? You don't say?"

"There are a bunch of pictures of you with Colin and some trophies. Do you sail too?"

He lets out an exaggerated huff. "Ah, sadly my sailing is limited to the volunteer search and rescue these days since this one here decided to focus his attentions elsewhere."

Colin glances at me from behind his glass before draining back its contents. "With Dad deciding to take off, someone had to take over. I can't leave it all to Grandda. The man works himself to the bone as it is." He sets the glass on the bar, lifting his chin to Steve. "And you know you have an open invitation to sail with me anytime you want."

"You got me there. Guess we all get busy sometimes," Steve concedes, before turning his attention back to me. "You've been out on the *Saoirse* then, yeah? 'Twas a right day for a sail."

"We were. It's incredible." I sigh and instantly feel my cheeks heat at the dreamy sound of my voice. I'm so transparent. I take a gulp of beer to shut myself up.

Steve shoots me an amused look. "You said you were a volunteer with search and rescue?" Steve nods, leaning a hip against the bar. "That sounds dangerous, though I can't imagine needing your services on a day like today."

"The sea, the wind, it's unpredictable. One minute you're sailing gentle waters, the next, the universe could turn against you. That's where a true sailor shines, Brie. The battle scars make us who we are." Colin huffs into his drink, and Steve pushes up his right sleeve of his shirt, revealing a fading silver scar the runs the length of his forearm. "Got this just before Ophelia hit in 2017, trying to convince this one to come in before she got too bad."

"It was nothing," Colin mumbles, annoyed as ever, his index finger slowly tracing the rim of his glass. Lucky glass.

"Nothing? Ya hear that, lads? Wee McGuire says the worst storm to hit Ireland in over fifty years was nothing." A chorus of shouts fills the bar area, causing Colin to shake his head and wave them off.

"You survived, didn't ya?" Colin fires at him.

Steve ignores him. "Truth be told, not everyone who sails is so lucky. We get our fair share of calls. People underestimating conditions, not knowing the currents, that sort of thing."

"Well, they're lucky to have you helping them."

"Ask him how his missus feels about that." Colin rests his forearms on the bar with a smirk.

"She's not my missus," Steve volleys back, and I can tell their banter is one born of years of friendship. It makes me miss Becca.

"Yet."

Steve flicks the towel in Colin's direction. "Shut it, McGuire." He turns back to me. "It's a bit complicated, you see."

A deep laugh from Colin causes my blood to heat. Even his laugh is hot. "That's one word for it."

"Ah. Say no more. I understand complicated." I tilt my glass to Steve.

"Aye. Enough about complications, even though *she* says it's not complicated." His palm slaps the top of the bar. "You just here for a holiday following the nuptials then, Brie?"

"I'm actually here for a few weeks, finishing up an office project."

"Office project?" Steve leans against the bar and I can see a hint of ink peeking out from the collar of the tight shirt, hugging his body like a second skin.

I start to speak, but Colin chimes in, "She works for O'Shea." His words sound gruff and bitter as he stares straight ahead at the coat of arms fixed to the middle of the wall behind the bar. It's quite impressive with the silver shield, black lion, and red crown, but what's more impressive is Colin's sheer annoyance at the mere word O'Shea. His jaw stiffens, veins popping in his neck. Clearly, something deep-rooted has gone down between them.

Steve's eyes widen as he stands a little straighter. "Please tell me you're joking."

"We've been working with the company on their redesign for almost a year now." Colin scoffs and then plucks a small menu from a tiny silver stand on the bar. "Why is that a problem? What happened between you two?" Colin ignores me, studying the menu.

"Not enough whiskey in the world for that conversation. Just watch yerself, yeah?" Steve says pointedly before he reaches over to tug the menu from Colin's hands. "And you know the menu by heart. You get the same thing every time. Cod and chips." He passes me the menu, opening it up with an exaggerated flare. "What do you fancy, then? The seafood chowder is mouth-watering, or maybe you're a mussels in white wine, cream and garlic sauce kind of gal?"

I get the feeling that Steve is trying to lighten the tense mood that dropped in like a heavy cloud, and while I'd love to know what ancient feud exists, I'm also starving. I decide to let it go, whatever went on between Colin and Patrick O'Shea shouldn't matter. I try to ignore the little voice in my head whispering that it matters because I'm starting to like Colin way more than I should.

I scan the menu, telling myself I don't notice, out of the corner of my eye, the way Colin and Steve exchange some unspoken conversation. *Just drop it,* I imagine is the gist, and I should do the same.

Everything on the menu sounds incredible—so many traditional Irish dishes, but I decide on the comforts of home. Best not to get too caught up in everything Irish. I have a feeling it could become addicting. "The burger looks good." Steve glances back at me, that easy grin of his back in place.

"A lady after my own heart." He takes the menu from me and taps it on the bar top. "Won't be too long." Steve disappears through a set of swing doors at the end of the bar, and I turn with my beer to listen to the band.

"They're really good," I say, turning to glance at Colin, but he isn't paying attention to the band, his focus is singularly on me, those steel blue eyes of his darkened. *Why does he have to be so damn hot?* There's a power in his intense stare. He blinks, giving me a tight nod as he clears his throat.

"They are. They've been doing this for a long time." He looks over to the band with feigned interest.

"Seems to be the Irish way. Tradition, history."

"It makes you who you are."

"But, we can always change who we are, don't you think?" I watch as his jaw tenses.

"Some things you can't change, Sabrina." I shut up then because it's all just too overwhelming—him, the day at sea, this live wire of tension that seems to constantly run through him. It's making me nervous as well as curious, and I know those two things are never a good combination for me.

Belly full from the delicious burger, I stare out the window of Colin's Land Rover as we wind our way through the darkened Irish countryside. Despite my attempts to pay, neither Steve nor Colin were having it. "Keep your shiny American credit card," Steve had said as Colin handed over cash for our meals.

Tack is asleep in the back, the occasional soft snore drifting up to us. An afternoon at sea in the sun must have wiped him out. Colin handles the Land Rover like he seems to handle everything—with quiet, determined focus.

I try—I honestly try *not* to notice his muscular arms or the way the silver from his watch glints in the dashboard light. It's one of those thick, expensive nautical watches with a few dials and all sorts of numbers around the face. I saw him glancing at it throughout the afternoon while we were sailing. I really try not to breathe him in, but the tempting combination of warm oak and spice that engulfs the car leaves me at a disadvantage. It's seeped into me, making me think things I really shouldn't. I've never felt this strong a pull to anyone so quickly—not even Laird. In fact, the longer I'm with Colin, the further away Seaweed Dick seems.

The silence feels heavy, awkward, and I've never been a fan of such feelings, so I do what I always do when faced with these types of situations, I start to ramble.

"Have you ever volunteered with Steve in the search and rescue?"

His eyes cut to mine for a moment before he focuses back on the road. "Not anymore. I used to." Five words from Mr. Conversation. It's progress.

"That must be a hard job. I can't imagine." A shiver rolls through me. Maybe I've seen Titanic too many times, but volunteering in the face of a potential marine disaster would wreak emotional havoc on me. I admire first responders. It takes a special kind of person to run headfirst into all types of disasters when everyone else wants to run out.

"'Tis to be sure. Like Steve said, we get our fair share of mishaps with the weather being what it is." I glance out to the blackened waters churning away in the distance. Those waters that were inviting, almost idyllic earlier today, now seem to have taken on something much more ominous. An unseen danger lurking. "It wasn't really dangerous when we were out there today, was it?"

"It's dangerous anytime you're out to sea, but not to worry. I know what I'm doing."

I try not to roll my eyes. What is it with men who think they are invincible? Laird had similar tendencies, surfing no matter what the forecast called for. I turn my attention away from the water. "What? You don't believe me?" There's a hint of amusement in his deep voice I don't like.

"I believe you. You're very..." I can't resist sweeping my eyes over him. So many highly toned muscles earned, in part, by hauling ropes on his yacht all day. I only just manage not to imagine various pervy pirate scenarios involving Colin and his buxom captive sea wench, who just happens to share my name. It's suddenly way too hot in this car. I clear my throat. "Capable."

"Capable?" He cocks his head, his brows rising. "Been called worse."

"Have you? Care to share?" It's fun to wind him up. He shifts in his seat, as if this topic of conversation makes him uneasy. I don't imagine that happens to him much. He always seems so completely in control of everything, his emotions included. His fingers tighten against the steering wheel, and I decide to give him a pass this time.

"It must have been incredible growing up here, in a castle and everything."

He shrugs, navigating the Land Rover smoothly around a bend in the road. "It was home."

"Right, but my childhood home was built in 1980 not 1580 like yours was." I glimpse at the darkened hills that hug the road. "And now I live in an apartment. A tiny apartment that's just like all the other apartments around it. Four walls and some windows that need repairing."

"Home is what you put into it. Who you share it with," he says rather cryptically.

"And you're sharing it now with your grandfather, but do you ever get lonely?"

"I don't really have time to get lonely." That's a non-answer from the Avoidance King if there ever was one.

"Hmmm."

He finally glances at me for a moment, a dark brow raised. "Hmmm? Just come out and say what you're thinking, Sabrina."

"I don't think loneliness has a timeline. I think everyone can get lonely—particularly if they live in oh, I don't know, say an old castle in the middle of nowhere."

He shoots me a dark look before turning down the road that leads to his home. We pass a few whiskey barrels set up in a display along the edge of the lane. "Is that how you spend your time? Making the whiskey?"

A small smile graces his lips. "When I have time, I do. Grandda still oversees most of it."

"But, you know how?"

"I do. It's quite the process."

"I'd love to learn about it." He unleashes a full smile at me that makes me tingle all over.

"'Fraid not. It's a family secret that exactly four people know about."

"Is the recipe hiding in some secret underground vault?" I stage-whisper.

He laughs—deep and rich. "Something like that. This business can be cut-throat. If people ever got their hands on the process—" He stops mid-sentence, shaking his head. "It's not all bad. There's some good lot in the business, some people I'm close to. Actually, when you're back home, you should check out Golden Hill Vineyard in Napa."

My mouth drops open. "You know who runs Golden Hill? I love their Sauv Blanc!" And any other wine that comes from Golden Hill or Napa in general.

He nods. "I'll be sure to tell Andrew next time we talk."

"How?" I shake his arm. "How do you know the person who runs Golden Hill? California is like a thousand miles away."

The corners of his eyes crinkle in amusement. "More like five thousand, but I met Andrew at a wine and spirits show in London ten years ago, when he was taking over the vineyard from his father. There's a few of us who have stayed in touch from that show over the years."

"There's more?" I ask, my voice rising. "Like who? What other secret friends in the business do you have?"

"A lot, actually. If you're ever in Italy, let me know. There's a prosecco estate I can hook you up with."

"You're just bragging now. Don't tease me with prosecco." I slump back against the seat dramatically. "I can't handle it."

The gravel crunches under the wheels of the Land Rover as it eases to a stop. Colin throws it into park, his accent a little deeper when he speaks, his gaze roaming over me. "I don't think there's much you can't handle, Sabrina."

Good thing I'm sitting down. Colin McGuire has a way of making me weak.

Colin

Gulls cry overhead as we walk toward the castle from the car park in back. Wisps of her blonde hair float in the light breeze, and I shove my hands in my pockets to keep from smoothing them down. My fingers are itching to touch that soft hair again. Dammit.

"It's so quiet," she says, looking around. "Don't you have any other guests right now?"

I lead her around to the main entrance, Tack scampering behind us. "We do, but I don't think there's a big event planned, like your friend's wedding. Just a bunch of tourists, probably."

I hold the door for her and inhale deeply as she walks past, her warm peachy scent making my blood race. Damn, she smells good. Tack ignores us, heading straight for the family staircase and his bed in my room. A day on the boat always wears the wee lad out.

"Well." She shuffles from foot to foot. "Thank you again, for the day and for dinner. I really did intend to pay, you know."

"I know." Like I was going to let a woman pay. Just her offer was more than any other woman I've ever known. There's no way I could take advantage of her generosity—my grandfather raised me better than that.

"Um, so, good night." Biting her lip, she edges away from me, her eyes darting from the floor to my eyes. "Maybe I'll see you around to-morrow before I leave."

"I'll walk you up." Not giving her a choice, I gesture toward the guest stairs and fall into step beside her. I rarely walk the guest floors. I don't know why I'm doing it now, except I'm not ready to part from her, this American girl that keeps plaguing my thoughts.

"This place is gorgeous," she says, brushing her fingertips along the wood paneling lining the hall. "I've never stayed anywhere like it. I'm so glad you've been able to keep it in your family."

"It will always be in my family, if I have anything to say about it."

"Um, this is my room." She comes to a stop and looks up at me, her honey-colored eyes large. "I was wondering—"

A door opens a little farther down and a trolley filled with towels and such is pushed into the hall. The young maid pushing it stares at me in shock. "Oh, m'lord! What are you doing in this wing?"

Oh, shite. Brie turns to me, eyebrows raised. "M'lord? You're a *lord*?"

Thankfully, Emily, one of the head maids, steps into the hall. "Sorry, sir; we had a late changeover in this room. Come along, Mary," she says briskly, prompting the gawking girl into movement. They push the squeaky trolley down the hall and around the corner, the young maid giving me one last look before they disappear. Brie's staring at me expectantly, a smile playing on her lips.

Rubbing my neck to ease the sudden strain, I try not to scowl.

"My grandfather is Lord McGuire, but both my father and I can technically be referred to as lords as well."

"Wow." She blinks at me, as if truly seeing me for the first time. "A real live lord. So, what rank do you hold, or title, or…I don't know the proper terms." She waves a hand at me, her cheeks pinking, and I stifle a laugh. Another golden tendril has come loose around her face, and my fingers are itching to touch it.

"Formally, Grandda is the Baron Crossmoor. But we don't usually get into all that." I lean my shoulder against her doorframe and cross my arms to keep from tucking her hair back. "It can make people feel awkward around us or think that we're too big for our boots. We're really just the same as everyone else."

She leans against the opposite side of the doorframe. "But not everyone lives in a castle."

"The fact that it's a castle doesn't make us better than anyone else. It's our home. We have the same problems—taxes, fixing the roof, tending the lawn—just on a bigger scale. Doesn't mean we're special."

She hums and contemplates one of the historic chandeliers lighting the hallway. "In my job, I've met lots of people who believe their fancy homes and fancy checkbooks *do* make them better and entitles them to special treatment." Looking back at me, she smiles. "I think it speaks well of you and your grandfather that you don't."

"Oh, um, thanks." My face heats, and I push away from the wall, shuffling from foot to foot. But then she tilts her head up, those kissable lips of hers quirking with amusement.

"So, do I have to kneel or curtsey for you now?"

My chuckle rumbles in my chest. I love her cheekiness. "Yes, but only on special occasions," I retort, my own lips twitching. The sudden image of her kneeling before me makes me twitch in other places as well. "Um, so," I continue, jerking my head to clear it. It doesn't work. "Where are you going to stay for the rest of your trip? How long did you say you were here for?" *Jaysus, McGuire, you sound like a laddie on his first date.*

"Three weeks or so. It depends on how well the work goes." She toes the wooden plank floor and looks up at me through her lashes.

"My company arranged for me to stay at a bed and breakfast in town. The Whiskey Rose?"

I nod, feeling a weird twinge of loss in my chest. If she must leave, as least she's going somewhere safe. "I know the owners. They serve up a great breakfast there, so I've been told. You'll be comfortable there."

She's really quite stunning. Cheeks still rosy from the sea air and the beer she consumed at dinner. Eyes sparkling with warmth and life. Her lips part as she stares at me and all I can think of is how soft and inviting her mouth is…

Bang!

A door slams shut somewhere down the hall, startling me out of my daze, and I snap upright again. Good god, I almost kissed her. *Jaysus, McGuire!* She takes a shaky breath, her eyes wide. Christ, I probably scared the poor girl to death. "Um, well. Have a good night, Sabrina. I hope to see you again before you leave."

I turn on my heel and let my long strides carry me out of the guest wing and back down the stairs to safety. What the hell was I thinking?

The morning dawned clear, but clouds are blowing in from the sea, an omen of rain later. And here I am, like an idiot, pacing and waiting for Sabrina to appear. Aileen let it slip at breakfast that the last American guest was checking out, and the next thing I knew, Tack and I were bringing the Rover 'round the front to the guest entrance.

What the feck am I thinking?

Actually, I know exactly what I'm thinking. Last night, after I'd run back to my own suite with my tail between my legs, I was tortured all night with dreams of Sabrina…Sabrina beneath me, Sabrina above me, Sabrina beside me. I was practically drilling a hole in my mattress when I finally gave up on sleeping and took matters into my own hands.

Now, I'm kicking at a few tufts of grass lining the drive, trying to appear nonchalant when I'm anything but. Tack is rolling around on the lawn, laughing at me with his squeaky growls. I frown at him.

"No treats for you today, traitor," I mumble at him. Ignoring me, he trots over and pees on a rock.

"Colin?" I turn away from my dog to see Sabrina standing next to a couple suitcases, confusion in her gorgeous amber eyes. She adjusts the tote slung over her shoulder and tugs her hoodie closed, wrapping it around her curves. "I didn't think I'd see you, um, so soon. Are you waiting for something?"

"You. I, uh, thought you might like a ride to town." Fuck, I hope that doesn't sound as lame to her as it does to me. Her face lights up, so I guess I did all right.

"That would be great. I was just going to call a cab." She wiggles her hand that's holding her phone. Tack bounds over to her, and she greets him with soft words and ear rubs. Lucky bastard.

"Eh, cabs cost a fortune out here. This will save you." I step closer and a wave of her gingersnap-scent wafts over me, making my mouth water. "Um, I'll load your bags," I mutter, swallowing thickly.

"Oh, you don't have to—"

"Colin! Fancy meeting you here."

Oh, hell. "Grandfather," I say, stifling a groan when I see the devilish twinkle in his eyes. I bet Aileen sent him out here to check up on me. Cheeky woman. "I thought you had to check on the new barley shipment." I give him a pointed look, which he ignores.

"Dermot's looking after it. Are you going to introduce me to your friend?"

I take a deep breath, preparing myself for the grilling he's going to give me later. "Grandda, this is Sabrina Worthington. Sabrina, my grandfather—His Lord, the Baron Crossmoor, Kieran Alexander Colin McGuire."

I quirk my eyebrow at him as I roll out his full title and name; if he's going to take the piss out of me about mooning over a girl, I'm going to have a go at him as well.

Brie's delectable mouth drops open. "Oh! It's nice to meet you, um, my lord."

Grandda shoots me a look, but I just smile innocently. He's not ashamed of his title, mind you, and he uses it when it's important, like when we're arguing to save a piece of national history or nature preserves. But he usually prefers to ignore it, just as I do. Neither of us share my father's hunger for the attention our title brings.

"Oh, never mind all that. We don't stand on ceremony here. Just Kieran will do," he says, returning his attention to her. "Sabrina. What a beautiful name. A magical name." He beams at her, and her cheeks pink. "What brings you here to our fair land?"

"My best friend was married here two days ago. And, I'll be staying on a bit for work." Her eyes dart to mine for an instant. Has it truly only been three days since I carried her from the pond? It feels like weeks, months.

"Oh, lovely, lovely. Marriage...what a fine thing. I hope your friends are as happy as me and my Aisling were." His eyes dim briefly as they always do when he thinks of the loss of his great love, my grandmother. The woman he loved, worshipped, cried with, argued with, and adored for decades. The love of his life.

The kind of love I've given up on, thanks to my father.

He continues to chat her up, learning that she lives in California and has no family, aside from an aunt in Seattle. She'd mentioned her home last night, but didn't elaborate, and I sensed it wasn't the time to push. California...that's a long way off. Too far. The thought of her leaving brings a sour taste to my mouth. *Oh, what does it matter, McGuire?* She'll get on a plane, go back to where she belongs, and that's that. Her delicious scent swirls around me, making my blood race. An image of her from my dreams last night flashes through my mind, and I gulp.

"So, are you off sightseeing this lovely morning?" Grandda's deep voice breaks into my thoughts. He's grinning like a Cheshire cat, his eyes bouncing between us. Tack winds around us, sniffing at Brie's luggage.

"I'm giving her a lift into town, is all," I state, managing to keep the growl out of my voice. I think. I seize her bags and move to put them in the boot, avoiding my grandfather's eyes.

"Oh, you don't have to do that," she blurts. "You're already saving me cab fare; you don't need to be my Sherpa, too."

My grandfather chuckles and waves a dismissive hand in my

direction. "Think nothing of it," he answers for me. "Just part of the guest services at McGuire Castle."

"Well, thank you," she murmurs, those amber eyes glowing as I slam the boot shut. "It was lovely to meet you, sir."

"A pleasure, Sabrina." He takes her proffered hand, but instead of shaking it, he leans over and kisses her knuckles. Her blush is instantaneous, and a pang of…something…stirs in my gut. "I hope you'll find time to stop by again before you return home."

"I will." She beams at him, before casting a curious glance at me. I round the car and open the passenger door. Tack jumps in and immediately climbs into the back seat.

"We should get going, aye?" She nods and walks around to get in. I move over to the driver's door, but before I can get in, there's a hand on my shoulder.

"Stop by my office when you return, yeah?" A smug smile plays at grandda's lips, but his eyes are serious. I nod, and he gives my shoulder a squeeze before heading back inside. I swing in behind the wheel, and then we're jostling down the drive.

"Your grandfather seems lovely," she says. I nod in agreement, lowering one of the rear windows enough so Tack can stick his head out.

"He is." I glance at her. "He certainly seems taken with you."

She bites her lip and looks away out her window. "It's so beautiful here. I'm looking forward to seeing more of the area." The town is laid out below us, the harbor beyond. It's a breathtaking view I never get tired of.

"Have you had any time to look around town?" She shakes her head, so I continue, "We have a thriving town center, full of shops and a small museum dedicated to our seafaring history. There's a stand in the town square where bands play in the warmer weather. If you're into history, you could tour the fort on the opposite bluff." I point toward the jagged cliffs on the other side of the harbor.

"I can't wait to see it." She grins and reaches back to ruffle Tack's head. He gives her a happy yip and resumes his stance at the window. Brie shifts forward again, tilting her head to look at me. "So, who is the *Saoirse* named after?"

I turn onto Rose Lane at the bottom of the hill. "My mother. She died when I was ten."

Her soft sound of sympathy wraps itself around my heart. "I'm sorry." She takes a deep breath. "I lost my parents when I was sixteen. Car accident. I was on a high school band trip to San Francisco." She looks away again, staring at the row of houses. "I'll never forget when the police came to get me after one of our performances."

Her hand grips the tote in her lap, and I wish I could take it in mine, give her the comfort she seems to need. "I'm sorry. Mine died of cancer. She wasn't diagnosed until it was too late. I was young, but I understood she was sick. What I couldn't understand is why she couldn't get better." I clear my throat. "So, you were in band, eh? Do you play an instrument?"

She nods, toying with the zipper of her hoodie. "Oboe."

"I like the oboe," I say, smiling at her fidgeting. "I'd like to hear you play sometime."

"No. No, you would not." She gives me a scathing look, and I laugh.

"Not concert hall-worthy then?" I quip, and it's her turn to laugh. We're skirting the edge of the harbor and turn onto Whiskey Lane.

"God, no. I'm not even good enough anymore to play in a closet, much less a concert hall." We pull up in front of the Whiskey Rose, and she smiles. "Oh, it's perfect! It looks just like the pictures I saw." It's at the end of one of the rows of brightly colored houses that frequently make the pages of tourist websites.

"You should be comfortable here, but, um, if you're not, you can always come back to the castle." The words are out before I can stop them and, based on Brie's shocked expression, she's as surprised as I am. "I mean, you'll probably be fine, but it's always good to have a backup," I stammer, frowning internally. I sound like an idiot. Before I can say anything else stupid, I climb out to get her bags. Away from her scent, my head clears a little. God, it's like I'm a schoolboy again.

I pull her bags out of the boot and when I close the door, I find her standing on the other side. Before I can stop her, she grabs the handle of one of her bags. "I'll help this time," she states, her lips pursed in amusement. "I know they're heavy. Knowing I'd be here for three weeks made it impossible to pack light this trip."

"They're not that bad," I protest, placing my hand over hers. The warmth of it makes my heart beat faster, and I can't help but stare. A blush spreads across her cheeks; she's fecking gorgeous. "What are you plans today?"

"Oh, um…" She blinks, as if trying to clear her head. "I thought I'd settle in, unpack, maybe take a walk. I need to go over some work files to prepare for a meeting tomorrow."

A meeting with fecking O'Shea, I bet, the bastard. A knot forms in my gut at the thought of her spending time with that shite. "Come out with me later." It's probably a bad idea, but at the moment, I don't care. "This afternoon or tonight. Dinner? A pint, at least. I can show you around if you'd like."

Her eyes grow big, but then an impish twinkle appears. "I'd like."

chapter
five

Sabrina

I FEEL A STRANGE LITTLE FLIP IN MY STOMACH AS COLIN PULLS THE Land Rover away from the curb. The little flip is ridiculous on many levels. I'm here to do a job—a job I've worked my ass off to get, and am extremely proud of. I need to stay focused and finish the office redesign at O'Shea and not get distracted by all things Colin, no matter how handsome and swoon-worthy he may be.

It was awkward when he delivered me into the lobby of the Whiskey Rose Bed and Breakfast. The building is adorable, set atop of a long, steep hill overlooking the sea, its exterior clapboard painted a soft yellow with inviting flowerpots blooming with bright colors welcoming you inside.

After a brief argument about not letting me carry my bags, Colin hauled them inside and set them down, giving the raven-haired woman behind the check-in desk a cursory glance, making her cheeks heat and her eyes widen. I know the feeling. One look from the man, and I turn to useless, melting mush.

He left with a grumbled promise to text me later. Somewhere in the back of my mind, a tiny voice reminds me that I now have his cell phone number, which is both dangerous and tempting. I think Colin could easily become a distraction if I'm not careful.

"That's quite a man you've got there," the woman says, and fans her face with a stack of papers. She leans over the mahogany desk to peer out the stained-glass window as Colin drives down the street.

"Oh, you're American." I smile over at her, and she nods. It's a bit of a shock to hear a non-Irish accent after spending a few days surrounded by it.

She nods. "Philly born and raised. And you?"

"California—Huntington Beach."

At this, her dark eyes light up. "Do you surf? I've always wanted to try." I try to quell the aggravation that rises at the mention of surfing. It brings up unwanted visuals of stupid Laird and his sun-soaked chest cresting the non-stop waves.

"I tried a few times, but I'm terrible at it." I thumb over my shoulder to the door. "He's not my man, by the way," I say way too quickly. *But if he was…* I give my head a shake. *Focus, Brie!* It's really hard to focus though with his unique oaky scent lingering, and the delicious promise of an afternoon with him taunting me.

"Hmmm. That's too bad. It would be nice to see Colin settle down after all that business with Brigid." The woman shakes her head and sets the papers she was fanning herself with down. She pushes a dainty looking plate, towering with sweets, toward me, but I'm momentarily stunned. *Brigid?* Could this be the obviously brain-cell challenged idiot who left Colin for his father?

"You know Colin?" I ask intrigued.

"Everyone knows the McGuires. They're an institution in this town. In the country, really. Salt of the earth people. Their whiskey's not too bad either." She gives me a knowing wink, motioning me forward. She's a few years older than me, probably in her mid-forties if I had to guess. She has an easy way about her that relaxes me.

"Here. Try some cakes and scones. I made them fresh this

morning." Her thick braid sways as she reaches under the desk to pull out some ancient looking, leather-bound guestbook. "Let's get you signed in."

"These smell amazing." I eye one of the fluffy cakes at the top of the pile and approach the desk.

"I'm not sure about the ones on the top." She motions to the stack. "I may have gone overboard on the lemon." She shrugs. "I'm still learning."

I smile at her and pluck a bite-sized treat, popping it into my mouth. Zesty lemon assaults my taste buds with the first bite, the tang making my eyes water. "It's delicious," I croak out after a not-so-subtle cough.

She laughs, opening the book. "You're lying, but thank you. I knew it was too much. There's always next time." She clears her throat. "Welcome to the Whiskey Rose Bed and Breakfast." She makes a show of spreading her arms wide. "I'm Brooke Flanagan. My husband, Connor, is out back with the rabbits and ducks, no doubt, or he'd be the one signing you in."

She glances out one of the open side windows, and I feel a light breeze rolling in. "Rabbits and ducks?" I ask, looking out the window to the yard. It's a sea of green gardens out there, and I can make out a few wooden benches along a winding path. It looks inviting and peaceful. I hope I get some time to enjoy it while I'm here.

"A few hens as well for fresh eggs. Connor's usually in charge of the kitchen, but I'm trying to learn. *Trying* being the key word there. Never really was something I was interested in until I met him. I'm a bit of a disaster in the kitchen if I'm being honest."

I finish off the sharp-tasting cake—it's really not that bad once you're used to it—and I can't remember the last time I turned down anything sweet. Seems like it should be a crime to do so.

"How did you two meet?" I ask her, digging around in my purse for my wallet.

She gets this faraway look in her eyes, as if remembering. "I was here on a student exchange during college. We met at a food festival." Her smile grows. "God that feels like a lifetime ago. I guess it was. I was twenty-three. Twenty-three! He was older." She looks around, and then drops her voice to a stage-whisper. "Thirty-five."

I just smile at her. "I didn't care. He was hot. Like…" She waves her hands, looking for the right word maybe, and then points to the door, "…like Colin McGuire hot."

"And you fell in love."

"We did. And we've been married for twenty-one years this year. I didn't think it would work at first. I flew home when my exchange was over. We only had a week together, but I was a total mess when I left him."

"So was I," a deep, male, thick Irish-accented voice drifts in, and I see a burly man sauntering toward Brooke, wrapping her up in his arms. "Ye took my heart with you when ye left." Holy silver fox hotness. Built vaguely like The Rock with salt and pepper hair that leans more toward silver, Connor Flanagan kind of reminds me of a jacked-up Daniel Craig. I can totally see the appeal.

He taps the end of Brooke's nose, and she scrunches it before turning back to me. "He flew to Philly a couple of days later and told me he couldn't live without me."

"Every word was and still is true, *cuisle mo chroidhe*." She all but melts, and I'm close behind her. I've never had someone look at me the way Connor is looking at Brooke. The two of them could set this quaint bed and breakfast on fire, if they're not careful.

"Cuisle mo chroidhe?" I try to pronounce his words, but I'm sure it comes out sounding like gibberish, kind of like *Q-mo-crudy*, which doesn't in any way sound as romantic as it does when Connor said it.

"Vein of my heart," Brooke whispers. "Or something close to that. Couldn't you just die?"

"Actually, I could. That's the sweetest thing I've ever heard."

"When you know, you know, so she tells me." He shifts so just one arm is around Brooke's waist. "You must be Sabrina," he says, holding out his free hand. "I'm Connor, and welcome. You're staying with us for a few weeks, then, aye?"

I take his massive, outstretched hand. "I am. Call me Brie. It's so nice to meet you. You have a beautiful place." I glance up to the wood-trussed ceilings. "I love it here already."

"It does tend to grow on you," Brooke says, leaning into her husband's side.

"We'll try to make yer feel right at home. The gardens are for you to enjoy," Connor says, nodding outside. "Watch out for the rabbits. They tend to think they have the run of the place. Don't be surprised if one of them tries to sneak inside the house behind you."

Brooke gives his barrel-chest a playful tap. "Don't listen to him. They're harmless and adorable."

"You'd be describing me now, would you?" Connor teases, glancing down at his wife with so much love, it makes my teeth hurt.

"Harmless and adorable?" She sizes him up. "Give or take a few other adjectives, I'd say so."

He shakes his head a little, before turning back to me. "You want to sign in, and I'll get yer key and take your bags up."

"Oh, I can carry them."

"Nay gonna happen. Consider it one of the many services we offer here at the Whiskey Rose." I sign their guestbook with a pen offered by Brooke, and hand over my credit card.

Connor passes over a key—an actual metal key that has a little white duck with a green head on the tag—not one of those swipe cards you get in every single chain hotel in existence. "You're in the Shelduck Suite," he declares, rather proudly. "Third floor. Brooke here just finished up with the trimmings on it last week. Has a view of the sea, so it does."

"It sounds perfect," I reply as Brooke hands me back my credit card.

"You're all set," Brooke says. "Let me know if you need anything, including wine. I can hook you up. We have a cellar." She looks positively giddy at the thought. I may just have to take her up on that.

Connor picks up my suitcases as if they weigh nothing. The man obviously works out. His muscles have muscles. "Now, you wait right here, Mrs. Flanagan," he calls to Brooke over his shoulder. "I'll be back down so you can tell me just how harmless and adorable I am."

I give Brooke a wave and admire the solid-wood staircase and stained-glass windows that mark our way up to the third floor. Connor dutifully deposits my bags at the door and offers a few tips on what sights to take in. There's an observatory housed on top of a castle that sounds like something out of a dream. Our conversation doesn't last long though, his wife is waiting and that, he tells me, "Is a cardinal rule not to break. Don't keep her waiting. Happy wife…"

"Happy life," I finish his sentence, and he leaves me with an excited smile, taking the stairs three at a time to get back to her.

The suite is a serene escape with a soaring, distressed wooden-beam ceiling, pale blue accent walls and billowing, sheer white drapes. As promised, I catch a glimpse of the sea, peeking through the gossamer fabric. I tug my luggage inside, immediately falling onto my back on the crisp white and blue comforter. Brooke is right. Ireland definitely grows on you.

Crossmoor has an old-world charm that I can't help but fall in love with. Traditional Celtic music spills out of the brightly-colored local shops and eateries, a delicious timbre of accents filling the air. Life here doesn't seem as hectic as the frenetic energy of California.

Colin picked me up this afternoon and has taken me to an open-air market close to the harbor. I'm already stuffed having sampled fresh artisan cheese and way too much local honey. "Aye, Colin!" A middle-aged man waves frantically from a booth set up across from the stand of honey, and Colin raises a hand in greeting before he moves to join him. I'm reluctant to leave the syrupy heaven I'm currently in, but I pat my cloth gift bag complete with a selection of honey, beeswax candles and soap that I've picked up for my co-worker Nat, and follow him over.

Colin shakes the man's outstretched hand. "Marshall, it's good to see you."

"Are ye coming to man the stand today?" Marshall glances down the cobbled-stone pathway, and I follow his gaze, seeing a huge marquee sign for McGuire Whiskey ahead. A crowd has seemed to form near the sign, blocking most of my view.

"Ah, no. I leave that to the experts." Colin rubs the back of his neck, his cheeks reddening slightly. He can't possibly be embarrassed about his own whiskey stand at the market, can he?

"They do a fine job, so they do," Marshall says, turning a smile on me.

"That's good to hear. Marshall," Colin says, motioning in my direction, "this is Sabrina Worthington. She's visiting from the States."

"Oh, welcome, Sabrina! How are ye finding our fair isle?"

"It's beautiful. I may never want to leave." Marshall's smile broadens as he sweeps his hand across the table in front of him. It's stacked with perfectly knit sweaters of every size and color imaginable.

"Well, we'd love for you to take a little piece of Ireland back if you do leave us. If not, these are perfect for cooler evenings here."

"These are amazing!" I run my hand along the thick wool of a navy sweater, glancing up at Colin. A fuzzy memory surfaces of him carrying me away from the lake, the warmth of the sweater he was wearing both calming and welcoming as I buried myself closer to his chest. I feel my own cheeks heat and focus back on the table.

"Shear our own sheep for the wool. Maggie, my missus, does all the dye for the wool and the knitting. If you left it to me, it would be one whale of a mess." He holds up his weathered hands, turning them with a laugh. "I'm useless, you see."

I laugh and pick up a soft grey sweater, holding it up to the afternoon light. "I doubt that."

"Maggie will be sorry she missed you, Colin. She's nipped off for tea with the girls. How did you like her last pie?"

Colin looks a bit stricken, but quickly blinks. "It was lovely. Tell her thank you again."

Marshall seems to bite a smile back as if they're sharing some unspoken secret. "I'll do that."

"I'll take this one." I pass over the grey sweater and Marshall beams at me. "Friends and family discount for you, Sabrina." I pass him over cash for the sweater, set it gently into my bag, and we say our goodbyes.

Colin turns, leading us away from the McGuire stand. "Are his sheep the ones we saw the other day when we were having lunch?" I ask, weaving through the crowd.

"They are. Marshall's family has been selling sweaters at this market for a long time. If you ever get offered pie by his wife Maggie, though, word to the wise." He leans down, his mouth close to my ear, which causes me to stumble a bit. "Don't eat it. Woman can't make a pie to save her life."

His hand catches my elbow, steadying me, and I let out a laugh. "You told him it was great."

"I can't very well be truthful to the man, can I?" He pauses, glancing down at his hand still fixed to my elbow, before he slowly pulls it away. "Plus, I suspect he knows it's awful. But Maggie is essentially a saint. There's no way anyone is telling her that her pies are anything less than perfect."

We make our way to a chocolate stand and I just about die from the rich toffee and mocha flavors of the sample offered to me. "This is to die for. You have to try," I mumble behind my hand that's covering my mouth. All the class in the world from me.

"Nora, how are you?" Colin asks the gorgeous brunette behind the table, who's eyeing up Colin like he's about to strip to a Magic Mike number.

I shove another piece of decadent goodness into my mouth. "I'm doing well. Surprised to see you here." Is it just my imagination, or did she just push her chest out farther in that t-shirt of hers that's a size too small?

Colin pops a piece of chocolate from the tray into his mouth, chewing quickly. "This is delicious," he says, after swallowing it down. I doubt he even tasted it properly. Also, the unenthusiastic tone of his voice doesn't match with this chocolatey goodness, and it doesn't escape me that he completely ignored her.

"It is delicious," I chime in. "I'll take a bar." I lift a neatly wrapped package and wave it at her, trying to draw her attention. She's not taking her eyes off Colin, though, not that I can blame her. The man is sex on a stick, and him eating chocolate? I'm surprised all the women aren't swooning as they pass by.

"That's five," she says, still holding Colin's gaze.

Five shots of whiskey? Five Euros? I have no idea, but I pass her over what I think is the correct amount, and she finally tears her eyes from Colin, glancing at the notes.

"I hope you enjoy it," she says dryly, as a few more customers wander to her stall. Translation, I hope you choke on it slowly.

"Good friend of yours?" I ask, heading to the market's exit.

He lets out a half laugh and shakes his head. "We had drinks. One time at Steven's, two years ago." There's so much to unpack in those brief words, but it's obvious the conversation makes him uncomfortable, so I decide to tread down a different path.

"You don't want to check out your stand?" I ask, glancing over my shoulder. The crowd has grown larger in just a few minutes. It's obvious McGuire whiskey is a huge draw.

"I don't want them thinking I'm checking up on them. Marshall's right. They do a good job. I would hate for them to doubt that."

"I get that. I'm always nervous when the execs come to one of the sites I'm working on, or sit in on a meeting I'm not expecting them to attend." He lifts his chin to the towering steeple by the harbor and we start toward it. "I don't know why. It shouldn't matter if they want to listen to a report, or want me to do a walk-through with them, but for some reason, it does."

He reaches for my gift bag, his hand grazing mine and sending a current that could light all of Ireland through me. "I can carry this," he mutters, and takes the bag from me.

"It hardly weighs anything, but thank you."

"I think they do it on purpose, to be honest. I mean, being an employer, you want to know your people are performing at their best. You need them to be. But at the same time, I never want my employees to feel intimidated."

I glance up at him, my eyes wide. "But you *are* intimidating."

He meets my eyes with a furrowed brow. "I am?"

"A little, yes. I don't think you're doing it on purpose. You just have this very…capable way about you. Confident. And confidence intimidates people sometimes."

"Mmm. There's that word again. Capable. You called me that the other night."

"Did I? Imagine." I grin, and he stops on the street, turning to the soaring cathedral on the corner, set next to the harbor and anchored at the bottom of the hill by a string of colorful houses.

It's stunning and an architectural masterpiece that takes my breath away. "It's from the early eighteen hundreds," Colin explains. "Well, they started work on it then. It wasn't quite finished for nearly half a century."

"It's magnificent." I fish around in my purse to find my phone, snapping a few pictures.

"It's Gothic –"

"Gothic Revival." I slap my hand over my mouth. "Sorry, I didn't mean to interrupt you. Continue, please."

"I should have known you would know the style."

"I may have done a few projects on Gothic Revival over the years. This is unlike anything I've seen before though."

"Want to go in?" he asks, and I see those creases at the edges of his eyes deepen a little. Why do I find that so sexy? He's just too damn tempting.

"Is the Pope Catholic?"

"After you then." He chuckles and sweeps his hand forward, and I make my way up the wide granite steps. I crane my neck up, noting the intricate detail of rose windows and pointed arches.

"I may get struck down by lightning when we enter. Just FYI," I warn, and he laughs, following me up the stairs.

"I'll catch you if you fall." I pause at the mammoth open doors and tilt my head up to meet his eyes.

"You know, I believe that."

"Good. Now, be a good girl for a change and…" My eyes widen at his words, and I watch as he makes the sign of the cross before stepping into the church.

Naughty, naughty thoughts whip through my brain, none of which I should be thinking in a church. He really just said that—really just suggested I may not be a good girl. I swallow back the lump in my throat and make the sign of the cross as well, and then we're standing at the aisle, and I am in total awe.

The craftsmanship and attention to detail is astonishing. The pews, the tiles, the stained-glass windows, granite with detailed mosaics,

and ornate wood as far as the eye can see. The people that built this…
Architectural geniuses. I'm consumed with inspiration, and I reach
into my bag to find my pencils and sketch pad.

"Is it okay if I sketch a bit?" I whisper, not wanting to disturb the
few parishioners who kneel quietly in prayer.

"Of course. Take your time."

"You don't have to stay. I could meet you after if you—"

"Shhh." His fingers delicately pressing over my lips sends a shock
of lust through me. It's a struggle not to bite down on them or suck
them into my mouth- it's truly a toss-up on what I want to do with
those fingers. Long, strong fingers…And it's official. I'm surely going
to hell. *You will not climb the man like a tree in church!* "Hush and start
drawing, woman. I'm not going anywhere."

He removes his fingers, his own eyes widening, like he can't quite
believe he just did that. He takes a deep breath in and then moves
down the aisle, sliding into one of the back pews. He sets the gift bag
he's so gallantly carrying for me on the seat beside him, stretches an
arm across the solid mahogany back of the pew and just stares ahead
at the altar, while I try desperately not to think about all the ways I
want ravish this man.

Jesus, Mary, and Joseph. I'm going to need to go to confession and
I'm not even Catholic.

"Where are ye taking me now? If I'd known we were going to be
on a marathon mission, I would have packed my trainers." Colin's
grumbled complaint doesn't sour my mood. It can't. And besides,
he's only irritable because he knows it riles me up. I think so, anyway.

I glance behind me inside the dimly-lit turreted castle wall, spotting his well-worn boots. "Please. Looks like you live in those. Don't
tell me you've got a blister or something. And here I thought you Irish
lot were made from stronger stock."

"Mind yer tongue," he says, an evil grin in place as he leans against the wall of the staircase. "You're on my turf now. If anyone knows their way 'round a castle, it's me."

"Yeah? You've been up here before?" I counter, winding up yet another dizzying curve in the staircase.

With dusk now falling, the guide at the entrance to the observatory told us tonight would be prime stargazing time. Whatever that means. I know nothing about constellations, other than what the Big Dipper looks like.

I feel my heart pound a little harder as the top of the staircase comes into view. I do have to admit, I shouldn't have had that last piece of chocolate, no matter how delicious and decadent it was. I'm feeling the sugar big time and not in a good way. Climbing in tight circles up this high also isn't great for my blood pressure, I'm slowly discovering. But, no way, no how, am I going to faint again in front of Colin.

"I haven't been here in a while. The view is incredible," he murmurs, his voice dropping slightly. And then, we're emerging onto a little landing with an enormous telescope cordoned off, a handful of people and nothing but the stars revealing themselves to us.

It takes my breath away, and I turn back to Colin, finding his gaze not on the constellations, but fixed on me. He's like a prowling predator as he advances toward me, never once taking his eyes off mine, and it feels like we're the only two people in the world. The blood rushes in my ears and I feel light-headed when he stops just in front of me.

His accent comes out thick and heavy when he finally speaks. "Told you the view is incredible."

Colin

"Incredible."

Her eyes flare as the word slips from her delectable lips. She's staring at me like she's seen the sun, even though the stars are beginning to pop out above us. Her hair is loose now, thank Christ, and I can't help myself; I slowly move a lock of the silky golden stuff behind her ear as I lean in. Her lips are beckoning, and fuck me if I can resist them any longer. I don't care that we're not alone. I don't care that it's only been three days, or that I'll never see her again after her work project is over. I need to kiss this girl.

But, as I lean in, her eyes glaze over and a tiny furrow of worry appears between her brows. "Oh, oh shit," she breathes, and her eyes roll back in her head.

Oh, fuck! "Sabrina!"

I barely have time to wrap my arms around her before her knees give way and she sags against me. "Sabrina? Can you hear me?" I sink to one knee, holding her as best I can, trying to keep her head from falling back. "Brie!"

There's a collective gasp from the onlookers in the turret, and we're suddenly in the spotlight. Not where I want us to be. "Is she all right?" a woman asks from behind me, and I can feel her looking over my shoulder.

"Should I get a medic?" a gentleman asks, but I can't speak past the sudden knot in my throat. Sabrina's sugar-spice scent envelops me, and I can't resist lowering my face to her soft hair and inhaling. It's like touching a cloud. Thankfully, her eyelids flutter, and she sucks in a deep breath. "Easy," I murmur, smoothing her hair away from her face. "Are you all right? You gave me a fright."

"I can't believe this." She groans, rubbing a hand over her face. "Oh my God. I'm sorry. I'm so, so sorry." Her cheeks flame in embarrassment when she sees the small crowd surrounding us.

"No worries." I flex my arm to hold her a little tighter against me. "Are you all right?"

"It's my blood pressure." She groans again. Her nose wrinkles, making the smattering of freckles there dance; even irritated with herself, she's adorable. "I'm cursed with low blood pressure, and all the sugar I ate, plus the stairs, must have triggered it. I'm sorry. I'll be okay in a minute."

A man huffs behind us. "Bloody tourists," he grumbles, and I can hear a soft thwack. "What?"

"Hush, Reggie." A woman growls. "It's not her fault."

Sabrina's breathing seems regular, and her face is slowly returning to its normal color. Reluctantly, I release her when she struggles to sit up, but I keep a supportive hand on her shoulder. The woman behind me comes into view, with a kind smile and a wealth of red hair held back with a kerchief.

"Don't worry," she whispers, casting a sly glance at me. "If I had a man who looked at me like that, I'd swoon, too."

Oh, Christ. Swiping a hand through my hair, I scowl down at the rough flagstones, hating that my own cheeks feel hot. "Do you think you can stand?" I ask, trying to ignore the helpful woman who's fluttering round us like a firefly. Sabrina nods, and I extend a hand to help her rise to her feet. Her hand feels small and soft in mine; I like it. "Do you need anything?"

With a shake of her head, she pulls away and starts to brush her pants off, and the well-intentioned bystander takes that as a signal to help; she starts patting at my girl, brushing off flecks of dirt, and it's all I can do not to swat her hands away and take over. Sabrina bears her attentions with a polite, embarrassed smile, until the lady finally leaves her be.

I shove my hands in my pockets, feeling a little lost. "Should we get you a bottle of water, or some food? I'm not sure what to do for low blood pressure," I admit, wishing I'd paid more attention in health class. "Is it like having low blood sugar?"

Sabrina flails her hands a little, blushing. "Kind of. Food would help. Non-sugary food," she hastens to add. "Really, I'm so sorry."

"Nae worries. I'm just glad you're all right." I smile, trying to ease her embarrassment. Most of our audience has either left or gone back to their stargazing, except for the one woman, who keeps watching us like we're the best entertainment she's had in years. "Do you want to stay and look around a bit?"

Sabrina casts a wary glance around and gives our audience a shaky smile, before turning back to me. "Another time," she murmurs, giving me an apologetic look.

"Well, let get some real food in ye, then." I hold out my hand, ridiculously pleased when she takes it again. "This castle isn't going anyplace," I assure her. "We can come back."

The sounds of the Crown and Cork surround us as I watch Brie devour her sausage roll. I'd offered to take her to a nicer place, but
she was all about visiting another pub, so here we are. Along with
Steven's place, it's one of my favorites. Dim and noisy, with dark
brick walls and heavy wood tables, it's a great spot for a pint and a
chat.

"This place is fabulous," Sabrina says, looking up at the thick
wooden beams overhead. "It feels ancient."

"It is ancient." I take a sip of my stout and nod toward Finn behind the bar. "Although Máire and Finn have only had this place for
about ten years, there have been pubs in this location for close to three
centuries." I catch Finn's eye; he gives me a friendly salute and goes
back to pouring pints.

Sabrina chuckles. "Do you know everyone in town?"

"Well, not quite everyone," I mutter. "Finn's a good friend." I stab
into my kidney pie, appreciating the savory aroma.

She shakes her head, a wry smile on her lips. "It's kind of remark-
able how casually you talk about something that's been here longer
than my country has been a country."

"That's because you colonists think you're the center of the world,
when really, you're just at the edge of it." I wink at her, and she laughs,
the sound making my insides light up.

"Did you find your inspiration today?" I ask her, curious on what
she sketched while we were in the cathedral. We were there for over
an hour, and it didn't bother me one bit. Watching her taking in the
stone and wood detail was truly something to behold.

"I did. I'll show you sometime if you're interested."

"I'd love to see your work if you'd like to share it." She smiles,
ducking her head slightly, but I don't want her to feel pressured or
embarrassed about what she does and how passionate she is about it.
That excitement I saw in her today reminds me of how I feel when
I'm working at the distillery with Grandda. "How are you feeling?"

"I'm fine." She raises her glass to mine, and we clink. I like that she seems to prefer the dark beers. "This is helping."

"It definitely has restorative powers. I've been trying to talk Finn into a joint venture, but he's just not interested."

Her brows shoot up. "What, like bottle it and sell it all over?" I nod, and she tilts her head, considering. "Well, it would definitely sell. It's delicious." She takes another sip. "But, some people don't care about 'taking that next step,' you know? Sometimes, keeping it small is where the joy is."

A warm spot in my chest grows as I regard her kind eyes. "You're right," I murmur, impressed with her insight. "That's one of the reasons Grandda and I haven't expanded, despite offers to do so from the bigger distillers. And we insist on hiring local, including our suppliers for the tourist events. We know every one of our employees and treat them well. Crossmoor is so dependent on tourist money; it's sometimes hard for folks to stay afloat in the off-season. We try to provide a stable living for as many as we can."

"That's admirable." She tilts her head, and it feels like she can see right through me. Shrugging off her praise, I take another bite and swallow.

"It's the least we can do. Everyone wants their hard work rewarded, right? We try to do just that."

"You sound very protective of them, the town, that is." She peers at me over the rim of her glass. "Have you lived here all your life?"

"Almost." I take a long sip of my beer. "After uni, I spent three years in Dublin, developing a brewery with a friend."

Surprise flickers in her eyes. "A brewery? You didn't come straight back here to the whiskey business?"

"I wanted to try something a little different. Something that wasn't tied to my family name." I finish my pie and shift in my seat, unaccustomed to talking about myself. "I'm sorry; I must be boring you."

"No!" she blurts, almost spilling her beer. She quickly sits back, gesturing for me to continue. "Not at all. I like to hear you talk. I mean...it's interesting."

I can't help my smirk. "Are you sure you didn't hit your head when you fainted?"

She playfully whacks my forearm. "You know I didn't. Keep talking. Was your brewery successful?"

"It was small, but yes. We were getting noticed and picking up a following. Mostly, it was fun." I smile, remembering all the small experimental batches that Jamie and I would cook up, debating which ones to focus on for bottling. We had a blast.

"I bet it was. So, why did you come home?" She pushes her empty plate aside and props her elbows on the table.

"Jamie—that was the friend I started it with—his mother became ill, and he needed to go home to Belfast. I thought about continuing on by myself, but I knew my grandfather wanted me to come home and help him, so I took it as a sign. We sold the business at a nice little profit and called it good. We'd accomplished what we set out to do."

"I bet your grandfather was proud of you." I look up to see those whiskey eyes of hers glowing with a warmth that sears me to my bones.

"You'd have to ask—"

A hand clamps down on my shoulder, and we both startle at the booming voice intruding on our bubble. "Well, if it isn't the famous Colin McGuire! And with a woman, no less. Saints be praised."

"Patrick." He releases my shoulder just before I pry his hand off, and he smirks at my cold tone.

"Come down off yer throne to mingle with the little people, eh *Lord* McGuire?" His pale grey eyes gleam with spite, despite the jaunty smile on his face. "How common of you."

"Colin's here so often, he knows the specials of the day. Nothing common about that." Finn's deep bass cuts through the sudden silence in the pub as he appears next to Sabrina's chair. He folds his arms across his barrel chest, his green eyes wary. "What brings you to town, Patrick? It's been over a year since *you* last graced our halls, hasn't it? I almost didn't recognize you." The tension in the air is palpable, and Sabrina's brow furrows as her eyes dart between them.

"I've a business project that's wrapping up. Big expansion. You may have heard of it." He sneers down at me, and my jaw ticks. It was a bitter pill, losing the chance to save that part of the woodland on the outskirts of town, knowing that this eejit is going to chop it all down in the name of *expansion*. Expansion, my arse; more like the all-mighty euro and his name in neon lights. Changing targets, the fucker flashes a charming smile at Sabrina. "Aren't you going to introduce me to your friend, *Lord* McGuire? Where are your manners?"

I'm surprised the glass isn't cracking in my hand. "Patrick, this is Sabrina Worthington." My voice is flat. "Brie, Patrick O'Shea."

"I'm the architect working on your office project, Mr. O'Shea. It's nice to meet you," she says, her soft voice sounding loud in the silence. At her revelation, a few patrons switch their gazes to Brie, eyeing her with suspicion. It's not surprising, since anyone associated with O'Shea tends to get a cold shoulder from the locals, but I hate that it's directed her way.

He leers at her and sweeps a hand through his hair. He's wearing it longer now, like a wannabe Richard Branson. "Oh, ho! This *is* a pleasant surprise. I was shocked to see Colin with a woman—it's been *years*. I'd thought he'd sworn off them after the last one. What was her name, Colin? Brigid, was it?" I grip the edge of table to keep myself from launching at him. Making scenes in public isn't my thing, especially in front of someone like Sabrina, but I may make an exception for this fucker. "But, now I see it's just business," he continues. "I believe I have a meeting with you in the morning, Miss Worthington. Or, is it missus? And, please, call me Patrick."

I'd roll my eyes at his clumsy effort if it was anyone but Brie he was stalking. Unable to stop myself, I shove my chair back, but Brie's confident tone stops me from rising. "It's Ms. Worthington, actually, Mr. O'Shea. It's nice to finally meet you." She rises gracefully, and I shoot up to my feet. "I'm sorry, but we need to be on our way. I'll see you at your office in the morning." She looks up at me and I nod, quickly handing some bills to Finn, who takes them without removing his gaze from O'Shea.

"Oh, yes, yes. I look forward to our meeting." He quickly steps back out of my way, but regains his haughty tone as I walk past. "Our Colin is a frosty one. I hope he isn't boring you."

Swinging around, I'm about to slam my fist into his face, when Brie steps between us, her hand comfortably on my bicep. "I hope you have a lovely evening, Mr. O'Shea," she says, as if he'd never spoken. With a polite smile for the surprised bastard and a bright grin for the now amused Finn, she turns and heads for the door. I can't help my smug smile as I follow, my eyes on her swaying hips.

The cool evening air is refreshing but doesn't do much to ease my temper. "Well, that was interesting," Brie muses. "And awkward. Awkwardly interesting."

I grunt in agreement and hold her door open as she climbs in the Rover. "That's one way to put it."

"What was with all that 'Lord McGuire' stuff?" she asks once we're back in the car. I grimace and shake my head as the engine roars to life.

"You caught that, eh?" I put us in gear and head down the quiet street.

She cocks an eyebrow. "Kind of hard to miss."

I turn the corner and head toward her boarding house with a sigh. "It's ridiculous. The O'Sheas used to be members of the peerage, had a barony over in Ballinscree, northwest of Cork. But their title was stripped. The fact that the McGuires have held onto their position is a sore point for Patrick. Daft bugger."

She huffs in amusement. "It was stripped? When?"

"1726…or thereabouts." She gapes at me. "Something about plotting to kill the king's brother-in-law or cousin…someone," I add, shrugging. She snorts out a laugh, and I smile at the sound.

"Long time to hold a grudge." She shakes her head.

"It's petty, of course." I shrug again. "But, O'Shea's a petty man. Mostly, he's just pissed because Grandda has been so successful at saving most of the land around Crossmoor." Land he wanted to ruin and exploit. The bastard.

"Hmmm." A smirk forms on her lips. We pull up in front of the Whiskey Rose, and I quickly get out and round the Rover to open her door. She pops out and stands there, toying with the zipper of her jacket. The beam of the streetlight makes her blonde hair glow gold.

"Thanks for this afternoon, and for dinner," she murmurs, her cheeks pinking as she looks at me. Shit, do I have something on my face? I swipe a hand over my nose and chin—nope, nothing there—and she quickly looks away. "I'm sorry about earlier. You know, with the whole fainting thing."

"I'm just glad you're okay." I can't help but step closer; her ginger-spice scent is too tempting. "I'm sorry our dinner was interrupted."

"It's all right." Her nose crinkles adorably. "I hope he doesn't make a big deal of it during our meeting tomorrow."

"If he does, tell me. If he puts one toe out of line..." My fists clench at the thought. "Fucker better watch himself."

"I can take care of myself." She sticks her chin out, her eyes narrowing. "It was an awkward way to meet a new client, that's all. I'm a professional, here to do a job. A job I do very well, thank you very much. And I'm not going to let some stupid ancient pissing match get in my way."

Damn, if I don't love this side of her. This feisty, confident, take-charge side that says she could kick my ass if she wanted to. But she doesn't understand.

"I bet there's not much you let get in your way." I drag my hand through my hair. "But, Patrick, he's a shifty bugger, both profession-ally and personally. You need to watch your back with him. Don't take my word for it: ask around."

She glowers at me. "Oh, and you're not biased at all, right? He seems pompous, but I've dealt with self-important jerks before. Besides, why does it matter it to you?"

"I don't know! I just know that it does." I heave a sigh and try to manage my roiling emotions. She frowns at me in confusion, and I can't blame her. I must sound mad. "Look, Sabrina, it's just that..."

"What? What is it, Colin?" She waves her hands in futility, and the words in my head disappear. All I can think of is...

"This." My hands cup her face, and my lips descend on hers. Her mouth is warm and supple, and my blood is roaring in my ears. My head is screaming at me to stop—I've never thrown myself at a woman in my life—but, just when I'm about to pull back, her hands sink into my hair and hold me fast. Her scent is intoxicating, and it's all I can do to stay upright. My hand slides down her neck and slips behind her; I tug her close, and her moan of yearning is almost my undoing.

The realization that we're standing out in front of her boarding house, where anybody could be watching, hits me like a freight train. Brie deserves better than being mauled on the front stoop. I pull back, leaving her in mid-pucker. She blinks rapidly and sucks in a tiny breath.

Oh, God, is she going to faint again? "Brie, are you all right? I'm sorr—"

The sudden onslaught of her lips cuts me off. Her arms wrap around my neck, and I squeeze her closer, molding her curves against my chest. "Colin," she murmurs against my lips, and I taste the beer we had earlier on her tongue, a toasty bitterness blending with her natural sweetness. It's a heady combination.

The sudden glare of passing headlights startles us apart. As the car passes, we stand there panting like we've run a marathon. Her large eyes look like molten amber, as she stares up at me with a satisfaction that warms my heart.

"Wow."

"Wow, yerself." I force myself to take another step back from her. She's starting her project tomorrow and probably needs to sleep. And I need to not be an arse and let her go to bed. I straighten and clear my throat, trying to clear my head of the Sabrina-fog I'm in. "Um, well. Goodnight, Brie," I murmur. "Sleep well, a mhuirnín. I'll call you to-morrow, if that's okay."

She nods, a smile playing on her lips. "Definitely okay. Goodnight, Colin."

I walk backward toward the car, my eyes not leaving hers until I sense the Rover behind me, and then I quickly open the door and swing up behind the wheel. As I turn the key, she slowly walks backward, up the walk toward the front door, that little smile of hers tempting me, until a light goes on inside. Then she swiftly turns, pops up the steps, and disappears.

Beidh an bhean sin mar bhás dom.

chapter
six

Sabrina

I CLOSE THE DOOR TO MY ROOM AND LEAN AGAINST IT—ONLY JUST managing not to swoon like some love-sick teenager in a coming-of-age rom com. The way I'm feeling, I'll be lucky if I don't float to bed on a cloud. It won't be long before I'm drawing hearts around our names in the back of my notebook or trying to figure out the best version of my new name— *Mrs. Sabrina McGuire, Mrs. Brie Worthington-McGuire.* God, what am I thinking? I'm acting like I've never kissed a guy before.

I give my head a shake, as my fingers come to rest on my lips. I can still feel his lips on mine, deep and consuming. Of course, the man can kiss. I wasn't wrong about him making me weak in the knees. Maybe I should have feigned a repeat fainting episode, you know? Just to feel his arms around me for a longer period of time.

Jesus, Brie. Get a grip! I've already fainted on the man twice, let's not go for a three-peat.

With monumental effort, and my head in a fog to get ready for bed, I feel like I've had one too many glasses of champagne. I can't seem to remember where I put anything when I unpacked this morning. Rifling through the dresser drawers, I finally find pajama bottoms and a shirt; they're soft and welcoming and exactly what I need to try to get some actual sleep.

Under the covers, with my long-dead phone charging on the nightstand (why they can't invent a battery that lasts longer remains one of life's great mysteries), I stare out at the harbor in the distance.

Pale light from the moon filters in past the sheer drapes, and I can't help but smile as I look out the window at the stars twinkling in the night sky. I can hear Colin's thick, sexy-as-all-hell accent from earlier tonight when we were on top of the observatory. "The view is incredible." I stifle a squeal and roll over to bury my face in the pillow. I need to calm the hell down and keep things in perspective.

It was one afternoon and one kiss. If nothing else comes of it, I can always say I got that kiss. That magical kiss on top of a hill under a blanket of stars. That weak-in-the-knees unexpectedly romantic kiss people dream of. And if that's all there is, I'm just fine with that.

"You're up early."

Ah sweet, sweet coffee. A giant, steaming mug is placed in front of me by Connor, along with an Instagram-worthy breakfast of crispy bacon, poached eggs, baked beans, mushrooms, grilled tomatoes and a mountain of potatoes. There's even a watercress salad and what looks like homemade bread, peeking out from underneath all of it. I'm not going to lie—the amount of food on this plate looks daunting. I couldn't eat all of this if my life depended on it.

Caffeine is typically my one and only breakfast requirement. And I need it today. Last night, despite my plan to get some sleep, I woke up around two a.m., with illicit thoughts of a certain Irishman in my head.

Beyond giving me a kiss that I will forever judge all kisses moving forward against, Colin has been extremely kind and giving of his time. Taking me out on his yacht, showing me around the picturesque city, putting up with me fainting on him—twice. I'd like to do something special for him. The wee hours between two and four this morning were spent scouring various websites for weird and wonderful things to do in Crossmoor. I now have a list of places we can visit in and around the village. I just need to work up the nerve to call him or text him. I groan at the thought. Texting the Irishman may just about do me in. I'll be reading his texts in that accent of his that makes my blood heat.

I glance up at Connor, who's moved to the open doorway from the garden and is currently blocking out the sun. Those muscles of his are something else. Perpetually flexed. He doesn't even have to try to show them off. I focus on the caffeine nectar flooding my veins.

"You made all of this?" I ask, scanning the plate once my brain starts to wake up.

"That I did. Eggs are fresh this morning, along with the vegetables. Picked 'em myself after my run."

I set the mug down and get busy shoveling a forkful of potatoes into my mouth. He probably ran with a thousand-pound weight on his back. You know? Just for fun.

I'm pretty sure I let out a moan at the sheer bliss exploding on my taste buds. These potatoes are the perfect mix of savory, crunchy goodness. Holy hell, Connor Flanagan *can* cook. "This is incredible," I tell him after a few more bites. "Seriously? How are you not booked out for breakfast?" I glance around the cozy sitting room that's currently empty.

Connor just shrugs. "That's not why I cook. I do it because I love it. Who needs all that stress of extra people queuing out the door and then complaining? If the guests who stay are happy, I'm happy. It's not like we've got a place like your Colin McGuire has."

I just about choke on a vine-ripened, perfectly roasted tomato. "Ah, he's not mine," I manage. *Oh, but would it be nice if he was.*

The corner of Connor's mouth twitches as I feel my cheeks heat. "Mhmm. Regardless," he carries on, "that's a legacy he's got there."

I look around the beautifully cozy room, the picture of a welcoming quintessential Irish home. "And this is yours."

"'Tis," he says rather proudly, casting his eyes over one of the stained-glass windows. "And we're just fine with our five guest rooms. I can't imagine dealing with busloads of tourists and keeping up traditions that date back a few centuries."

I point the fork at him. "It's perfect here. I may never leave."

"Yer welcome to stay as long as you like."

"Will Brooke be down for breakfast?" I ask. I've barely made a dent in the tower of food, but my stomach is already in knots about making a good first impression this morning at O'Shea's office. No matter how mouth-watering this breakfast is, the last thing I need is for it to make an unexpected reappearance during my meetings.

Connor glances toward the staircase just outside the sitting room with a gleam in his eye. "My Brooke isn't exactly a morning person."

I lean back in the chair to take a break from eating, and nurse my coffee. "Now that I understand."

Connor pushes back the sleeve of his Henley to look at his watch. "It's not even half five and yer up and about."

"First day and everything. Normally, I'm not up this early. I'm just nervous, I guess."

"I reckon you'll be just fine. What is it you're working on while you're here?" He nods to my blueprint storage tube propped up against the wall beside the table.

"My firm is finishing off the redesign the O'Shea Pharmaceutical headquarters." There's no ignoring Connor's frown. "O'Shea?" Connor asks, his jaw set.

"Wait." I hold up a hand. "I need to watch myself, right?"

"Well, yeah. Ye do." I furrow my brow, and Connor's accent gets more pronounced. "He's out of his bloody mind."

"I'm sure he's not that bad. I have a meeting with him this morning, and then I'll probably never see him again." Connor lets out a non-committal snort. "It's only because we're almost finished that he's even coming to this one." I glance at my phone to see that my ride is two minutes away.

"Thanks again, Connor. You really should think about opening up for breakfast so everyone can enjoy it."

I push back from the table and reach for my bag and the tube with the blueprints. "And let 'em all in on the best kept secret in town? Never." Connor walks with me to the front door and holds it open. "You have our number if you need anything, aye?"

"I'll be fine, *dad*." Connor laughs, but it sounds forced, doing nothing for my already churning stomach.

The office is a buzz of activity when I arrive and pass-through security. Saws whirl and hammers fly, the smell of fresh paint permeates every inch of the place. The finishing touches are one of my favorite parts of a project. My dad always said it's the little things that will make people stop and take notice, and I try to remember his words of wisdom with each project I'm working on.

Being sent by security to Patrick O'Shea's office, I make my way through the curved hallway, dodging crews of workers on the way. The office design is anything but normal. Inspired from the meandering streets of Crossmoor, the space is fluid, with open breakout spaces and dotted wood-grained signposts that direct you to various meeting rooms, all named for various Irish landmarks and O'Shea inventions.

Patrick's office is uncharacteristically on the first floor. When the team questioned the location, we were told O'Shea likes to be at the center of things. His office takes up the entirety of the floor, and is fronted by a massive slate reception desk, that currently sits empty.

The nervous flutter in my belly intensifies with each step I take past the desk. The red flags that both Connor and Colin raised regarding Patrick O'Shea seem to be winning the battle, making me more anxious than I typically would be.

I can hear more rhythmic hammering ahead, though it sounds weird, like there's some injured animal howling. It wouldn't be the first time crews came across wildlife at a design site. Oh God, I hope it's not some bird nest. On the last build we did in Los Angeles County, the crew found a nest of western snowy plovers living on the shore, and the entire project ground to a halt while we waited for the nesting season to finish. Something tells me, Patrick would not like to hear about any delays caused by birds, regardless of how adorable those birds may be.

A bank of glass comes into view around another corner, and I soon find out what the intense shrieking is all about. I stop short, cursing the full floor-to-ceiling glass design of his office. There's Patrick O'Shea, with his pants (designer probably, and costing more than my rent), down around his ankles as he drives into a woman from behind. Her inky, black hair is spilled over his glass desk, and he takes a handful of it, yanking her head back and saying something against her ear that makes her howl louder.

Holy, holy hell. I am not getting paid enough to witness this, but it's like a train-wreck. You can't stop watching. I feel my cheeks heat and my mouth drops open as he hikes her leg up on the desk, continuing to plow into her. Thank the lord they are turned toward the windows that face the sea. For him to catch me watching would be a level of embarrassment I'm not equipped to deal with at this moment or ever.

His almost white hair is a disheveled mess, sticking up in every direction. I guess mine would be too if I was going at it like this. A thud from something down the hall yanks me from the X-rated scene in front of me, and I quickly flatten my frame against the far glass wall, inching back and away from the scene.

I'm going to need brain bleach.

I tilt my head up, keeping my palm on top of my hard hat as I take in the living wall of plants that runs from floor to roof in the All Hands meeting space, in the center of O'Shea's building. The alternating green hues are highlighted by the large windows that face the rocky landscape overlooking the sea. I don't think I'll ever get over that euphoric feeling of seeing something you've helped create come to life.

Nolan Riley, O'Shea's Executive VP of Development who's been leading the project, glances over at me. "What do you think?" he asks.

I take another picture of the space with my phone. "I think it's unique and inviting. I hope it's what you were expecting." I also hope Patrick doesn't think he can somehow climb up these planter boxes and try to screw someone three stories up.

Nolan pushes his glasses up his nose, casting a shrewd eye over the space. Nolan is probably in his late fifties, with thinning salt and pepper hair. I always get annoyed-principal vibes from him, like he's just waiting for the team to make a mistake so he can send us all to detention.

"It's a little more green than I imagined," he says, and I have to bite my lip to avoid reminding him, *he* was the one who wanted to, and I quote, *'bring the outside in.'* "But I think the employees will appreciate it," Nolan adds with a firm nod.

"Perfect." I can't help but give him a satisfied smile. I'll have to text Nat back at the office to let her know that we got the closest thing to a compliment we're ever going to get from him.

For his part, Patrick has been completely absent from the redesign, leaving the work to his chief minion, Nolan, who made it very clear what the O'Shea vision was. Avoid the traditional primary colors that so frequently show up in a lot of offices, and make sure the company logo is embossed in at least four places in every room—in the floor, in the glass, and two in the wooden walls. Our team agreed that was a little over the top, but when the client is paying ten million on a redesign, you give them what they want.

We went with a muted color palette of timber and grey, with white oak floors and wooden dividers and panels throughout. There's no space that doesn't have a massive window looking out either to the sea, or to the impressive gardens the company maintains.

As Nolan and I continue the tour, he apologizes again for Patrick missing our meeting. I don't say a word. I just want to erase that visual of his morning quickie from my memory. We round the bend of another curved hallway and stop in front of one of the open labs. It's just as impressive as the rest of the space. A few dozen state of the art microscopes are strategically placed along wooden tables, with at least forty computers strewn throughout the room, and more lab equipment than I'll ever understand how to use in a lifetime, taking up the space.

Nolan clears his throat and narrows his eyes at a woman, dressed in a white lab coat, perched on one of the artful leather stools, peering into a microscope. "Kathleen," Nolan says in that authoritarian way of his. "You aren't supposed to be in here yet." Poor Kathleen. I wonder how often she gets scolded by him.

Kathleen doesn't move her gaze from the microscope. "Tell that to Patrick. I've got a deadline." Kathleen has platinum blonde, obviously dyed, hair piled on top of her head in a haphazard bun.

"Then work at the office in Shearing," Nolan says, his eyes narrowing in her direction.

She lets out a little huff. "You mean the sweatshop? Where I have to fight to get time in *my own* lab?" She glances away from the microscope to jot something down in a notebook. "No, thank you."

"We haven't even cleared inspection yet," Nolan presses on, folding his arms across his chest. "It's scheduled for later this week."

"Mhmm," Kathleen murmurs, moving back to the microscope. "Trust me when I tell you, nothing here is going to be as bad as things are at the Shearing Lab."

"What's wrong with the Shearing Lab?" Nolan takes a step into the room, and I follow him, drawn in by the drama.

"I don't have time for this, Nolan." Kathleen turns to the computer set up beside her and starts feverishly typing.

"Kathleen," Nolan hisses through gritted teeth, and she finally tears her attention from her microscope, letting out an exasperated breath.

"What?" Her voice is raised, and her palms slap against the wood table in frustration, before her gaze drifts to me, and she realizes she has an audience. She falters, reining in her obvious anger, her burgundy stained lips fighting to flash an extremely fake smile. "I didn't realize we had company, what with the building not having passed inspection yet," she grinds out, shooting daggers at Nolan.

"Yes. Sabrina Worthington, Kathleen O'Shea." Nolan sweeps his arm between the two of us, and I tentatively approach the table, take off my hard hat and hold out my hand.

She lifts a brow, glancing between Nolan and me before she takes my hand in a firm grip. "And you would be?" she asks with just a hint of an Irish accent.

"Sabrina is one of the architects on the redesign," Nolan answers for me.

"It's a pleasure to meet you. Your last name's O'Shea?" That perfectly manicured brow of hers rises again, and she withdraws her hand, her lips pursed in annoyance. "Are you related to the family?" I nod around the pristine lab.

"Yes." She cocks her head to the side. "I'm Patrick's wife." My heart stutters as I get a flash of what I saw in Patrick's office earlier, and the raven hair of that woman he was plowing into from behind. That woman who is obviously not his wife. Oh shit.

Colin

Aileen doesn't bother to hide her grin as I push myself back from the table in the family kitchen. "Finally!" She presses a hand to her cheek in mock shock. "I swear, Colin, you did us proud this morning. A body would think that we've been starving you, based on how you devoured that breakfast."

I shoot her a smirk as I grab one last piece of Mrs. Sullivan's delectable fresh-baked bread and slather it with honey. "Just keeping you on your toes, woman. Don't want you to think you can slack off just because I'm not a tourist." On the floor by the door, Tack is finishing his own breakfast with gusto. One of the kitchen staff mixed leftover scrambled eggs in with his food. I've never seen his tail wag so fast.

Aileen huffs at me, trying to repress a smile, and makes a shooing motion. I stand, snatching the remaining strip of bacon before she can pick up the platter. Honey oozes out the edges when I wrap the bread around the bacon and take a healthy bite. Sheer heaven.

"Colin!" She laughs at my blissful expression and playfully shoves me toward the door. "What's gotten into you this morning?"

Sabrina's gorgeous amber-colored eyes come to mind, and I can't help my grin. "Oh, I just slept well. You know." My God, that woman can kiss. Soft, supple lips that molded themselves to mine, giving as good as she got…she's damn addicting. It was all I could think of as I drove home, all I could think of until I finally fell asleep, spent after another Sabrina-induced wank-fest. And again in the shower this morning, pulling on my cock with my mind full of her—her smile in the sunshine, the wind blowing her hair, and those lips… I roll my eyes at myself; I'm like a fucking teenager. The weird part is that I don't think I really mind.

Aileen hums and narrows her eyes as she regards me, a smile playing on her lips. "Hmmm. Okay, we'll go with that," she drawls, obviously not buying my excuse. "Although, I rather think a certain American architect might have something more to do with it."

I look at her with wide-eyed innocence, until she bursts out a laugh. "Aye, well, off you go then," she says, starting to clean up the table, "you have a busy day."

"Aye. C'mon, Tack." I give Aileen a wink and head out the door, her chuckles ringing behind me as I walk toward the offices attached to the malting shed. Tack trots ahead of me, chasing a bug flitting just above him. I finish the bacon sandwich in a couple more bites, and then lick a few drops of honey off my fingers as I walk.

Aileen was right about one thing. This girl…this amazing,

unbelievable girl…has completely upended me. I don't know what I'm doing. It can't be sustained, after all; she's an American. She *lives* in America. She will return in a few weeks to *America*. California, to be exact. Not just on the other side of an ocean, but another whole fecking *country*. Thousands of miles between us.

I rub my chest as I walk, trying to ease the odd ache there. Ugh, I'm a fecking eejit. Starting something like that, with her? What am I thinking? I huff a laugh; I wasn't thinking, that much is clear. All I know is that I *had* to kiss her. Had to feel those sweet lips, breathe in her scent, and hold her close. If that makes me an eejit, so be it.

And then she'll leave. *Fuck.*

Grandda is stepping out of the offices as we approach and holds the door open so Tack can scamper in. "What's wrong?" he asks, peering at me with concern.

"What? Nothing. Why?" He gestures toward me, and I realize I'm still rubbing my chest. I immediately stop, shoving my hands in my pockets. "I'm fine. Just ate too much. Where are you off to?"

He steps aside so I can enter and pauses on the stoop. "I need to run to town for a minute. Can I pick anything up for you?"

"No, thanks," I reply, shaking my head. "I may be going to dinner again tonight with…um, just some people, you know." I rub the back of my neck, hating the feel of my cheeks warming.

"Just some people, huh?" He turns away to look back at the castle, but there's no hiding his broad smirk. "Right. Well, I'll see you later." He shoots me a grin. "Say hello to Brie for me."

"I didn't say it was Brie!" I call toward his back as he walks away, but all I get is his laughter.

My morning is taken up with meetings and paperwork, but it's not unpleasant. Grandda has been letting me take over most of the daily work of the business, only getting involved for formal events and what he calls 'the fun stuff,' like tastings. It's a lot of responsibility, but I'm proud of—and grateful for—the confidence he has in me. I am glad that we aren't any bigger than we are, though. It's nice to not spend every waking minute in the office.

"Okay, I think that's about it, aye?" I rise and reach across the desk to shake Mack's hand. He works with the local group of farms we sell the spent mash to for cattle feed. "Any questions?"

"Aye, we're good," he says with a smile. I've known Mack for years; he's the typical Crossmoor resident. Salt of the earth, solid. Stoic on the surface, but would give you the shirt off his back if you needed it.

I escort Mack out of my office and to the main door, where he turns and claps his hand on my shoulder. "Thanks, Colin." He looks past me and smiles. "Ah, great photo. You looked like your grandfather even then."

I follow his gaze, and feel my smile stiffen. My grandfather's office door is open, and Mack is looking at a photo on his wall. It's of Grandda and me…and my da. It was from before my mother died. Back when my father was my father. I'm about eight and clutching my first sailing trophy in my arms, grinning like a fool, and still wearing my lifejacket. They're standing on either side of me with proud smiles on their faces. Mack's right—even then the resemblance between Grandda and me was obvious. Da has our bright blue eyes, but his face is rounder and his hair a light nut brown. He looks like my grandmother, which, I suspect, is why Grandda has never given up on him.

No matter what a shit he became after my mother died.

I take a deep breath and manage a sincere smile for Mack as I wave him out, standing and watching while he drives away. I'm not sure how long I stand there observing the empty drive, but a shrill whistle jerks me out of my reverie. Looking toward the barrelhouse in the distance, I see my grandfather wave me toward him. In his other hand is a tasting ladle, and I automatically smile. This is the best part of the job.

"How's your day been?" he asks when I join him and Theo, our foreman, beside a cask of our latest batch.

"Good, but I think it's about to get better." He laughs as Theo pries the access cork out of the cask and dips in the long, skinny ladle. This batch has matured in American oak bourbon casks, which impart a smooth mellowness to the whiskey. Inhaling the scent rising from the cask, we watch as Theo carefully draws out the sample and pours it into a glass beaker. He sniffs the contents before swirling the amber liquid and holding it up to the light.

"Beauty," he mumbles, and we both grunt in agreement. Theo pours the liquid into three tall shot glasses and hands one to each of us.

"Sláinte." We all clink and sip. I smile, savoring the taste as I swish the whiskey in my mouth, a slight burn making its way down my throat. Next to me, Grandda lets out his breath in a whoosh that makes Theo laugh.

"Oh, now there's a proper drink," he says, a note of deep satisfaction in his voice. I nod and raise my glass to examine the contents in the sunlight streaming through the doorway. It's a perfect golden hue. The exact color of Brie's eyes.

Closing my eyes, I take another sip and let the liquid roll over my tongue. Smokey, with notes of honey and almonds. Perfect. I can't wait to share this with Brie.

"This is ready," Grandda proclaims, to which Theo and I nod in agreement. It's perfect.

"What are you calling this one?" Theo asks, pounding the cork back in the cask. While this cask and its mates have been maturing, they've only been identified by a number.

Grandda takes another sip and gazes at the beams overhead, considering the question. "It's a worthy brew," he muses.

"Worthy…Worthington," I blurt, the rightness of the name striking me. "Worthington Proper."

One bushy eyebrow rises, and I'm pinned under his blazing blue gaze for a second before he grins. "Worthington Proper, it is," he agrees, clapping a hand on my shoulder and giving it a squeeze. We discuss a few details with Theo, and then take our leave, walking back toward the castle.

"So, I take it your *friendship* with Sabrina is getting serious?" he asks, casting a sideways glance at me as we walk. I reach down, pick up a stick, and toss it for Tack to chase.

"Not exactly." Tack dutifully brings the stick back, so I toss it again as we continue walking. My grandfather grunts.

"Not exactly," he repeats. The gravel crunches under our feet as we walk. "And yet you're naming a batch after her?"

"I didn't say that—" I stop my feeble protest when he looks at me.

"Colin, it's been five long years, and I'm glad a lass has finally caught your eye. But you know she's leaving, aye?" That weird ache in my chest appears again at his words, and I rub at it absently.

"I know." I huff out a breath in frustration and throw the stick for Tack again. "It's not…serious. I know she's leaving. It's just that…" I groan and rake my hand through my hair. "I don't really know what I'm doing."

He chuckles. "Well, don't worry about it. Just enjoy the time you have. She's a lovely girl. And ignore me; I'm just happy to see you take an interest again. I'd almost given up hope."

"Oh, please," I start with a frown, but then see his teasing smile and the twinkle in his eyes. "Yeah, well, I'm just full of surprises, aren't I?" I mumble, rolling my eyes as he laughs and bumps his shoulder against mine.

"That you are, my boy. That you are."

chapter
seven

Sabrina

"**H**IS WIFE?" MY VOICE SOUNDS HIGHER THAN NORMAL. Why I'm feeling embarrassed is a mystery. I'm not the one who was bent over Patrick's desk, howling like a werewolf on a full moon. I suppress a shudder. Patrick is clearly the dog that Colin and every other male I've come across in this country warned me about. "I didn't realize he was married," I manage over the lump that suddenly has appeared in my throat.

"He doesn't most of the time either." Kathleen folds her arms across her chest, giving me the shrewd once-over. One of her manicured brow rises, and now I'm flailing, the words spilling out of my mouth, because it's obvious what she thinks here.

"Oh, God. No." My hand flutters around in the air as if this explains everything. "I would never. I mean, I just met him last night." I groan at my word vomit. *How To Make a Bad Situation Worse, a Novel in Career Implosion by Sabrina Worthington* coming soon to a bookstore near you.

Kathleen and Nolan exchange a skeptical look, and I stumble to find my voice. "That sounded even worse. I meant that Nolan's been handling the project." I glance at Nolan, and he gives a subtle nod. "I was at one of the pubs last night on a date, actually. And the man I was with knows him. Well, they sort of hate each other, but anyway, that's the first I've actually laid eyes on him." *Stop rambling, Brie!*

Kathleen's eyes widen, her interest clearly piqued. "You mean Colin McGuire?" she asks, leaning forward a little.

"Yes!" I say a little too loudly. I want there to be no room for misinterpretation here. There's no way, no how, I would ever get involved with a client. "That's who I was with."

"Colin McGuire on an actual date?" Kathleen shakes her head. "And he spoke to Patrick without blood being shed? Well, maybe hell has finally frozen over."

"You know about their history?" I struggle to find the words. How do you explain a hatred between families that has gone on for centuries, when you don't really understand it yourself?

"Oh, everyone is aware. It's ridiculous." She rolls her eyes. "Boys will be boys, I suppose."

From some muffled place, a phone buzzes, and Nolan reaches into his suit jacket pocket to pull out his cell, clearing his throat. "If you'll excuse me, I need to take this. Will you two be okay here?" Nolan gives Kathleen a pointed look and she waves him off.

"Of course. You do what you need to do, and I'll see you at the meeting at 10:30."

"Sabrina?" Nolan turns to me. "Patrick should be out of his meeting shortly." I force a smile. *Oh, he'll be out of her shortly, I'm sure.* "I'll let him know you're here. I don't know how he got the times mixed up." I want to tell him I know exactly how he mixed up the times. "You can find your way back?"

I fight the urge to roll my eyes. There's that condescending tone of his again. *Can I find my way back?* Of course I can, you stuck-up suit. I helped design the place. "I can, and thank you for the tour, Nolan.

I'll get with the designers on the paint changes you want for the work-space on the third floor."

He nods and makes a swift exit, the sound of his shoes fading as he hurries down the hall, leaving me with Patrick's wife, who seems intent on burning lasers into me.

The silence spreads between us. Awkward silences are the worst, and I break her hawk eyes to wander across the room. I stare up at the O'Shea name, embossed on the muted grey wall above a massive, complex sketch of a chemical compound. I remember being fascinated by it when Nolan asked for us to recreate it in larger-than-life form. I take a few deep breaths, feeling the weight of Kathleen's gaze on my back. No matter how uncomfortable this first meeting is, I can't afford to screw this up. It wouldn't be wise to have Patrick's wife pissed off at me. *Just talk to the woman!*

"How long have you been a scientist?" I ask, turning away from the wall.

"I've been the Chief Scientific Officer and President of Worldwide Research and Development here for ten years. So, a while." She makes it sound like nothing. Like being the CSO of a multi-billion-dollar organization isn't impressive.

"That's amazing. You must be incredibly proud."

She tilts her head. "Because I'm a woman?"

"No. Because that kind of responsibility, whether you're male, female or identify as a dragon is impressive."

Her mouth quirks slightly, and I take it as progress. I move back to her. "Have you –" I start, but she interrupts me.

"You know, you aren't his type." Her voice is flat, very matter-of-fact.

I stop in my tracks. "I'm sorry...His type?"

"Under twenty-five." *Ouch.* I set the hard hat on the table and try to gather my wits.

"No. I passed that a decade ago, but even if I was under twenty-five, I would never get involved with someone I work with. Particularly someone who's married." Kathleen's expression softens slightly, and I take that as my cue. "I should probably leave you to it. It was nice to meet you, Kathleen."

I grab my hard hat and try not to race out of the room. The sooner I'm away from Mrs. O'Shea, who clearly has a host of issues to deal with, the better. The sound of the stool scraping across the hardwood echoes as I reach the door.

"Wait. Sabrina, I'm sorry." I turn to find her standing behind the microscope. "I was just a right cow to you, and you don't deserve that. I'm just… Not used to meeting women who haven't slept with my husband," she says in a cool, measured tone, like we're simply talking about the weather or what to put in our coffee.

"Why do you stay then? I mean, you're obviously accomplished, brilliant to be running this." I spread my arms wide and step back into the lab.

"Because I get to do this." She motions to the microscope. "I get to make a difference."

"With Sharexa?" I ask. I suppose erections do make a difference for millions. I glance at the Sharexa tagline etched into the wall between the windows behind Kathleen.

Share the Moment. Make it Last.

A little cheeky, but it obviously works. O'Shea stock is soaring. The fact is they can afford imported hand-scraped sandalwood without batting an eye. The price per square foot costs more than my monthly car payments. Sex is clearly a big business.

"You've heard of Sharexa?" Kathleen asks with, if I'm not mistaken, an actual smile teasing at the corners of her mouth.

"Everyone in the world has heard about Sharexa. But if your erection lasts for more than four hours, get yourself to an emergency room." Kathleen laughs at this and motions me over to join her at the table.

"Well, that could be problematic, you're right. And painful, though some would deserve it." She shifts the stool to the side and pats the top. "Sit down and I'll show you why I stay." I glance at the stool then back at her warily. "I won't bite. I promise. And it would be nice to talk to a woman who's a grown-up for once." Carefully, I take a seat on the stool and scoot forward, setting the hard hat back down. "I stay because Sharexa lets me do the research I want to do."

"Which is what?" I ask, intrigued as she looks into the microscope before leaning back.

"Research into prostate cancer. My dad passed away from it two years ago, before I could make much headway." There's the first sign of a waver in Kathleen's voice, and it tugs at my heart.

"I'm so sorry, Kathleen." My voice is quiet, and she gives me what I assume is a practiced, tight smile before she lets out a shaky breath.

"Once it spread, he was gone quickly." She pauses, glancing over the notes that are scribbled out on an open book beside her. "I just wish…" She shakes her head and glances back at me. "I had more time, you know? Research takes so long, and then there's the clinical trials and approvals, and don't get me started on the patent process." She lets out a huff, squaring her shoulders. "So that's why I stay." Her accent is thick with emotion, and I feel my own tears threaten. "I can't make a difference for my dad now, but maybe I can make a difference for someone else's dad, their brother, their husband, their friend."

I reach out to touch her arm, my hand landing on the pristine white of her lab coat. "Of course you can. It's going to make a difference."

Kathleen glances at my hand on her lab coat and then back to me with a watery smile. "I hope so." Then, she's clearing her throat and gesturing to the microscope, all business. "Have a look. Tell me what you see."

My eyes widen. "Ah. I didn't go past grade twelve bio." I cringe at the expensive looking microscope. I don't even want to know how much something like this costs.

She laughs and taps the top of the microscope. "That's okay."

Carefully, I look into the microscope, seeing a blurry mass of squiggles and dots. "It's all blurry."

"Just adjust the eyepiece," Kathleen instructs. I lean back and gingerly fiddle with the focus, hearing Kathleen chuckle. "It won't bite you either."

I glance back down into the microscope, turning the eyepiece until the view comes into focus. "It's still a bunch of random lines and dots. What am I looking at?"

"I'm measuring changes in prostate-specific antigen velocity." I glance up at her, perplexed, and she gives me another smile. "PSA levels," Kathleen patiently tries to explain. I think she'd make a great teacher. She clearly has the patience of a saint to deal with the likes of Patrick. "We're using imaging and AI. Initial results are suggesting if PSA levels change over a certain period of time, there may be a higher risk of developing prostate cancer."

I lean back, floored. This woman is a genius, and I suddenly feel small and insignificant in her presence. "You're trying to predict when it might develop?"

She nods slowly. "If we can figure that out, we may be able to catch it earlier, and patients have a fighting chance then. Not like my dad. It was just too late for him."

"This is incredible," I mumble, looking back into the microscope.

"It's early days yet," Kathleen says. "The AI piece alone is a massive project."

"What's this massive project now, darling?" I lurch back at the booming male voice, narrowing my eyes at Patrick O'Shea as he saunters into the lab, a petite woman with long flowing black hair trailing behind him.

Holy hell, it's the wolf-howl woman. I feel sick, and like I'd like to take one of these microscopes and whack him in the nuts with it.

"I found Emily roaming around looking a little lost, but I showed her the way, didn't I, Emily?" I just bet he showed her the way.

He has the gall to place his hand on Emily's back, guiding her forward. "Yes, sir." It's a meek response from Emily that makes me want to gag.

Kathleen's practiced mask slams back into place, and she gives Patrick an icy glare. "The PSA research project. This is Sabrina Worthington, one of our office designers. I was just showing her some of our research." Patrick's bravado falters a little when he finally spots me, but it's only for a brief moment. Then, he slides in behind the table and plants a kiss on each of Kathleen's cheeks.

I steal a glance at the raven-haired woman, watching as she winds her hair up into a high ponytail. Ah yes, she's definitely under twenty-five, and clearly knows Patrick is married. How can people like this sleep at night? How can you just carry on like nothing has happened when less than an hour ago, a married man had you bent over his desk with his dick inside you?

"Ah." Patrick holds Kathleen out at arm's length, his gaze roaming over her before he turns to me. "Sabrina and I met last night at the Crown and Cork."

"It's nice to see you again, Mr. O'Shea." I manage to sound somewhat normal despite my gritted teeth. "I'm sorry we missed our meeting this morning." *I'm sorry I saw you with your pants down around your ankles. I'm sorry Kathleen feels like staying with you is her best option.* Are all men dogs? Seaweed-dick Laird, Colin's father, and now Patrick. The list is growing by the minute.

Patrick makes an attempt to smooth out his wild, almost stark white hair. "These things happen. We can reschedule." He gives me a nod that feels very much like I'm being dismissed, before he turns his attention back to Kathleen. "You spend far too much time on Artificial Intelligence, darling. How's the Sharexa research advancing? And I thought you were at the Shearing Lab today." He totally ignores little miss homewrecker as she opens up one of the lockers on the far wall, and tugs out a lab coat. Holy hell, she works for Kathleen. I look up frantically at Kathleen, but she's giving nothing away. Nothing that suggests she knows anything is going on between her husband and this woman.

"Shearing is overrun with interns this week. I thought you would know that." *Point to Kathleen.* I almost want to clap for her. She moves away from Patrick and toward her husband's mistress. "Emily, if you could get the specimens from the Paradigm Lab, we can get started."

"That's my Kathleen," Patrick says. "Always work, work, work." Kathleen's jaw ticks in annoyance, and Emily scurries from the lab. "I'll leave you to it. Sabrina, maybe we can have that meeting now? I think the coffee station on the Encore floor is finally operational. Fancy a cup?" My stomach dips. I was beyond ready for this meeting an hour ago, but now, after seeing what I've seen, after meeting Kathleen and knowing what a philandering prick Patrick is, I'm not sure I'm ready at all. But confidence is everything, so I push back from the stool and stand. Fake it until you make it, right?

"That would be great. Kathleen, it was so nice to meet you. I'm here for a few weeks. Maybe we can grab a grown-up drink some night if you're not busy." I hold my hand out, and she shakes it firmly.

"I would really like that," she says, and I know she means it. Lord knows she probably needs a vat of Irish whiskey to deal with Patrick. And quite frankly, so do I.

Sadly, there's no Irish whiskey at the coffee station, but there are a slew of different types of coffee available that I wouldn't mind trying. I go with good old reliable American roast, avoiding the tempting nitro shots that sit nearby. I don't think I need to be more amped up than I already am for this conversation.

Patrick makes a show of brewing up some sort of espresso from an elaborate machine that looks like it came from NASA, chatting amicably with a few employees who drift into the area. If I didn't know what I know, and believe me, I wish with everything in me that I didn't know, I would think he's a really good boss, who seems genuinely interested in his employees. But I do know, and everything he says or does just comes off as contrived.

When he finally takes a seat across from me at one of the custom wood tables, he lets out a long sigh, as if he's just sprinted a mile. He takes a sip from the tiny, steaming cup, eyeing me over the rim.

I take a delicious sip of caffeine, practically scalding my mouth in the process. "So, Colin McGuire, hmm?" One of his bushy white eyebrows rises, and I slowly lower my cup. Oh, hell no. There is no way I'm going to sit here and listen to him slam Colin or the McGuire name. I'm here to do my job, not get in the middle of some ancient soap opera that shows no signs of slowing down. Still, I need to tread carefully here. I've got three weeks to finish up this project and not piss off our client in the process.

"Mr. O'Shea, I—"

He interrupts my train of thought, his voice low and measured. "Call me Patrick, please. I mean, you're already on a first name basis with my wife. I think that's only fair." He leans back in the booth, stretching one arm out across the expensive leather, waiting for my next volley.

I take a deep breath. Fine. I can use his first name. No lines in danger of being crossed there. It's normal, right? "Patrick," I finally say, "I like to keep my personal life to myself."

"Mmm." He regards me for a few moments longer than are comfortable, his pale grey eyes slowly sweeping over me. He's not quite leering, but it's pretty damn close. "Privacy and discretion are important in business, don't you think?"

I don't like the direction this is going. The icky flag is waving like crazy, and my hands suddenly feel clammy, like my body senses an impending threat. "I think I'd add integrity to that list." There, you misogynistic creep. That should give you a clue to where I stand.

"Lots of things could be added to the list. Luck, timing, compatibility, fate…" I almost choke on my next sip, having to cover my mouth so I don't spew expensive coffee across the table. It would be a shame to waste what I'm sure costs a small fortune, but it might be worth it if it landed on him. *Compatibility and fate? Is he serious?*

I swallow thickly before answering, "Your company was built on years of research and hard work. Do you honestly think fate and luck had anything to with it?"

Patrick moves around in the booth, and leans forward, his forearms on the table. "My company was floundering before I took it over from my father." I just blink at him. Does he have no sense of loyalty to his family at all? "We had two drugs for hypertension and the stock was at an all-time low. Do you know how Sharexa came to be?"

I shake my head. "No. I don't. I assume with a lot research."

"Another thing to add to the list." He tilts his head, his eyes never leaving mine. "Never assume in business." I fight the urge to throw the rest of my coffee in his face. Could he be any more condescending? I can see where Nolan gets it from. "It came from a running joke at Trinity College we had about sex and how long we all could stay hard." I feel my face flush. In no universe is this an appropriate conversation to be having with a client.

"Ah—" I start to voice my opinion, but he's on a roll, plowing over me like the narcissistic caveman he is.

"I was in a clinical microbiology class with Kathleen. We were lab partners. I didn't pick her. We just sat at the same table." He holds up his hand, counting out on his fingers. "Timing, luck, and fate. We used that joke about getting hard as our lab project. A different table, a different person, a different time and Sharexa never would have come to life. I wouldn't be sitting here, I wouldn't employ over eighty thousand people, we wouldn't have twenty plus drugs to our name, and you wouldn't have this job." He relaxes back against the booth, clearly proud of himself. "So yes, I honestly think fate and luck had something to do with it, Sabrina."

"But even with those things, it's the research and the time that went into bringing it to life that made it successful. A joke and an idea you dreamed up in a lab class will just stay a joke and an idea if you don't put the work in." He thinks about this for a minute, studying me carefully.

"You still think that all you need is hard work and you'll be rewarded." It's a statement not a question from him, and I don't like it.

I set my cup down before it ends up in his lap. "Yes. I do."

"And yet there are thousands, probably millions of people who work very hard and have nothing to show for it."

"Maybe it's not about showing anything for it. Maybe the hard work is the reward," I fire back at him.

He leans forward again, steepling his fingers. "That's a very interesting perspective. It's entirely wrong, but it's interesting. *You're* interesting, and that's rare, Sabrina. Very rare indeed." I feel like I need to bathe in hand sanitizer to rid myself of the ick factor.

I clear my throat. I need to get out of this conversation and fast. "Yes, well, how about we talk about the interesting items remaining on the project then. I'm sure you're busy, and I have another meeting with the interior designers soon." I reach into my bag for my tablet. "Just a few questions."

He gives me an amused smile and, his hand sweeps across the table. "By all means. Fire away, Sabrina. I'm all yours."

Yep. It's official. I'm buying a case of hand sanitizer.

Later in the afternoon, I'm standing on a side street close to the Whiskey Rose, dreading the next few hours of my life. *At least the building is cute.* I shake my head slowly at the lavender painted exterior and the iron sign hanging beside a flowerbox bursting with a kaleidoscope of color that reads, 'Clinic.' At least there's a bar next door. I gaze longingly at the tiny patio beside the medical clinic. A few small round tabletops are set up under a series of expansive orange umbrellas outside of a tiny, crooked stone tavern. I'm going to need a drink after this. A serious drink.

Miraculously, the small reception area is empty when I open the door and slip inside. Perhaps the visit to the church has brought me some form of luck. A young woman behind a desk glances up from her computer, giving me a warm smile. "How can we help you?" Her accent is thick and rich, but does nothing to calm my annoyance at having to be in a medical clinic in a foreign country because my ex is an absolute dog.

"Well…" I shift nervously, my hand tightening against the strap of my purse, "it appears I may need a quick test."

She tilts her head and I reach for a pamphlet on the desk beside her, absently turning it over in my hands. "A quick test?" she asks, her tone encouraging.

"I mean, it's probably nothing." I wave the pamphlet in the air, mortification growing when I see a word in large black font on the leaflet, *Sharexa.* I stuff it back into the pile. "I had a physical before I came over and we were always safe. Always had protection. Condoms, I mean. That probably should have told me something, given I've been on birth control forever, but when you find your boyfriend…" Words fail me for a moment, and I clear my throat. "Suffice to say, I would feel better if I got things checked out."

The woman shakes her head with a scowl. "Bastards. The lot of them." She types something into her computer, hitting the keys so hard I think she may actually break the keyboard, and then hands me over a clipboard from a filing cabinet behind her. "Fill this out and we'll get you looked at."

Colin

After the gargantuan breakfast I had, I settle for a pasty for lunch, followed by a run. I should have hit my weight room, but I just couldn't stand being indoors any longer. So I hit my favorite path up the hill where I took Brie for our picnic lunch. It's a perfect day: a few clouds scudding through blue sky, but a nice breeze keeping it comfortable. Now, after a few miles, my feet thud on the dirt track as I near the castle. I wonder if it's too early to call Brie. She should be done with her meeting today. Her meeting with O'Shea. I squeeze the empty water bottle in my hand until it pops. That fucker had better watch himself around her.

I don't trust him. A few hundred years of animosity between our families will do that to you. But beyond the history is the simple fact that O'Shea himself is a certifiable prick, interested in only two things: bedding as many women as he can and being at the top of the list of the richest people in Ireland.

He's a ruthless businessman, intent on bulldozing over anyone and anything in his path to get what he wants. I slow my pace as the lake in front of the castle comes into view. If he had his way, he'd scoop up every acre of land in a five-kilometer radius of Castle McGuire. Thankfully, we've still got over four hundred acres that will forever remain untouched by O'Shea, and I'll move heaven and earth to keep it that way.

When I make my way into the grand hall, my phone chimes with an unexpected, but welcome text.

Sabrina: After the day I've had, I need a drink. Maybe 10. Heard you may know a good place?

I can't help the smile that her simple message brings. I don't waste any time responding.

Colin: A good place? I know maybe 500 or so.

I pick up my pace, heading toward my study, watching the little dots on my phone bounce and disappear a few times before her answer finally appears.

Sabrina: I'm just on my way back to the Whiskey Rose. Are you up for a tour?

Flopping into my leather chair behind my desk, I hit the button to ring her. I want to hear her voice. Scratch that... I *need* to hear her voice. That sexy American accent I can't get enough of.

She answers on the third ring, but I can barely hear her beyond a rush of air in background. "Sabrina?"

"Colin?" I pull the phone away as her yell fills my ears. I put her on speaker.

"Where are you?"

"Sorry, just in a cab. I had the windows down." I close my eyes, imagining her blonde hair whipping in the breeze.

"Aye. What's this tour you're on about now?"

"A tour—you know? I thought I would take you to a few places." Damn, the places I'd like for her to take me. I try to bite back a groan.

"You want to take me for a tour in my own town?"

"Yes. Yes, I do. But there's a rule. No talking about work. At least for a while."

I turn the chair to glance out at the lake, spotting a small group of tourists taking photos near the family of ducks at the far edge. "I'm intrigued. Can I ask where you're taking me?"

"You can, but I won't answer. I'm surprising you. I mean, if you're interested."

I shake my head though she can't see me. The last time a woman surprised me, it was finding her in bed with my father. I pinch the bridge of my nose. No more thinking about the past. It can't be changed and look what good it's done for me to dwell on it.

"Colin?" Sabrina's voice comes out softer now, laced with concern. "If you're busy, I completely –"

"No, I'm not busy." I look at the mound of paperwork on my desk.

I've got two articles I'm supposed to approve for travel blogs, about five months of expenses to enter into our system, and employee reviews coming up. This would be my typical Monday night. It all needs to get done, but as Grandda says, I need to move forward. No more looking back. I push off the chair, striding from my study. "What time can I get you?"

chapter
eight

Sabrina

"I**T'S A BRIGHT YELLOW DOOR,**" COLIN DEADPANS, HIS EYES light with amusement while he scans down one of the tiny side cobblestone streets I've dragged him to. "And there's a pink one, and a dark blue one down farther, and a purple building over there." He nods down the charming winding street, just as the lamp posts flicker to life. It casts him in an almost mystical glow, making him seem other-worldly.

Glancing at the purple building, I'm actually grateful I stopped at the clinic to set my mind at ease, no matter how embarrassing it was at the time. All tests negative, all systems go.

I give a playful smack to his bicep— his clearly-defined, taut and sexy as hell bicep encased in a dark green button-down shirt that makes me want to rip it off him and send the buttons flying into the crevices of the cobblestone. "I know it's a yellow door. But do you know *why* it's yellow?"

He grimaces slightly and then nods. "I do actually." I frown, looking up at him.

"You do? Seriously?"

"I mean, I know most of the legends about why they're painted. I don't ever want to lie to you, Sabrina. Not even about something like this."

"Damn." I let out a frustrated sigh. "I wanted to show you something that you've seen, but not really seen before, if that makes sense." I shake my head. "I'm such an idiot. Of course, you know about these." I flail my arm toward the cutest canary yellow door in existence, glancing up at the antique iron ice-cream sign above it. At least I can drown my embarrassment in some dairy goodness.

"Hey." The sharpness of Colin's voice cuts through the air, making my momentary disappointment vanish. Gently, as if I'm made of glass, he sets two fingers under my chin, tilting it back to meet his gaze. "I don't ever want to hear you say things like that about yourself again. You are not an idiot. Do you hear me?"

His eyes darken to almost black, and blaze with determination. I hit a nerve. I bite the inside of my cheek as I nod, trying to get a grip. "And I don't know about them through your eyes," he says, the edge gone from his voice now, his own eyes darting down to my lips. "Why don't you tell me why they're painted."

He slides his fingers away from my chin, turning back to look at the door as if it's a Rembrandt.

I swallow back the lump in my throat. This man is way too intense, but oddly, that's more of a turn-on than I ever imagined it could be.

I clear my throat. "Okay, well, the most common theory is that there used to be a habit of coming home drunk, after a few too many pints at a pub, and ending up in the wrong house. The doors were painted different colors, so people wouldn't get confused."

He folds his arms across his chest, nodding as if deep in thought. "Mmm. There's also another twist to that."

"There is?" I smile up at him and see his eyes crinkle at the corners while he studies the door.

"There is. Legend is that women painted the doors because their husbands often ended up in the wrong house and the *wrong bed* after a steamin' night out."

I laugh, taking another look at the candy-colored doors sporadically dotted down the narrow street. "That's even better."

"'Tis. But I'll let you in on a secret." He reaches for my hand, giving it a tug as he leads us toward the yellow door. "I'd never need a colored door to find my way to you."

It's a good thing he's holding on to me, because I'd trip and fall over the cobblestones with a statement like that. I have no time to recover. Up the three stone stairs we go, and then he's pushing open the door, motioning for me to head inside.

We're assaulted by a rich, sweet aroma. Chocolate mingles with lemon and berries, making my mouth water. There are a few small iron bistro tables off to one side of the room, all occupied with customers enjoying a frozen treat.

I peer into the freezer case, before glancing up at the chalkboard sign suspended by a chain above the cash register. "Whiskey ice cream floats?" I turn back to look up at him. "You can get your whiskey as a float! Did you know about this?"

He nods his head slowly. "We sell it at our café as well." He leans an elbow against the wooden counter. "Whiskey brownies, truffles, fudge, candies, cupcakes. You name it, it's there."

"So you've had this before?" I try not to drool at the perfect steel containers of colorful ice cream behind the glass. Every possible flavor is in there.

"Not here I haven't. But I'm going to stay away from whiskey tonight."

"So, what's your pleasure, then? My treat—and don't try to talk me out of it." I quickly add on as he opens his mouth to protest.

He studies the freezer, before unleashing the Irish again. "Imreog." I'm going to melt. Right here. Right now. Just let me slide into the Imreog and I'll be happy. "In a waffle cone." The kid behind the counter, who doesn't look at day over sixteen, gets to work.

"Make that two."

"Do you even know what Imreog is?" Colin asks while he tries not so subtly to inch me away from the cash register.

"It doesn't matter. It sounds delicious, and so it will be." We jostle in front of the counter until the cones are handed over. Somehow, I win the battle and tug a few notes from my bag, handing them over. I'll take that as a small victory.

The first lick is like heaven. Creamy, butterscotch heaven. "It's made onsite here, you know?" Colin sets his hand on my lower back, guiding me out the door once more. "All-natural, farm fresh cream, cane sugar." I try not to linger on his tongue as he takes a sweep across the golden goodness. "Even the sea salt is from here."

"Mmm." It's all I can manage. The man can make anything sensual. We head along the winding street, with chatter from a few restaurants and pubs spilling out to us. "What would you be doing if you weren't here?" I ask as we cross over to the street that lines the harbor. It's a beautiful sight with the moored yachts listing in the slow-lapping waves.

"Something terribly boring, I'm sure."

I roll my eyes at him. "I doubt that." I slow down my devouring of the cone before I get a brain freeze.

I watch as he crunches into the waffle cone, trying to ignore the way his Adam's apple bobs. I am in so much trouble here. "It's completely true. Essentially, I drown myself in paperwork, take Tack for a walk or a run, go to bed, and repeat."

"That isn't true. I heard something about a poker game the other night."

He tosses the napkin from the cone into a nearby bin. "I haven't been in a while, though you also heard from Steven."

"Why not? If you're bored, why not go to poker night?"

"I don't know. I mean, they've all been mates of mine for a long time." He shrugs, glancing out to the sea with a look of longing I recognize. "Guess I was just bored of that too."

I stop in my tracks, not liking that answer. "So, you get bored easily. Is that it?"

"I don't think I'd say that. I'm just... looking for something different."

"And am I something different?" He takes a step toward me, lifting the cone that I've left foolishly dangling in my hand, and popping the rest of it into his mouth. He holds my gaze as he slowly chews and swallows.

"You are definitely different in the most beautiful, unexpected way."

"It's a merrow," he explains, the corner of his lip curving up slightly in that way that makes me want to bite it. I've shown him a tiny mermaid etched in a stone wall that runs the entrance to the harbor—which of course he knows about. "It's from *muir*, the sea and *oigh*." He pauses, studying me while the waves lap against the rocky shoreline. "Maid, roughly translated."

"So, old maids of the sea then?" I bite back a smile.

"Mhmm. I don't think I'd describe them as old. There are too many variations to count, but merrows, or mermaids…" he tries the word in a non-Irish accent, and I shake my head at him with a laugh, "…are typically sirens, beautiful, mystical creatures with long hair and webbed fingers."

"Legend has it that if a sailor or fisherman is lucky enough to come across one, merrows will charm them." His voice is like liquid sunshine, seeping in and putting me in a trance of my own. "Bewitch them. Beckon them to the depths of the sea where they'll live out their days obeying their every wish."

"You know, I don't think I've ever heard the word bewitch used outside of a Jane Austen novel, but I think I might like these merrows." I draw my finger against the outline of the mermaid.

"You'd like your every wish fulfilled?" His voice has a rough edge to it that heats my blood.

I lift my eyes to his, finding a burning intensity drinking me in. "Name someone who wouldn't."

"Maybe you'll tell me more about your wishes sometime," he murmurs. His eyes dart to my lips, and I press my back against the stone wall, needing it to hold me up. I have a feeling I could get pulled under by *him* and never resurface.

I take a steadying breath and push off the wall, feeling over-whelmed, the fading sounds of gulls echoing overhead as we move away from the harbor. "Maybe you'll tell me more about your legends sometime."

He falls into step beside me as we start the climb back to the Whiskey Rose. At least I know I'll work off the copious amounts of ice cream I intend to devour during my stay here, hiking this hill every day.

These few fleeting hours with Colin have been—well—magical, if I'm being honest. And because he said he always will be honest with me, I need to be honest with myself. I want this man. It doesn't matter that I'm coming off a terrible experience with Laird, or that my time here has an expiration date. Maybe, that's why I want him more.

I can do casual and uncomplicated. He glances over at me as the Whiskey Rose comes into view. "What's going on in here?" he asks, gently tapping my forehead as we stop in front of the door.

"Just… thank you for this. For indulging me." That's what he feels like. An indulgence. Pure fantasy. And I want to get lost in him.

"It was my pleasure. And thank you for the tour. Maybe I can repay the favor again, let you in on more legends and secrets, if you're free sometime this week?"

I look up to the sky, pretending to contemplate, tapping my finger against my lips. "Let's see. Am I free?"

A strong arm wraps around my waist, and he pulls me against his chest, and then his mouth is on mine. He steals my breath when his tongue sweeps in, making me dizzy. *I will not faint…I will not faint.* That kiss the other night was just a preview to the main attraction. Holy, holy hell.

My hands grip his defined shoulders as he explores my mouth desperately. Blood sings in my veins, my nipples drawing tight just from a kiss. A searing, devastating, reducing me to a shaking mess kiss that I want to experience again and again.

Taking one last taste of me, he leans back with a subtle groan and my eyes flutter open. I watch as he takes a deep breath before moving to his Land Rover. He opens up the door and leans against the frame, the silver of his watch glints in the light from the streetlamp. His voice comes out all raspy and deep, rough with want when he finally speaks. "Just for the record. You're free."

Colin

Driving home with blue balls isn't fun. I'm sure she was going to invite me up. Hell, I was going to invite myself up. But I want to savor this time with Sabrina. Make it last.

When I reach the castle grounds, I scowl at the sight of a strange car in the family car park. Damn tourists parking in the wrong area again. I'm surprised Dermot hasn't moved it yet. Tack runs out to meet me as I shut the door, struck by the quiet. It's weird; there's not a soul to be seen. Not by the malting shed, or the barrelhouse, or even in the carport. Huh. But then, as I approach the back door, Aileen appears like an apparition.

"Saw me coming again, did ye?" I give her a playful look, but my smile dims when I see the distress written in her face. "Aileen, what's wrong?"

She starts to speak, but instead looks over my shoulder and claps a hand to her mouth, prompting me to turn. Grandda and another man are walking toward us from the offices. My grandfather looks stricken, his usual ruddy face pale. "Colin."

Frowning in confusion, my eyes swivel to the other man...and I freeze. His skin is pasty, and his tall frame looks thinner than when I last saw him. His coat hangs on him and he's wearing a beanie pulled down low on his forehead. It looks...odd. But the blue eyes under that hat still blaze the same blue as mine.

Da.

I can feel the blood drain from my face and my fingers go slack. It's like I'm seeing it from outside my body. And then I'm moving. Ignoring Aileen calling my name, I step off the stoop, my long strides carrying me across the yard. My vision narrows to the gaunt figure before me. I'm halfway there when another thought hits me—*Brigid*. Holy fuck.

I look around wildly, and my face must have told everything, because Grandda immediately says, "She's not here, Colin." *Oh, thank Christ.* I'm not sure I could take both of them right now.

"What are you doing here?" I grate, stopping a few feet away. I'm bouncing on the balls of my feet, my hands clenching and unclenching as I try to cope with the adrenaline surging through me.

"Colin," Grandda warns, his voice low and rough with emotion. God, it had to have been a shock for him, too.

"What are you doing here?" I say again.

Da sighs and passes a hand over his face, and it's then I notice how waxy his skin looks. What the fuck is going on? He gives me a tentative smile. "Colin. You're looking well. Da tells me you're seeing someone? She must be good for you."

I feel like he's punched me in the gut. Oh, he did not fucking go there. *After what he did?* My vision goes a little blurry, and I lunge. I vaguely hear Aileen's distressed cry somewhere behind me as my hand closes on the collar of his jacket. "You fucking stay away from her, you bastard!"

"Colin!" Grandda's strong for an old bugger; he grabs my other fist that has drawn back ready to fly at Da's face. "Stop it! Jaysus!" He wrestles me back, glaring at me until I lower my hands. It's then that Da reaches up and slowly pulls his beanie off; his thick head of hair is gone. Completely gone.

The bottom drops out of my stomach. "What's going on?" I demand, my patience gone and my dread building. "What's wrong with you?"

Grandda keeps a firm hand on my arm, as my gaze shoots back and forth between them. After what seems like an eternity, Da sighs again. "I've come home, Colin. For good. I...I'm sick. I have cancer."

My eyes shoot open, and I take a step back, out of Grandda's grip. "What the fuck?" I dig my hand in my hair, and for a second, I'm a small boy again; standing in the kitchen and wondering why Da had been crying, and then hearing my mother say those same words. *I have cancer.*

"Colin," Grandda murmurs, his voice full of pain. "It's terminal."

I gape at him, feeling cold all over. This can't be happening. My stomach churns, and I have to choke down bile.

"You're dying." My words are barely a whisper, shock rendering me almost mute. And then my anger returns, my volume increasing as I start pacing in front of them. "You're telling me, you've come home to *die*?" I stop, wheeling around to face him. He's wearing that same expression of wary pain that he had as he stood behind Mum as she tried to explain without scaring me. But all I heard was that my world was ending.

"How fucking dare you," I hiss, ignoring my grandfather's groan of frustration. "You traipse around the world for years, partying it up and acting like a fucking degenerate, sponging off the estate and leaving all the real work—*your fucking heritage*—for your father and son to handle without barely a word of your whereabouts, and you have the fucking gall to come back here to die?"

"Colin, please," Da croaks, his voice thick with emotion. He reaches out for me, but I jerk away.

"Don't touch me." I take another step back, unable to look away. My chest is heaving and I can barely get the words out. "So, what… you're back and the fact that you're dying is supposed to make up for all the shit you've thrown our way? We're supposed to be a happy little family and play nice until the end to ease your conscious? I don't bloody think so."

Seeing his eyes well up with tears makes my heart clench, and I recoil. I don't know what to do with all this, this *emotion*. "Colin, you don't mean that. You're upset. We're *all* fecking upset." My grandfather edges closer to me as he talks, like I'm a wild animal about to bolt. Maybe he's right. "Let's go inside and talk." I look at him, surprised that my own vision is blurry. Fuck, I'm crying. It's too much.

"I'm sleeping aboard tonight," I choke out, sweeping a hand across my eyes. Turning on my heel, I yell for Tack and run to the Land Rover. He jumps in as soon as I open the door, and I climb in after, immediately turning the key and hitting the gas, causing the gravel to spit up behind me. In my mirror, I can see the two of them staring after me. One man, the greatest support of my life, and the other, the biggest disappointment.

It only takes a few minutes for regret and shame to wash over me. I had a tantrum worthy of Finn's three-year-old son. I know this. But I'm not turning around.

I lower the window and let the sea air fill my lungs and calm my jangled nerves. A nudge at my elbow draws my attention and I look into Tack's soulful, deep brown gaze. "Well. I've cocked things right up, haven't I?"

He doesn't disagree.

On the boat, I manage not to think about anything while I charge my phone, shower, and change into fresh track pants and a hoodie. My earlier anger and shock have morphed into a smoldering ball of guilt lying like lead in my gut. I behaved like an eejit, this I know. But for Christ's sake, seeing that bas—no, that would be an insult to my granny—that utter fecking asshole again was a bigger shock than if Aileen had stripped down naked and danced a jig around the yard at midnight.

Shaking my head to clear it of *that* disturbing image, I lift my phone, jog up the hatchway barefoot and out into the burgeoning night. The clean, crisp sea air fills my lungs and calms my churning thoughts. I stretch out on one of the aft loungers, folding my arms behind my head, and stare up at the sky. This is my favorite time of day: when the stars begin to pop out and the small sounds of the evening start. Not that I can hear crickets here. Beyond the gentle slosh of water against the hull and the creaking docks, there are faint traffic sounds and music from somewhere as Crossmoor settles in for the evening.

The rapid click of Tack's nails on the stairs alerts me before I feel the weight of him on the lounge. He crawls over my legs and hops up on the ledge above me before lying down with a huff. All I can see of him is his tail hanging over the edge, but I know his head is probably on his paws in preparation for a nap. I wish I could join him.

My phone vibrates in my pocket, and I groan. It's probably Aileen, checking on me. Grandda knows better; he knows I'll need a while to process, and then I'll come skulking back to face...whatever.

But the name flashing on the screen makes my heart leap. "Sabrina?" I answer, sitting up abruptly.

"Oh, good, you picked up." Her rich voice vibrates in my ear, warming my blood. "I hope I'm not disturbing you."

I huff a laugh. "No. Not at all."

"Oh, good." It's only then, when I hear her relief, that I realize her voice carried a thread of nervousness. I scrub a hand through my still-damp hair and swing my legs over to plant my bare feet on the deck.

"What are you up to right now? Shall I come pick you up?" I offer, the thought of seeing her again erasing my earlier angst. Every muscle is ready to leap into action. I'm not sure how simply hearing her voice can do that to me, but it's a welcome distraction. A very welcome distraction.

"No need. I'm coming to you." The thump of steps down the gangway at the end of the slip comes to me from over the phone as well as behind me. I swing around, startled, my eyes shooting open at the sight of her walking toward my berth, a large tote bag flung over one shoulder, her phone held up to her ear. "Surprise." She gives me a crooked smile, and I laugh, shoving my phone back in my pocket.

When she reaches the boat, I take the heavy bag from her and help her down, her small hand warm in mine. She's dressed casually, wearing some stretchy pants that cling enticingly to her curves. "Welcome aboard. How did you know I was here?" Her answering smile eases the heaviness in my heart. Tack startles awake at the sound of her feet hitting the deck, and he explodes off his perch, almost falling off his ledge, as he wiggles in ecstasy at her feet.

"I called to the castle when I couldn't reach you. Aileen answered." She bends swiftly and ruffles Tack's ears, making his tail wag even faster in response. "She said she thought you'd be staying on your boat tonight and, um, might need someone to talk to."

Oh, I bet she did. Ignoring the stab of guilt at the worry I undoubtedly caused Aileen and my grandda, I grunt noncommittally and heft the bag carefully, hearing a faint rattle. "What have we here?"

"Dinner." My eyes shoot open again in surprise as she rises to her feet, Tack squirming between us. Her thoughtfulness gives me a warm glow. I can't remember the last time a woman surprised me with dinner that I didn't have to pay for. Certainly not Brigid. "I couldn't remember how to get to Finn's," she continues, slowly rubbing the shoulder where the bag had rested. "So, I stopped at Steven's pub across the street. He seemed to know what you'd like. Man cannot live on ice cream alone."

The smell of fresh-baked meat pasties wafts from the bag. "That's sad but true," I assure her, nodding toward the companionway. "Thank you. Let's go below." She moves ahead of me, with a grace that makes my balls ache, and I moan in my throat at the sight of her firm, round arse. *Dia, cuidigh liom*. Once in the cabin, I move past her and set the bag on the galley table. She immediately reaches in to start pulling out takeaway boxes and setting them beside the bag.

"Here." She draws out a beer jug and hands it to me with a triumphant smile. "This is the most important part. I got that stout you seemed to like last time. Do you have glasses?" I nod and open a cabinet in the galley to remove two pint glasses.

"I asked him if he sold growlers, and he almost choked," she continues, sounding puzzled and eyeing me suspiciously when I snort in amusement. "Don't you call them growlers here?"

"Um, no. Beer jug works just fine." I bite my lip to hide by smirk and avert my eyes. Lord, please don't ask me…

She props a hand on her hip. "Okay, so what's a growler, then?"

Clearing my throat in resignation, I look down at the golden brown pastie she just uncovered, my mouth watering a little. "Um, it's…a rather rude term for a woman's…ah…lady bits."

A delightful shade of pink blooms on her cheeks. "Oh." Flustered, she digs around in the bag, hiding her face.

"It's not usually used in general conversation," I murmur, removing the jug's stopper so I can pour. I can't help my grin; she just looks too cute. "If it's any consolation, he was probably as embarrassed as you are now."

"Hmmm. Okay, moving right along," she mutters dryly, and then pulls out another box. I hand her a foaming pint, and she accepts it with a grateful expression; we clink glasses and take deep drinks. "Oh, that's so good." She gasps in appreciation. She plunks down on the padded bench, slips her shoes off, and draws her feet up to sit cross-legged, facing me.

We munch the savory meat pies and sip quietly for a moment, tossing the occasional tidbit to Tack. We're silent until I refill our glasses.

"So, I know you said no talking about work, but I have to ask. How did your meeting with that wanker go?"

Her eyes darken and my internal alarm goes off. That bastard better not have tried something. "It was fine." She takes a long drink, and then lets her breath out slowly. "And, you were right. You, and Finn, and Steven, and Conner, and every other man I've met here who warned me about O'Shea."

Damn it. "What'd he do?" I almost growl, a bizarre feeling of possessiveness that I can't explain surging through me. I lean forward, my eyes urgently searching hers. "Tell me he didn't touch you."

Tack whines quietly, and she tears off a tiny piece of pastry and lets him nibble it from her fingertips. "He didn't." Her lush lips flatten in disapproval. "However, I almost walked in on him banging some woman I found out later was one of his wife's assistants."

"Oh." My worry suddenly morphs into a combination of relief that it wasn't her, and the usual distaste I feel for O'Shea. I swallow a mouthful of pastie with difficulty, and wash it down with the dark, frothy brew. "I wish I could say I'm surprised, but I'm not."

She huffs and takes another drink. "I mean, the flipping idiot's office has glass walls! Glass! And he thinks it's okay to just…just…argh!" She jabs at the air with a finger, the movement making the beer slosh in her glass. "*Anyone* could have walked by! The sheer *arrogance*, not to mention the general assholery of fucking around on his wife, is just astounding. What if I'd been a reporter or something? What if his *wife* had been there instead of me?"

Her face is flushed, either from exasperation or the beer. I love her feistiness, but my admiring grin is tempered with empathy. This must strike close to home, considering her recent experience with that arsehole surfer. "Kathleen is so used to him by now, she may not have noticed. Or cared." Frowning into my glass, I feel a jolt of pity for the woman. Everyone knows Kathleen deserves better than that git.

Her eyes narrow to slits. "Oh, she would have," Sabrina mutters with a steeliness that makes my cock twitch. "On both accounts." Then she sighs and shakes her head. "It's just so sad, that a woman as brilliant as she is stays with a pig like O'Shea because she thinks it's her only choice. She'd be hired by another company in a heartbeat."

I pick up a second pastie and take a healthy bite. "I don't know Kathleen well," I admit after swallowing. "But I have a feeling that she has as much pride of ownership in the company as that asshole does. They certainly owe their current success to her discoveries. I can imagine that would be hard to walk away from."

"I suppose." Sabrina shakes her head again, the wisps of hair that have escaped her ponytail floating around her head, and takes a deep breath. "So, why are you sleeping out here tonight? Aileen didn't say, but she seemed worried."

The tender pastie in my mouth turns to ash, but I manage to choke it down. After refilling our glasses, I drain mine in a long, continuous draught. I don't want to think about that train-wreck at the castle, but when I look down into her patient, amber gaze, the words spill out. "My da came home. Out of the fecking blue."

Her delectable mouth drops open. "Wow." Then she eyes me warily, like I'm a bomb about to go off. "That must have been a shock. How long has he been gone?"

"Not long enough." I rise abruptly, banging the table with my hip and making the various wrappers and boxes bounce on the tabletop. Turning away from her, I grip the edge of the galley counter, trying to control the sudden churning in my gut.

"Why did he return? Is he here to stay?" Her soft voice behind me sounds like warm honey, and I close my eyes, suddenly longing for… something. Comfort. Safety. Something.

I huff a laugh, but it cracks with emotion I can barely contain. "You could say that. He's dying. Apparently."

"Oh my God," she murmurs. I hear her stand, and then her hand gently covers one of mine on the counter. "Colin. I'm sorry. What can I do to help? Are you okay?"

I turn and look down, into those whiskey-colored eyes full of concern, and feel as if I could drown in them. "I don't know." I hate how weak I sound, but let my fingers twine tightly with hers. Suddenly, a hard little knot in my heart—that I didn't even know was there—dissolves in a rush of heat. *Tá sé í.*

We move at the same time, and then my lips are on hers, warm, soft, and oh-so-inviting. A groan rumbles in my chest as I wrap my arms around her, pulling her tightly against me. My cock is trying to burst through my pants; I can't hide it, but she doesn't seem to mind. Her fingers thread in my hair, tugging deliciously, and making the blood roar in my ears. Everything falls away; my father's betrayal, the lingering sting of Brigid's infidelity, O'Shea's bastardy. The glorious woman in my arms obliterates it all, filling my senses and setting my body on fire. I don't know what I'm doing, but God, I can't hold back. I need this woman. Now.

Pulling apart for air, I search her face in desperation, hoping to Christ that we're on the same page. "Bed," she gasps, and I swear my cock weeps with joy. I reach down and lift, my hands full of her round arse, and she wraps her legs around me as I stagger toward the bedroom. There's not a lot of room to move—this isn't the castle—but I'll be damned if I'm stopping now. The door bangs open, and I stumble, landing us both on the bed with a yelp.

She's laughing, and it's the best thing I've ever heard. "Sorry," I mutter, gently brushing a few golden strands of hair out of her face. "Not very graceful, huh?"

"It was perfect. *You're* perfect." I'm about to protest, but her lips return to mine, and I forget what I was going to say. We only stop kissing long enough to strip each other out of our clothes. The bedroom is dark, but there's enough light from the galley, thankfully. I wouldn't want to miss this.

"God, you're beautiful," I whisper, my hands smoothing over her curves, cupping her full breasts. It's true; she's the most gorgeous woman I've ever seen.

"Flatterer." She smiles at her joke, but I sense that she's not comfortable with hearing it, as if she doesn't really believe it. Well. That will change, if I have anything to say about it.

I gently remove the elastic from her hair, letting the waves cascade over her shoulders. I nibble down her throat to her breast, and she lets out a needy whimper. "It's the truth." We're a tangle of writhing limbs, learning each other's bodies, eager hands sliding over skin. I rise over her, breathless, and she looks down between us, her hooded eyes snapping wide open.

"Oh, holy—" With a wry smile, she looks back up at me and raises an eyebrow. "Don't break me with that thing, all right?"

I snort a laugh. "Should I stop, a mhuirnín?" My whisper floats between us, and she closes her eyes for a second, a smile playing on her lips.

"God, no! Don't stop."

Her soft moan echoes in the cabin as I slide home and a tremor of blinding pleasure ripples through me. Bloody fecking hell. I try to control my pace, wanting to savor her, but after a dozen thrusts, it's obvious I'm fucked. I need *more*.

Something crashes out in the galley, but it doesn't matter. Nothing matters but the soft, squirming woman in my arms. Her tight, wet heat, her stuttered pleas for *more*, and her sugary scent all draw me in, obliterating every thought. Fuck, I'm acting like a man possessed, all groping hands and pounding cock, but she doesn't seem to mind. She clutches my shoulders, her nails digging in, but the sting only makes me need her more.

The cabin is filled with the scent of sweat and sex and Sabrina. It's intoxicating. "Holy God," she gasps against my neck, rolling her hips to meet mine. "Do that…do that again."

I grab her knee and push it up, so I can get deeper, and am instantly rewarded with a series of breathy little squeals and moans that light up my heart. God, those little noises she makes—fuck, they're hot.

My balls feel like they're about to explode, but I'm desperate to stay with her, to keep this delicious fire burning until we're both consumed. Just when I think I can't wait a second more, her golden eyes squeeze shut and my name falls from her lips as she shatters around me, triggering my own release. I shudder and jerk against her, shockwaves burning down my spine until I'm spent, my head lolling forward as I collapse on top of her with a groan, boneless.

When I manage to pry an eye open, I'm curled around her like a cat, every muscle in my body humming. I'm bone-weary, but happier than I've ever been in my life. "Sabrina?"

She lets out a squeaky little hum. "Can't…talk…oof."

My chuckle quivers in the air around us. "Did I break you?"

"Not sure." She gives me a saucy little smile, stretching luxuriously beneath me, and I'm both shocked and gratified when my cock twitches appreciatively. I'm still encased in a tight warmth I never want to leave. "We may need to do some additional research to know for sure." She leans in, but before her lips meet mine, there's a happy little yip and some loud rustling noises from the galley. I grumble and glance over in the direction of the sound. Tack has obviously decided to clean up the scraps from dinner.

Brie giggles softly. "Do we need to do something about that?"

"Nah." I sink my hand into her hair and draw her face to mine. "He'll be fine until morning."

chapter
nine

Sabrina

*D*EFINITELY NOT A SEAWEED DICK. I CAN ACTUALLY FEEL HIM twitching and starting to harden again inside me. It's a delicious, euphoric feeling that someone needs to figure out how to bottle. No. No. Forget that. I want to keep it and him all to myself.

When he closes his lips around my nipple, it feels like heaven, until his teeth graze my heated skin. His firm, defined muscles seem to lock, and he slowly glances at me with darkened steel blue eyes. His teeth tighten for a moment before he releases my nipple with a leisurely stroke of his tongue that does nothing to bring me back to reality. "Did you just say seaweed dick?"

I swallow, feeling supremely idiotic. I didn't say that out loud, did I? "No." My voice comes out as a squeak—not convincing at all. He pushes my arms up over my head, his grip firmly on both wrists as he gazes down on me like I'm someone he wants to devour and claim.

"I'm pretty sure that's what you said, mo mhuirnín."

I shake my head quickly, biting down hard on my lip. When he breaks out the Irish, I'm done. Just melt me into a puddle. I clear my throat, trying not to focus on the fact that I can feel his hips rocking forward and his heated gaze on my breasts. I'm completely naked and exposed, and while it should feel intimidating, it just feels... right. "No. No. You must not have heard correctly. The sex was that good, it's blown your eardrums."

He drops his forehead to my chest, his breath a hot laugh against my hypersensitive skin. "Is that what happened? You've blown my mind *and* my eardrums?" He lifts his head, his palm pressing against my wrists as if he wants to keep me here forever.

"I blew your mind?" I try to lean back against the pillows to take his words in, because it's monumental. Never in my life has anyone said I've blown their mind during sex.

"I'd say so. But I'm also sure of what I heard. Care to explain that?" He accentuates each word with a press of his hard body against mine, and I draw in a hitched breath.

"Nope. No. Definitely not."

"Sabrina..." Dear God. If I die now, with his accent in my ear and his glorious, thick cock inside me, I'd be happy. "Were you comparing my cock to seaweed?"

I try to arch up to meet his hips as he deliberately presses forward, but the man has a grip of steel, and his raspy words are turning me to liquid. I'm helpless, and I love it. "I wasn't. Honestly."

"Then what?" He doesn't really sound like he cares, to be honest. His lips are too busy teasing my breast, a shudder wracking his body as his fingers brush a path up the curve of my neck. "What were you comparing?"

A low groan escapes me in my lust-filled haze. "Laird." It's a mumble from my obviously oxygen-deprived brain.

"I'm sorry, what?" Colin's voice has a dangerous edge to it that clears my thoughts slightly. His muscles stiffen with barely contained intensity.

"No! Oh God, no. It's just, when I saw him screwing Alison against your stone wall, I kind of wished a seaweed dick on him. You know, because he spends so much time in the ocean. I was hoping it would shrink." Colin narrows his gaze, and I ramble on like the fool I am. "And then I thought I really shouldn't do that because what if the wish backfires and somewhere down the line, I get stuck with someone who has a seaweed dick. And yours is definitely not. Obviously."

"Obviously." He slides forward just enough so I can feel the clear intention of said non-seaweed dick. "I think we need a rule."

"Rule?" I wish he'd let my wrists go. Being with a man like Colin is something I'd like to explore. So many solid, toned muscles and de-fined lines just begging for my touch.

"No talking about exes when I'm inside you," he murmurs against my ear, making me shiver.

"When you're inside me, and I can feel everything." I curl my legs around him, trying to bring him closer. "And I mean *everything*. We didn't use anything." My voice comes out as a whisper. He blinks as if coming out of a daze and leans back studying me. "You know, protection?"

"You don't have to worry. I mean, I'm essentially a born-again vir-gin. I haven't had sex in two years."

My eyes widen in surprise. That's a long time without this man having sex. Talk about mind-blowing. "You sure know your way around a woman for a virgin," I tease, trying to wiggle an arm free, but it's pointless. He's got me pinned.

"What about you?" he asks, letting out a breath.

"I take the shot thing. And we always used condoms, which now that I think about it should have been a red flag." I shake my head. It's amazing what you can see with a healthy dose of perspective. "I had my physical before we came over, and then another…" I wave my hand. "All clear."

"So, we're good then?" He raises a brow and I give him a nod. "And no talk of exes."

"None at all. Just one more thing though."

"What's that?"

"I'd like to touch you now." I give my arm another little tug, and he releases his grip immediately, his hands finding much better places to explore.

It's only taken me twenty minutes or so to figure out this little game he's playing of *Name the Stars* is utter crap. Crap in that swoon-worthy way he seems to have. We're lying on the deck, fully clothed, sadly, staring up at the stars winking down at us. They're fading slightly as dawn pulls at the horizon in pale pink wisps.

I'm deliciously sore and exhausted. Multiple orgasms will do that to you, I've discovered. Also, sex in a yacht-sized shower is not the easy feat romance novels will have you believe. We abandoned the slippery shower floor, and I wound up bent over his dresser. I did not complain.

I've been woken up three times since then with the feel of him sliding into me from behind, or to the tickling of his tongue between my legs. When I said indulgence earlier, I was spot on. I feel illicit and like I'm living in some kind of dream sequence.

"And this one is Arianrhod." That low, rich voice of his murmurs in my ear as he points skyward and traces some random pattern across the same cluster of stars he used earlier. I turn my head to grin at him, his ruggedly classic profile making the butterflies feel like they've taken an LSD trip in my stomach. Every possible cliché skips through my head on what this man makes me feel— bolts of electricity, explosions of fireworks. All of it has me gone over this man.

"Aria what?"

"Arianrhod Celtic Goddess of fertility and fate."

I let out a laugh. "Fertility and fate?" He turns his head to glance at me. "I call bullshit."

"Bullshit?" He flops a hand over his heart as if he's wounded.

"You pointed to the same stars that were allegedly also Reithy, or whatever name you made up."

"It's pronounced Réithe and it's Aries, as in the star sign."

"Mhmm. A likely story. I thought you said you would always tell me the truth." I feel the weight of him over me, all-encompassing, and he gently brushes a strand of my hair from my face.

"I will always tell you the truth. Those *are* the stars up there. I was trying to impress you."

I set a palm against his neck. "You don't need to try. You're pretty impressive as is, Shrek."

His lips claim mine once more, and as much as I want to just stay on his yacht and let the gently sway of the hull lull us further into our dream, I can't. I have a jam-packed day of meetings, and I'm running on less than three hours of sleep.

"I need to go."

"No. You don't," he murmurs against my lips between kisses.

"I really do. It's almost dawn –" I flatten my palm against his chest reluctantly. I can feel his steady heartbeat, the warmth of his body that I'm already addicted to.

He rolls off me, propping his head in his hand. "And you're about to turn into a pumpkin?"

"I have meetings all day." I pick up his wrist, squinting to see the dial on his watch, as I try to avoid getting drawn in by the veins in his arms. It's impossible. It's also impossible to ignore the feel of his lips against my neck. "If I go now, I can get some actual sleep before 9:30."

"Poor Sabrina. Sleep-deprived. What can I do to help?" He asks this while running a single finger against the band of my jeans. *Damn magic hands.*

"You can let me go," I whisper, pushing to sit up.

He props both hands behind his head, watching me. "I'll let you go, but I don't want to."

Leaning forward, I press a lingering kiss to his lips. "If it's any consolation, I don't want to go either. Drive me home?"

"Anything for you, mo mhuirnín."

I try not to swoon. I also try not to read too much into it.

But I know trouble when I see it. And I'm in so much trouble.

Colin

We don't speak much on the short drive to the Whiskey Rose, content to hold hands over the console and shoot each other small looks. Tack is knocked out in the back seat, his wheezing snores filling the space.

I'm surprised at how natural it all feels. I expected it to be awkward somehow, to not know what to say. Instead, all I can think about is the *rightness* of being with her. My body still tingles with the feel of her underneath me, and the way she responded to my slightest touch. *My God, cad is bean ann.*

We reach the inn too soon. The gravel crunches beneath my feet as I walk around the car, meeting her on the other side as she slides out of the seat. "You don't have to walk me to the door, you know." She squints up at me, but doesn't pull away when I take her hand.

"Yes, I do." Her fingers twine with mine, making my heart thump erratically. "You might get lost."

She snorts in amusement, making her ponytail bounce. "Between the car and the front door? You think your sexing powers are so strong that I've lost all sense of direction?"

We reach the door, and I pull her against my chest. Her eyes glow as she looks up at me, her cheeks flushed, and I tighten my arms around her shoulders. "Better safe than sorry, mo mhuirnín." Her breath catches, and her eyes glaze a little.

"Oh." She bows her head and leans her forehead against my chest, her hands clutching my jumper. "Smooth talker," she murmurs with a breathy laugh.

I lower my face to her hair and breathe in the intoxicating scent of Sabrina and sex…and of *us*. God, the things this woman does to me. There are warning bells ringing somewhere in the back of my mind, a vague annoyance like an insect buzzing around my head that

I mentally swat away. All I want to do is bask in the Sabrina-induced euphoria that surrounds me.

She looks up at me again, but doesn't pull away. "I need to go inside."

"I'm not stopping you." Even though it's the last thing I want, I loosen my hold a little; instead of pulling away, she leans in, planting a soft kiss on my chin. I can feel it, all the way down to my toes.

The stars are fading, the sky turning that soft color of indigo that heralds the dawn. It's quiet, but I can feel a sense of anticipation in the air, as if the new day is eager to shake off the night and get started. Sabrina's lips twitch in a smile, a dimple popping out on her cheek. "You're not letting go."

I glance down to where she's fisting my jumper, my own mouth curling into a smug smile. "Neither are you." She tugs at me, and I lean down to capture those luscious lips again when the porch light pops on and the door suddenly swings open with a screech of hinges. Sabrina jumps away from me as if she'd just touched a live wire, her face aflame.

Connor steps out on the stoop, eyebrows raised in surprise. "Oh! Morning, Sabrina." He rubs a hand over his mouth, hiding a smile, and nods to me. "Colin."

"Morning, Connor." I return his nod, striving to match his nonchalant tone, despite my heart pounding like a trip hammer. No longer concealing his grin, he goes off around the back of the building, whistling to himself. Sabrina's face is as red as a tomato, and I have to stifle a laugh.

"Well, that wasn't awkward at all," she mutters, rolling her eyes. Seizing the moment, she grabs the door and steps inside, but quickly turns back on the threshold, her brow furrowed. "Colin…"

"I'll see you later," I interrupt, making my intentions clear—I hope. It's all I can do to keep from pulling her into my arms again. "Call me when you're done with your meetings, aye?"

Her eyes soften. "I will. But, Colin," she says, hesitating. "You should talk to your father today." I jerk back, my euphoria vanishing. I try to move aside, but she touches my arm; a current runs under my skin, stopping me cold. "I know what he did to you, but Colin, he's the only father you have. Talk to him. I'm not saying you need to reconcile with him, but at least open up a channel of communication. You'll feel better for it. And, I bet your grandfather will be glad of it, too."

The memory of my grandfather's disappointed frown as I drove away yesterday hits me, and my heart squeezes uncomfortably. I manage a jerky nod, knowing she's right, but not able to admit it, at least not at the moment. I clear the lump in my throat roughly. "So, um, call me. If you want to see me later," I add, my voice raspy.

Her hand tightens on the doorsill, and she smiles, her beautiful eyes full of understanding. "I will."

I walk back to the car without thinking. I don't look back to the inn until I'm behind the wheel; Sabrina has gone inside, no doubt wondering why she should continue seeing an arsehole like me. Damn it. As I pull away, Tack climbs from the back to the front passenger seat and braces his paws against the dash, so he can look out the windscreen. His tail beats out a rhythm against the seat that echoes in my head.

Brie's right. I know she is. But knowing it and knowing what to say to the bastard when I see him are two different things.

Fuck.

The scent of coffee teases me out of sleep. The leather sofa creaks as I stretch, trying to work out the kinks. Instead of going upstairs to my room when I returned home, I sprawled out on the game room sofa to catch a few more winks. Delaying the inevitable, I suppose.

Dreams of Sabrina mingle with the scent of her on my clothes and I automatically smile. My dreams have triggered something else automatically, too, which takes more than a few minutes to will away. It'd be easier to deal with it directly, but after everything, I'm not really up to the shock it would give Aileen if she walked in on me wanking.

Sounds of the household beginning the day tell me it's time to face the music. Slinking into the family dining room, I'm almost bowled over by Mrs. Sullivan, our cook. "Good morning, Colin," she says with a smile, slipping a laden plate in front of my grandfather. He looks at me calmly across the dining table, as if it's just another day, which makes me feel even more like an eejit, if that's possible. Mrs. Sullivan—Fiona—pats my shoulder as she bustles past, heading back to the kitchen. Aileen is reviewing guest-planning charts on her laptop while sipping her coffee, studiously ignoring me. Her husband Dermot gives me a friendly nod and pushes away from the table. There's no sign of Da, thank God.

"I need to get moving," he mumbles, rising and picking up his empty plate to take it through to the sink. "We're taking down that dead rowan behind the malting shed today. Otherwise, it'll take out the shed roof when the next big storm hits." He bends and kisses Aileen's cheek, before giving me a friendly nod and shuffling down the hall.

Tack is curled up in his basket near the door, snoring softly, his manky stuffed squirrel clutched in his paws. The whole scene feels a little surreal. It's as if yesterday's drama was a dream. But then I catch my grandfather's eye, and I'm brought back to reality. He's looking me up and down, measuring. "How are you this morning?"

"Um, okay, I guess," I mumble, feeling supremely awkward. I take a spare mug from the sideboard and fill it with coffee from the pot. Aileen huffs softly behind me, and I groan internally. Knowing I need to man up, I clear my throat and face them. "I'm, ah, sorry. For yesterday. I was an ass."

Aileen's mouth twitches and her face softens, but she keeps her eyes on her screen to give us the illusion of privacy. Grandda nods, giving me a wry smile, and the tension in my shoulders lessens. "Understandable. It was a shock for everyone," he murmurs, the master of understatement. "You should have seen *me* when he walked in— nearly shat myself." I snort in response, and his smile grows a bit. "I take it Sabrina found you?"

My gaze shoots to Aileen, but she merely smiles, tapping at the keys. "Um, aye. She did." I take a long sip, leaving it at that. To my relief, he simply nods and smirks at his plate. The warmth of the coffee spreads through my chest, and I know I need to take the next step. Brie was right. "Where is he?"

Aileen sighs softly and finally looks at me, sympathy in her eyes.

"Fiona said he'd come down early and went for a walk. He said he was heading to the shooting range."

"Colin, he's sick. I know he's been a bastard these last few years, well, for a long time, but…" Grandda stops and drags a hand through his thick, white hair. The pain in his deep blue eyes stabs at me, and I walk over to place a hand on his shoulder.

"I know. I'll find him." I squeeze his shoulder, and he reaches to place his large, knobby hand over mine. "It will be all right. I promise." Fuck me if I know how, but I need to reassure him. This must be tearing him up, too. Aileen gives me a soft smile and, with another squeeze of Grandda's shoulder, I turn and head out, coffee cup in hand.

There's a mist in the air as I make my way across the yard toward the shooting range. I snagged a coat from a peg next to the door on my way out, and I'm glad of it now. My thoughts are jumbled: images of Brie laughing, my grandfather, Da and my mother when I was a wee lad, the sight of Brie spread out beneath me. Her expression as I left her this morning, with that mix of empathy and concern that tugs at my heart, still. As much as I wish yesterday's drama hadn't happened, I'll never regret my night with Brie. I pray it's not my last.

I head up the grassy slope and spy Da sitting on the lawn next to the range, looking out over the valley below. The defeated slump of his shoulders makes my heart ache, despite the anger that still simmers below the surface. He looks…small. Diminished, somehow. A far cry from the vigorous man I knew. Taking a deep breath, I steel myself, not knowing what to expect. I still don't know what I'm going to say to him, but I suppose that's not as important as listening to him. For the moment, at least.

He glances toward me at the sound of my feet and sighs before resuming his gaze over the land that was once to be his. Well, most of it still will be. When he and Brigid…did what they did… and left, Grandda changed his will so that the business, the castle, and the land surrounding the main keep will go to me. He'd said that he'd be shivering in hell before he'd allow a *fraochÚn* like her to get her hands on our ancestral home. The title still goes to Da, of course, and the vast remaining acreage, but he can't develop it due to conservancy restrictions. He can't even sell it—that was another of Grandda's conditions.

I sit down near him, sipping my coffee in silence. Clouds scud overhead, but some bits of soft blue manage to show through. I'm not sure what to do next, but the manners Grandda took such pains to distill in me kick in, and I offer him my mug silently. He shakes his head, a ghost of a smile on his pale lips. "Thanks, but no. I used to love coffee in the mornings, but it doesn't sit well now since the chemo."

Chemo. The strong brew loses its taste in my mouth at the word and a shiver runs through me. Well, I suppose that's somewhere to start.

I clear my throat. "We'd thought you were in Spain. Costa del Sol."

"I was. I was trying to decide what to do, and a friend offered his villa. It seemed like a pleasant place to contemplate my next steps. Such as they are." He frowns and draws his knees up to his chest. His coat seems too big for him. The absence of his usual morning scruff is unnerving. It's not his usual shaven look—it's like his thick beard never existed to begin with. But then he drags his slouch hat off and his pale baldness is even more shocking. If I needed more evidence that something was seriously wrong, that would have done it for me.

"Perhaps you'd better start at the beginning." It comes out sharper than I wanted, and I grimace; I need to keep this civil. But he simply nods.

"It was six, no, seven months ago. We were staying with friends on Tortola," he begins, glancing at a bird flying overhead. "I started having shooting pains in my gut. I wrote them off as simple indigestion or a pulled muscle after my daily gym session, but they kept coming back and getting more intense. I finally went to a doctor and when the tests came back, he said it was pancreatic cancer. Stage four."

Suddenly, it feels like there's a steel band around my chest, and it's a struggle to breathe. He shifts and stretches his long legs out in front of him, mirroring me. "He explained there were a few treatment options available to maybe prolong the inevitable, but that basically,

I was fecked." He's silent for a bit, the words falling heavily between us. "The treatments weren't offered there on the island, and a friend recommended an oncologist in Madrid, so we flew there so I could seek treatment. The cancer had moved to my liver and one of my bile ducts was blocked, so I had a bypass. Surgery went well, and I began chemotherapy. That's when Brigid left."

I flinch at hearing her name, and he grunts. "Actually, I'm surprised she stayed that long," he mutters, and then looks at me directly, the blue eyes we share still bright inside his gaunt face. "Colin. I'm sorry." He takes a deep breath, his voice ragged. "I'm sorry for it all. For leaving after your mother…" Shaking his head, he looks away abruptly, dashing a hand over his face. "I was weak. After she died, it was like the world disappeared for me. I couldn't face it; I couldn't face life without Saoirse. And every time I looked at you, I saw her. I told myself that Da would care for you better than I could, that you'd be fine, but the truth was, I was a coward. I abandoned you when you needed me most, and I'll never be able to make it up to you. Never be able to take back all those missed years. And then, what I did with Brigid…" He chokes off, but I hardly notice his emotion—the bile has risen in my throat, and I can barely swallow it back down.

"I don't want to hear it. I can't. Not now," I grate, gripping my mug like a lifeline. The vision of Da plowing my fiancée from behind in a guest bedroom is seared into my brain, but I shove it away with grim determination. "Just finish the rest. What happened with the treatment?"

He nods and scrubs a hand roughly over his scalp before pulling his hat back on. "Chemo was hideous. Pills for the nausea, injections for pain, bag after bag of infusions… I couldn't eat anything, and when I finally could keep something down, it tasted like shite. And then, my hair fell out. Haven't had balls that smooth since I was a wee lad."

I snort a laugh in spite of myself, and he cracks a smile. But it fades with his next words. "I'd almost finished chemo when my oncologist sat me down. My last blood tests had come back poorly, and she said the prognosis had worsened. She said I could either try radiation to slow it down, which would sap what little strength I had left, or I could stop everything, except the pain meds, and try to enjoy what time I had left. So, when Philippe offered me his villa, it seemed a godsend—I was so fecking sick of feeling sick, especially when it was merely delaying the inevitable. I just wanted to lie in the sun and think. Why try to eke out another month or two, only to feel miserable the entire time? What difference would it make?"

I take a shaky breath, looking out over the lush green fields below. What difference indeed? What would I choose if it were me? Probably the same.

"So you decided to come home," I murmur, and he nods.

"I should have come home as soon as I got the diagnosis. I need to try to make amends with you and Da, as much as I can, before it's too late. I need you to know that I'm sorry." He reaches out, but lets his hand drop when I don't reciprocate.

"Sorry." My derisive snort makes him flinch. "You're sorry. Well, isn't that nice."

He sighs softly, his eyes misty. "Colin—"

"No," I interject, sharply tossing the remaining coffee in my mug onto the grass. "You've talked, and now it's my turn." I can't sit still any longer, so I jump to my feet, looking down at him. "I barely saw you that year after Mum died. You were either holed up in your suite with a bottle or out on your boat. If it wasn't for Grandda and Aileen and Dermot…I was ten when she died. Ten! You say you couldn't live without her? How do you think *I* felt?"

I stalk over to a boulder embedded in the grass a few meters away and kick at it. Behind me, I hear him groan as he rises to his feet. "I was eleven when you finally left. I've seen you once, *once* in the last twenty years. You came home five years ago for a visit, full of platitudes. 'I want us to be closer now,' you said. 'I've missed you, Colin,' you said," I recite with a sneer. "It was obvious that you weren't going to stick around permanently, but I actually had hope that maybe we'd at least be able to text each other on occasion. And then, what do I find? You, fucking my fiancée!" The empty mug flies from my hand when I throw my arm out in frustration. "You're my *father*, for Christ's sake. Who the fuck does that?"

He closes his eyes in a brief grimace, but then faces me, shoulders bowed in resignation. "I…I have no excuse. I was fucked in the head, obviously." He shoves his hands in his pockets and blows out a breath. "I was a fecking eejit for years, come to that. But, for what it's worth, I'm sorry."

I glare at him, the pain in my chest so acute that it feels like I'm about to explode. Then he cocks his head at me, his eyes narrowing. "It does take two to tango, though, you know," he says, and I momentarily see red.

"*What?*" The sound is so sharp I'm surprised the stone at my feet doesn't split. The fact that he's right makes my gorge rise. As loathsome as his behavior was, she'd clearly embraced it. "Oh, so I'm supposed to thank you for exposing her for a gold-digging harlot? You don't think I would have figured it out?"

"No, you would have, eventually. At the time, though, you were too love-struck to see straight." He rocks back on his heels, the wind fluttering the collar of his coat. "You couldn't see all the little looks she'd been giving me for weeks. I knew what Brigid was instantly. You met her when she sailed in one afternoon and rented the slip next to yours, right? Well, do you know who paid for her boat? Her last bhfaighteoir, a man named Kohler. He was a banker in Bern."

I gape at him, incredulous. "You *knew* her?" He shakes his head, the cap slipping a little.

"I recognized the type. I'd seen a hundred girls like her on my travels. She *was* familiar besides that, though, and eventually, I remembered why. I'd seen her at a party a few months earlier," he says, pulling his cap back in place. I grab at my hair, stunned by his revelation.

"Why didn't you say—"

"You know what did it for her?" he interrupts. "Why she switched targets from you to me? She finally realized that she wasn't going to get her hands on your trust fund."

I rear back in confusion. "What?"

He walks over to the other side of the boulder and retrieves my coffee cup from the grass. "She finally accepted that you weren't joking about living off the salary you get from your position at the distillery. She thought that she'd be able to convince you to use your trust fund to pay for the lifestyle she wanted for herself. That's the whole reason she came to Crossmoor. She'd heard about you at some tasting event in London, apparently."

"Holy shite." Sitting down on the rock, I lean forward and brace my elbows on my knees. "She told you that?" I ask, scandalized. Honestly, I'm not sure which is more shocking—confirmation of her plan, or that she actually admitted it to my fecking father.

He nods. "Oh, aye. Eventually. Alcohol is a great truth serum."

Cold dampness from the stone seeps in and starts spreading up my spine. "But, how the feck could she think that? I never touch that fund," I protest. When I was born, my grandfather had established a trust fund for me with a portion of the estate money, putting more into it over the years to celebrate birthdays, holidays, good marks at school, my sailing trophies, whatever. I never thought about it and hadn't really paid attention to how much was actually in it until I went to university; I almost passed out when I saw the sum. Grandda had been *more* than generous over the years. I was able to pay for college and left the rest. I only dip into it occasionally for special things, like the *Saoirse*.

Da shrugs and sits beside me, letting the cup dangle from his fingers. "Well, she'd heard that you'd given money to Finn and Conner and a few other people, and thought you'd do the same for her."

"I didn't give it away! Finn needed help to stay afloat until his insurance money kicked in after the kitchen fire, and Bonnie couldn't qualify for a loan for the ice cream shop after that arsewipe ex of hers fucked up her credit." I pop up from my seat and begin to pace, jamming my hands in my pockets. My arse is almost numb from sitting on the cold rock. "And Conner simply wanted to renovate the Whiskey Rose's kitchen as a surprise for his wife. None of them asked for money—I just heard they needed help and gave it. They all paid me back, eventually."

I scrub one hand through my hair in frustration. Jaysus, it's not like I'm fecking Robin Hood. I mean, it wouldn't have mattered to me if they'd paid me back or not, but still. They're good people, every one of them. I had the means to help, so I did. Simple as that. "How the hell did she even hear about all that?" I demand, feeling a little exposed. "It's not exactly common knowledge."

He shrugs again. "Eh, she can get people to talk. It's one of her few gifts. That and fantastic blowies." I bark out a laugh in spite of myself, and he grins. Then the awkwardness descends again and he looks at the ground.

"Okay, so that explains her motivation," I say, clenching my jaw to keep my emotions in check. "What was yours? Are you trying to say you did it to save me?" He grimaces at my mocking tone, but meets my gaze after a beat.

"You won't believe this, but yes, mostly." His smile is wistful, and my heart twists. "You're a good man, Colin. Listen to yourself. Think of all the good you've done for people here. And as you said, you did it simply because they needed help. A lot of people wouldn't do that. Brigid would have sucked you dry and left your carcass for the crows." He frowns again and fiddles with the cup in his hands. "It was also as I said; I was fucked in the head back then. I should have thought of a better way. But she initiated it, and I didn't dissuade her. She had a great set of tits."

I swallow the knot in my throat, surprised that for the first time, the thought of Brigid doesn't make me want to retch. And I know it's because of the sweet, funny American girl I held in my arms this morning. Brigid, with her fake tits and faker smile, could never hold a candle to Brie.

But that doesn't make hearing my father talk about my ex's tits any easier. Clenching my fists, I tilt my head skyward, looking for the strength not to throttle him. The clouds are darker, meaning rain isn't far off. I should go check on Dermot, see if he's doing all right with that tree removal.

"Well. So, I guess we'll be seeing more of each other then. At least for a while." I shove my hands in my pockets again.

I turn and start to walk back toward the malting shed, where I know Dermot is working. "Da says your new girl is lovely. Reminds him of mum—" I spin around, cutting him off with a glare.

"Not one more word," I grate, jabbing a finger at him. His mouth drops open. "I am *not* discussing Sabrina with you."

He nods quickly and heaves himself off the rock. "Yes. Fine."

With a final glare, I try to leave him there. "Colin!" I can't help myself—I stop again at his anguished cry. "Colin," he repeats behind me, his voice softer, defeated. "I know I don't deserve it, but do you think you can forgive me? Please?"

My gut roils with a toxic brew of resentment, frustration, and—if I'm being honest—twenty years of heartache because my father didn't want me. Brie asked me to talk to him—mission accomplished. I got some answers, I suppose. But forgive him?

I take a shaky breath. "It's good you came home. Grandda is happy to have you here." Without another word, I walk off into the morning mist, wishing I was still aboard with Brie.

chapter
ten

Sabrina

"I DON'T THINK IT'S BIG ENOUGH." PATRICK O'SHEA IS IN FINE form this morning as he stands at the front of the Waterford boardroom, turning in a full circle.

The man is clearly insane. It's the biggest boardroom I've ever seen, taking up the entire back half of the second floor. There is no way to change it either, despite what he's currently complaining about, given the western facing wall is load-bearing.

I roll out the blueprints, yet again, on the expansive table that took a lifetime to get right. The table is a feat of pure magic, seemingly floating in the air and handcrafted to the tune of six hundred grand. I take a deep breath, not wanting to relive the no less than eighteen conference calls we had with Nolan about this table and this room specifically. Give me strength.

"Patrick, I can assure you, there's plenty of room given the specs we received from your team. The AV has already been dropped in." I press a button on the remote that lowers the automatic shades halfway over the curved windows, and springs the video walls to life. Various video conferencing apps light up on the walls, with the latest O'Shea stock numbers burning brightly in the wall at the front of the room as instructed.

NASA could launch a rocket with the tech embedded in here. This kind of money is staggering when you think about it. Patrick glances at the stock numbers, tilting his head as he studies the screen.

He turns back to me with a satisfied grin in place. "Up two percent since the bell this morning." He pushes the sleeve of his suit jacket up, studying his watch. "Not bad."

I have no idea if he's telling me the truth. I don't pay attention to stocks, but maybe I should. My mind wanders to my one and only credit card, and my modest savings account. There isn't much left of the small inheritance left over after Gran dealt with the house, funeral, and various bills that had piled up after the accident that took both of my parents. They were never good with planning or with their money. To be fair, I was sixteen at the time of the accident, and in shock. It's a good thing Gran was there to help, or I wouldn't have had the first clue what to do. She took care of everything, including me.

Dealing with a teenage girl battling grief could not have been easy for her, but she was always there to support me. She's the one who encouraged me to major in architecture after high school, just like dad. It was a way I could hold onto him, to honor his memory, and I try to do that with every project I work on.

I should invest what I do have in something. That would be the smart thing to do, to start planning for the future.

I never got around to it with Laird. That's probably a good thing, given how things turned out. I scowl, glancing at the remote in my hand and press the button to raise the shades in the room again. Carting Laird around and paying for all of his equipment and entry fees burned through a lot of what I had saved up to now.

He always talked about paying me back after he would have endorsement conversations with various sporting companies, but nothing ever came of those. My skin prickles with something unfamiliar. Something I don't want to think about. Could he have been using me the whole time we were together? I'd like to think I'm smarter than that, but –

"Sabrina?" Patrick brings me back to the present and is standing far too close for comfort when I snap out of my haze. "I lost you there for a moment, didn't I? Away with the fairies?"

"Away with the what?"

He waves his hand dismissively and moves to the table, taking a look at the blueprints. "There's no way we can move this out?"

I join him at the table and suppress a laugh. He's not even pointing to the right room. I turn the blueprint slightly, pointing out the boardroom. "We're here." I glance up at him, watching as he lifts a bushy eyebrow. It's as if no one ever questions him, and why would they? The man is in charge of a multi-billion-dollar company, and is clearly used to getting his own way.

"This…" I run my finger across the lines of the load-bearing wall, "is something we can't move. It's a structural wall that's integral to the building." I pause, turning back to him. "We've designed the entire floor around it."

"In your opinion."

It's my turn to give him a derisive look. "In anyone's opinion who's an architect and understands the structure of buildings," I bite out through gritted teeth. Probably should not have said that, judging by the look of disdain on his face. I open my mouth to speak, but he holds up a hand, as if I've been dismissed.

"I'll just check with Nolan." And with that, he turns on his heel and leaves me silenced. I glance at the Waterford name etched into the door of the chic boardroom, and shake my head. I may as well be in Gilead. Under his eye.

I'm still annoyed as I sit cocooned in one of the private café spaces a few hours later, on yet another video conference call with Nat, one of the other architects on the project. My day started out blissful and dream-like, my thoughts swirling with everything Colin McGuire. I should have known there's only one way to go after that kind of euphoric feeling.

"He doesn't know what he's talking about," Nat says, pushing her glasses to the top of her head. "That wall can't be moved unless we strip the building to the ground. We've run every possible scenario."

"I know. He doesn't believe me. He went off to find Nolan. You know? Because someone with a penis, who doesn't actually have a degree in architecture, clearly knows better."

"Fucking men," Nat snarls, shaking her head.

"My thoughts exactly. As if we need more mansplaining." I take another sip of caffeine, hoping it soothes away my growing irritation. "It will be fine. I'll find a way to smooth things over with him." My stomach churns at the thought of having to be nice to Patrick. I should have listened to Colin, but I like to give people the benefit of the doubt. Clearly a flaw I need to work on.

"I know you will. It's just rough, you know?" Nat waves her hand around. "We have to work twice as hard to get a seat at the table, and then we're questioned about everything we do."

"At least he likes the table," I offer with a smile.

"He should. It cost him enough." Nat laughs a bit, and then grows serious. "I wish I was there to help."

"You *are* helping. Seriously. Thank you." A knock on the high wall of my hideaway has me looking up from my laptop and turning to see Patrick, his arm outstretched with a coffee cup in hand. "I need to go, Nat. I'll give you a call later on." I close my laptop and pull out my earbuds, lifting up my own coffee cup.

"Already working on my fifth." Patrick nods to the luxurious bench seat across from me.

"May I?"

"Of course." I shift a little higher in the seat, squaring my shoulders.

"I need to apologize," he starts, turning the cup between his hands as he studies me intently.

"Apologize?" Well, well, well. What a turn of events this is. I glance out to the sea churning in the distance far below to see if there are signs that hell is freezing over.

"I, ah… I'm not used to hearing no."

At least he's honest. "I'm sure you're not. Though maybe I could have been a little less—" I struggle to find the words, but he shakes his head.

"No. You were right, and I just didn't want to listen to you." He takes a sip from the cup. "I want what I want." He shrugs his shoulders, and leans back against the seat. That's as simple as it is for him. He wants something, he gets it. I wonder if he's ever experienced failure or disappointment in his life. I wonder what drama has gone down between his family and Colin's that influences both of their behaviors. Best not to dwell on that, I think.

"Well, like Mick Jagger says, you can't always get what you want. But if you try sometimes, you just might find you get what you need." I go for something I hope will make him laugh to ease the tension between us.

He smiles a little. "Like a load-bearing wall for example?"

I give him a nod, feeling the tension ease from my shoulders. "Exactly. Like a load-bearing wall. Really, when you think about it, Mick and Keith are philosophers."

He laughs loudly, tapping his cup on the table. "I'll tell them that the next time I see them."

I barely resist the temptation to roll my eyes. Of course he knows them. Of course he feels the need to tell me that he knows them. Even in his apology, he can't tame the air of superiority he carries around with him.

"I'm sure they'll be riveted at the revelation."

"So, then the wall stays," he states emphatically, ignoring my frustration. I don't know how Kathleen stays with him. It must be infuriating to live with a man who wants his own way all the time, and stalks off in a tantrum like some toddler when it doesn't happen.

"Yes, it does." He lets out an exaggerated huff, and I try another tactic. "You need to trust the team that's been working on your project for over a year." I pause, choosing my words carefully. Confidence is everything, and I have a feeling Patrick takes great pleasure in squashing people like bugs if they show any signs of weakness. "You need to trust me. I'm very good at my job."

He seems satisfied with my answer. "Where does that leave us, then?" He leans forward, cradling the cup between his hands.

"Well…" I pull open my laptop again, waiting for it to spring to life. "That finishes the first and second floors, all of the breakout rooms and social spaces. I'd like to check with Kathleen on the lab on the third floor to see if it meets with her—"

He reaches to my laptop, pushing it closed. "No. I mean, where does that leave us?" He motions between us.

"Excuse me?" I lean back in the seat, trying to put as much distance as I can between us. The alarm bells are ringing again, and I don't like it.

"I don't want there to be tension between us," he says, his voice lowering.

"I think we're good. Mick and Keith saved the day. We can just move on." *Please just let it go.* But of course, he can't.

"I know women tend to hang onto things."

"Is that what you know?" I feel my jaw set at the misogynistic comment.

He nods slowly. "You do. I just don't want it to be an issue between us." I want to tell him *he's* the one making it an issue, and that there is no us. "We'll be working closely together. We may disagree on other things."

"Patrick, this is your office, and I want you to feel comfortable in it, but there are some things that we just can't change, structurally speaking. And if we disagree on something, we'll work through it."

"As simple as that?" He gives me a skeptical look, his grey eyes hardening.

"As simple as that."

He's silent for a moment as he regards me, then pulls his phone out of a pocket in his jacket, giving it a glance. "I knew I was right when I said you were interesting, Sabrina. I'm looking forward to next time. I need to take this."

And then he's gone, leaving me unnerved, and not knowing who exactly won that round.

"I'm really glad I didn't go to the Shearing Lab today," Kathleen yells over the roaring sound of the band playing in the gastro pub, where we're currently enjoying our second pint.

After the meeting with Patrick, I found Kathleen heading into her lab. Despite Nolan telling her the building isn't due for inspection until the end of the week, she told me she gets more work done in the new lab, where she can work undisturbed. I was glad to see the dark-haired homewrecker wasn't with her today.

When she asked if I'd like to go for a drink after work, I jumped at the chance. I'm missing Becs, having not heard from her since her honeymoon started, and I'm in desperate need of some down time after the stress of the day.

"It's been years since I've actually been out!" she says, clapping as the band wraps up its first set.

"Years is a long time." I finish off my bold lager, glad for the break from the band. They're great, but constantly having to shout to hear each other isn't easy.

"I know. Patrick says I work too much."

"Do you think you work too much?"

She shakes her head. "If I could put more hours in, I would. But at some point, sleep becomes a requirement."

"I totally understand. There are never enough hours in the day on some projects."

"Like this one?" she asks with a grin.

"At first, it never seemed to stop, but that's typical when a project starts. We're at the end now."

I take a bite of the pub mac and cheese, enjoying the rich flavors. "This is amazing. I didn't realize how hungry I was."

Kathleen eyes me from across the table. "I saw you were a bit shaky there when we first came in. Is everything okay?"

I wave her off. "I'm totally fine. I just have an issue with my blood pressure sometimes. I've been known to faint every now and then." Or you know, when a certain delicious Irish man is in the general vicinity.

Kathleen nods, and I continue, "I get lost in my work sometimes and today was *a day*. I just didn't have time to eat."

"I should probably apologize for Patrick's behavior," she says after a pause. I look at her confused.

"How do you know what Patrick has—"

She touches my arm. "Listen, I don't know what he's done, but I do know he's not an easy man to work with or for. So, whatever he's done, however he's made you feel, I'm truly sorry."

I fiddle with the napkin under my glass. "I know I asked you this the other day, but seriously, why do you stay with him? You're brilliant and your work is groundbreaking. I'm sure you could find another position easily."

She runs a hand across the back of her neck, tilting her head from side to side. "I couldn't. That's the sad thing. Patrick owns this industry. No one would touch me with a ten-foot pole; he'd make sure of that. And, I have a non-compete clause that bans me from working for another pharma for at least five years if I ever quit."

My heart aches for her. What a horrible position to be in. "What about starting your own company?"

"That would take years, and again, he'd put up every roadblock he could to stop me, and he'd probably succeed." She lets out a long breath. "There are days I think about it though." She meets my eyes and I can see the pain there. "Giving it up and becoming a professor or something. But, I'm almost four years into my research on prostate cancer, and at the end of the day, he owns it. I can't take it with me. All of that work would be lost, and I'm close. I'm so close, Sabrina, to finding something that could truly change people's lives." She takes a long sip from her glass before gently setting it down. "So I stay because giving up means giving up on making a difference and I can't do that. I wouldn't be able to live with myself."

"Does he know that you know about his…" I wave my hand in the air.

"Inability to keep his dick in his pants? Yes, he knows I know. He's not particularly good at hiding it. I guess in some ways, you could say we're ahead of the curve. Isn't an open marriage the in thing right now?" She uses air quotes, and I laugh.

"I'm not sure. There's a few reality TV shows out there that seem to suggest that."

She smiles at me, but it seems forced. "It didn't used to be this way. When we first got together, it was all-consuming. We were madly in love. You know that feeling?" She absently traces the condensation on her glass, lost in her memories. "That first little while when you're just getting to know each other and feel like you're in a dream?"

I nod, listening to her. I know exactly how that feels. It's how I felt this morning, and every day since I've met Colin. My stomach flips as I listen to her. "But, then I was busy with research on Sharexa, and he was busy rebuilding his family's empire, and we just kind of…" Her shoulders lift, resigned. "Stopped trying, I guess."

I swallow a lump in my throat. "I'm so sorry, Kathleen."

"Don't be sorry. I get to do what I love, and I'm not exactly innocent in all this either." She gives me a sly smile, and my eyes widen.

"Go on! What does that mean?"

"It means, a woman has needs too, and when her husband is screwing half of Ireland, that woman finds a way to have her needs fulfilled. Discreetly, of course, and without complications." She finishes off her pint and sets it down with a flourish.

"No complications," I repeat her words, a little floored by her admission.

"That's the key, Sabrina. Get out before your heart gets broken." I wonder if it's already too late for mine.

An hour later, I manage to pass my credit card over to the waiter while Kathleen is searching for hers. "Put it on mine."

"No, I couldn't let you do that," she protests, rooting around in her Hermes bag.

"I insist. Please."

She smiles at me, hugging her fire engine red purse against her chest. "It's my treat next time."

"Deal." I grin as the waiter swipes my card against the portable reader and then frowns.

He grimaces and wipes the card with the end of his shirt. "I'll give it another go. Tricky machine sometimes."

I watch in horror as his grimace deepens and he holds the card back out to me. "Says unable to process."

"What?" I feel heat rise in my cheeks. "That's impossible. There's a three-thousand-dollar limit on that card." My heart hammers as he turns the machine to me, and I see the terrible message on the little screen." That can't be right. Can you try it again?"

Panic starts to rise as I watch him try my card again. I've only given my card to the Whiskey Rose since I've been here, there's no way it's maxed out. Could someone have stolen my number somehow? I try to remember the websites I've been on, but I hate paying for anything online for this very reason.

"Sorry. Got another?" He passes my card back and I turn it over as if the reason it's maxed out will magically appear on the back.

"No. I can give you cash, hang on."

"It's okay, Sabrina." Kathleen passes over her card. "You can get it next time."

"I just… I don't understand. There's nothing on that card." Kathleen gives me a sympathetic smile.

"Maybe call them when you get back? I'm sure it's just a misunderstanding."

I shove the card back into my wallet, my eyes falling to a neon green wristband at the bottom of my purse from the last surfing competition Laird was in, and my heart stops.

That absolute shit.

Laird has my second card. I gave it to him on one of the many wedding errand runs he took with Alison.

Kathleen was right about getting out before your heart gets broken, but she missed another part of it. Get out before they ruin your credit.

Colin

"Sorry to miss your call. Out with Kathleen at a pub. I'll call later. Promise!"

I slap the book I'm not really reading down on my side table and continue to mull over Brie's text. Out at a pub? Which pub? And, with Kathleen O'Shea? I remember Brie saying they'd talked, but I didn't realize their acquaintance was at the pub-mate level. Well, at least she's with the safer O'Shea.

Her text was sent at dinnertime, and she didn't answer when I called a few minutes ago. "Jaysus, McGuire, get over yourself," I mutter, dragging my hand through my hair. She is here for a purpose—her job—not to be at my beck and call. It was one night. One fucking, glorious night. Even if it's the only night, I'll remember her forever.

But it won't be the last—not if I have anything to say about it.

Tack is sprawled in his bed in the corner, oblivious to my mental turmoil. He turns over and grunts in his sleep. It's the only warning I have before the foul fumes from his arse waft over me, scorching my nose hair. "Holy fecking hell, dog!" Gasping, I stagger to the window and push it open, letting in the night breeze to dissipate the noxious cloud. Jaysus, he must have gotten into the spent malt again. It's the only thing that makes him fart like that.

Sticking my head out the window, I suck in a lungful of clean, bracing air. Oh, thank God, that's better. I shoot Tack a glare over my shoulder; he's on his back now, his paws twitching as he chases squirrels in his sleep, and I roll my eyes. It's impossible to stay mad at him when he's lying there so innocently, completely unaware of the biohazard he's created.

It's a clear night, although clouds are gathering over the sea and heading this way. There's a breeze off the ocean that clears my nose and my mind. At least Brie won't get rained on when she heads back to her room. Is she still at the pub? My fingers tighten on the windowsill at the thought of some unnamed git making a pass at her. I wonder how much she's had to drink. I don't know Kathleen well, but she doesn't strike me as a sot. And Brie can take care of herself. They're all right. Probably.

I throw back my head with a huff. What the fuck is wrong with me? I'm Colin Kieran McGuire, not some pathetic boy with a crush. And yet, here I am. That lovely, funny, amazing American has turned me completely upside down, and I've been powerless to stop it.

"It's ridiculous," I mutter into the night. What the hell am I doing? She's only *visiting*. She's going to leave and return to her life, and that'll be that. I just need to enjoy the time I have with her while I can.

But I can't do that when Kathleen flippin' O'Shea is monopolizing her time.

Turning, I lean against the windowsill. Maybe I should head into town. There aren't that many pubs in Crossmoor, wouldn't take long to figure out where she is. I could give her a ride home, save her from a long walk after a day dealing with the O'Sheas. I hope she's eaten today. What if she has another one of her blood-sugar faints and some arsehole at the pub takes advantage of her?

Fecking hell.

I'm in the process of scooping up my keys and wallet from the side table when there's a knock behind me, and I hear the door swing open. "I thought I saw a light under your door—Christ and his angels, lad, close the bloody window! It's colder than the devil's arse in here."

Grandda waves one hand at the window, scowling in disapproval as he steps into my suite. With a sigh, I set everything back on the table and hurry to close the window as requested. "I didn't expect you to be home tonight. Thought maybe you'd be with Sabrina," he continues, leisurely pouring two whiskeys at my bar.

"She's out with Kathleen O'Shea." I head back to table, but before I can reclaim my keys, Grandda gracefully blocks me, handing me a glass. "Um, thanks. But, I was thinking of heading to town—"

He cocks a bushy brow. "To do what?" he asks, refusing to take the crystal tumbler I'm trying to hand back to him. "Did she invite you?"

"No, but—"

"So, she's out with a friend, enjoying the fine nightlife of Crossmoor. Good for her!" He chuckles, not bothering to hide his knowing smirk. "Sit and have a dram with me, lad. I haven't seen you much today."

Swallowing my growl of frustration, I join him at the pair of leather armchairs by my fireplace. Looks like I'm going nowhere for a while. The frosty old man grins at my squirming, and I roll my eyes, making him laugh. But then his smile dims and I know he's getting down to whatever brought him here.

"Your da said you talked with him this morning," he says, cautiously. I take a deep breath, my chest clenching at the thought of my father.

"Yes." I take a sip, savoring the burning warmth as it slides down my throat. "Got a few answers. Can't say they were satisfying, though."

He grunts. "Aye, I know what you mean. He told me what he said to you." I nod, unsurprised, and he continues, his brow furrowing. "When Brian first left—when you were wee—I thought he'd be gone for a short time. That once the worst of his grief had passed, he'd return. As the months and years went on, no matter how disappointed and hurt I was, I had to come to terms with it, for your sake if nothing else." His blue eyes are full of past sorrow as he looks at me. "We managed well enough, didn't we?"

"How can you ask that?" I choke down the sudden lump in my throat. To see him—my champion—doubting himself is almost too much. "You were, you *are*, amazing. I wouldn't be who I am without—"

He cuts me off. "And then that mess when he showed up five years ago…" He shakes his head, and we sip in silence for a few minutes, each of us mastering our emotions.

"We have a rough few weeks ahead of us, ye know?" He raises his eyebrows at me, and I hum in acknowledgement. As much as I tried to ignore it today, burying myself in paperwork in my office, the presence of my father loomed over everything, covering the entire household in a kind of grim determination. You could feel everyone battening the hatches, preparing for the storm ahead. In addition to the stress of having to interact with him while he's here, there will be other inevitable things to handle…medical things. Legal things. The things of death and dying.

And I know that despite all the pain my father has caused us, I must stand with my Grandda through it all, supporting him, consoling him when the end comes. He is losing his only son…for the last time.

Grandda shifts in his chair. "Well. There's time to discuss all that later." He takes a sip. "Another thing your da did mention to me today was that you're a little touchy about Sabrina."

"I'm not 'touchy' about her." I frown into my glass. "I just didn't want to talk about her with *him*."

"Understandable." He glances at me over the rim of his glass and takes a drink. "Will you talk about her with me?"

My gaze darts to his. "What do you mean?"

He smothers a grin, although his cheek still twitches. "Weeell, you seem a wee bit taken with 'er."

I groan and look down at Tack for backup, but he's still dozing peacefully in the corner. I want to tell Grandda to mind his own business, but that would be a dead giveaway. Better to be play dumb. "Taken how?"

He huffs in amusement. "That's what I thought." Damn. But instead of taking the piss out of me, which is his usual practice, he smiles reflectively into his glass.

"She reminds me of my Aisling. Aisling was a redhead, of course, with a temper to match, but there's just something about Sabrina." He cocks his head, considering. "She's strong. You can see it in how she carries herself. Straight ahead and damn the torpedoes. It may just be the American in her, but I think it's more than that. I hear she gave O'Shea a right telling off today."

I jerk in surprise. "What? When? Did he do something?" If he had, I was going to rip his head off.

He grins at me. "Apparently she told him 'no.'" I'm halfway out of my chair; he waves me back down and hurriedly adds, "Not like *that*; sit your arse down, boy. About this project she's working on for him. He was being his usual fuckwit self, demanding the moon and the stars, and she stood up to him."

A warm feeling spreads through my chest at the thought of her standing up to that prick. "I bet he didn't like that. How did you find out?"

"Eh, the usual." He shrugs. In a town as small as Crossmoor, word travels fast, and Grandda knows everyone in town. "Word is, he had a meltdown when his crew told him the same thing she had. Something about a wall or a pillar." He shrugs again and takes a sip, relishing his story. "Took him quite a while to get over it."

My chuckle rumbles in my chest. "I'd have paid good money to have seen that." He laughs.

"Too right." He takes another sip and smiles wistfully. "I met Aisling in London. I'd just attended a meeting with my da in Parliament, and she was part of a protest outside. She literally ran into me—almost knocked my head off with the sign she was carrying," he says, chuckling. "It was an accident, of course. When I opened my eyes, she was leaning over me, wiping the blood from my forehead, with such a look of concern that it took my breath away. I knew then that she was the one for me."

I smile into my glass; I've heard the story many times, but that doesn't matter. "What was she protesting?"

"Ooch, I can't remember exactly. I think it was workplace rights for women. It was the sixties; another generation was waking up and discovering their power to change the world. There were protests every day about one thing or another. Aisling was in the middle of it all, fighting for better access to healthcare, voting, workplace equality… you name it, and Aisling had a position on it."

"She was a confident woman who knew what she was about, and I thank my lucky stars everyday—still—that she'd decided I was what she wanted, too." He takes a sip and looks at me. "Your mother had that same strength, although she expressed it differently. Saoirse's father was an MP, so she was taught early to keep her feelings inside, away from the cameras. Doesn't mean she didn't have opinions, mind you; she just expressed them in private."

I swallow the remainder of whiskey in my glass, smiling at the memory of my mother. She was the sweetest person alive. When I was seven and fell out of the tree by the barn and gashed my head, I scared both my grandmother and mother to death. My grandmother showed her fear and love by scolding me 'til my ears burned off, but Ma just cleaned the wound and bandaged my scalp, kissing away my tears. Grandma expressed her love loudly. Ma showed it with smiles, and kisses, and warmth.

"Sabrina strikes me as having that same strength," he says, eyeing me before emptying his own glass.

A thrill runs through me at the thought of her, but I try to maintain my expression, conscious of his eyes on me. "How can you tell? You only spent five minutes with her the day she left after her friend's wedding."

He shrugs, a smile playing about his lips. "Maybe it was the way she rolled her eyes at you when you loaded her bags into the car, or the set of her shoulders when you introduced us. She was taken aback by all the titles, but squared herself to face them. That's why the gossip about O'Shea today doesn't surprise me." He cocks his head. "Can't you see it?"

An image instantly comes to mind of Brie during our sail, hand on the rail as she stands confidently, smiling into the sun, and her hair blowing about her face… Her first time on a boat, yet she looked as comfortable as a seasoned sailor. And then there was the gleam in her eye when she took my cock in her mouth… I look down into my empty glass to hide my smile. "Of course I can."

"You can't hem a woman like that in; it just causes resentment and mistrust. She's free to do what she likes; be grateful when she chooses to include *you* in what she likes."

I huff and look at him. "Well, she'll be gone in a week or so, so it's kind of a moot point."

"So? Doesn't mean she can't come back. Or that you can't visit her," he points out, rolling his eyes at me. "There's an airport two hours away, you know."

"No shit," I deadpan, and then wave my hand at him. "You know what I mean. She has an entire life on a different continent. And I'm sure as hell not leaving here. So, that's that."

A mysterious little smile plays about his lips. "Maybe, maybe not." Before I can respond, he slaps his hand on the arm of the chair and heaves himself to his feet. "Well, I know you've been showing her all around Crossmoor, but this might be a good opportunity to expand her horizons. Do something other than the usual tourist fare."

He fishes in his back pocket and draws out an envelope; he hands it to me and takes my tumbler in exchange, then steps to the bar to set both glasses down. "What's this?" I ask, opening the envelope and peering at the creamy paper inside.

"An invitation to the nature trust's spring meeting." He winks at me. "Might be a good way to show her more of what it means to be a McGuire. Show her that not all Irishmen are like O'Shea."

'Meeting' isn't exactly the word I'd use for it. Even though there are a few speeches given and votes taken on which projects will be funded by the charity, the Nádúr Charitable Trust spring meeting is mostly an opportunity to dress up, enjoy a lavish dinner, and drink. Since we're one of the trust's founders and a major contributor, it's expected that a McGuire attends. Our association with the trust and its work to preserve and thoughtfully develop the land and wild areas of Ireland is one of the things I'm most proud of, but whenever I've gone to the spring meeting with Grandda, it's usually an exercise in not rolling my eyes at the pretentiousness. Why can't we just give money, vote on stuff, and celebrate with a pint without all the PR frippery?

However, the thought of going this time with Brie on my arm...

I cock an eyebrow at him, slapping the envelope lightly against my knee. "Are you sure? You normally enjoy being able to put your stamp on the decisions made."

He waves a dismissive hand. "It's your turn. You know what our priorities are for the fund grants. Go, enjoy yourselves. Besides—gah! Jaysus!" Gasping at another foul cloud of stench Tack has unconsciously released, we jump frantically in different directions—me to the window and Grandda to the door, flinging them both open. "Oh, lord. He's got into the spent malt again, didn't he?" Grandda splutters, wiping at his eyes. He glares at Tack.

I sigh in resignation. "Apparently."

"Come on, lad. Come down to the game room and try to beat me at darts. It'll be a while before you can breathe in here tonight." He casts a baleful glance at the beagle sleeping peacefully in his basket. "Better leave the window open, or he'll gas himself in his sleep."

"How fancy is 'fancy?'" Brie asks, her brow furrowed. The gravel crunches under our feet as we walk toward the warehouse as part of our tour of the castle grounds.

"Well, I need to wear a suit, if that helps," I offer, wondering what's going on in that beautiful head of hers. "There'll be cocktails, followed by a few speeches and dinner. We shouldn't be gone more than three or four hours." She's been busy with work at damn O'Shea's for the past few days and we hadn't been able to see each other until today. Although she let me take her to a late lunch, she seemed preoccupied. Distant. Her kiss when I greeted her was warm and genuine, though, and she was intrigued with the invitation to the spring meeting. It wasn't until I suggested a tour of the distillery and warehouse that she seemed able to shake off her troubles.

"Hmm, I'm not sure if I packed anything suitable." She purses her lips, worry in her eyes.

I squeeze her hand. "How about the dress you wore to the wedding?"

"What?" she laughs. "I don't think so. It's a bridesmaid dress!"

"So?" I shrug. As far as I remember, it was maybe a bit floaty, but otherwise okay. She looked beautiful in it—at least, before she jumped into the lake.

She hums noncommittally, shaking her head with an amused smile on her lips. "Men." Then her face lights up when we approach the cavernous entrance. "Wow. This is fantastic."

I let Brie walk ahead of me into the vast warehouse, enjoying the view. She's wearing jeans that hug her spectacular ass just right. "What's through there?" She points at the opening for the conveyor belt in the wall, upon which a row of filled barrels are making their way steadily into the warehouse.

"The barrels come from the distilling room through there," I point to the rectangular opening, "into here for aging, up there." I gesture to the four open floors above us where we can glimpse the stacks of barrels on each level.

She follows the conveyor belt to the wall, where the automated lift clamps onto each barrel and carries it up the brick wall. "That's a neat trick. I've seen pictures of wall conveyors, but I've never seen one in operation. Where are they going?"

"Those are destined for the fourth floor." I hold out my hand. "Come on; I'll show you."

She smiles and slides her hand into mine, as if it was always meant to be there. I guide her into the open, two-person lift that runs parallel to the barrel lift. I close the safety gate, press the button, and the lift begins its jerky ascent. She leans into me and hums in contentment when I slip my arm around her. "I love old brick buildings. They have a charm that modern construction seldom matches. When was it built?"

"There has been a distillery on this land since 1692. Those first structures are long gone, of course. This section of the warehouse was built in 1910. There's an older section on the other side of the office. It was built in 1860."

"You've done a beautiful job preserving it. I'm glad you didn't cover the brick over with cement or steel reinforcement."

"Well, preservation is kind of a passion of ours, blending the old with the new." I return her smile.

"It's a passion of mine, as well. I love being able to take an older property and incorporate more modern elements, while keeping the flavor of the original design," she says, her eyes alight with enthusiasm that mirrors mine.

"Exactly."

We reach the floor with a shuddering jerk of the lift. I take her over to watch the crew move the barrels off the lift with a forklift and maneuver them over to the long row, where they'll sit until ready.

"How long before you can sell these?" she asks, running her hand over one of the rough barrels.

"This batch has already aged ten years in American oak barrels. We've transferred it to these port pipes—casks that used to hold port— to age for another two years. Makes the whiskey richer, sweeter."

Leaning against the opposite row, I can't help feeling proud as she reviews the long line of barrels.

"Impressive."

The foreman parks the last forklift near the lift and waves at me in farewell; another crew will be along in about an hour for a short evening shift, but for now, we have the warehouse to ourselves.

Brie turns and steps closer, placing her hands on my chest; I take the initiative and pull her closer. "I'm glad you like it." She's warm and soft in my arms, sending a thrill through my veins. "You, ah, seemed distracted earlier. Tough day?"

She stiffens. "You might say that," she says with a sigh, and rests her forehead against my chest.

"Work related?" If that prick O'Shea was an arse to her again…

She huffs a rueful laugh. "No. That's going swimmingly. Work is the least of my worries right now."

"Brie." She raises her face so I can look into those lovely whiskey-golden eyes. "You can talk to me, you know. Is there anything I can do to help?"

"No!" Her eyes widen with alarm, and she takes an abrupt step back, out of my embrace. "Um, no," she says more softly, with a small smile in apology. "Sorry. It's just something I need to work out for myself."

"All right." She steps into my embrace again, sliding her hands across my back, and my worry eases a bit. "Just know that I'm happy to help if I can. You need only to ask," I murmur into her hair. It's down today, a fragrant cloud of gold silk.

"I know. Thank you." She raises her face to mine; her lips are soft, but with a growing insistence that matches mine. "It feels like a long time since we were on the boat," she says breathlessly, her hands locked in my hair. The yearning in her voice strikes a chord in me.

"Let's remedy that." Reaching down, I flip the button on her jeans—she gasps in surprise, but then eagerly does the same for me. Quickly yanking down her jeans, I lift her and plop her down on a cask; she yelps—and then laughs—as I flip her over, exposing her creamy arse. An appreciative groan escapes me as I rub my cock over her opening. She's more than ready for me. "Last chance to back out," I gasp.

"Are you kidding?" she blurts, and then bubbles with laughter. The next second, her laughter turns to a deep moan of pleasure as I plunge home. Holy God—she grips me like a vise that almost makes me lose my load on the spot.

"Fucking hell, Brie." I groan. "Bloody fantastic."

"Colin, please!" She wriggles against me, making needy, frantic noises, her hands clawing at the wooden cask. She's completely at my mercy, and it sets my blood on fire.

"Hang on, mo mhuirnín." I set a quick pace, plunging deeper with every stroke. Her gasps and squeaks bounce off the brick walls and her arse turns a lovely pink. She's intoxicating; my heart is hammering in my chest, the blood roaring in my ears. I never want this feeling to end. It doesn't take long before she's shuddering and bucking against me, her knuckles turning white as she clings to the cask.

"Oh my God, my God," she chants softly, her breath stuttering. It causes my balls to tighten, and suddenly I'm pouring myself into her, fire ripping down my spine. My knees buckle, and I brace myself on the cask, my head hanging down to rest on her back.

"Holy God." I can't suck in air fast enough, but I manage to rise and help her off her perch. She stands on wobbly legs, clinging to me for support.

"Wow. That was…unexpected." She chuckles, still trying to catch her breath. "Unexpected and so *hot*."

"Och, aye? Well, that's good." God, she makes me feel ten meters tall. I reclaim her lips, loving the way she melts into me. Jaysus, this woman. We're still standing bare arsed and shaking, and I'm wondering if she'd be up for another round when I hear a loud metallic clink and footsteps far below. We both freeze.

"Colin? Are you in here, man?" It's Grandda. Brie stares up at me, eyes wide, her lips smashed together, and it's all I can do not to laugh. She breaks first—a high-pitched giggle-squeak escapes her, and she buries her face against my chest to muffle the noise. There's dead silence below.

"Ah, I'll just be heading back to the kitchen now…in case anyone wants to join me." His voice is quivering with humor, and I know this time I won't escape his teasing. The footsteps retreat and there's silence below once more.

"Oh my God!" Brie whispers, her face red as a tomato, as we pull up our jeans. "Did he know it was us?"

"Aye, probably." I pull her close and kiss her softly, enjoying the smell of sex clinging to us. "Would you like to go down for a nice cup of tea?" I fix her with a direct gaze, my voice rumbling in my chest. "Or would you like to see the office space downstairs? There's a loft with a cot."

Her lips curl in a sensual smile, her eyes glowing. "I've always been a fan of cots."

chapter
eleven

Sabrina

AFTERNOON TEA IS CLEARLY AN *EVENT* AT CASTLE MCGUIRE.
After freshening up, Colin and I are now parked in luxurious
royal blue velvet chairs by a marble fireplace, the smouldering
peat in the hearth warming the massive room that faces one of the
magazine-worthy gardens.

Any thoughts of visiting Colin's office flat and his cot went out
the window when I caught a glimpse of the trays of food that were
being carried into this room. He seems happy to indulge me, which is
new, at least for me. Past men who shall remain nameless always had
their own agendas. There were times I was literally forgotten at various
events and get-togethers. I was an afterthought. I've never feel like an
afterthought with Colin. His focus and attention are always squarely
on me, and that's equally thrilling and scary, if I'm being honest.

There's more cutlery on the table than I know what to do with.
Work from the outside in is the only thing I vaguely remember from

some rom-com I saw a dozen years ago. I'm frazzled by the whole afternoon. Seeing where Colin's prize-winning whiskey is made and the sheer magnitude of the operation is overwhelming. Not to mention being bent over a wooden cask and rocked into pure bliss. I feel my cheeks heat as Mr. Calm, Cool, and Collected grins at me across the small round table, one ankle resting on his knee as he relaxes into the chair, looking like the lord of manor that he is.

I swallow the lump in my throat as a waiter dressed to the nines gingerly sets down a sterling silver tiered tray, layered with Michelin star quality sweets and golden baked scones. You know, just your typical Tuesday afternoon.

I try to steady my hand as I take a sip from the delicate china teacup that probably dates back to the 1800s. A malty taste explodes in my mouth with a hint of cocoa. Even the tea has hints of whiskey in it.

"Can I get you anything else, my lord?" The waiter asks, all dutiful and proper. I bite the inside of my cheek as I watch Colin shift in the chair. It's the first sign that he's uncomfortable today.

"That will be all, Daniel. Thank you," he murmurs, not taking his eyes off me.

"Very good." The waiter bows before he strides off to another table.

"Wow. My Lord. You really don't like that title, do you?" I whisper before I make a show of setting down my teacup on the saucer, keeping my pinky up.

Colin watches me in amusement. "No, I don't."

"But that's what you are."

He rolls his eyes, settling back in his chair. "Technically speaking, yes. But it's not something I like to broadcast. Besides, it means very little now."

"Seems to me it means more than what you let on." I pluck a miniature pastry coated in gleaming chocolate from the upper tier of the tray.

He hums a response, his typical go-to when he's not interested in answering a question. I bite into the pastry, tart raspberry greeting me after the rich chocolate glaze. Holy hell that's decadent. I close my eyes, savoring the taste, and when I open them, his gaze has darkened, his eyes focused on my mouth. Glancing around the room, I clear my throat. As much as I'd love to straddle and ride him like a stallion right now, that's not going to happen in a room full of primly-dressed diners.

Instead, I wave what's left of the pastry at him. "This is fantastic, by the way. Kudos to your chef."

"She won pastry chef of the year at the Wine and Food Awards last year."

"I can see why." I pop the last bite of pastry into my mouth with a nod.

"Do you bake, Sabrina?" he asks, taking a sip from his teacup.

I try not to choke on the last bite. It would be a shame to die and not experience more of this— more of him. "Only when forced. There's a lot of takeout happening for me, I'm afraid. I'm a bit of a disaster in the kitchen. How about you?"

The silver from his watch glints against the light as he lowers his cup. Damn his arms are something else. So much tightly wound muscle just aching to be touched. Now that I know what those arms feel like when they're around me, pulling me close and coaxing me against him, I'm not ashamed to admit that I'm becoming addicted to them… maybe even to him.

"I can get by. My mum taught me a bit before she passed, and then Aileen tried to carry that on." He smiles fondly, as if the memory is a good one. "I can slow cook a mean stew."

"I'd love to try it sometime."

His fingers trace the side of the teacup, and I can feel it everywhere. I can still feel him *everywhere*. I'll never look at a whiskey barrel the same way again. "I'd love for you to try it sometime." My phone buzzes from the table, and I grimace.

"Sorry about that. I thought I turned it off."

He waves his hand as the phone continues to vibrate. "Not a problem. Take it if you need to."

I turn the phone around, only just managing not to growl when I see the caller. "I need to take this." I haul myself out of the cozy chair and answer, moving to push the ornate doors to the garden open. "What the hell have you been doing?" I whisper-yell into the phone, hurrying along the meticulously groomed path to the corner of the garden.

"Hello to you too, Brie." Laird's laid-back voice that I used to enjoy, but now officially loathe, comes through the phone.

"In what universe did you think it would be okay to use my credit card?"

"You did give it to me," the idiot answers, and I stop beside a white rose bush.

"I gave it to you to use for buying stuff for the wedding, and when you were my boyfriend, both of which are officially over." Even surrounded by the serene garden, engulfed in the sweet aroma of blooms and freshly cut grass, he has me seething. "You absolute prick!"

"I needed a few things," he says dismissively.

"So get your own damn credit card! Do you know how embarrassing it is to have your card declined? Oh, wait, you don't. Because you're a man-child who doesn't actually have credit."

"I do have a new board though, and sunglasses." I'm having a nightmare. That's the only explanation for this. I let out a sigh and glance skyward.

"Let me guess, you lost one of the twenty pairs of sunglasses you already own?"

"I looked everywhere at our place."

"It's not our place!" I grind out through gritted teeth. "You're supposed to be moving your shit out. Did you conveniently forget that minor detail?"

"Brie, baby…"

"Do not baby me!" I turn and see an older couple on the other side of the garden, wide-eyed, staring in my direction. I give them a friendly wave and turn down the path, hurrying away from them. "I'm not your baby. We are not a couple anymore, and you have no right to use my credit card, you asshole!" I'm hissing now, sounding like some deranged person no doubt.

"But-"

"No buts! I put a freeze on that card, and you owe me three thousand two hundred and forty-nine dollars. Though I'm not going to hold my breath waiting for it. God! You're unbelievable. Do you know how long I had to spend on the phone with the credit card company, trying to convince them it wasn't me spending all that money?"

"I'm working on an endorsement."

I stop by a gentle water fountain surrounded by pristine blossoms, seeing the calm lake in the distance. There's a couple in a rowboat, the man leisurely rowing as the woman lounges back with her fingers dangling in the water. A family of ducks floats on past without a care in the world. It's all so peaceful and dream-like. Not like the train-wreck I seem to be in the middle of here. It seems like a lifetime ago that Colin carried me out of that lake.

"Just like you were for the last four years? Save your breath, Laird. I don't care, do you hear me? Just pack your stuff and get out of my apartment. Today."

I'm going to have to bleach the entire place when I get back. Who the hell knows what he's been up to since he's gotten back to the States. "Just give me a couple of days. I'm sorry about the card. I didn't think."

"No. You didn't think. That's not a strong suit for you, is it?" No response from the surfing god, probably because he just doesn't get it. I follow the path out of the garden and head to the edge of the lake.

"I think we should talk about us."

I stop abruptly by a row of stones along the water's edge. "No. No, we should not. The time for talking has long passed, Laird. You made a choice, and I've made mine. I don't know how much clearer I can be. Pack your shit. Get out of my apartment and don't ever contact me again."

There's a long pause and for a minute I think we've been disconnected. The truth is we've been disconnected for a long time.

Finally his voice comes through the phone. "For what it's worth, I am sorry, Brie. I didn't mean to hurt you. I'll finish packing up and be out of your hair soon."

"Yes. Yes, you will be. And good luck with the surfing. Don't let your dick permanently shrink from all that ocean water."

"Don't let my what?" I punch at the end call button, fighting the urge to hurl the phone into the lake. Men can be so clueless, and Laird reigns supreme. King of the clueless.

I take a seat on one of the rocks, turning my phone in my hand, telling myself it's an experience that I'll learn from. Learn and move on, Becca is always saying. Don't make the same mistake twice.

"Back to the scene of the crime, I see." Colin's buttery accented voice comes from behind me, and I turn to smile up at him. Speaking of mistakes… Even as the thought enters my head, I know that my time with Colin is not a mistake. He's shown me more attention and care in the week we've spent together than Laird did in four years. I probably should feel guilty about jumping into something with another man so soon, but I don't. Colin is funny, kind-hearted, and sexier than anyone I've ever been with. Regardless of what happens next, I'll have nothing but good memories about what we've shared.

"Back to my lake." I motion to the water, and he laughs.

"You mean *my* lake." He crouches down beside me, his eyes searching mine. "Everything okay with the call?"

I nod, giving him the answer he always gives me when he doesn't want talk "Mhmm. All good."

He reaches for my free hand, his thumb running a slow circuit over my wrist. "I can help if you let me."

Leaning forward, he presses forehead to mine, and I whisper, "You already are."

"What do you think? Too much?" I ask Brooke as she sits on the edge of her bed, practically bouncing. I twirl in front of her beveled mirror, feeling the delicate silver material swish around me.

After Colin dropped me back at the Whiskey Rose, I found Brooke, seeking her advice on where to shop for a dress for tomorrow night. I certainly didn't bring anything that would be deemed formal wear. She insisted we go through her closet first, and I have to admit, she was right. It's like Narnia in here.

Apparently, Brooke and Connor attend their fair share of weddings and formal events, and she's got a virtual treasure trove of dresses to choose from. But, when I saw the backless silver dress glimmering in the light of her closet, it reminded me of the watch Colin had on today, and I had to try it on.

Backless isn't my usual style, but the spaghetti straps and built-in bra under the crossover bodice give it a glamorous feel. I run my palms down the dress's layered skirt.

"It's incredible on you." Brooke grins. "He's going to faint."

"No. That's my department." The dress is a little big in the chest as Brooke has a generous amount of cleavage, and I do not, but otherwise, it's perfect.

"Shoes! You need shoes!" She bolts off the bed, opening up another door to reveal a few rows of high heels.

"I have a pair of black wedges with me."

She casts me a look like I have four heads. "Ah. No. This dress needs heels. What size are you?"

"Seven usually." She hums, reaching up to a pair of silver strappy sandals.

"These might work!"

"Are you sure this is okay? The dress, the shoes…" She passes me the sandals and I take a seat on the edge of her bed to try them on.

She waves me off, taking a seat beside me on the bed. "Oh please! I wore this once like two years ago at Molly Walsh's wedding." Her voice drops and she mock whispers, "Married a Scotsman, she did. Shhhh! It was quite the scandal."

I laugh, fiddling with the strap around my ankle. "I bet it was."

"And God forbid I wear the same dress twice. I've already been there, done that. You would have thought I murdered the Pope with the looks I got."

"That bad?" I slide the other sandal on and fasten the tiny buckle in place. The shoes are a little big, but I don't intend on walking a marathon in them.

"You have no idea."

I push up from the bed and steady myself on the shoes. I can rock a stiletto if given the chance, but I'm typically in wedges or flats. "Do I pass inspection?"

Brooke stands up, clapping. "I'd say so! It's perfect for Lady McGuire." I stumble back, gripping her dresser before I topple over.

"Ah, definitely not. There will be no Lady McGuire here." I turn to her mirror, trying to calm my racing heart. *No, no, no. You will not read anything more into this. It's a date. That's it. Nothing more.*

Brooke steps beside me, glancing at me in the mirror. "I'm just teasing. But it does have a nice ring to it, right? Lady Sabrina McGuire." She holds her hand up like she's tracing a marquee sign.

"Stop it." I nudge her in the side, shaking my head. "Hair up or down?"

"Definitely down with those loose beachy waves everyone raves about. Can't let him forget you're a California girl at heart."

I give her a nod, feeling my heart stuttering. That's right, just a California girl clearly out of her element here.

The next day, I give Nat a wave on our video conference as I show her the serene relaxation space complete with a mature Monterey Cyprus tree and brass fixtures that accent the flowing waterfall. I don't even want to think about how much it's going to cost Patrick to keep this going. The maintenance of the tree and accompanying foliage wall alone is going to be off the charts.

O'Shea wanted a zen-like space, where their employees could relax and unwind, and this definitely fits that bill. I'm rather proud of the curved walls that we managed to incorporate, and the inviting plush seating.

"It looks amazing!" Nat gushes. "Show me the brass chandelier again." I angle the phone up, so she can see the piece that she hand-picked herself, and I hear a squeal from her. "It's perfect."

"It really is, Nat. You did an incredible job."

"No. *We* did an incredible job." I sink down onto one of the chairs, glancing over at the waterfall. "I can't wait until the professional pictures come back. This is going to vault the company to the next level," Nat says excitedly.

"I think you might be right." I can't help the rush of excitement and pride I feel. Over a year's work, countless hours, gruelling conference calls, insane requests, and here we are. Finally. At the end of a project I can honestly say is one of the best I've ever been a part of. It was a challenge for sure, and dealing with Patrick has certainly been a trial, but the results are incredible. I wish my dad could see this. I think he'd be impressed.

She scoffs. "Of course I'm right. Is Patrick behaving himself today? No more meltdowns?"

"I haven't even seen him today. I've been with the building inspection crew all day."

She squints at me. "Everything okay there? I only saw a few questions come in to the engineering team."

"Everything's fine. Just a few minor clarifications they wanted on the A/C and duct work. The engineers said they'd be back with updates to them tomorrow."

"I'll check on it in the morning if I don't see an email when I come in." I watch as she scribbles a note into her book.

"Thanks, Nat. You're the best."

She grins and tosses her hair over her shoulder. "I know." We share a laugh and say our goodbyes, and for the first time in what feels like forever, I finally start to relax.

Sadly, it doesn't last long as I hear footfalls enter the space. I steel myself as Patrick sidles onto the chair across from me. "This is quite something, Sabrina. I'm impressed."

I blink at him, wondering if I've entered an episode of the *Twilight Zone*. Was that an actual compliment? "I'm glad you like it."

He studies the waterfall, his lips pursing slightly. "I wonder. Do you think it will cause an issue with productivity?" He glances slowly back to me, his head tilting, challenging.

I lift a brow. Is he serious? He's the one who wanted a space like this. I sit up as straight as the all-encompassing seat will allow. "The request was for a place where your employees *could* get away and relax. To recharge if they were feeling stressed. I remember the details and the conversations we had with Nolan. I can pull up the meeting minutes if you like."

He lets out a low laugh, holding his hand up. "No need for

that. I believe you." He leans forward, his elbows on his knees. "Sometimes I wonder if I'm too easy on them. But you know, competition is brutal out there. You have to give them some perks. This is a good perk, don't you think?" He spreads his arms wide, leaning back.

"I think so. I think they'll enjoy it, at least that's the intention."

"Mmm." His grey gaze slowly roams over me. "That's the intention. And what are your intentions when you're done here?"

"I have a few projects lined up back home."

"What if I wanted you?" I lean back abruptly, the hairs on the back of my neck rising. What in the ever-loving hell is he talking about?

"I'm not sure I understand."

"You're good at your job, Sabrina. You said so yourself, and it's obvious you have a passion for it. I'm always looking for people with passion."

I just bet he is. "You need a full-time architect?" I ask, not being able to hide the dubious tone in my voice.

"I have ten R and D facilities located around the world. Offices in over thirty countries. They all could use a little…" He waves his hand in my direction. "Sabrina magic."

I don't know whether to be offended or flattered. Patrick is such a dichotomy. I know he's a cheating husband, and clearly loathed by at least half the town, but then I've seen glimmers of a different man when he interacts with his employees. But this? A job offer? Never in a million years did I see this coming.

"Sabrina magic?" I ask with a laugh.

"Yes. Just so we're clear. I'm offering you a job. Chief Architect of O'Shea Pharmaceuticals. Name your price." He leans forward, and I can see the true negotiator start to come out in him.

"You're serious?"

"As the stock market at opening bell."

I struggle to find the words. I'm totally unprepared for an offer like this. "Whatever they're paying you is inconsequential," he continues, "I want you. Working for me. Money isn't an object."

"I don't… I don't know what to say."

"Yes. Say yes."

"I can't… I have a job, Patrick. A job I love, with a team that I respect and am truly blessed to work with." I can feel my heart race, my mind whirling at the possibility he's presenting me.

"Bring them with you," he volleys back.

My eyes widen. "Bring them with me?"

"Yes."

I shake my head, confusion mixing with sheer disbelief. "I can't do that."

"Yes. You can. Just think about it. You would have free rein to design what you want, in virtually any country in the world. With your own team, your own designers, your own vision."

I study him, the warning flags that Colin raised slowly waving at me. "Why me?"

"I told you. You're good at your job and I like you, Sabrina. I like your vision, I like what you've done here, and I like that you don't cave to my every whim." Ah, so, I'm a challenge. I get it now. It all clicks into place. I wonder how many other decisions he's made based on a challenge.

"Thank you, Patrick. It's an amazing offer, but I'm afraid I'm going to have to –"

He holds up his hand, stopping me. "Don't say anything right now. I'll have my assistant send you an actual offer. Read it over and then if you decide to say no…" He shrugs his shoulders. "No harm, no foul."

My mouth opens, but I've got nothing. Speechless isn't a good look for me, I know. His phone blares at him, and he fishes it out of the inner pocket of his blazer. "I need to take this." And then he's pushing out of the seat and striding away, barking into the phone. "O'Shea here." There's a pause as I watch him turn the corner out of the space, his voice fading. "No. I told you…"

I sink back into the chair, staring at the waterfall, wishing it had the answers for me.

Later that evening, I'm fidgeting with my clutch as I stand inside the foyer of the Whiskey Rose. God, this is worse than prom night. I'm looking for a much better result than a two-minute pump and a boob grab in the back of a limo from drunken Brad Lancaster, let me tell you.

Why am I so nervous? "Relax, Brie." Brooke gives my shoulders a squeeze as she looks out one of the stained-glass windows. "You look amazing and you're going to have a great time."

I give her a rueful smile. "Thanks, Mom." I smooth down the front of the layered skirt, the silky material calming me slightly.

"Oh! He's here." Brooke is practically giddy. "I'm just going to disappear." She thumbs in the direction of the office behind the front desk. "Don't worry, I won't be spying or anything." She gives me a wink and disappears into the office as I pull open the door.

Holy hell. Colin is mouth-watering at the best of times, but nothing could prepare me for the man in a suit. And not just any suit. A three-piece, midnight blue, obviously custom-made suit complete with a dark blue tie and a checkered pocket square. An actual pocket square. I didn't think anyone owned one of those outside of David Gandy himself. I've lost the ability to speak as his tall frame fills the door. Those chiseled cheekbones and half a day's scruff he's sporting are enough to make me swoon.

"Just..." He shakes his head, his eyes sweeping over me in a way that is far too illicit. I'm never going to make it through this dinner, cocktail hour, whatever the heck it is we're going to. He'll be lucky if I don't pounce on him before we get to his Land Rover.

"Wow. You're stunning, Sabrina. This dress is..." I beam up at him. "Magnificent."

"This old thing?" I move the skirt from side to side. "Every girl travels with a gown nowadays, don't you know?"

He laughs and the deep sound seeps its way into my heart. "You clean up pretty well yourself there, Shrek."

He gives me a half bow. "Why thank you, my lady." My heart flutters a little as I try to push away the conversation Brooke and I had yesterday. *There will be no Lady McGuire. No. No. No.*

I clear my throat. "Should we go?" My voice sounds high and out of control, my pulse already racing.

But instead of leading me out the door, his arm wraps around my waist, his lips finding mine in one of the hottest, deepest kisses I've ever had. My hand flattens against the rich fabric of the lapel of his jacket, and I can feel his heat, breathe in that unique oaky, amber scent that seems to radiate off him, and I'm falling. Falling hard and fast with no safety net in sight.

He pulls back, his talented fingers tracing the tiny silver strap over my shoulder, his breaths slightly ragged. "Now we can go."

"Are we there yet?" I tease, and he tightens his hand in mine while he navigates another curve in the road.

"Almost." His thumb runs that enticing circuit over my wrist like he did the other day when we were at his lake. Damn man knows exactly what he's doing to me. It's been all kinds of touches and glances since we got in the car. It's driving me crazy, and he knows it.

"What can I expect tonight?"

His brow furrows at the question. "There's a cocktail hour, a few speeches, a meal."

"I mean, will people ask who I am? What do you want me to say?"

He glances over at me. "The truth. Always."

"I'm banging you while I'm here on a job?"

He laughs loudly. "Is that what you're doing?" He pulls into a parking area where a few valets are milling about. "Maybe don't mention you're working for O'Shea to this lot. They're likely to burn you at the stake."

"Burn me at the stake? Where exactly are you taking me?"

"Right here." He throws the Land Rover into park and opens the door, handing over his keys to a valet before rounding the hood and opening up my door. I flounder my way out as gracefully as one can in shoes that are a half-size too big and a dress you're not used to wearing, and gape at the sight in front of me.

"Are those photographers?" I see a few flashes up ahead in front of a sprawling estate. I watch as couples meander to the imposing double front doors.

He glances casually at the mansion. "They are indeed." I narrow my eyes. "It's for the society pages and the gossip sites. There are a few slightly famous people who are members. You never know if they'll show up or not."

"Famous people?" He holds an arm out and I take it, hanging onto him or dear life. "What kind of famous people?" I ask under my breath. "You didn't say anything about famous people."

"You didn't ask. And it's no one really. A couple of players from the national football team, a few brewery owners, an actor, a guy who owns a distillery. You know? The usual."

"The usual? Wait?" I pull him to a stop, teetering slightly on my heels. "You're one of the famous people?"

"Normally it's Grandda, but tonight, they get me. They won't even notice. Trust me. I'm no one. Come on. Cocktail hour has already started."

I take a deep breath and steady myself beside him. I may need more than a few cocktails to get through this.

Colin

Holy fecking hell.

I sneak another peek at the creamy skin exposed by that incredible dress and stifle a moan. If I can make it through cocktails without ravaging her in an alcove like a fevered bear, it will be a bloody miracle.

I don't think I've ever had my breath taken away like that before.

Having the air well and truly snatched from my lungs, leaving me gasping like a landed trout. But it happened when I opened the door at the Whiskey Rose and saw Sabrina standing there, wearing a dress that looked like it was spun from moonbeams.

Handing her another flute of champagne, I can't help my smile as she takes in the room around us. Her golden eyes are as round as saucers as she surveys the walls lined with books and the groups of well-heeled people chatting and gossiping around us. Gossiping *about* us, probably. I've caught more than one sly glance in our direction from busybodies trying to figure us out. I've never attended before with anyone besides Grandda, so Sabrina—especially looking like she does tonight—is a revelation for them.

"So, what do you think?"

She pauses in her gawking to cock an eyebrow at me and shrug. "This? Eh, it's just your usual, run-of-the-mill ancient castle library," she drawls, flipping her hand. "I've seen better."

My grin widens. "Impressive, isn't it?"

She takes a sip, the bubbles making her nose wrinkle. "Very. I've obviously never been here before, but this room seems familiar, somehow," she murmurs, gesturing to the huge windows on one wall.

"Well, it's used all the time for films and the like." A waiter appears with a tray of nibbles and she daintily selects one, popping it in her mouth. She closes her eyes, savoring the treat, and I fight the overwhelming urge to kiss her. "In fact, the whole estate was used for…oh, I can't remember the name of the show. Aileen was a huge fan. The one about backstairs intrigue that was big a couple years ago? Maids, and footmen, and whatnot?"

"Backstairs intrigue?" Her eyes pop open. "Oh! You mean Broadmoor Lane? Oh, I loved that show!"

I chuckle at her eagerness. "You and a gazillion other people. They still do a very healthy tourist business here based on that show."

"I can believe it." She glances toward the door. "Do we need to stay in this room, or can we look around?

Excellent. A chance to get her away from all these prying eyes. Maybe we can find an obliging alcove… I place a hand on her back, ostensibly to escort her, but also so I can touch that flawless skin. "I think we can manage that. You'll love the staircase—"

"Colin! Great to see you tonight, man. How are you holding up these days?" A hand claps my shoulder, and I mentally curse the interruption. At least it's someone I actually like.

I turn and give him a warm smile as I shake his proffered hand. "John. Wonderful to see you again." Slipping my hand around Brie's waist again, I give it a slight squeeze. "May I introduce Sabrina Worthington? Brie, this is John, Earl of Tratshal. He's a member of the board that manages the Trust."

"Lovely to meet you, er, my lord," she murmurs, an uncharacteristic note of nervousness in her tone, and I give her waist another squeeze in support.

His eyes light up. "An American! Lovely to make your acquaintance. Are you visiting, Miss Worthington, or have you relocated to our fair isle?" He sweeps his hand through his iron-grey hair; he wears it on the longer side, giving him the air of an aging rock star.

"I'm here on business." She flashes him a confident smile, but I can feel the tremors running under her skin. Is it nerves, or something else? "I'm an architect managing a project for O'Shea Pharma."

His bushy eyebrows quiver. "O'Shea Pharma? Hmm, I see." He gives me a look, but I merely give him a bland smile. "Well, I'm so pleased you joined us this evening."

"Thank you." She gestures to the room. "I am, too. It's a beautiful location for such an event."

"This was John's family home," I comment, exchanging my empty glass for a full one from a passing waiter. "He grew up here."

"Wow." Her eyes widen. "You have a lovely estate, my lord."

"No need for formality tonight," he says with a dismissive wave of his hand. "Call me John. And, thank you, but it isn't mine any longer, unfortunately. Between the expenses of upkeep and taxes, it made more sense to sell it. The LLC that owns it now is committed to maintaining the history of the place, and that takes the sting out of seeing the busloads of bloody tourists swarming over the grounds."

The regret in his eyes strikes a chord in me. Even with the distillery, I know that if it wasn't for our tourism business, my family would likely also have to go that route. I dislike having to rent out my child-hood home to a bunch of vacationers who don't give a damn about the history, the lives that have come and gone there, but it would be worse to lose it forever. So, we put up with the odd bits of thievery and vandalism—people who think it's okay to steal a copper cup or carve their names into a 100-year-old oak—and just get on with it.

"I can imagine," Brie murmurs, a small wrinkle appearing in her smooth forehead. John cranes his neck to look over the heads of the guests behind us, and grimaces. "Oh, damn. Vivien is chatting up the Reynolds. If I don't intervene, she'll probably buy another bloody horse, and we've already got too many. Excuse me." He nods to us and gives Brie a charming smile. "Sabrina, it's been enchanting. Have a lovely evening."

Sabrina, enchanting. The perfect description of the woman beside me whose light, sugary scent is filling my head, conjuring up hopes for later. She grins up at me. "Wow, first a baron and now an earl. Know any dukes you can introduce me to, so I can fill up my bingo card?"

I bark out a laugh. "One or two."

"What did he mean about horses?" She beams at a passing waiter, and he instantly stops, taking her empty glass, and handing her a full one.

I smile at her over the rim of my own glass. "He and his wife, Vivien, raise horses. In fact, one of their stallions won the Irish Derby two years ago."

"Hmm. Horse racing is a rich man's sport." Her smile falters. "And he still had to give his estate up?"

I nod. "Well, there's rich, and then there's rich. John's real love is horses, and after the last property tax increase…" I shrug. "It was an easy decision for him, I suppose."

She frowns. "It doesn't sound easy."

"Well, there's easy, and then there's easy." She rolls her eyes at me, and I laugh. As if on cue, a butler appears at the door and taps a small chime, giving the signal for dinner. I offer her my arm with a flourish, and she giggles as she takes it. "Shall we? We'll see if we can't check off a few more titles from your card."

"It would be nice to meet just one person who doesn't give me that look whenever I mention O'Shea," she fumes.

"What look?" I tighten my hands on the steering wheel, wishing I'd thought to hire a car tonight.

She huffs. "You know. The look like they've just discovered something nasty stuck to their shoe. Connor, Steven, your grandfather, John the Fancy Earl…they all do it. You do it yourself, every time I mention Patrick—see? Like that." She jabs an accusing finger at me.

Suddenly realizing I'm scowling, I let my face thaw and a reluctant smile tugs at my mouth. "Oh. Well. It's not something I can control, I suppose."

"Hmph." Brie looks out her window and crosses her arms, which makes her cleavage more pronounced. A low-hanging tree limb brushes my side window, and I jerk my eyes away from her tits and back to the road. *Jaysus, pay attention, McGuire.*

"You know, there's more to him than you think," she says after a few minutes.

"Who? O'Shea?" I keep my face carefully neutral; it's more difficult than I thought. "How so?"

"I mean, sure, he's a pig and an asshole—" She breaks off, frowning, then shakes her head and continues, "He's also a hell of a businessman, according to Kathleen."

"She's his wife," I point out, and she waves her hand, impatient.

"True, and if anyone had a right to say bad things about him, it's her. And she doesn't, really. Say bad things about him, I mean." She looks out the window again, her brows drawn. "He certainly knows how to negotiate," she murmurs.

I grunt. My hands tighten on the wheel at the thought of O'Shea's smarmy face. "There are several people in town who've lost their businesses or their homes due to his business tactics. Why don't you ask *them* what they think of him?"

Tense silence reigns for a few minutes before she sighs. "You didn't tell me you were receiving an award tonight," she says, thankfully changing the subject.

"I didn't receive anything. I was merely accepting something for my grandfather." I grin at the memory of her surprise when they called my name, and then her proud smile as I went forward and said a few words on behalf of Grandda. Her reaction sent a warm wave through my chest, and I felt taller somehow.

"You were very eloquent."

There are few cars on the street when we reach Crossmoor, and before I know it, I'm pulling up in front of the Whiskey Rose. I feel my heart wrench when I realize the night is over.

I know I should get out and open her door, but instead, I take her hand. "Sabrina." I move without thinking; my hand sinks into her hair a split second before my lips cover hers. Need blazes in me and I kiss her, hard—her wanton moan only drives me further. Suddenly, she pulls away, panting. Oh, God, did I push too hard?

I'm about to apologize when a slow smile curves her lips. "Come inside with me? It's not a large bed, but it's more comfortable than a whiskey barrel."

There are no lights on when Brie opens the door and we enter. The yeasty aroma of rising bread fills the small lobby. My eyes slowly adjust to the darkness, but Brie doesn't hesitate; she takes my hand and leads me past the desk and up the narrow stairs. The wood floor creaks underfoot, and I chuckle. "This is a first. I feel like I'm sneaking into my girlfriend's room with her parents sleeping down the hall."

"You never snuck a girl into your room at home before?" she whispers back.

"I did, but it's different. Stone floors don't squeak. Not much of a challenge."

"Lucky. My grandmother's floors used to squeak so loudly, the whole block could hear. It was a major deterrent." She opens a door and hauls me inside. The shade is up, and moonlight floods the room. It's not a large space, but it's comfortable, with a lot of homey touches. Connor and Brooke have built a great place here.

Brie steps out of her shoes with a sigh of relief and stands before me, a teasing smile flickering on her lips. "Well, now that we're here, whatever are we going to do?"

In answer, I draw a fingertip slowly down the length of her neck, making her shiver. The straps easily slip off her shoulders, and my breath catches as the dress slithers down her lithe body to form a silver pool at her feet. She's fecking amazing. She stands shoulders back, her full breasts glowing in the moonlight, and the sight steals my breath. All the blood in my head has rushed to my cock. "You're bloody gorgeous, Brie," I manage to choke out, and her answering smile is like the sunrise.

She slides her arms around my neck and grunts softly when I pull her hard against me. "It's been a long time since I've snuck a boy into my room."

My trousers are uncomfortably tight. "I'm honored." My heart hammers in my chest as she starts unbuttoning my shirt.

Her lips brush mine. "So am I."

I peel an eye open and blink a few times to clear the blur. We never got around to closing the shades last night, so it's disgustingly bright in here. There's also an annoying tapping coming from somewhere, and I wish it would stop. Brie shifts beside me, her head resting on my chest. We're sprawled diagonally across the bed, and still my feet hang off the end, sticking out ridiculously from under the quilt we pulled over ourselves a few hours ago. At least, I think it was a few hours ago. Feels like a few minutes ago.

Still, even squished into a too-small bed, sweaty and sticky from fucking Brie into oblivion, I've never been this comfortable. Every inch of me is happy. I turn my head on the pillow and smile when I spy my shirt hanging off a floor lamp. After I got her naked, everything was a bit of a blur. I do have a vivid memory though of her shocked face when I picked her up, pinned her against the wall, and drove my cock into her tight, wet heat. Christ, that was fun.

My stomach growls. "Mmm, bacon," she mutters, making me chuckle.

"What?" But she only snuggles closer, her breath warm against my skin. It's soothing, and my body starts to sink back into sleep.

The damn tapping returns, this time accompanied by a creak. "Brie? Are you up?" a feminine voice asks, and my eyes snap open. "I'm sorry, but I can't wait anymore! How was your date with Col—"

To my horror, Brooke's face eases around the edge of the door. Her eyes pop open in shock. "Oh my God!" she blurts in a choked whisper. "Oh. My. God!! I'm so sorry!" Her now flaming face instantly disappears and the door shuts, a chorus of "I'm so, so sorry," and "holy shit" trailing away.

Brie jolts awake and looks around wildly, her tangled hair a golden cloud floating around her face. "Did I...was that *Brooke*?"

I let my head flop back onto the pillow. "Yep. Well, it could have been worse. At least we had the quilt pulled up; otherwise, she would have gotten a real show."

"Oh, my God," she mutters, burying her face against my chest, laughter bubbling out of her. My stomach is definitely awake; it unleashes another unholy growl, and her laughter doubles. The vibrations wake another part of my anatomy, which pokes into her belly with increasing urgency.

She looks at me, her humor melting into desire, and I swiftly roll her over, making her yelp. Kissing her neck, I'm rewarded with a breathy moan. "I guess there's no need to be quiet now, right?"

Her grin is all the answer I need.

chapter
twelve

Sabrina

THE MORNING IS A LITTLE SURREAL AND DOMESTICATED AS WE
try to share the mirror in the bathroom. Given it's tiny and
he's not, I quickly find myself hoisted up to the counter
while he contemplates my razor.

"I kind of like you scruffy." I pluck the razor from his hand as
he examines his jaw, turning his head from side to side. He steps
between my legs with a grin, his hands skimming my inner thighs as
he parts them farther.

"Is that right?" He grins at me, making my stomach flip again.
It's been doing that a lot. The more time I spend with him, the more
it flips, like I'm on some rollercoaster with those upside-down loops
that terrify and excite you simultaneously.

"That's right. And besides, this won't do." I toss the razor into
the sink, and it clangs against the porcelain.

His fingers caress my sensitive skin, my own tracing the leather belt on his pants because sadly, he's half-dressed—an issue that needs to obviously be corrected. I'm still in the towel he wrapped around me after he pressed my torso against the tiles of the shower and had his wicked way with me. The fact that he's started to get dressed is clearly a crime. "You sure you like me scruffy?"

"I think I do." He flashes me a wicked grin, his palms tightening against my thighs as he lowers between them, nipping at my side like. The fluffy towel that was wrapped around me finds its way to the floor. "Jury is still out. Keep trying." I lean back against the wall, opening my legs wider, feeling his tongue sweep from knee to hip.

"More?" he asks, glancing up at me as his fingers tease against my throbbing clit.

"More. Definitely more." I sound desperate, because I am. Desperate for more of him. I'm not sure I'll ever get enough.

My head hits the wall, my hips lifting as he slides two fingers inside me. Some sort of raspy groan fills the small bathroom, and I'm not sure if it's him or me, or both of us. My legs tighten around his head, dangling over his broad shoulders, and then his tongue is teasing me, the scruff from his jaw tickling and torturing me in the most delicious way.

My breaths are all choppy, and I'm slack-jawed, that tingly sensation stirring low in my belly. I wouldn't have thought it was possible to have this many orgasms in one morning, but the man seems intent on proving a point.

It's almost embarrassing how quickly his tongue can push me closer, how the coarse hairs on his jaw can have me writhing and calling out his name. My hands dive into his hair, tugging and urging him forward. His fingers curl back into me, in a magic dance with his tongue, and I'm flying.

He doesn't let me fall, though. He gently brings me down, gingerly wraps the towel back around me, and leaves the bathroom with me calling after him, "Jury's back. Definitely keep the scruff."

I'm disoriented and flustered, having trouble with the side zipper on my skirt while he stands at the desk near the bed, his shirt open with the sleeves half-rolled up, studying the blueprints for O'Shea's office.

"Are these yours?" he asks, glancing at me over his shoulder.

"Well, not mine specifically. The whole team worked on the design." I finally yank the zipper up. Why designers don't make it easier to pull a zipper without breaking into a sweat, I'll never know.

"I think you're being modest." I feel the heat rise in my cheeks.

"And I think all modesty went out the window this morning when you… you know." I wave my hand at him, memories of our morning shower flooding me. Holy hell that was hot. Colin turning to press my stomach against the slick wall, his tongue teasing and exploring while the shower rained down over us, isn't something I'm going to forget any time soon.

"When I what? Say the words, Sabrina." That damn grin of his lights me up, his gaze holding mine. He's irresistible and way too tempting.

I clear my throat dramatically. "Ahem… When you licked me from front to back, lingering on the back."

He lets out a laugh that lights his whole face. "That is a lovely way to put it."

I put my hands on my hips, trying to hold back a laugh. "You think ass play is lovely?"

Those steel blue eyes of his seem to darken as his gaze slowly rakes over me. The way he looks at me is illicit. "It is to me." We're never making it out of this room. I'm going to be so late for work.

"Come show me these." He motions me over, and I join him at the desk where the blueprints for O'Shea's office are laid out. "I have no idea what any of it means."

"Now you know how I felt at your distillery the other day."

His brow creases as he looks down at me. "The distillery isn't confusing."

"Not when it's been your life. But for someone like me?" I shake my head. "It's overwhelming. You're pretty impressive there, Lord McGuire."

"No. I'm just following traditions and very specific instructions. This is something so much more. You're creating something here, and it's beautiful, even if I don't understand it." He turns back to the blueprints, and I feel a swell of pride. No one has ever described blueprints I've had a hand in that way before. "What is all of this?"

His hand sweeps across the blueprint of the first floor. "Well, this is actually Patrick's office."

He scowls at me. "I'm liking it a bit less now."

I hit him in the chest, his strong, powerful chest that I've spent a lot of time resting against. Colin seems to like people to think he's closed-off, but in reality, he's a big teddy bear, holding me close as I cuddle up against him.

"Stop it." He gathers my hand in his, pressing a tender kiss to my palm. The man is so confusing. He's commanding and intense one minute, sweet the next.

"I'll try to be good."

I roll my eyes at him. "Promises, promises."

He gives my side a squeeze. "Please continue."

"So, this is the lounge area." I point out the area on the blueprint and hear him huff.

"He has an actual lounge in his office?"

"The entire first floor is his office. A personal workout room, fully functional kitchen, a private boardroom, media room." I trail my fingers along each of the areas. "The man could actually live here if he wanted to."

"That's convenient for when Kathleen kicks him out." I nudge him with my hip before moving in front of him.

"Something tells me he probably has a few homes he could move into if that were to ever happen." Colin mutters something under his breath that I can't quite hear, and I start fastening the remaining buttons on his shirt.

"We're having an opening next week. You should come. See the finished product."

I push another button into place, flattening my palms against his chest. "While I would love to see something you've done, you don't go storming your enemy's castle unless you're planning on taking it."

I shake my head at him. "Okay, Sir Lancelot. But, I'm not sure it's healthy carrying around this kind of animosity all of the time. Are you two ever going to let this go?"

He tilts my chin up, his expression serious. "No. It's been this way between our families for literally centuries, and we've learned to live with it."

"Mhmm. Until it's showdown at noon at the O.K. Corral."

He laughs, tapping my nose. "Not quite right there, my American girl. Try again."

There's that damn spin in my stomach again. *His girl.* Is that who I am now? "Hmm." I tap my lip, pretending to think on it. "Medieval jousting on horseback?"

"Closer." He lowers his mouth to mine with a slow kiss that steals my breath. "In all seriousness, it sounds amazing. I'm sure O'Shea is pleased."

"I think so, I mean, he offered me a job."

Colin's arms tense around me and he leans back. "He did what?" He takes a step back, eyeing me warily.

"He offered me a job. Chief Architect of O'Shea Pharmaceuticals. He sent over the offer yesterday."

"Of course he fecking did. That bastard." Colin turns from me, stalking across the room, tugging his jacket aggressively from the chair it landed on last night.

"Excuse me?"

"This is classic O'Shea."

I feel my anger spike. I don't like where this is going. "How so?"

"He saw us together at the bar. He knows hiring you would get to me." Colin's voice is hard, annoyed, as he starts pacing.

"So, there's no way he would offer me a job based on my ability then? This is all about you? Is that what you're implying here?"

He stops his pacing, turning to me. "That's not what I said."

"That's what you meant though."

"No, it's not." He crosses back to me, his jacket draped over his arm. "Look, Patrick doesn't do anything without having an ulterior motive."

I fold my arms across my chest, stiffening in place, beyond incensed that what I thought was a generous offer based upon my skills and ability has turned into a testosterone-filled pissing match.

"I know that you're a gifted architect, Sabrina. That's not even a question." There's a conviction in his voice that make me bristle a little less. "Patrick offering you a job makes sense. It also means he gets to gloat about having you as an employee. Don't think that he won't use that any chance he gets. It's who he is. That truth, however, doesn't diminish his offer to you in any way."

"They have over thirty offices. This is a tremendous opportunity, Colin, one I only ever dreamed of getting. I kind of thought you would be happy for me. It might mean I get to spend more time here... with you."

The tension in his jaw eases, and he lets out a long breath, touching his forehead to mine. "Forgive me," he whispers, leaning back to hold my gaze. "I'm afraid that when it comes to Patrick, I'm always going to think the worst. I didn't mean to offend you. Not at all."

He wraps his arms around me, and I'm pressed against his crumpled dress shirt and the warmth of his chest. It feels so good to be enveloped in his arms, inhaling his unique masculine scent. He presses a kiss to the top of my head. "I'll work on it. I promise. This is all very new for me, mhuirnín."

Resting my chin against his chest, I look up at his handsome face. "How do you think I feel? I have no idea what's happening. All of a sudden I'm spending time with royalty."

"I'm not royalty, not really." He shakes his head, his fingers curling around a lock of my hair.

"I'm meeting lords and dukes and who knows who else. I mean, you live in a castle. You own hundreds of acres of land and a boat."

"Yacht. She's a yacht," he says, his voice a little amused at my rambling.

I wave my hand dismissively. "Yacht, whatever. I can't even talk to my best friend about this right now, whatever *this* is. And there's Laird at the apartment."

He tilts his head in question. "Laird? Is there a problem?"

"Yes. Actually, no, not anymore. I handled it. He racked up my credit card, and he's still at my apartment when he was supposed to move out when he got back to the States."

Colin's brow takes on a deeply creased wrinkle. "Jaysus. What an arse." I'm not going to lie, I kind of like it when his accent gets deeper, inching into that intense timbre that makes me want to climb him like a tree.

I pat his chest. "Take it easy there, Shrek. I slayed that dragon myself. I don't need rescuing, you know."

"This all started because you needed rescuing, remember? In my lake?"

"I had that completely under control." I try and fail in protesting, because let's face it, if he hadn't carried me out of that lake, I would have died of embarrassment when the wedding party found me. It's hard to believe that was over three weeks ago. So much has happened, it's all beena whirlwind.

"Sure you did. In any case, I'm glad I carried you out of my lake and into my bed."

"You know, I haven't actually been in your bed yet?"

"Let's remedy that, shall we? What are you plans this weekend? I was going to take the *Saoirse* out Friday night."

"Hmm. I've been in that bed." He takes a firm handful of my ass, making me squeal before he continues on.

"I'm aware. But, we can sleep under the stars, spend the day at the beach. Give you a taste of home, hmm? It's not a proper Californian beach, but I think you'll like it. I promise to have you back by Sunday."

"It sounds perfect." I glance over at the closet. "I don't have a bathing suit."

His eyebrows lift before he lowers his lips to my ear, the stubble on his jaw brushing my skin. "Who said anything about needing one?"

It's been a few days since Colin took me to the benefit. We've fallen into alternating between nights spent exploring the streets of Crossmoor, stealing kisses in darkened alleyways and ending wrapped up in each other at the Whiskey Rose, and spending time with Steven at his pub. They share a love of sailing and can dispute for hours over their definition of the perfect day at sea. Seeing how close they are makes me miss Becca.

Since she moved to Ireland with Liam in the months before the wedding, I've missed my best friend. Knowing she would only be a few hours away rather than a plane ride and an ocean is another reason why I'm seriously considering Patrick's job offer.

It's a dream job, with a salary that is almost triple what I'm making now. The promise of running my own team is one I'm not sure I can pass up. While I can't ignore Colin, I also need to be logical about this. We've only known each other for a few weeks. My reasons for upending my life in California cannot and should not rest solely on him.

With thoughts of my decision on an endless loop, I survive another intense Friday morning meeting with Nolan as we iron out the final details on the project. Colin's promise of a weekend on the *Saoirse* is exactly what I need before we dive into the grand opening of O'Shea's offices.

After the meeting, I knock on the open door to the lab where Kathleen is engrossed behind a microscope. "Thought you might need this." She looks up with a smile, pushing back from the table.

"Gods yes. How did you know?"

"Just a hunch." I head over to the table and set the cup down along with creamers and a few packets of sugar. "I didn't know how you take it. How's it going?"

She pops the lid off the coffee cup and tears open two packets of sugar, dumping them in. "It's not going."

"I'm sorry to hear that. I'd offer my help, but I don't know a thing about this."

She lifts the cup in a salute before taking a sip. "This is perfect help."

"Maybe you just need a break from it for a while. I know when I'm working on a design, I need to walk away sometimes, get some air."

"You're probably right. Some days it's so frustrating." She shakes her head, looking down at her notebook. It's scrawled with equations and notes, and things I have no hope of understanding. I'm once again in awe of Kathleen.

"It will get better. I know it will."

"Take my mind off of this." She stands up, motioning to the door, and I fall into step beside her. "How's everything going with the office? Nolan said the inspection is finished."

We make our way along the curved corridor, to the panoramic windows at the end of the hall. There's a bench that faces one of the gardens and the sea churning in the distance. In the span of a couple of hours, the morning sunshine has turned to an overcast afternoon with the threat of rain in the distance. The weather here is so unpredictable.

I smile at her, taking a seat on the bench. "It did. We're good to go now. Just a few minor changes that Patrick is asking for, but they're cosmetic, not architectural. The big move-in is going to start over the weekend."

She takes a long sip of her coffee, gazing out to the garden. "You've done an amazing job here, Brie. Patrick is thrilled with it, though I doubt he'd say it to your face, so I will."

"Thank you. It's one of our more ambitious projects. We're excited about it." I fiddle with the lid of the cup, wondering if I should talk about Patrick's offer with Kathleen. She's starting to become a friend, and regardless of her screwed-up relationship with her husband, I value her opinion.

"I know he offered you a job," she says, surprising me. "He does share a few things with me, you know?"

"What do you think about it?"

"I told him if he didn't extend you an offer, I would have." She waves her hand in an arch over the space. "This is incredible. You transformed this place, breathed new life into it. It's not just bland offices and cubicles anymore. The question is, what do you think about the offer?"

"It's an amazing opportunity." I glance down at the coffee cup before looking back to her. "To have my own team and be able to create my own vision? That's pretty much all I've ever wanted."

"Why do I hear a 'but' in there?" Kathleen asks.

"Colin said something about Patrick using it to get a rise out of him. It didn't sit well with me."

She shakes her head. "Well, he will, because it's Patrick, and he can't miss an opportunity to annoy Colin, but Brie, I'm serious. When I said I would have offered you a job, I meant it, and that has nothing to do with Colin McGuire." She reaches over to squeeze my arm in encouragement. "You know, some of our offices haven't been re-designed since the eighties, and honestly, you're a perfect fit for this. Don't let their petty feud make you think you're anything other than fantastically talented."

I glance up at the O'Shea logo embossed into the curved ceiling and can't help but smile. "It is pretty fantastic, isn't it?"

"Damn right it is." She touches her cup to mine. "And don't you forget it."

"Tack!" The most adorable beagle in the world wiggles in excitement as I approach Colin's yacht later on Friday night. It's a cool, but clear evening, and the threatening clouds from the morning have now fully disappeared. The marina looks like something out of a fairy tale, with white lights dancing over the water. "I didn't know you were coming." He sets his paws up on the metal rail of the yacht, and I lean over to scratch behind his ears.

"He wanted to join us. I hope that's okay." Colin emerges from the lower deck, a dark blue t-shirt stretched across his broad chest, his legs covered in worn denim jeans that look sinful.

"Of course. Permission to come aboard, Captain?" Colin holds his hand out for me, and I toss my overnight bag over the rail, watching it land with a soft thud before taking his hand as he helps me in.

He pulls me against his chest, his lips descending over mine with a kiss that makes my knees buckle. "Permission granted."

"Is that the way you welcome all of your passengers on board?" I ask, my voice a little breathless when I pull away.

"Only the really important ones."

"Mmm. I like that answer." I hold up the brown paper bag from the Crown and Sparrow. "I had Steve make us fish and chips."

His eyes widen at the bag. "You didn't have to do that. I have food on board, you know."

"I know, but I wanted to bring something."

"He does make a mean fish and chips. But you're all I need." He draws me closer and my stomach starts its inevitable gymnastics routine. I know I'm falling hard and fast. I just hope that this weekend escape doesn't make me crash and burn.

Colin

"This is heaven." Brie sighs and leans back on her elbows, staring out across the blindingly blue water, where the *Saoirse* bobs gently at anchor in the sheltered cove. "For some reason, I never thought about Ireland having sandy beaches. I only ever pictured rocky shores and forbidding cliffs."

We're relaxing on a blanket after a picnic lunch—an extremely late lunch, thanks to her distracting me with a spectacular blowie. I'll never be able to enter the galley again without getting hard.

My chuckle rumbles in my chest. "Well, we have plenty of those, to be sure. But we have hundreds of spots like this, as good as anything you've got in California. You can even surf here, if you fancy it."

Her smile falters, and I mentally kick myself. The last thing I want is to bring up anything that makes her think of the infamous Laird. Bloody wanker. The thing with her credit card made me see red; the fucker's lucky he's not in town anymore. Our dungeon hasn't been used for anything but storage in centuries, but I'm sure there's a spare cell down there near the Christmas decorations...

"This is even better than the places I've been to back home because we have this all to ourselves. No dealing with hundreds of tourists."

She shades her eyes with one hand, peering around the cove. "I can't believe there isn't anyone else here. You don't own it, do you?"

My laugh startles some gulls perched nearby; they take flight, arcing over the water. "No. It's a public beach, but it's not easily accessible except by sea, so it tends to be less visited." Her gaze follows as I gesture to the rugged terrain behind us covered with boulders, sea grass, and thistles.

"Well, it's perfect. Thank you for bringing me here." She stretches her long legs and digs her bare toes in the sand. Dressed in shorts with windblown hair and drowning in one of my old jumpers, she's unspeakably beautiful. "In fact, thank you for the whole weekend. It's just what I needed."

It's what I needed too—uninterrupted time with Brie. We moved along the coast at a leisurely pace to show her a few of my favorite spots. Since she's been here, she hasn't had much time to sightsee beyond Crossmoor. Watching her enjoy the scenery glide by has become one of my favorite things. Unlike others I've taken on cruises, friends who visit from abroad, Brie doesn't ooh and ahh every five minutes or gush about how everything is so 'charming.' She simply takes it all in with a quiet and almost reverent appreciation.

Leaning closer, I press a gentle kiss against her temple. "It's been entirely my pleasure."

She twists so her lips meet mine, making my heart race. "I wouldn't say entirely," she murmurs, her smile growing.

"Oh no?" I quickly roll over her, making her yelp, and maneuvering until she's resting on top. My erection strains against my jeans in response. "Nice to know I'm holding up my end," I say, flexing my hips to make my point.

She giggles and lowers her mouth to mine. Kissing Brie is *definitely* one of my favorite things. Right along with suckling Brie, licking Brie, and driving my cock into Brie's—

"Ack! Jaysus, dog!" Nothing like a wet dog nose in your ear to break your train of thought. Sabrina laughs as I wipe the slobber off my ear, and Tack gives one of his tortured yips, wriggling all over like a maniac. Daft dog.

"Aw, he just doesn't want to be left out." She rolls off me and sits up to rub Tack's ears. "Poor guy."

"He hasn't been left out. I've thrown the ball for him so many times, my arm is likely to fall off." I cock an eyebrow as he blinks at me, full of false innocence. "Don't make me regret bringing you," I warn him. He yips again and promptly rolls over on the sand, so Brie can rub his belly.

"Pay no attention, Tack," she informs him, giving him a firm ruffling, to his everlasting joy. "Shrek's just naturally grumpy."

There is it again…Shrek. Well. It's time to clear this up. I give her a stern look, but I can't keep my lips from twitching. "Ye do know that Shrek is Scottish, right?" She stills, her fingers deep in Tack's fur.

"He is?"

My smile broadens. "He is."

"Huh." A faint blush stains her cheeks, and her lips quiver with laughter. "Um, oops."

"You Americans." I groan, shaking my head in mock dismay, but her giggles make me smile. "All accents are the same. You can't tell a Scot from an Irishman or even an Englishman, much less discern between Cork, Dublin, or the North. Heathens, all of you."

"Oh yeah? I'll show you a heathen." Abandoning Tack, she leaps on me with a laugh, but stops mid-wrestle as a dark shadow passes overhead. "Wow," she says, looking up. "Where did that come from?"

Bugger. "The pressure wall must have broken. Sooner than I expected, though." The clouds that were holding about twenty kilometers offshore are now looming overhead, no doubt bringing rain with them. "Come on—let's gather this up and head back."

We quickly bundle up the leftover food and shake the sand out of the blanket. Brie carries Tack to the inflatable dingy we came ashore in and helps me turn it around for the return trip. Brie holds Tack in an iron grip on her lap, per my earlier instructions, making me smile. I love how seriously she takes the safety rules. It takes only a few minutes to reach the *Saoirse*. I hold us steady, so Brie can scramble up the ladder, and then I hand her our gear and Tack. Thanks to the rising waves, it takes a little longer than usual to secure the small outboard and fasten the inflatable to its stern mooring, but it's finally done, and I go aboard myself.

Brie pops out of the companionway, her brow furrowed. "Do you need help?"

I shake my head, checking the fastenings and hitting the button; the electric winch buzzes reassuringly, and I watch with satisfaction as the inflatable rises and nestles flat in its spot against the transom. "Nope. All done. Let's get below."

Fat raindrops start to fall as I usher her below and secure the hatch behind us. Tack is ahead of us; he's already curled up in a ball on his cushion, licking his paws. Brie laughs and shakes a bit of wetness from her hair. "I can't believe this! It was so gorgeous all day. It's a little shocking how unpredictable the weather is here."

Taking the food bag to the galley, I unzip it and start to put the leftover cheese and fruit in the small fridge. Glancing at her, a twinge of uncertainty shoots through me. "You're used to days of endless sunshine, I suppose?"

As much as I loathe O'Shea personally, and distrust his intentions for offering Sabrina a job, I'd be lying if I said I wasn't excited at the prospect of seeing her every day. But entwined with that excitement is the worry that she might somehow find moving here too much of a stretch. That all it would take is one small thing, like the food or the weather, and she would ultimately decide against it. It would be a daunting—and courageous—undertaking, after all: to uproot oneself from the familiar to the very unfamiliar. It would be quite a leap of faith.

Will she think that it's worth it—that *I'm* worth it—to take such a leap?

Pushing a strand of hair behind her ear, she comes over to help me. "Unpredictable isn't necessarily a negative," she says slowly, drawing a packet of cheese out of the bag. "Endless sunshine can be boring. Plus, there's draught, smog, wildfires, earthquakes…" She looks at me, her eyes darkening to the color of our 30-year special reserve. "I think maybe I'm tired of endless sunshine."

A thrill runs down my spine. "Really?" I manage, my throat suddenly dry.

Dropping the cheese on the counter, she draws a fingertip down my scruffy jawline, making me shiver. "I think so. There's a lot to consider still, but I think so." Her whisper sends my heart into high gear. I grab her arms to hold her still and crush my lips to hers. I try to be gentle, but I just can't. It doesn't seem to matter; she throws her arms around my neck and clings to me, making the small whimpers that I love. I lift her, and she wraps her legs around my waist as I walk us, staggering a bit because of the rocking of the ship, to the bedroom.

Rain thrums against the deck above, and I can't get her clothes off fast enough. She seems to be thinking the same thing. "Who the fuck made these buttons, a locksmith?" She snarls, fumbling at my jeans, and I laugh. "The same person who made your fecking shorts."

Between bursts of nervous laughter, we manage. Her skin feels like silk under my hands. Despite the need raging in my blood, I try to take my time as I work my way down her body. I love her tiny noises, especially when I—

"Colin!" Brie's squeal echoes in the cabin as she shudders beneath me, dislodging me from my spot between her thighs. Her fingers dig into my shoulders, as if she's unsure whether to pull me forward or push me off. Not giving her time to think about it, I crawl up her body and quickly plunge deep inside her.

She moans and claws at my back and arse as I repeatedly drive into her. God, I can never get enough of this woman. So warm, and wet, and *responsive*…sex with Brie is unlike anything I've ever experienced before. Every time feels like the first time with her. My name falls from her lips in a breathy loop, until I capture them in a bruising kiss. She doesn't seem to mind. Likewise, I don't mind when she flexes and squeezes my cock like a vise, making me gasp and my vision go a little blurry.

A line of fire burns its way down my spine, and my heart feels like it's pounding out of my chest. Brie switches her hold to my hair, tugging enough to cause pain, but it doesn't matter. Nothing matters except the feel of my cock sliding inside her tight, slick heat. Pounding again and again and again.

Time is suspended as we buck against each other with the rhythm of the waves, and then I'm melting, pouring myself into her as we both dissolve into a boneless heap. Our panting is almost as loud as the waves slapping the hull, and it takes a few minutes for my head to stop spinning.

Jaysus.

"My goodness." Her cheeks are flushed, and she sounds dazed. "If that's the reception I get when I say I'm just *thinking* about moving here, what am I going to get if I *actually* move?"

Rolling onto my side, I rest my hand on her flat belly, savoring the warmth of her skin. "Brie, I know it's a huge decision for you." Her smile softens in response to my tone, and she lays her hand over mine. "Wherever you decide to work—here or there, with Patrick or on your own—" Her eyes pop open at that suggestion, but I blunder on, "I just want you to be happy. That's the most important thing to me."

Her eyes sparkle with tears, and she cups my cheek. "Colin—"

"I'm not very good at this," I blurt, and then chuckle at her doubtful snort. "Expressing myself, I mean. I don't know how to say what I'm feeling." I shake my head slowly. Grandda would laugh if he saw me so tongue-tied, but I can't seem to shut up. "All I know is that I want you, Brie, any way I can have you. Whether that's here or...in California..."

I blink as the gravity of what I'm suggesting hits me. A knot of fear forms in my stomach, but there's a jolt of possibility, of *hope*, too.

My mind races. Technically, the paperwork part of my work could be done anywhere, but I love the physical part. And it can only be done here, in Crossmoor. Checking the quality of the grain, the smell of the malting shed, testing samples, and the clink of the bottles running through the automatic labeler...I take an active hand in it all. It's a part of me.

But I realize, with a jolt that runs down to my toes, so is Sabrina. And that's what's causing my churning belly. It's the realization that it's real, this thing I feel for her. I'm afraid to put a name to it, but it's there—I can't deny it. I don't want to.

Her eyes widen in surprise and her lush mouth drops open. "But, but what about the distillery? It's your life, your family's legacy. And your grandfather? Colin, you can't leave him, especially now." I kiss the soft crease of worry between her brows.

"I'm not saying it would be easy." I pause and toy with a strand of her silky hair, rolling it between my fingertips as I try to put my roiling thoughts into words. "I'm not even sure it would work; I'd have to fly back here several times a year, and I've no idea what Grandda would say. But if you decide—"

She interrupts me with a quick kiss. "Thank you," she whispers against my lips. She shifts to lie on her side and cradles her head on her arm, mirroring my pose. Her eyes seem large in her face, dark pools of amber that I could easily lose myself in. "Thank you for being willing. It's a huge thing, what you're offering. You're so connected to this place, Colin. Not just to the castle and the distillery, but the whole town. I see it in your face wherever we go, and in the faces of your friends, as well. Crossmoor is your *place*. I've never been connected to a place like you are here."

"But, if you—"

"I know," she says hurriedly. "And I love that you're offering. I know you're serious, and I can't tell you how much it means to me." She sniffs, giving me a watery smile, and places her hand on my chest, over my heart; I wonder if she can feel how fast it's beating. "We have time. My project isn't officially over for another week. I need to consult with my team back home, too. There are a lot of logistics to work out, and not just mine."

A sudden rustling of fur and mad jingling of dog tags from somewhere beyond the edge of the bed interrupts us. "Um, do we need to do something for him?" Brie asks, batting at an errant dog hair that drifts by.

"Naw. He's got food and water in his bowls, and I put down a fresh pad in the spare bedroom before we went to the beach." I had incorporated use of the pee pads onboard when I first adopted Tack and, clever wee lad that he is, he took to them in a surprisingly short amount of time. It's the only way I can keep him onboard with me for more than a few hours.

Brie slips her arms around me, rolling us until she rests on top. "Okay then, so, going back to my original question. If I do move here, what other, um, *inducements* might I expect?" Her lips quiver in amusement, and she blinks innocently at me, golden hair streaming over her bare skin.

I flip us over, making her squeal-laugh, and slip a hand between her legs. She gasps and squirms, but I'm relentless. "I'll just have to show you."

The Rover comes to a stop and I put on the parking brake, only half-thinking about what I'm doing. The other half of my brain is consumed with Brie. When I dropped her at the Whiskey Rose, she practically floated up the stairs past the amused looks of Conner and Brooke. She'd made me swear not to follow her, saying that she needed a full night's sleep before work tomorrow; it took everything I had not to follow her, regardless.

Tack hops out as soon as I pop the door open, making a beeline toward his water bowl that sits outside the kitchen door. He plunges his face into it, his tail waving like a flag as drops of water fly everywhere. Daft dog.

The soft violet light of early evening cloaks the castle and grounds. I climb out and heave my gear out of the back, whistling softly to myself as I slam the door shut. The smell of something baking makes my mouth water; I hope pasties are on the menu tonight. A small group of tourists are walking in the field beyond the shooting range, their torchlights bobbing in the twilight. Thank God there's a light booking of guests this month. I'm not sure I could stand a castle-full of tourists right now.

Gravel crunches under my feet as I heft my duffle over my shoulder and fill my lungs with rain-freshened air. I feel more relaxed than I have in weeks. The taste of Brie lingers on my lips as thoughts of her dance in my mind. Maybe after dinner I'll—

"So, you're back."

My contentment evaporates. I jerk to a stop, my head snapping up to see my father coming around the corner of the castle. He's clinging to his walker, rolling toward me steadily, his eyes hard. "What do you care?"

"I care. More than you know." He scowls at me, but his diminished frame robs it of its power. "Been out with your girl?"

It sounds almost like an accusation. "I have. Not that it's any of your business." I tilt my head, suspicious. The last time I talked to him, when he was begging for forgiveness, he was full of supportive curiosity about Sabrina.

"It is my business. You're my son."

A derisive snort escapes me. "Now, you remember. Well, better late than never, I suppose." I try to walk past him, but he grabs my sleeve. I jerk out of his grasp and glare. "What the hell are you doing?"

"Stop for five seconds and listen to me," he rasps, his voice weak, but urgent. "Do you know that she works for Patrick O'Shea?"

"Oh, for the love of…" My eyes practically roll out of my head. "She works for an architectural firm. She's finishing a contract job for O'Shea—she's not his employee." At least, not yet, I remind myself, ignoring the nagging twinge in my gut. "Again, what business is it of yours?"

His jaw clenches. "I realize I fucked up in the past. And although my methods were extreme—" he grimaces, glancing at the ground, "—I saved you from Brigid. She would have drained you dry."

"So you've said," I growl. The last thing I want to think about right now is Brigid. "Do you have a point, or can I get on with my evening?"

I start to walk on, but the asshole maneuvers the damn walker in front of me. "Listen! I did save you from Brigid, and I'm going to save you from this one too. You know what Patrick is—how do you know this Sabrina isn't his doing?"

"What the fuck are you talking about?" I demand, my eyes popping. He's short of breath from the exertion and has a death grip on the walker as he glares at me. "Have you completely lost your mind?"

"No, but maybe you have." His chin juts, and for an instant, I see a glimmer of the powerful man from my youth. When I was small—before mother died—he seemed able to do anything…like my very own superhero.

But not any more.

"You know what he's like," he persists, letting go of the walker long enough to wave a hand in irritation. "Patrick can't be trusted.

Not for one second. He's an even bigger ass than his father, amazing as that is. Aiden was an adulterer and a drunk, but at least he had an honest interest in the county. Patrick has all his worst traits and none of the good ones."

I step back from his flailing arm and give him my own glare. "I know exactly what Patrick is. But beyond that, I know Sabrina. She isn't whatever you're accusing her of...which is what, exactly? That's she's some kind of spy? That's mental!"

"How do you know she's not?"

My duffel falls off my shoulder as I spread my arms; it lands on the gravel with a dull crunch. "This is insane. You've never met her. You know *nothing* about her. She's an incredibly talented architect and an amazing, intelligent woman. She's nothing like Brigid!"

"Maybe, maybe not." He's breathing heavily and his face is alarmingly pale. "Don't you think it's quite a coincidence that her friend's wedding just happened to be in the same town as this 'project' she's working on?"

"You have completely lost your mind." My tone could freeze lava. "When I need advice on how to be an international playboy who sponges off his father and abandons his son, I know who to ask. Until then, shut the fuck up."

He sways, and I reach out to help in spite of myself, but he jerks away from me. Leaning heavily on the walker, he rallies and levels me with another glare.

"Fine. Stubborn ass. But you'd better start thinking with your head instead of your cock or you'll find yourself arseways before you know it."

"Fecking hell," I mutter, and snatch up my duffle. I turn back toward the kitchen door but stop and swing back around as my outrage spikes again. "What would he gain? He has zero interest in distilling. His only interest in life is in making millions of euros selling hard-ons to the male population and cheating on his wife. That's it." My voice bounces between the walls of the garage and castle, and I notice Aileen stick her head out the kitchen door. Her brow creases with worry, and she darts back inside, probably to fetch Grandda.

The wheels on the walker jam against a rock, and Da angrily jerks it free. "You can't trust an O'Shea." He growls, jabbing his finger at me. "Haven't you learnt your family history? Don't you remember what they did to the magistrate?"

I snort in disbelief. "That was two hundred years ago!" In 1802, my family won a land dispute over the O'Sheas, and within 24 hours, the O'Sheas cut the presiding magistrate's throat in his own garden. There weren't any witnesses, so no arrests were made, but the O'Sheas had never denied it.

"Some things can't be forgotten!"

Words fail me and I stare at him, shaking in righteous anger despite his obvious frailty. Generations of animosity between the O'Sheas and the McGuires shines in his eyes. And I suddenly see the ridiculousness that Brie sees. The crimes and insults from two hundred years ago no longer matter. Yes, Patrick is an arrogant prick. But so what? If his sole purpose in offering a job to Brie is merely to tweak my tail, then he's an even bigger fool than I thought, because having an architect of her caliber on staff *does* make sense for a conglomerate such as his. The fact that he would be her boss won't matter to me if I don't let it matter.

What *will* matter to me is if Brie uproots herself and moves here, only to have O'Shea pull the rug from under her to spite me. If that's his game, he *will* have to answer to me. But that's a problem for another day.

I look at my father, a shadow of the man he was, and my anger and frustration drain away, leaving only hollow disappointment. This is not how I want to live my life, beholden to the past. "I know our family's history. But I make my own choices for my own reasons. Not because of some ancient grudge."

Turning on my heel, I hike the duffle higher on my shoulder and stalk toward the door. Grandda comes out as I reach it, Aileen behind him. Their anxious looks tweak my heart. I try to give them a reassuring smile, but I'm not sure how successful I am. "I'm going up to my room. I need a shower."

chapter thirteen

Sabrina

I

T'S MONDAY, AFTER OUR IDYLLIC WEEKEND ABOARD THE *SAOIRSE*, and I'm finally catching up with Becca on a video call. "You're glowing. You're actually glowing!" Becca laughs before she buries her face in a nearby towel as she lounges poolside. "Seriously. Did you go to Cabo? Because that doesn't look like Ireland at all." She turns her phone again, showing me the swanky pool deck where she's relaxing away in honeymoon bliss.

"We're only a couple of hours away from you." I scowl out the window at the menacing grey clouds whirling over the choppy sea in the distance. This morning, we were treated to a handful of sunbursts through the clouds, but now, a chilled wind has descended and the clouds have amassed, taking over the sky completely. It would be nice to have the weather Becca's having for the grand opening today at O'Shea, but what can you do?

I show her my view, which is not nearly as inviting as her

sun-soaked five-star resort, where she's sipping some pink cocktail with an actual umbrella in it. "How can it be that sunny there and like this here?" I wave my hand at the window.

She adjusts her sunglasses with a shrug. "It's Ireland. We've seen everything from this to a wicked storm where the rain was freezing and coming down sideways. We got completely drenched. Give it a while, it'll change again."

Becca has given me a rundown of their honeymoon so far. The stuff fairy tales are made of. I've given her an update on the last few weeks. Has it only been weeks? It feels like longer. It feels like, somehow, I've always been here. It's starting to feel like this is where I belong.

"But enough about me." Becca relaxes back in her plush lounger. "Tell me more about Colin McGuire!"

I've literally told her about Colin and Patrick, the job offer and everything in between. Becca and I don't have secrets. Truth be told, we probably share too much. But this is who we are, and I wouldn't change it for anything in the world.

"Is it weird? It's weird, right? I mean, it hasn't been that long and he's talked about..." I shake my head.

"A future? Upending his whole life?" Becca pushes her sunglasses to the top of her head. "Sound familiar?"

"Like Liam did for you." Liam and Becca met during our first year of uni. He was visiting for an epic Golden Bears vs. Tar Heels football game. In a crowd of 63,000 frenzied, revved-up fans, they found each other. Liam, finishing up his PhD, with Irish roots tied to UNC spent the weekend at our tiny off-campus apartment. It took him all of two weeks to apply for a transfer, uproot his entire life, and move to California.

"Everyone's story is different, Brie. Some people end up with their next-door-neighbour they've known since they could walk, others find their soul mate in the blink of an eye. The question isn't how long it took, it's how does it make you feel?"

"Like I'm in somebody else's life." I turn away from the window and move to flop onto the bed. "I was with Laird for four years and never felt this way. What does that say about me?"

"It says he wasn't the one. And maybe Colin isn't either. But maybe you should just focus on you." She drains whatever cocktail is in her glass and pouts, glancing into it before setting it down on a nearby table. "What do *you* want?"

"I think I really want this job."

"There's a sure statement if I ever heard one. You *think* you want the job?"

I sit up, squaring my shoulders. "No. I know. I know I want this job."

"Then that's where you start. As for your castle owning whiskey connoisseur? I say take as many tours of the secret rooms in that castle you want."

Later in the evening, my face actually hurts from smiling. So many photographers and press that I was completely unprepared for. Nolan mentioned there would be a ceremony and coverage of the official opening of the office, but I had no idea there was this level of interest. I feel like a fish out of water. I can imagine this must be what it feels like as an actress to go to your first big awards ceremony.

There was an actual carpet leading into the building. Not red, because as Kathleen told me once I found her in the mayhem, Patrick thinks red carpets are jarring. Slate grey in keeping with the aesthetic of the redesign was chosen. I can't deny that it does look good. Whoever he has working on his events team knows what they're doing.

We're surrounded by the buzz of business and society elites, so Kathleen has explained anyway. I don't recognize anyone, but judging from the amount of expensive suits and designer wear in sight, Patrick invited all of Ireland's rich and famous to this. I've given a dozen tours and interviews of the office and am now officially exhausted. I know I've represented our company well, and I can't help but feel a sense of pride about this project.

Kathleen snags two fresh flutes of champagne from a passing

waiter as we take a much-needed breather in the corner of the atrium. "No whiskey, I'm afraid," she says, grinning as she raises her flute to me.

"Patrick didn't want to ask Colin for his services?"

Kathleen nearly spits out her mouthful of bubbly. Shame to waste it. I take a long sip. "Can you imagine? He'd sooner be thrown into a pit of crocodiles than ever ask Colin for anything."

"It's too bad they can't just put the past in the past."

Kathleen snorts and covers her mouth quickly, her eyes widening before she recovers. "I'm afraid that's never going to happen. No double dates for us in the future. You know? If you do decide to move here." She gives me a nudge with her hip and I smile.

"I've been thinking about it—" I start, but a frazzled Nolan appears, breathing like he's just sprinted a mile.

"You need..." He bends over, hands on his knees, heaving in breaths.

"Nolan? What on earth is wrong?" Kathleen sets her hand on his back, and I hear a wave of murmurs in the crowd. With a surge of anxiety, I realize we're drawing attention. Nolan is white as a sheet. Something is very, very wrong.

"Patrick..." Nolan blurts out, unfolding himself and blowing out a breath of air.

"What about Patrick?" Kathleen asks with a clear tone of worry in her voice.

"He's... Oh, God, we need the PR team." Nolan searches the room with wild eyes as he rubs his temples furiously.

"The PR team? What's happened?" Kathleen's voice is uncharacteristically higher now, latching onto Nolan's panic.

"I was giving a tour, you know?" Nolan heaves through a pant. "Of his office with all the windows?" He shots me a hairy eyebrow.

I stare back at him, confused. "The ones he specifically asked for, yes. And?"

Nolan turns his attention back to Kathleen. "Kathleen, I'm so sorry—"

"Mrs. O'Shea! Kathleen!" It's a chorus of shouts getting louder by the second, and I turn to see the press weaving their way amongst the guests in the atrium like a swarm of bees seeking out their target.

"Sorry for what? Nolan, tell me what's going on!" Kathleen whisper-yells, her hand gripping the sleeve of Nolan's jacket.

"Kathleen O'Shea!" I'm jostled by a throng of press, shoved to the side as the horde lands in front of Kathleen. Rapid fire questions seem to bounce unintelligibly off each other until one voice rises from the horde. "Victoria Marlowe, Irish Times." An invasive microphone is thrust in front of Kathleen's face. My stomach plummets. *What in the actual hell is happening right now?* "How do you feel, Mrs. O'Shea, about your husband being found having sex in his office on the day of your grand opening?"

Night has fallen, and I'm sitting with Kathleen on a bronze bench under an alcove in the empty garden outside of O'Shea Pharmaceutical. The press has finally gone, the news now viral—in Ireland at least—that Patrick O'Shea was caught quite literally with his pants down at his grand opening event.

Kathleen passes me her phone, taking a healthy sip of what I think and sincerely hope is the last bottle of champagne in the place. "Look, in this one you can actually see a photo of us on our wedding day." She points with her free hand to the grainy picture that's currently making the rounds on social media. "Right here, beside his bare arse."

"Okay." I gently pull the phone from Kathleen's hand and turn it off. "That's enough show and tell for today. No more thinking about this."

Kathleen traces the rim of the champagne flute and is quiet for a while, watching the lightning storm put on a show over the choppy sea. "You know, he's actually done me a favor here."

"A favor?"

"I can get out from this marriage now and not have to worry about losing my job, my work." She lets out a strangely satisfied laugh. "It's funny. I should feel something beyond relief, but I don't."

"Kathleen." I place a calming hand on her arm.

"No, Brie. You don't understand. It's like a weight has been lifted off my shoulders and I just feel…" She pauses, searching for the right words. "Free."

"Free?"

She nods, polishing off the last of the champagne. "Does that make me a horrible person? A horrible wife?"

"Not even a little." She sets her glass down and gives my hand a squeeze.

"Thank you, Brie. For being here and listening. I know today didn't turn out how you wanted."

"Oh, I'm not sure about that. The press coverage will be huge."

She laughs, and it warms my heart to hear it. "If you ever need to talk, Kathleen, just know I'm here, and I'll always listen."

"I know, and I can't tell you how happy that makes me." She stands up, teetering a little on her heels, and I grip her elbow.

"Let's get you a cab home, hmm?"

"Not home. I've got someone I need to talk to." She wiggles her eyebrows at me, and I guide her out of the garden.

"The non-complicated one you mentioned at the bar?" I steer a wobbly Kathleen to the elevators, laughing as she leans against me. She bops the tip of my nose as we wait for the doors to open.

"The very one. I think he's going to be happy about this. At least I hope he is."

"Well, he's a fool if he's anything but thrilled."

"Why can't we take the stairs?" Kathleen waves her arm in the general direction of the staircase. "They're so beautiful. You did such an amazing job, Brie."

I laugh, ushering her into the elevator. A tipsy Kathleen is entertaining. "I didn't make them, but they are lovely and any other time I would happily take the stairs with you, but the way you're swaying here…" I laugh as she props her hip against the mirrored wall of the elevator. "I think we should try to limit ourselves to one apocalyptic event a day, hmm?"

"You have a good time at the party?" the cab driver asks me after I've put Kathleen safely into her own cab.

"Well, it was memorable." I relax against the back seat, thankful this whirlwind of a day is over. I need a long bath, Colin, and a solid night's sleep.

"Aye, our fair town is full of surprises tonight. Must be the full moon."

I glance out the rain-soaked window into the darkened night. The moon is nowhere to be found. "I don't see the moon."

"She's up there behind the clouds. It's blowing a gale, probably what caused Mr. McGuire's yacht to go off the grid."

My heart stops, any lingering buzz from the champagne obliterated. "I'm sorry? Mr. McGuire's yacht? As in Colin McGuire?"

"The very one."

"What do you mean off the grid?" I put my hand on the headrest of the passenger seat and pull myself forward, my stomach churning.

"The *Saoirse*. She didn't return to the harbor before the storm really started kicking up." I swallow the lump in my throat, watching helplessly as the windshield wipers try to keep up with the menacing rain.

"Oh God." My hands feel clammy, my chest tightening. He wouldn't be foolish enough to go out in a storm, would he? There's got to be some kind of mistake.

"They've got search and rescue out now. We should be hearing something soon."

"Take me to the harbor. Please!"

"'Fraid not. You'd never get close to it. They've got enough folks out lookin'. Yer best to sit tight."

"Please." My voice cracks. "There's got to be something I can do. I know him. I know his grandfather." I set my hand on the cab driver's shoulder, and he gives me a side-eye. My voice sounds strained, and I'm dizzy, my breaths coming faster. Horrible, wild scenarios roll through me like a tidal wave, each one worse than the last.

"Kieran's at Steven's pub waiting it out. It's the closest to the harbor. I can drop you there if you like."

Fresh tears sting my cheeks, and I barely croak out, "Please hurry!"

Colin

My left eyelid is stuck shut. I have no idea what time it is, but I do know I wish Sabrina was next to me. But today is the big opening at O'Shea's House of Horrors, and she needs to concentrate. Which, she says she can't do when she's, "worn out by my ginormous cock." Fuck, if that girl isn't good for my ego.

Deciding that prying my crusty lid open probably isn't a good idea, I crawl out of bed with a groan and stumble to the loo to splash water on my face until my eyelid releases. My eyes are a little bloodshot, but there's no pain. That's what I get for drinking into the wee hours with Grandda and Dermot. When I got back from dropping Brie off, I discovered them locked in a billiards deathmatch that involved copious amounts of single malt. Joining them seemed like a good idea at the time.

The face staring back at me in the mirror is haggard with a thick scruff of beard. It's soft to the touch, though, which is good, considering how much time I spent between Brie's thighs yesterday. My grin is automatic when I recall her shooing me out of the Whiskey Rose last night, her face flushed from spending the afternoon on *Saoirse*. She'd entertained me with stories of growing up in California with her free-spirited parents and practical grandmother while I washed down the deck. She helped me polish the railings, and I told her stories about my mom and grandmother, my grandfather teaching me to fish, stupid stuff I did at uni.

I have not told her about my father's insane industrial spy theory.

What a crock. He came up with a half-arsed apology the next day, looking suitably embarrassed. I'm not sure if Grandda had a hand in that, or if Da realized how stupid he sounded. Regardless, he stumbled through it, and I let him, for Grandda's sake. And maybe for mine, I don't know. Gripping the edge of the sink, my eyes blur as I picture the miserable look on his pale face, eyes pleading for me to understand and forgive him.

I'm not sure I ever will.

After a quick shower and shave, I jog downstairs, following the enticing aromas coming from Mrs. Sullivan's kitchen. Tack is already in his corner basket, snoozing on his back with all four paws in the air. If I did that, I'd be arrested for public indecency.

I pour myself a cuppa and sit at the table with a sigh of gratitude as Mrs. Sullivan herself sweeps in and plops a laden plate in front of me. "Eat up, now, my boy," she says with a wink. "You're way too skinny these days. Your girl is wearing you down!"

My chuckles ring in her wake as she breezes past Grandda on her way back to the kitchen. He follows my lead and is soon seated across from me with his own steaming cup and plate. We dig in, making happy yummy noises whenever Fiona's in earshot, just to make her laugh. He winks at me over the rim of his cup, and my heart warms at our shared efforts.

"Um, have you seen Da yet this morning?" My eyes drift over to the empty corner where Da's walker usually resides.

"Not yet." He swallows his bite of eggs as Mrs. Sullivan sweeps in with a basket of scones. "He looked a bit peaked last night. Probably having a lie in."

Mrs. Sullivan pauses, looking between us. "I hope so; he looked like a stiff breeze could blow him over yesterday. I'll bring him a tray straight away."

"Thank you, Fee." Grandda beams at her, sending her bustling back into the kitchen with a chuckle. He then looks at me, head tilted in thought. "How are you doing with your father? He apologized for that daft idea about Sabrina, did he?"

I grimace at the memory. "He did. Things have been a bit stilted since, but…" I shrug and take a hasty sip of coffee. "I want to try to… well, make more of an effort, I guess," I huff, feeling my face heat, but I see only compassion in his frosty blue gaze.

"I think he wants to, as well," he murmurs, sipping from his steaming cup. "It would be good for both of you to spend time together."

"I thought I'd maybe ask him to look over the order from the Chapmans. They want to partner on a special blend for their parents' anniversary." The man may be a world-class guitarist, but Cameron Chapman also has an amazing palate. The special blend we did with him and his brother two years ago won top awards in Glasgow, New York, Sydney, and Paris.

"Excellent idea." He nods, a smile stealing across his face. "I've been thinking—"

A clatter of dishware and the sound of someone rushing down the backstairs interrupts him. Mrs. Sullivan bursts from the stairwell, carrying a laden breakfast tray, and the look of worry on her face has me instinctively rising to my feet.

"Excuse me, sirs." She's red-faced and breathless, and I quickly relieve her of her tray and set it on the table. "Lord McGuire's bed looks like it hasn't been slept in."

"Oh, well, he probably fell asleep in the library again," Grandda says with a sad smile. "I found him there last week, as well. He likes that red chair by the tall window; he can sink in it and sleep, without his book falling on the floor."

"Oh, well, then…" She starts to pick up the tray again, but I stop her.

"Let's see where he is first." I wink at her. "No need for you to lug that thing all over the house. In fact, I'll nip in there and check for you."

Snagging a piece of toast off the tray, I head toward the library, munching as I go. I've seen Da in there myself, usually dozing or staring out the window at the moors. However, when I pop my head in this time, the library is empty. So is the billiards room, the sitting room, the games room, the small library, the smoking room, and the formal dining room. I'm not sure why, but I even run down to the wine cellar. I startle a couple kitchen maids, but there's no sign of my father.

My heart beating a little faster, I return to the kitchen; Grandda glances at me, then does a double-take and shoots to his feet. "What's wrong?"

"He's not in any of the family rooms." I suck in a steadying breath. "Do you think he could be over in the public areas?"

"No. He's been avoiding that side of the castle like the plague," Grandda says, pressing a hand to his forehead. I know that's true; because of his reduced immune system, Da avoids crowds and especially tourists.

The back door opens, and both Grandda and I whirl to face it, but it's only Aileen and Dermot, coming in for breakfast. "Aileen, could you please check to see if Brian happens to be over in the public areas?" Grandda asks, as he steps over and grabs our coats from the pegs by the door. "I don't know why he'd go over to that side, but Fee says it looks like he didn't sleep in his room last night, and he's not in any of the family rooms."

Aileen blinks in surprise, but she nods and hurries past, heading down the hall. Grandda hands me my coat, and we both shrug into our jackets as we go down the steps into the yard. Startled awake, Tack shakes himself and quickly follows us. "How far do you think he could go?" Dermot asks, falling into step with us, a grim expression on his face. The gravel crunching under our feet sounds louder in the quiet of the morning.

"Not far." Grandda clenches and unclenches his fists as we walk. "Couple days ago, he insisted on going out to the malting shed with me, and he had to sit on his walker to rest twice on the way there. Wouldn't let me help him, the fool." He jerks to a stop, catching us off-guard, and my throat closes when I see him fighting back his emotion. "It's not like him to wander off without a word. He knows we worry."

Dermot clears his throat. "How about I head over to the offices and the distillery? I can get the warehouse boy to help. You two take the malting shed. Those are the most likely spots, if he's not in the house, aye? He probably just wanted some air."

Grateful for the direction, I nod, and he jogs off. Slipping a hand across Grandda's shoulders, I guide him toward the malting shed. It doesn't take long, and our mutual frustration and dread grow when we come up empty again. "Oh, for God's sake!" He slams a hand on the shed door, making it rattle on its hinges.

"Did he mention anything last night? An early doctor's appointment maybe?"

He shakes his head, shrugging helplessly. My stomach is in knots, apprehension and irritation roiling in equal measure. With a huff of frustration, I scan the landscape and get an idea. "Come on." I lead him toward the shooting range, and my heart leaps when I spot the tracks of Da's walker. "Look!"

We start jogging, following the tracks. And I realize where he went.

I spy his walker first, parked near the boulder where he and I had talked when he first arrived. The morning mist has mostly dissipated, and the view of the fields and sea beyond is breathtaking. A rusty sigh escapes my grandfather, and I grip his arm in support. My throat closes with dread as we round the boulder.

Da is sitting on the grass, legs stretched out in front of him and leaning back against the rock, his coat buttoned up to protect against the morning chill. His eyes are closed, mouth curled in a slight smile. If it wasn't for the mottled grey of his face, I'd think he just laid down for a kip.

"Oh, oh Brian, my wee lad." Grandda lets out a strangled sob, and sinks to his knees beside Da. My vision blurs, and it's only when the dampness seeps through my jeans that I realize I'm kneeling on the other side of my father. His hands are folded in his lap, and I place a hand over his. He's so cold, but not stone stiff yet; he must have come out just before dawn.

With a shaky hand, Grandda gently pulls the thick beanie off Da's head and smooths his palm over the fuzzy skull. Bowing his head, he murmurs something in Irish, a blessing I remember from my childhood. After a few moments, we both rise to our feet, looking down at the man who was the link between us. I'm not sure what to do; I'm numb, but I can't seem to swallow down the painful lump in my throat.

He looks so small, a far cry from the strapping man who let me ride on his shoulders as he and Mum walked through town after church. Even with the tang of death in the air, it doesn't feel real. None of this does.

A hand clasps my shoulder, and I sense Dermot there. "Oh, Brian." He sighs, his hat clutched in his other hand. "I should have guessed that you'd want one last look before going." I follow his gaze; a flock of birds rises from the far field, the sun flashing on their wings. Beyond, I can see ships heading into harbor. It's a stunning view.

The sun is well up, bathing us in its glow, but I don't feel warm.

Grandda clears his throat. "Dermot, call Kerry's funeral home, please; they'll know what to do." He looks across to me, blue eyes swimming with tears. "We'll just wait here."

After the constable and the men from Kerry's have left with my father, I find myself sitting in the library, in the red chair where he spent so many afternoons reading or staring out the window. The plate Mrs. Sullivan brought me for lunch sits on the ottoman, the savory pasty uneaten. I'm not sure any of us can eat anything, but food is her favorite way to show us she cares. Tack keeps edging closer to it, while pretending not to know it's there. He's ridiculous.

I wait until he's practically leaning against the ottoman before giving in. "Oh, all right, ye daft bugger. Take it." The words are barely out of my mouth, before he snatches it off the plate and bolts out of the room with his prize, his nails clicking like gunshots in the hallway.

"I'm glad someone has an appetite."

Startled, I look up to see Grandda come in from the East door. "The world could end, and Tack would still be able to eat."

He huffs a laugh. "True enough." He pauses beside my chair. "Did you ring her?"

I stare dumbly at my grandfather until he nods toward the phone in my hand. "Sabrina. Have you called her yet?"

"Oh. I was going to, but I don't want to distract her. It's her big day at O'Shea's opening." As much as I want to hear her voice and wrap my arms around her, I can't quite bring myself to ring her. She's worked so hard for this opening; I don't want to spoil it.

He nods. "Tomorrow is soon enough." His eyes are red, and he looks a year older than he did this morning.

"Is there anything I can do for you? I've already talked to Theo, and he'll handle getting the latest stuff to bottling. But is there anything else that needs to be dealt with today?"

Patting my shoulder, he shakes his head. "No. Theo and the others know what to do." He sits on the ottoman opposite me. "What about you? What are you feeling?"

"I'm not sure." I blow out a breath. "Empty, mostly, and exhausted. It's only mid-day, but I feel like I've run a marathon. I feel like I should be doing something but have no idea what to do."

"Me too." He takes a deep breath, and pulls two envelopes out of his pocket, handing one to me. I stiffen when I recognize my name scrawled on it in my father's messy hand. "I found these in his room. I have one, too."

I hold it delicately as if it's going to explode. "Have you read yours yet?" He shakes his head and rises to his feet.

"I'll be in my room if you want to talk afterward." He squeezes my shoulder, and I automatically reach up to pat his hand. "Love you, boyo," he mutters gruffly, and then shuffles off in the direction of the family staircase.

I sit for a moment, staring at the envelope through blurry eyes, and then finally tear it open and pull out the note.

Colin,

I love you. I'm sure you find that hard to believe, but it's true. From the moment I knew your mother was expecting, I've loved you. I'm sorry I haven't been here for you as I should have. I'm sorry I selfishly let my grief consume me, and I'm sorry I wasn't brave enough to face it until it was too late. I've let both you and your mother down. I'm sure she'll give me a right bollocking when I see her again.

I wish I had met your girl. It's obvious how much she means to you; it's written all over your face every time you speak of her. Warms my heart to see it. Again, I'm sorry for my daft comments about her motives—I don't know what I was thinking. Chalk it up to a dying man's desperation to show his son he cares. Because I do care, more than you know.

All I want is for you to be happy and safe, Colin, whether you believe it or not. And if Sabrina does that for you, either forever or for just now, then that's all I can ask. Enjoy it. Live your life to the fullest and have no regrets. Take care of Da for me. If you think of me, think of the days before your Mum died. That's the real me, not this shell I've become over the years. Forgive me if you can, for abandoning you, for Brigid, for all of it. It's easier than having anger and pain weigh you down all your life. Believe me—I know.

I'm so proud of the man you've become. I know the McGuire legacy is safe in your hands. May you always have fair winds and following seas.

Da

Cold rain lashes against the cockpit, and I tighten the hood of my jacket around my face. Thank God for Gore-Tex. I promised Grandda that I'd be out for just a few hours, that I needed to clear my head. It seemed a good idea at the time.

After reading Da's letter, my head was just so full of...of...*stuff*. Emotions I didn't know what to do with. The walls were closing in and the only things I could think of were Sabrina and *Saoirse*, and since I was trying to let Brie enjoy her opening, the boat was the only option. Grandda understood. I think he was trying to digest whatever was in his own letter from Da, so he simply clapped me on the shoulder and asked that I be back for dinner. Judging by the rough seas ahead, however, I'll be lucky to make it.

When I slid out into the waters beyond Crosshaven Harbor, the weather wasn't ideal, but it wasn't bad either. There was a front expected overnight, but the afternoon was supposed to be fine. I figured I'd get about 20 or so kilometers offshore, then shoot up to Ballyvale to pivot and return home. But after I made the turn, the clouds rolled in, and the sea woke up. Now, faced with about four-meter seas and pissing rain, I wished I'd docked in Ballyvale and gotten a ride home.

I reefed the mainsail in lieu of the storm jib and trysail, and now although she's slower, I have better control. But it doesn't really feel like it at the moment. Every once in a while, I think I can hear the tinny crash of Tack's food bowls rattling around below. Thank God I left him home.

Peering through the rain, I try to imagine Brie's night. God, I hope that arse O'Shea is giving her the credit she is due. My hands tighten on the wheel. Fuck, what am I going to do if she takes that job and she's working with him all the time? A gust of spray hits me in the face and I laugh, shaking off the sting; I wonder if that was Da or Mum giving me a smack? *It's not about you, Colin, my wee lad.* I know. It's about her and what makes her happy. Always.

I should really see some lights by now. The bearing is right, but I'm not seeing anything beyond the gloom. I should really—

"Holy shite." I blink the dripping water out of my eyes, realizing with a jolt that I'm sprawled across the deck, in the stern. My head is throbbing like a bastard and for a few seconds, twin images dance before my eyes. What the fuck? When everything becomes one again, I finally notice *Saoirse* is heeled hard to port, and scramble to drag myself into the pilot chair and grab the wheel. Jaysus, what happened? The sea is rough, but not *that* rough. I've sailed in worse weather than this. Wincing at the pounding in my head, I sweep the dripping hair off my forehead, shocked when I see the blood on my hand. "Fuck."

The wheel isn't wanting to turn; it's like pulling it through cement. Something must have fouled the rudder. Blood keeps dripping into my eye—fucking head wounds. I've got to get a bandage. The boat shudders as I swing open the hatch and...

"Jaysus!" Water is swirling in the galley. I stare dumbly at it until it hits me that the hull must be punctured. I've hit something. Debris, or...I don't know. Fucking, fucking hell.

I stagger back to the cockpit and grab the radio. "Mayday, mayday, mayday. This is *Saoirse* out of Crossmoor. I'm taking on water and require immediate assistance." I swallow down my growing panic and the realization this is my first mayday call. I repeat the call with my position twice and check the hatch again. The water is higher, and I know I don't have a choice.

Nor do I have much time.

Bracing myself against the railing, I reach the winch for the inflatable and hit the button. The smooth winding sound of the electric winch calms my jangled nerves, and I sigh in relief. Thank fuck. It won't be easy in these waves, but at least I'll have a motor and—

No. No, no, no, no, no... Do not fucking do this to me! I push against the inflatable in vain, the waves splashing over the stern drenching me. Jesus fucking Christ... It's stuck good. Not moving another inch. Doesn't look like anything's fouled in the mechanism, but I can't lean over the transom enough to see. Fecking hell.

She's really listing to port now. *Get your arse moving, McGuire!*

It's hard to maneuver on the slippery deck. No time to make another radio call. Clinging to the railing, cleats, anything I can grab, I grope my way to the starboard emergency raft. The port raft is probably already underwater. My fingers are so cold and stiff, it takes several tries to flip the catches on the capsule. The blood dripping in my eyes doesn't help. The painter line is already attached to a cleat, so all I need do is heave the raft off the deck. Easier said than done, considering the rolling of the ship, but finally it falls off the side. I slip the painter tether over my wrist and prepare to jump, but the deck rises under my feet, and the world tumbles.

I try to control my fall, but everything is slippery as hell, and I can't grip the rail. Stars explode behind my eyes as I slam sideways into the gunwale. Oh, fucking hell. Everything hurts, even thinking hurts. But I'm out of time. Fuck, fuck, fuck...

The tether is still around my wrist. My hand closes over the rail with a death grip and, with my teeth clenched against the throbbing in my head, I haul myself up and over the edge.

The cold I felt onboard was nothing compared to this. Fecking hell. But at least it gives me something else to think about beside the stabbing pain in my chest and head. The raft has inflated and is bobbing about 10 meters away; I can see the beacon blinking at the top, merrily sending out it's radio signal. Hand over hand, I follow the painter line, spitting out mouthfuls of seawater. Reaching the raft, I take one last look across the heaving sea at my beloved *Saoirse* and drag myself aboard. It's a lot harder—and a fuck-ton more painful—than when I practiced with the yacht club in harbor. Shivers rack my body, and it takes forever to cut the painter line free from the sinking craft. Once the raft is free, I've got just enough energy to pull one of the flimsy metallic blankets from its pocket and wrap myself in it before collapsing. Now the waiting begins.

Lying on my back, I can see the darkening sky out of a crack in the overhead cover. My ears are buzzing, thanks to the drumming rain and the slapping waves. Everything aches and the cold is bone deep. It even hurts to breathe. Tears blur my eyes as I sob, deep racking sobs that tear at my heart. The pain, fear, and overwhelming loss of the day consumes me, and I thank God that I made it to the raft. Grandda couldn't take it if he lost me today, too.

Memories of Da when I was young tumble through my mind. I can't grab just one to focus on. He and Mum walking in town. Eating ninety-nines after church, trying to keep the ice cream from dripping down our hands. Teaching me to bait a hook. Posing with him and Grandda after winning my first race. I remember the love on his face when he looked at me, and I know everything he told me in his letter is true. He's right—that's my real father. And he loved me.

The years of anger, hurt, and regret drain out of me, leaving me limp and exhausted, and despite the chill seizing my broken body, my heart feels light.

Da, I'm sorry. And I love you, too. Sleep well.

I close my eyes, smiling. Brie will be so pleased.

chapter
fourteen

Sabrina

THE SPRINT FROM THE CAB TO THE DOOR OF STEVE'S PUB IS short, but I'm drenched, assaulted from the frenzied wind and the downpour when I haul the door open. I must look like a drowned rat, judging by the hush that falls over the full bar upon my entrance.

It's packed in here and I glance frantically around the unfamiliar crowd until I find the face I'm looking for. Colin's grandfather's face is sheet white, his hands clasped firmly around a short glass, holding it for dear life as he sits huddled at a table close to the door.

There's no Irish band playing a rousing song of celebration this time. No deep laughs of friends sharing a drink and a memory. Only an eerie quiet before murmurs resume after the wind catches the door and it slams shut with an all-mighty thud.

Kieran lifts his head in the direction of the sound and his anxious eyes find mine. My heart stutters and the lights flicker overhead as the wind howls outside. I push my way through the crowd that has gathered close to his table, their faces pressed to the rain-soaked windows.

I put a tentative hand on Kieran's shoulder and his hand slowly reaches up and covers mine. It feels cold, and his fingers tremble slightly. "What's happened?" My voice sounds tight as I crouch beside his chair. He shakes his head, glancing down at me, his worried eyes burning into mine.

"He went out earlier. It should have been fine." He swallows thickly. "His father..." Kieran's voice trails off.

I turn my hand to envelop his with mine, giving it a squeeze. "He's with him?"

Kieran blinks at me with a slump of his shoulders and a slow shake of his head, as if he's carrying the weight of the world and this simple action is barely manageable. "He passed this morning." His voice is raspy, laced with sadness.

"Oh God." I wrap my arms around Kieran. "I'm so sorry," I whisper, and he weakly pats my back.

"We found him on the grounds. Against one of the stones. It's like he was just having one last look at the sea." I lean back, kneeling on the cold stone floor. "I shouldn't have let Colin go out today."

"It's not your fault," I croak out through the sandpaper in my throat.

"Aye, listen to the girl," an unfamiliar voice drifts from the crowd at the window. "Colin has a mind of his own. More stubborn than you, Kieran. If that's possible."

"He'll be fine," another deep voice declares with a rich Irish accent. "Best yachtsman I know."

A chorus of ayes seem to engulf us. A chair is pushed my way through the crowd and I'm grateful for it. The stone floor is cold and unforgiving on my knees, and it takes me a moment to push up and flop into the stiff chair.

A familiar half bark drifts up from under the table and I see Tack spring up from his spot at Kieran's feet, his little paws landing on my soaked pants. "Tack, come here." I lift Colin's precious dog, cradling him against my chest. He gives my cheek a lick before turning his head toward the windows with the rest of the crowd.

"He's worried sick," Kieran mutters, reaching over to scratch the soft fur between Tack's ears. "Been whining since we got here."

"He'll be okay, Tack." I press a kiss to his fur. "Right?" Lightning flashes, illuminating the harbor enough to see an emergency vehicle parked close to the bar, and distorted shadows dancing across the rain-slicked docks.

There's a sudden gasp from the pack keeping watch at the window and the entire bar seems to hold a collective breath. "'Tis nothing, Jamie. Yer eyes are playing tricks on ye," a hushed voice trails off.

The prickle of unease that's been brewing since the cab ride inches a little further up my spine. Kieran absently reaches over and strokes Tack's fur, his eyes fixed on the blackness of the harbor.

Silently, a glass of beer is placed in front of me, and I tear my gaze from the window, surprised to find Kathleen giving me a worried smile, any traces of the drunken state she was in earlier gone. "What are you doing here? I put you in a cab."

She drops into a chair beside me. "It's a small town, and cab drivers like to talk." She slides over a small plate with a selection of cheeses and vegetables to me. "And you need to eat something. I can't have you fainting on me now." There's no mistaking those tears brimming in her eyes and a new sense of dread washes over me. "Plus..." She leans closer, her voice lowering. "Remember the non-complicated one I told you about?"

Tack wiggles against me and nudges his head in Kathleen's direction, looking for attention. She sets her hand on his head and gives a few slow strokes, making his tail wag. "He owns the bar, and he's on the search and rescue crew."

I stare at her in disbelief. "Steve is your..."

"My non-complicated one?" She gives me a watery smile. "That's him. And I probably shouldn't even be here, I mean..." She glances around the bar, tightening her hand a little on Tack as if he's grounding her. "I didn't know what else to do, so I came, but no one knows," she whispers, "about us."

Kieran shifts to look our way, leaning into our little huddle. "Some people know. McGuires only, love. No need to fret," he soothes in hushed tones, patting Kathleen's hand when her eyes widen at his admission. "He'll be fine. They all will. They have to be." There is an air of finality in Kieran's words, as if he's willing them to be true, but as he looks back out to the churning sea, there is no mistaking the hard set of his jaw, the pain in his features.

"It'll be okay." My voice comes out as a whisper and is not convincing at all. Tack whines a little, snuggling in closer to my chest. "You're just here supporting a friend. Supporting me." Kathleen nods quickly and moves her hand from Tack's back to give my arm a squeeze. I take a bite of a cheese cube, but I can barely stomach it.

"What's taking so long?" a hissed, impatient voice asks from the window. "It's bucketing down now."

"It's only been an hour or so since they went out," another answers from the crowd that seems to be growing unsettled.

Kieran glances down at his watch. It's similar to the ones I've seen Colin wearing: all thick silver with dials that glint in the dull light of the bar. His frown deepens. "When did he go out?" I'm almost afraid to ask, but the words come tumbling out.

"Half four." Another stab of pain shoots through my chest. It's almost one in the morning now. He's been out there for hours. They've only just started looking for him. I tilt my face forward, burying my cheek against Tack's fur. Tack whimpers and wiggles his way even closer.

The truth that I've been ignoring slams into me. Fear of getting hurt again has kept me from admitting what my heart already knows. I cannot lose this man. It doesn't matter that I've only known him a few weeks. It doesn't matter that our future is unknown. It doesn't matter that I live in California: an ocean and several thousand miles between us. All that matters is that Steve and the rest of the rescue team find him. Because things need to be said to Colin McGuire. Things that I've kept close to my heart. Things I didn't want to allow myself to feel fully until now. Why is it that it's when something could be taken away that we suddenly realize how important it is? Why does it take a crisis to strip away our fears and speak our truths?

It was simmering there right under the surface when he opened up his heart on the *Saoirse*. When he said he just wanted me to be happy, that he wanted me any way he could have me. Like a fool, I told him we have time to figure it out. The truth is you don't know how much time you have, and now? Now I may never get the chance to tell him how I feel.

A hand rests on my shoulder, and I hear Kieran's distinct accent. "It'll be okay. He's been through much worse than this." He motions to the shrouded darkness of the harbor, wincing as another crack of thunder rattles the windows.

"There!" Excitement from the mass seems to swell, and Kathleen, Kieran and I strain to try to see above them. Looming out of the blackness, in the distance, is a flash of light, subtle at first, then burning brighter as it draws closer to the harbor. "It's the rescue boat!"

Disjointed scrambling ensues as the pack rushes for the door, throwing it open to march out into the darkness. I take a firm grip of Kieran's arm. Either I'm holding him up or he's holding me. It's impossible to tell, but the three of us, Tack still pressed close as I carry him, follow out in the wake of the crowd.

We're assaulted by a gust of wind and rain, but duck our heads and hurry across the street. Tack's whine turns sharply into his signature yelp, and he strains against my hold. "Tack!" He manages to wiggle himself free and launches to the ground, eating up the distance between us and the approaching boat. "They must have him!" Kieran shouts above the pelting rain as we push forward, following Tack and the crowd down the dock.

My heart pumps wildly, adrenaline coursing through me. My grip tightens against Kieran's arm, and I feel Kathleen press closer. From the lights that line the dock, it's a chaotic orchestration as shadowy figures race to tie ropes and secure the boat.

A shouted, "One, two, lift!" rises above the chaos, and the three of us stop to see a stretcher being lifted from the rescue boat into the waiting hands of strangers on the dock.

"Clear the way!" It's an authoritative command, and we edge to the side, the crowd parting in front of us as the stretcher bobs along, carried by drenched volunteers.

A siren blares once from the street, and I turn to see an ambulance backing up to the entrance of the harbor, its back door flung open, the battering wind almost taking it off its hinges.

"Is he?" Kieran's voice, laced with anxious worry, almost breaks my heart as the volunteers surge forward with the stretcher.

"He's okay," that commanding voice calls again, and we look up to see Steve, rushing toward us with the stretcher behind him. He pauses, setting a hand on Kieran's shoulder. "He's unconscious, but breathing. Took in a lot of water, has a nasty cut we tried to bandage. Probably looks worse than it is."

Kieran lets out what sounds like a half-sob, half-groan, and I try to steady him on shaking legs of my own. Tack is leaping beside the stretcher as the volunteers move along the dock, almost tripping over him.

My hand flies to my mouth as the volunteers rush past, my eyes falling to a dark, crimson stain, crusted along Colin's forehead. There's a makeshift bandage resting just above his brow, but the blood has seeped in, soaking it through.

His face is a ghostly blue shade under the harsh overhead lights on the dock, his jaw slack, lips open and unmoving. His head lolls to the side of the stretcher, his eyes staying shut, and if it weren't for the rise and fall of his chest under the thick rescue blanket that covers him, I would think he wasn't breathing at all.

"Steven!" It's a hushed whisper-gasp from Kathleen, and he whips his head in the direction of her strained voice.

"What are you..." He either can't find the words, or doesn't want to cause to a scene, but the searing look he gives her as the rain whips against his face speaks more than words can say. *What are you doing here, you fool?* And perhaps most importantly, *I'm okay. I love you.* It's all there in the intense moment between them. His eyes soften briefly at her with a subtle shake of his head before his large and in charge demeanor takes over.

"Who's coming with us?" He looks between Kieran and me,

and I don't hesitate for a moment, practically shoving Kieran toward Steve.

"You go. We'll meet you there." Kieran gives me a pained look over his shoulder, before he moves with Steve along the wet road to the ambulance. Tack yips frantically, racing after the stretcher, and I bolt forward to scoop him up.

I manage to hook my arm under Tack and lift him into my arms as he whines and fusses. "It's okay," I murmur against his fur, stepping into a shallow puddle. "He's going to be okay."

I watch as the stretcher is loaded into the back of the ambulance, and Steve helps Kieran up before he jumps in and disappears inside. Another volunteer slams the doors shut, a struggle in the relentless wind, and then slaps the door twice once it's secure.

Blue lights on top of the vehicle spin to life, and the siren pierces the night. Kathleen and I stare in shock with the rest of the crowd as the ambulance takes off, spraying water from a puddle and fading down a curve in the road into darkness.

Hospitals officially suck.

I feel zero guilt thinking that and I know I'm not alone in my assessment. Stale coffee, the antiseptic, sterilized smell that seems to permeate within, the incessant squeak of shoes against the floor, the most uncomfortable chairs in history. Not that I'm sitting down, mind you. Wearing a hole in the pristine floor? Maybe. But there will be no sitting down. Not until we know something more than, "He's in observation."

"Sit, Brie. You're driving us all mad." Steve's voice drifts to me as I start lap four thousand of the waiting room. "There's nothing to be done now." I give him a weak smile, grateful he's stayed along with Kathleen.

They've been doing a good job of trying to hide what's obvious between them, but every once in a while, his hand brushes against hers, or they share a look for a beat too long. It must be torture to hide your feelings like this, to live in fear of people finding out your secret. Maybe now that Patrick's true colors have been revealed for the entire country to see, Kathleen and Steve can finally be together the way they clearly want to be.

The three of us left the rest of the crowd behind at the pub, and Dermot, one of Colin's faithful employees, took Tack with them back to McGuire Castle. The hospital is no place for a dog, even if that dog is as adorable as Tack. It broke my heart a little more watching his sad eyes as Dermot carried him off.

I glance down the hallway before moving to the window. The fog is a slow roll this morning, burning off in wisps as the storm clears. A glimpse of sun between the overhanging clouds reminds me I haven't slept yet.

A beige paper cup appears in front of me, and I look up to an exhausted Kieran. "Here. Something a bit extra in this one."

I gingerly take the cup and give it a tentative sniff. "This isn't Batch 41, is it?"

Kieran lets out a half-laugh at my wrinkled nose. "No, it's not."

"Good, because I'm not sure I could stomach that right now."

"Aye, that's not for everyone, to be sure. This one's more subtle with the almond notes, but it does surprise you a little at the end." He takes a sip from his own cup and lifts his brow as if inviting me to do the same.

I tip the cup back, smooth, rich whiskey exploding on my tongue and soothing my throat. "I like this one," I say with a lift of the cup.

"Right that you should. It's named after ye, so it is."

I almost choke on the next sip, making Kieran's blue eyes light a bit. It's a welcome sight after the stress I've seen in them over the last several hours. He's already lost his son; I cannot imagine how Kieran would deal with losing Colin too. "Wh-what?"

"'Tis the truth. That's Worthington Proper you're drinking."

I lift the cup up to the light, wishing I could see the color of the whiskey through the paper. "This is not named after me."

"I'd never lie to you, Brie." He lowers the cup, turning it in his hand. "Our Colin's never been the best at sharing how he's feeling, but he shows it in other ways, you see."

I stare back at Kieran, floored, overwhelming emotion brimming to the surface. *Our* Colin. "He's going to be okay, right? I mean it's taking forever."

"He'll be okay. His pride'll hurt more than anything. Losing the *Saoirse?*" He lets out a long sigh, shaking his head. "Damn shame, but she belongs to the sea now."

Hot tears sting my cheeks again. "Don't start now or you'll get me going." He reaches over to grip my arm. "We'll get a new one. Don't you worry. He'll be back out on the sea in no time." He smacks his lips with a huff, lifting his cup. "This needs to be in a proper glass not a bloody paper cup," he grumbles, turning to march down the hall, in search for a glass or a place to be alone is anyone's guess.

"He's all yours, Brie," Kieran says, relief evident in his tired eyes as pushes the door to Colin's room open for me. "I'll see you a little later." He sets a gentle hand on my arm before heading down the long corridor.

It's closing in on noon and we *finally, finally* are allowed to see him.

Even with the warning from the doctor that he's bruised, battered, and highly medicated, my heart stutters in my chest when I see him.

The door shuts with a soft click, and I freeze at the sight of this big, strong, and always in charge, man tucked under a blanket, an IV dripping away beside the bed. I swallow against the lump in my throat. Vulnerable. It's not a word I would ever have thought would be associated with Colin. "Mhuirnín…Yer too far away." It takes me a few seconds to realize that faint, raspy sound is coming from him, and it kicks me in the heart and into gear at the same time.

Somehow, I make my way to the bed, battling between wanting to fling my arms around him and keeping a distance for fear of hurting him. "Closer. I'll not bite ye."

It's only now that I notice a male nurse, lurking in the corner, clipboard in hand. He steps closer to the IV, glancing up at the bag of fluid slowly dripping into the tube. "It's okay," he declares in soothing tones. "Just try to be gentle. Our Mr. McGuire has a few broken ribs, so he does."

"It's nothing." A weak reply croaks out from Colin as he drops his palm to the bed, his eyes staying shut.

"A few broken ribs?" My stomach churns as I run my eyes over the blanket covering his torso.

"Five to be exact," the nurse chimes in.

"Five?" I squeak out. "That's bad, isn't it?"

"I've seen worse. Luckily there's no internal organ damage. A little rest, he'll be right as rain."

I narrow my eyes at the nurse. "Isn't rain what got him into this situation to begin with?"

"I saw you, Mhuirnín." Gingerly, I sit at the edge of the hard bed, and set my palm over his hand. He's warmer than I thought he would be, given the blue tinge his skin had on that stretcher, but he's here. Flesh and bone and breathing. I feel a sob threatening to burst through, but I bite it back.

"I'm here," I whisper, lifting his hand to set it against my cheek. I close my eyes against the feel of his palm, his fingers twitching slightly.

"No. In the sea. I saw you, but you had green hair," he murmurs, and I glance up at the nurse who purses his lips together, hiding a smile.

"Are you spinning tales about a merrow now?" the nurse asks, moving to the end of the bed to slide the clipboard into a slot. Memories flash to the harbor and Colin's story of merrows enticing sailors and pulling them under. "He's got a concussion. Might be a little out of sorts for a while. I just topped up his pain medication. He should be out like a light soon." The nurse tucks a pen into a deep pocket on his scrubs.

"The doctor said the concussion was a bad one," I mumble, turning back to watch the deep, shuddered rise and fall of Colin's chest.

"We'll set him to rights in no time." I glance over my shoulder and the nurse gives me a small smile. "You're not to stay too long now. Mr. McGuire needs his rest." I answer with a nod, lowering Colin's hand back to the bed. "I'll be back to check on him."

The door snicks shut, and it's just Colin and me, and the staccato scraping of a branch outside the tiny window. "You're not going to scold me?" Colin's words sound a little breathless, like it's a struggle for him to speak.

He still hasn't opened his eyes and it's jarring not to see that steel blue intensity burning into me. "No. Of course not."

Colin's hand skims along the bed as if in search for mine. "Mmm. You smell good."

I can't help the clipped laugh that escapes. "I smell like rain mixed with hospital."

Blindly, his hand finds mind, and he gives it a drained squeeze. "No. Like sunshine." He takes a shuddered breath on a groan, and a fresh sting of tears streaks my cheeks.

"Stop talking. You need to rest."

"I'm fine," he counters. "Probably could use a good knock to the head, truth be told."

"Stubborn man," I grumble under my breath.

"Brie?"

I study his strong jawline, graced now with stubble and a few bruises. My eyes track along the fresh bandage swathed pristine white against his skin, any traces of the crimson blood having been sponged away by the nurses or doctors most likely. My fingers itch to touch him, to press my lips to his, but shock and fear paralyze me. I can only hold his limp hand, afraid to move. "Yes?" It's a struggle to get any words out, my throat constricting.

"I thought..." And then he's gone, pulled under by the pain medication again. At least it's not a merrow.

Colin

"Not so fast, Colin, or you'll give yourself a headache!" Mum shakes her head at me, but I know she's not mad. She's never mad at me.

I finish my ninety-nine in two gulps and grin up at her while she wipes my mouth with a wet napkin. "You haven't ruined your supper, have you?" Da asks from my other side and gives my hair a ruffle. "Fiona won't be happy with us if you have."

"Nope!" Mrs. Sullivan is making shepherd's pie for supper, and I always have room for that. We sit quietly in the sunshine while Mum finishes her ice cream. Da was done first, like always. It's really hot today, and the harbor is so blue it almost hurts my eyes. There are so many people on the boardwalk that it's hard to see them all. On another bench across the way, Mrs. Pouffer's daughter is making kissy faces with the boy who works in the ice cream shop, and I gag. Ugh!

"Colin?" Mum looks at me, then she and Da look where I'm looking. Da laughs. "Oh, my fine lad, one day, that will be you."

"Nuh uh!" I shake my head, my nose wrinkled in disgust. "I hate girls. They talk too much, and they smell like manky, old boots." I shoot a look at Mum. "Er, not you, Mum. Other girls, like Sally Kerry and Bonnie Fleck. You smell good."

Da laughs again, while Mum grins at me. "High praise, indeed." She smooths my hair back and kisses my forehead before standing. "Colin, love, I guarantee you that one day, many years from now, you will find a girl you can't live without. A very special girl who lights up your life and makes everything better."

"And she won't smell like a manky, old boot," Da adds, giving Mum a wink that makes her laugh. "Now, come on. Time to go home."

My eyes flutter open and the salty tang of the harbor in my mind is replaced by the sharp smell of disinfectant. It takes a moment to focus; a box with blinking lights is attached to a pole near my head. Guess that's the source of the soft beeping, too. Keeping my eyes open takes too much effort, so I let them close and try to concentrate on my body. My head throbs, my side feels like someone hit me with a belaying pin, and everything feels heavier than normal. It's an effort even to breathe. Bloody hell.

"Sabrina, you need to take a break."

I know that voice. What the hell is Steven doing here? A second later, the memories of bone-chilling cold, frantic yelling, and grasping hands dragging me aboard the rescue boat come flooding back. Aw, fecking hell. My poor *Saoirse*.

"I will. I just want to see him wake up again, and then I'll let Kieran take over. He just went to get more coffee." *Brie.*

"Trust me. Colin's so stubborn, it will take more than a few broken ribs to keep him down."

I can hear the smile in his voice. "Weren't you the one calling me a bloody fucking gobshite a few hours ago?" I croak. Several gasps hit the air, and when I open my eyes again, two beaming faces hover above me. Brie's eyes are huge over her watery smile, while Steven's grin broadens.

"Maybe. That was when I was hauling your frozen arse out of your life raft. You weigh as much as a draft horse. A pregnant one."

Vague memories of Steven swearing at me on a heaving deck swirl in my head. "Thanks, man."

"My pleasure." He pats my arm and backs away so Brie can move in closer. "I'll go find Kieran. Talk to your girl."

I don't really notice him leaving. Brie slips her hand in mine and squeezes. "Is this okay?" she whispers, her eyes glassy. I squeeze back harder, and her smile breaks through.

"More than okay." I try not to wince; my throat feels like I swallowed sandpaper. "Are you okay?"

She snorts. "Me? I'm not the one who almost drowned in a sinking ship."

"I wasn't even close to drowning." She looks down her nose at me, and I sigh. "All right, it was a bit dicey, but the life raft deployed as it should, and I got to it. Easy."

"Easy. Right." She closes her eyes and shakes her head. "Okay, we'll go with that." With her free hand, she smooths my hair from my forehead, which feels fabulous. "Do you know what happened? Steven said something about the hull?"

I lean into her hand, and she takes the hint and keeps stroking my hair, a smug grin flickering on her lips. "I must have run into some debris that punctured the hull. She went too fast for anything else. Whatever it was also fouled the dingy, so the life raft was my only option."

"I was so worried. And your poor grandfather was beside himself." Her amber eyes start swimming with tears again. "I'm so sorry about your father, Colin."

Rubbing her knuckles with my thumb, I savor the feel of her hand in mine. She smells heavenly, like warm caramel and sunshine. Closing my eyes for a moment, I remember my parents' wisdom that day at the harbor. They were so right. "That was my fear when I realized *Saoirse* was going down—that Grandda couldn't lose us both in one day. But worse than that was not seeing you again."

"Why didn't you call yesterday after you found him? I wish you had."

I give her what I hope is a reassuring smile. "Ooch, it was your big day for the opening. I didn't want to distract you. You'd worked so hard for it."

A tear finally rolls down her cheek, and she swipes it away, blinking hard. "Colin, I—"

I interrupt her with a coughing fit and groan, the stabbing in my side taking my breath away. "Shite, that hurts."

Her eyes pop open with alarm. "Oh! Let me get the nurse. You're probably due for more pain meds. And Kieran wants to see…" She tries to pull her hand away but stops when I squeeze hard.

"Don't go." My vision suddenly blurry, I look up at the beautiful woman whom my parents foretold.

Her soft brows draw together. "I'm just going to get your—"

"No." I raise her hand to my lips. "Don't go back to California. Stay. Here with me. Please."

Another tear rolls down her cheek, but this time it's accompanied by a soft smile. "I'm not going anywhere." She leans down, and

I instantly relax when her soft lips meet mine. "Now, close your eyes and rest. I'm going to find your grandfather. Okay?"

"Okay." I close my eyes, and as I sink back down into sleep, I remember something else. "Brie?"

"Yes?"

"I love you, mhuirnín."

Her breath catches. "I love you, too, Colin."

Sunlight streams in the library window, warming me. Tack is sprawled on his back in the sunbeam, shamelessly exposing himself to the room. Daft dog. He's barely left my side once in the two weeks since I've been home. Movement is easier, but I still have a few weeks before I'm back to normal. Between Brie, Aileen, and Mrs. Sullivan, I've spent most of my recovery on my arse. Every time I try to lift something or even throw a ball for Tack, one of them swoops in, ready to scold me. They're my own personal guardian angels.

I glance at papers in my hand; they're the sketches for Da's memorial stone. Seeing his name, Brian Angus Kieran McGuire, spelled out in such formal type makes his death even more definitive.

His funeral was five days ago, conducted in the family cemetery on the castle grounds. It was quiet, with just clergy, family, and household staff—and Brie, of course—in attendance. I think Grandda was gratified that so many of the community attended the wake that followed. Brie had never been to a wake before; it wasn't as raucous as those in the past, but there was still a sizable number of toasts and speeches. It was good to see people who knew Da in his youth share stories about sailing races and friendships. People overlooked the years of his absence and focused on the good days, when he was the real Brian. Which is as it should be.

Having Brie in the castle has also been good for my grandfather; she's listened for hours to his stories of my father as a child, allowing him to work through his grief. And me to work through mine as well, to be honest. Although I made my peace with Da on the sea, I still have bouts of guilt over not coming to it while he was still alive. And when I do, Brie is there. She's acted as a balm for the hurt of Da's passing and brought sunshine and light back to our lives.

The sound of Aileen greeting Sabrina in the kitchen floats into the room, warming my heart. I never believed I could be as happy as I've been since she moved her things from the Whiskey Rose to the castle. She's technically staying in one of our guest rooms, but everyone knows she spends her nights in my bed. Which is just as it should be.

She walks into the room and my heart lights up. "Showing off the goods again, eh Tack?" She shakes her head in amusement, but Tack merely huffs softly in his sleep. "He's shameless."

Closing my laptop, I set it and the sketches on the side table and pat my lap in invitation. She looks smart in a clinging sweater and trousers that hug her curves. With a grin, she gingerly climbs on and places a soft kiss on my lips. "Is this okay? I'm not hurting your ribs, am I?"

"Better than okay," I reply, ignoring the ache in my side. She hums in contentment and lays her head on my shoulder. "How's Kathleen?"

"Amazingly great, for someone whose marital troubles have been splashed all over international media. Patrick has agreed to settle."

"Already? Damn." I never believed that O'Shea would give up that fast. "Did she tell you the terms?"

"She'll be the majority shareholder, and he's agreed to step aside from all management involvement. He'll keep his shares but has effectively lost control of the company. Her lawyers kicked his ass. Besides the media exposure, they discovered several sexual harassment claims he'd managed to sweep under the rug and old memos proving how little he really had to do with the development of Sharexa. And, of course, the line of women he's cheated on her with goes around the block, and they're all willing to talk."

I grunt in satisfaction. "He's always been his own worst enemy, the fuckwit."

She raises her head and cocks an eyebrow. "Gloating doesn't become you, McGuire."

"Gloating? Me?" I release her to hold my hands out innocently, but she takes one and puts it on her waist again, so I wrap my arms around her once more.

"Yes, you." She kisses my cheek, then lays her head on my shoulder again. "But I love you anyway."

"Good," I murmur, kissing her soft hair. "Did you talk about the job?"

"When I go back to California, I'm going to give my notice." She sighs softly. "I would love to convince Nat to come with me, but I'm not sure if my powers of persuasion are up to the task.

"I have every confidence in your powers of persuasion. They worked on me, didn't they?" I lean back in the chair to look at her. "And what do you mean *go back to California?*"

"I'd like to give them my notice in person, and I need to clear out my apartment there. Decide what I'm going to ship over."

"Can't you do that all over the phone?" Even I can hear the whine in my voice. *Nice, McGuire.*

"I could, but I'd really like do it face-to-face." At my scowl, she brushes her fingers lightly against my lips. "It won't be for long. Maybe two weeks at most. Becca is going to come with me."

"I could go with you and help."

She shakes her head. "While you're recovering? No way. You shouldn't fly with a concussion anyway; you could end up hurting yourself."

"I'm not made of glass, you know. No one is letting me do anything. I feel completely useless." I huff, glancing out the window at the distillery in the distance. I feel her lips against my cheek, making me smile. "I know you're not. Oh—I forgot. Kathleen said there was a flat coming available near the ice cream shop. It's in that cute row with the colorful doors. And she'll assign a car and driver to me my first six months, so I don't have to worry about getting my own vehicle for a while. What if while I'm gone, you take a look at the place? You could check it out, send me a video. And I'll send you one of my place. You can see my four walls and sketchy windows that need replacing."

Wait, what? "Why do you need a flat?" My heart starts beating a little faster. "You're here. And Aileen had the maids preparing my parents' old suite. It's enormous. You can have all your things shipped here. I thought we decided this?" She kisses me quickly, stopping my babbling.

"We talked about it, but nothing was decided." She sighs and sits up to look at me. "I can deal with Aileen and Fiona's smug looks every time we come downstairs together. Sometimes I mess up the sheets in my room just to keep them guessing. But when I move here, to Crossmoor, I need to be in my own place for a while. Not very long, perhaps, but long enough to not feel that I'm taking advantage of you."

"What? Who said you were?" The thought of someone—especially someone on staff—gossiping about her makes my blood boil.

"No one has said anything," she hurries to say, resting her hands on my chest. A smirk flitters on her lips. "Calm down, Shrek. It's me; I need to establish myself first, into my new job and into the community. I need to prove to myself I can stand on my own before I get swept up into the McGuire lifestyle."

Brushing a lock of hair off her forehead, I then slip my hand down her neck. "But you stand on your own now, in America. You don't need to prove anything to anyone. Especially me."

Her eyes soften. "Thank you. After having someone else take advantage of me for years, I need to be sure I'm not doing the same thing to you."

That fucking ex of hers. I want to argue, but I can hear the hint of steel in her voice and know it's best to let it go. For now, at least. "Whatever you need, mhuirnín." I manage a smile. "You're turning your whole life upside down to move here, and I'm beyond grateful for it. Just let me know what you need from me, and you'll have it."

Her answering smile calms me, and her lips on mine seals the deal. "Thank you. You are all I need."

"Excuse me." We look up to see Grandda leaning against the

doorway, grinning at us. "How long have you been in that chair, my boyo? Have you done the stretches your physio recommended?"

"I've been looking over the orders for the next six months," I protest, but stop when Brie frowns at me. "What?"

She slides off my lap and stands, avoiding my grasping hands. "Colin, you need to keep up with your physical therapy. Come on, let's go for a walk." Dutifully I stand, grimacing only slightly at the twinge in my side, and laugh at Tack when he snaps awake in a flurry of feet and fur. Silly dog. He follows as I let Brie lead me out of the room. Grandda gives me a frosty wink and a pat on the shoulder as we pass, and I grin back, knowing how happy he is for me.

It feels good.

Tack yips and runs after a dragonfly as we approach the lake. Little did I know the night I found Brie drunk and wading around out there in her bridesmaid gown, that I would have found the woman to complete my life. *Lady McGuire...someday.*

Pausing at the water's edge, Brie slips a shoe off and dips a toe in, sending ripples across the smooth surface. "Feel like a dip? Shall I fetch a bottle of Batch 41?"

I laugh as her nose wrinkles in distaste. "Good God, no. Never again, please." She turns and steps into my arms, sliding her hands around my neck to spare my ribs, smirking up at me. "But...I wouldn't complain about a glass of Worthington Proper."

My heart thumps. "Oh?" I lean back slightly so I can see her better. "Who told you about that?"

"A little birdie, about six-foot-two with frosty eyebrows and blue eyes like yours." She tilts her head, her honey-colored eyes warm. "He shared a flask of it with me in the hospital waiting room right after they brought you in. It's quite tasty."

"Ah." Grandda told me how afraid she was that night, but how well she bore it. I was so proud of her. "Did I tell you they found

Saoirse? She washed up on the rocks near Drummenhall. I was on the line with the salvage company all morning."

Her eyes shoot open. "What? No! Can they save her?" I shake my head.

"No, but some of her parts have value. Based on the wreckage, they think she ran into a floating hulk of a fishing trawler that went down three weeks ago. Just bad luck."

"Right. Bad luck." Her eyes dim with the memories of that night, and I kiss her brow.

To change the subject, I say lightly, "I was hoping you'll come to Dublin with me in a couple days to visit the Oceanis dealer. I need your help selecting a new boat."

"Really? That would be fun." Her grin is infectious. "A new *Saoirse*?"

"No, I don't think so. I'll always remember her fondly, but it doesn't feel right to put her name on a new vessel. I have a new name in mind."

"Oh?"

"The *Sabrina*." Her mouth drops open and her golden eyes well with tears. "Is that all right?"

"More than all right," she whispers, smiling back her tears. Squeezing her tightly, I relish the feel of her arms around my neck and the sugary sweet scent of her hair on my face. Murmuring against her neck, I pass along my father's blessing.

"And may we always have fair winds and following seas."

chapter
fifteen

Sabrina

"**A**RE YOU SURE YOU DON'T WANT ME TO COME WITH YOU?" Colin asks for about the millionth time over this past week as I load my bag onto the conveyor belt at the check-in desk at the airport. To say he's not happy about me going back to California, even if it is only for a couple of weeks, is an understatement.

"One day, when you're back to normal and not wheezing with every step you take, we'll go visit. Deal?"

He gives me a resigned nod, but the set of his jaw tells me all I need to know about how he really feels. "Hey." I take his hand, giving it a squeeze as we make our way to the security gate with Becca and Liam following us. "It's only two weeks."

"Twelve days. Do not make it sound longer than it is."

"Okay, grumpy Shrek. I won't." I grin at him when we stop at the line that leads to security. "You're cute when you're not getting your way. You know that?" He gives me a scowl, and I pull my phone from my purse. "Take a picture with me. You know we don't have any of us together?"

I hold my arm out to try to take a picture of us, but I am and always have been awful at this. I try a few times and fail miserably, cutting off half of my head in most of the shots. Colin chuckles under his breath, taking my phone and quickly snapping a picture. "I have a picture of us," he says, passing the phone back to me.

I lift a brow in surprise and tuck the phone back into my purse. "You do? When did you take a picture?"

"Wouldn't you like to know?"

"You are full of surprises, aren't you?"

He lets out a rough huff and slips an arm around my waist, pulling me against his chest, catching me off guard. "I feel like part of my heart is leaving," he whispers against my ear, his tone solemn.

I bite the inside of my cheek to try to keep control of the emotion that threatens to spill over. "You can't say stuff like that when I'm about to get on a plane, Colin."

"It's the truth. And I told you I would never lie to you," he mumbles against my lips.

"Ahem." Becca's voice causes me to lean back and I glance over to see her shaking her head at me. "Geez. You would think that you're the ones who just got married. It's only a few days." I laugh, watching as Liam plants a long kiss on her lips, lifting her up in the process.

"And don't you forget it, Mrs. Swanson," Liam says, letting her back down.

"How could I, Mr. Swanson?" She beams at him before giving him another kiss and tugging me with her into the line.

"Text me when you get there. Go dté tú, a mhuirnín, slán." Colin's voice rises as Becca drags me away from the warmth of his arms.

I shout over my shoulder, "What does that mean? I never know what you're saying half the time."

"Does it matter?" he hollers back, stuffing his hands into the front pockets of his jeans with that irresistible smirk of his.

"No. Just keep talking to me in tongues and I'm yours." We're drawing attention now, with a few impatient travellers muttering behind us in the line.

"You always were, mhuirnín." With warmth radiating through me, I give him a final wave before we're ushered forward and through to the security check.

"Was it always this horrible to fly?" I ask Becca as we're finally in a cab, travel-weary, and on our way to my apartment in Huntington Beach. Flying coach really is the worst. At least there weren't any two-year-olds going ballistic this time. I spent the flight over to Ireland trying to help a single mom calm her toddler down by drawing pictures on demand. If you think adult clients are difficult, try entertaining a toddler with a hundred different ways to draw a cat. 'Cat' was the only word the kid knew and he cried when my sketches weren't up to his standards.

"God no. My neck is killing me." Becca grips the nape of her neck, rolling her shoulders. "We need to get upgraded on the way back. And what time is it?"

I laugh, taking a look at my phone. "Here or in Ireland?"

"I don't even know," she groans, resting her forehead against the window. "We need sleep and wine. Not gross airplane wine. That was awful."

"We'll get real wine. Don't worry." I smile at my phone, seeing the stream of texts from Colin, the first one coming about a minute after I texted him that we had to turn our phones off for takeoff.

CM: Miss you already, mhuirnin.

And then about an hour later, there's a picture of Tack, looking adorable on one of the rocks by the lake in front of the castle.

CM: Tack is looking for you. Wondering if you've actually fallen into the lake.

It's so sweet, it almost makes me ask the driver to turn around so I can catch the next flight back to Ireland.

"Now who's glowing?" Becca asks, grinning at me. "You've got it bad."

"I know. Is it that obvious?" I throw my phone back into my bag, fighting between wanting to read every line he's written right this second or taking my time to savor them.

"It really is. I'm not sure I've ever seen you like this before."

I shake my head, glancing out the window. There's no lush green rolling hills, no sheep blocking our way. No rows of historic colored houses with crooked signs and winding cobblestone streets. Even though Huntington Beach has been home for years, I feel like a stranger. "I don't really know what I'm doing," I say, looking back at Becca.

Becca reaches for my hand, giving it a squeeze. "No one ever does, hun. But I can tell you this, that man is all in with you. Just embrace it and enjoy the ride."

The next afternoon, Becca and I have separated my tiny apartment into piles of ship, toss, and donate. It's taken longer than we wanted it to, given the two bottles of wine we had last night.

It was somewhat of a shock to find that Laird was actually true to his word and did move all of his shit out. There's not a single trace of him left, and while I think some part of me should be a little sad about that, I'm not.

It's a trip down memory lane as Becca and I find old photo albums from our university days, and JT concert tickets from when we followed his Future Sex/Love Show tour around in 2007. I still have my Golden Bears hoodie from Cal. I'm wearing it while Becca sings off key in the background to "Rock Your Body" on my old CD player as I video call Colin. He's going to give me a walk through of the loft Kathleen found, and I can't wait to see it.

"You two sound like you're having fun." Colin grins at me as I step onto the miniscule balcony.

"We are. There's a lot of history here. Not history like you have, mind you."

He chuckles, the sound making me miss him even more. "Show me your place," he says, and I hear Tack's distinctive yip in the background. "Oh, hang on. He wants to see ye."

Colin picks up the adorable beagle and I practically squeal when I see him. "Tack! Are you making sure Colin is doing his exercises?" Tack squirms in Colin's arms with a whine, and Colin sets him back down.

"He is indeed."

"You're not overdoing it, are you?"

Colin runs a hand over his jaw. Stubble has started to grow, giving his handsome face that rugged look I crave. "How could I when I have the helicopter crew keeping watch 24/7?"

Glad to know Aileen and Fiona are keeping him in line. "They're just worried about you."

He blows out a breath. "I know they are and I do appreciate it. Now, let's see this apartment that has pulled you away from me before I show you this one."

I turn the phone, panning the parking lot. "This is the stellar view from the balcony that's about as big as a postage stamp. Isn't the cracked asphalt amazing? There are even weeds growing up here and there, you know? To give it a pop of color."

Colin laughs and I move inside. Becca jumps into view and gives Colin a wave. "Colin! You missed the dance-off." She twirls before stepping into the bedroom.

"Dance-off?" he asks, the corner of his eyes crinkling in amusement.

"You don't want to know."

"Oh, I think I do want to know."

"Some other time, maybe."

He taps his temple. "I'm holding that up here, mhuirnin. I'll have you dancing for me in no time." His words make me lightheaded. I have no doubt that Colin could make me do just about anything.

I clear my throat. "Moving on to the famous four walls and sketchy windows that are painted shut." I scan the living room/kitchen/dining room/entryway. "It's amazing that I lived here as long as I did. I'm an architect! You would think I'd live in a place with more character!"

I turn the phone back around to look at him. "There's nothing wrong with your place, Brie. It's…"

"Boring," I supply. "It's boring." I move into the bedroom, showing it to him. "Another four walls, a closet and a bathroom, where the hot water only gets to tepid at best."

"See? We also tend to have that problem."

"Says the man with the castle from the 1600s." I swivel the phone so I can see him. "I showed you mine, now you show me yours."

"Promises, promises." His voice drops to that deep, rich tone full of promise. "Okay, we've got an open fireplace here, original wood floors that have just been redone." I smile, watching as he slowly scans the loft. Tack jumps up onto a colorful seat along a large bay window in the bedroom. "You can see the harbor from the window seat here."

"I can watch you coming home," I say, and he stops, appearing in the frame.

"I rather like that idea. The idea of you welcoming me home after a day at sea."

"Me too. What else? Show me!"

He grins as he continues the tour, stopping when he's outside at a small community garden that sits in the backyard of the building. I can hear the faint sounds of Irish music drifting in the background from one of the pubs nearby. "It's small, but I can see you here. I think you'll like it."

"I love it. It's perfect." I heave an exaggerated sigh. "I'll miss the weedy parking lot though." He laughs again, but then his voice grows serious.

"I miss you, mhuirnin. It's not the same without you here."

My heart hurts being away from him and it's only been a day. "I miss you too."

Becca shimmies her way back beside me. "We miss our Irish men! It's true! But, we'll see you soon. She really needs to go now. This place is not going to pack itself! Bye, Colin!" I laugh as she tries to hit the button to end the call.

I pull the phone away from her. "I'll text you later!"

"More promises," he says.

"I'll keep them all."

"How do you feel after giving your notice?" Becca asks as we walk the HB Pier. It's been a week since we landed and we've accomplished a lot. I've sold my Jeep and we've cleared out the apartment. We've delivered about twenty bags of donations to the local Salvation Army and packed two large boxes of my stuff that I simply can't part with that I'll ship over to Ireland.

Giving my notice was hard. Freeman Architects was my first real job out of school, and they've provided an exceptional learning experience. I'll always be grateful. But, the time is right for this move. I did ask Nat if she would be interested in joining me, but her roots are firmly planted here.

"Brie?" Becca nudges me while I watch the Pacific. As always, it's other-worldly, spread out before us with the sunset looming. A few die-hard surfers remain in the twilight, their shadows darkening as they bob in the water, waiting for the perfect wave.

The ten miles of sandy beach along the Pacific Coast Highway are picture-postcard perfect, but all I can think about is Colin. About how he would guide a yacht on this ocean. About how Tack would play and try to bark at the waves at the HB Dog Beach.

I stop at the end of the pier, wrapping my arms around myself. The air here feels different, infused with Californian warmth and sunshine. It's nothing like the secluded beach Colin took me to with its unpredictable winds, but I'd give anything to be back there with him. "Oh no," Becca says, gripping my shoulders, her brows drawn. "You're not having second thoughts are you?"

"No, no. Not at all. I'm just thinking about him. About what he would think about all of this." The breeze from the ocean kicks up, and I glance out to the muted-orange sky, wisps of light pink brushing the horizon.

"I miss him, Becs. So much. I know we've only been here for a week, but –"

She wraps her arm around my shoulder, and I lean against her. "I know. I miss Liam, too." We spend a few moments watching the waves, and I take a couple of pictures, sending them off to Colin.

It's the middle of the night in Ireland, so I'm surprised when I see the bouncing dots before getting his text.

CM: That's quite a view, mhuirnin.

My heart clenches when I read his words.

SW: Would be better with you in it.

Becca and I start back down the pier, making our way to one of the gastro pubs close by. I used to love this place, but now, it falls short compared to Steven's pub. We're tucked into a booth with a view of the ocean and a pitcher of sangria when Colin's final text of the night comes.

CW: Come home soon.

I remember one of the conversations we had at the beginning. When he said home is who you share it with. Colin's become my home, and the flight that will take me back to him cannot come soon enough.

epilogue

One Year Later

Sabrina

"**D**AFT DOG." COLIN LAUGHS AS TACK NUDGES HIS NOSE between us on the bed in a move that is now all too familiar in the morning. "I'm trying to get a proper wake up." I grin against Colin's strong shoulder as he ruffles the soft fur on Tack's head.

"You mean more proper than the one you got twenty minutes ago?" I ask, stroking my hand along Tack's back as he settles between us for his morning cuddle.

"I always want more. I'm greedy like that." I try to bite back a smile. Colin is the least greedy person I've ever met. The man gives more to the people of the community here than he would ever let on, and he never asks for anything in return.

Since settling into life in Crossmoor, I've started to discover the layers of this complicated man and found myself falling a little more each time another one is peeled away.

He's provided loans to no less than ten families in town when they've found themselves in need of help. He continues to let farmers use the many acres of land that roll around the castle for their sheep to graze and roam. He donates substantially to the charitable environmental trust that his family has been a part of for generations. The list just keeps going on and on, but he's never told me any of this. I hear it all from the people of the town, usually with conversations that start off with, "Oh, Colin would never want me to say anything but…"

"I don't mind you being greedy with me," I say, pressing my lips to the warmth of his skin.

"I like hearing that." His hand stills on Tack's back, and he turns his face to me. "What would you change about this place if you could?"

My eyes widen. "About the castle? Nothing."

His brow furrows as he leans back to regard me. "Nothing at all? Even with that brilliant architectural mind of yours?"

"I learned a long time ago, you don't mess with perfection."

Colin lets out a huff and sweeps his arm to the vaulted ceiling of his bedroom. I say bedroom, but really, it's the size of small cottage. I still have to pinch myself that I get to wake up here sometimes. I stayed in the perfect little apartment in town for about six months before moving into the castle. While Colin sometimes complained about me not moving in right away, I secretly think he enjoyed the time we spent at that loft.

"Some mornings it's drafty in here," he complains, and I can't help grinning at his messed-up hair.

"It's a castle. That's to be expected, but body heat can help with that," I fire back at him, enjoying his little rant, but he ignores me and plows on.

"And the paint is chipping in the corner of the main dining hall."

"That's cosmetic, not architectural." I'm so helpful.

He gives me one of his signature Shrek-like scowls. "You don't want to make any changes?"

"No. I can't imagine changing anything here." I lean up, propping an elbow against the pillow. "What is this about?"

"I just want you to feel like this is your home." His fingers lace with mine after he adjusts the rock that's been sitting on the ring finger of my left hand for two months now. My engagement ring is nothing short of magical with its simple, sleek platinum band and a halo of diamonds around a single perfect oval center stone. When the light catches it, I actually want to cry sometimes.

"You're here. That's all I need for it to feel like home." His lips press against my temple before he leans back once more.

"If there's anything you want to change or improve upon, I want you to know that you can. You're a brilliant architect, I just thought you might want to, I don't know, put your mark on the place somehow." He's actually pouting a little as he stares at me with an intensity that heats my skin.

I know that incorporating me into his life is a huge step, because the castle isn't just his family home, it's his livelihood, and a key feature of the community. When I think about it too much, I get a little overwhelmed to be honest. I'm not just going to be marrying a man, I'm marrying into a legacy.

I take his face between my hands, pressing a soft kiss to his lips. "Thank you. You'll be the first to know if I get any wild ideas, but for a while, can we just enjoy this beautiful room, and this amazing castle without a construction crew barging in on us during our first few years of marriage?"

"I didn't think about a construction crew." His lips press into a hard line.

"Yes, well, sadly, I can't just snap my fingers and magically make changes happen. They haven't figured out how to do that just yet." I push forward to kiss the frown from his lips.

"Damn shame."

"Yes, it is." Turning my head to give him access to my neck, I spot the sketch I drew for him of Shrek beside a turret. It's sitting in a black frame on his dresser and makes me smile every time I see it. "I love that you kept that."

"Mmm," he murmurs against my neck. "Kept what?"

"The sketch I did." So much has happened since then, it feels like a lifetime ago.

He lifts his head, following my gaze to his dresser. "Aye. The one you drew after I rescued you."

"I didn't need rescuing." I give him a playful hit in his strong shoulder.

"I'd rescue you a thousand times, mhuirnín."

His words make warmth flow through me. "You can be very sweet, you know, Shrek?"

"Sweet?" He narrows his eyes, gingerly picking up Tack and leaning over to set him on the stone floor. He's back quickly, rolling me to my stomach, his palm greedily skating down my back before settling on my ass. He leans forward, covering me with the warmth of his body, his mouth wicked against my ear. "Let's see just how sweet I can be."

"You sure this is the place?" Colin asks, that grin on his face deepening as we stand in front of the lake at McGuire Castle. It's November and this morning, we woke to a light layer of frost covering the grounds with an almost magical glow. The lake is a pane of glass, reflecting the rising stone turrets of the castle in mirrored perfection.

Winter in Ireland is really something else. There are moments when the Californian in me still has a craving for the sun and warmth, but Colin has learned to recognize those times. The tucked-away beaches he takes me to may not be high on any travel blog's listings, but they will always be on the top of mine.

"The scene of the crime? Can you think of a more perfect place?" He moves behind me, his strong arms tightening around my waist before he drops a kiss to the curve of my neck.

"That I cannot, mhuirnín." I lean back against him, feeling the warm wool of his sweater against me. We watch silently for a few moments as Tack sniffs at the rocks that line the edge of the lake.

I turn to face him, still getting that weak in the knees feeling I always do when he's this close to me. "We can do it in December. Becca and Liam can drive down. We can see if Kathleen and Steve are free, and maybe Connor and Brooke. It doesn't need to be a big production."

I try to fight back a grimace and tighten a fist in his sweater. Since word was announced in the local paper of our engagement, there seems to be an ever-growing expectation that some lavish, once-in-a-lifetime event on a grand scale is going to be taking place. People are always asking me for details: when I'm checking out at the grocery store, at the harbor when Colin and I are minding our business on his new boat—excuse me—*yacht*. Even Steven's pub can't provide us relief as hushed murmurs are followed by an inevitable peppering of questions about the wedding.

Plus, some industrious busybody created an Instagram page that's been set up, dropping various suggestions on dresses, food, and venue, as if there could be any other venue than this. I mean come on… a winter wedding at a castle? Crackling fires in the hearths, mulled whiskey (I'll have to ask him if that is even a thing), flaming torches lighting the way to the ceremony at the lake as fresh winter snow cascades around us? It's a no-brainer if you ask me. Maybe weddings don't have to suck after all.

"Whatever you want, you can have. You know that," Colin says. "I'll marry you today. Right now, if you want." His hand finds its way into my hair. I had it cut short in the summer on a misguided whim, and it's finally starting to grow out. Who would have thought a simple haircut could whip strangers into a frenzy, but there it was in trending Instagram glory, with a comment from @Whiskey2049 which simply read, "She looks like a wood nymph. She must be pregnant. He's not the marrying kind." Some people really are the worst. I quit looking at all things social media shortly thereafter.

I glance down at his jacket, about four sizes too big for me that I threw on before we wandered out into the crisp morning, at my worn jeans and battered hiking boots before meeting his gaze. "You'd marry me when I look like a lost lumberjack or something?"

"Yeah, but you're my lost lumberjack, and I'd marry you any

place, any time." His palm caresses my cheek, his thumb stroking my jaw. "You just say the word and you'll be Lady McGuire before nightfall."

I blink at him, leaning away from the temptation of his strong chest. "What exactly does being a Lady entail?"

He laughs, a deep and rumbling sound I've decided is my favorite thing in the world. "Is that what you're worried about? I've told you it's nothing. It's a title only."

I raise a brow. "Last month we were introduced over a loud-speaker at your buddy, the Duke of Fairfax's, horse race as Lord McGuire and the future Lady of McGuire Castle." I try my best to put an Irish accent on, but fail miserably.

His eyes shine with amusement. "His name is John and he's the *Earl* of Tratshal. Not the Duke of Fairfax." He studies me closely, his expression growing serious. "You're nervous about the title?"

I throw my hands up in the air. "I don't know! The only Lady I know is Lady Macbeth and things didn't work out so well for her with the whole murderous tyrant, slowly driven into madness thing."

He shakes his head at me, pulling me back into the warmth of his arms. "What about Lady Gaga?" he murmurs against my temple. "She's a badass. Goes after what she wants. Doesn't care what anyone thinks."

"So I can wear a meat dress when we get married? No, Tack would think I was a giant hors d'oeuvre. Oh, wait! Maybe I'll arrive inside of a silver egg pulled by shirtless men." Colin gives me a half growl, lifting me off the ground and taking a few steps toward the lake.

"No shirtless men other than me, or I swear I will dump you into my lake so fast..." I let out a squeal that echoes off the forest as I try unsuccessfully to squirm away from him. Tack yips as he hops between our legs.

"*My* lake!" I manage to throw in between a laugh as I find myself swooped up into his arms, much like I was the night of Becca's wedding. I didn't realize then that this man would come to mean so much to me. That I would crave his touch, his words, his steady but slightly annoying sureness.

"*Our* lake. Better?" he asks, striding across the frost-covered grounds back to the castle. I crane my neck to watch as Tack bounds forward, pressing his little paws against the huge wooden door that leads to the family wing of the castle.

"Our lake is much better." I lean forward, tightening my arms around his neck, coaxing his lips to mine.

Our lake. Our life. Our future.

acknowledgments

Thank you, readers for coming along with us on a new adventure. We hope you will enjoy this series as much as we love writing it.

To the amazing Annette Brignac and Michelle Clay of Book Nerd Services: we love you and your endless energy, support and friendship.

Thank you to our ARC team and pre-readers for taking the time to read and for providing your incredible insights.

To the multi-talented Jada D'Lee, we always love your vision and creativity. Thank you for being part of our journey.

To our fabulous editor, Rebecca of Fairest Review Editing Services, thank you for your patience and observations!

A world of thanks to Stacey and Champagne Book Design for your beautiful work.

We are beyond grateful for the supportive community of authors, bloggers, Twitterloves, Facebook friends and groups, Goodreads friends and reviews for Indie authors.

And as always, a huge thank you to the Facebook Dream Team for providing ongoing inspiration and laughs.

Sneak Peek of *A Spirited Heart*
Book Two in the Spirits Series—Coming Soon

THE CROWD IS ANXIOUS, BUZZING WITH ANNOYANCE. I'M ONCE again lost to the timbre of accents and rapid words being thrown around, making the tightness in my chest ache a bit more. I wish Nonna was here. She was always good at simplifying things for me. Unlike me, Mamma easily cruises from English to Italian and back again without missing a beat. Sure, I catch the basics, and can carry on fragmented discussions, but the nuances of conversation are foggy even after thirty-five years.

There's shuffling around on the raised stage at the front of the hall, and the murmurs in the crowd fade out, replaced by a high-pitched squeal from a poorly-equipped microphone. My ears burn with the unwelcome noise, and I crane my neck, along with everyone else in the crowd, to try to get a glimpse at the stage.

Just once, I wish Papà's genes could have helped here, giving me some height, but no. I'm stuck trying to peer through the breaks in the crowd with my vertically-challenged Mamma.

The group in front of me shifts a bit, allowing me to see Giorgio Romano, the President of the local vineyard association at the podium. "Buona sera, amici e benvenuti." He continues on in Italian, thanking us all for coming before he switches to his heavily-accented English. "And now, it is my pleasure to introduce to you the Director of the Stanford Archaeology Center, Dr. Micah Tyler. Dr. Tyler is from America. He's been an associate professor at Stanford for ten years and will lead us tonight. Dr. Tyler, if you please."

A collective groan of displeasure rolls through the crowd, and I see Giorgio step aside. From somewhere near the back of the room, comes a heightened shout, "Chiunque tu sia, sei un cretino!" followed by a few barks of agreement. My view becomes obstructed once more before the two men in front of us move a bit, giving me one hell of a stellar view of Micah Tyler.

Sadly, my original suspicions of him being some old, grey-haired idiot are dead wrong. Instead, I'm staring at an Adonis come to life in a finely tailored suit. Sun-streaked brown hair, a defined, clean-shaven jaw, probably over six-foot-four of pure, sexy-as-all-sin man. A woman to my left whispers under her breath, "Questo sì che è un bell'uomo." Understatement of the year. The man should be walking runways, not about to unleash chaos onto our otherwise calm little piece of paradise.

about the authors

Over a decade ago, an American carnivore and a Canadian vegetarian bonded over their mutual love for shoes, the perfect cocktail, and swoon-worthy story telling.

From her home in Portland, B.B. Miller spends her days with friends and family in search of the perfect pear martini.

Leslie Carson lives in Ottawa, with her busy family and two cats. She's not at the rink so much anymore, but the Zamboni drivers still know her by name.

Together they enjoy visiting vineyards and distilleries, and writing about romantic adventures.

They would love to hear from you.

Join our Facebook team: The Dream Team
www.facebook.com/groups/46308339723003

other titles by the authors

Rock the Dream

Live Your Dream

Chase the Dream

Wildest Dream

www.ingramcontent.com/pod-product-compliance
Lightning Source LLC
Chambersburg PA
CBHW030239200626
46816CB00002BA/427